CHRISTMAS MASQUERADE

An eternity passed before
Andrew spoke

"Were you afraid I was going to demand a reward, Florence Nightingale?"

Jo Marie's heart went still. "You do remember." They'd spent a single, golden moment together so many months ago. Not once since Kelly had introduced Andrew as her fiancé had he given her the slightest inkling that he remembered.

"Did you imagine I could forget?" he asked quietly. "I went back to that hospital every day for a month," he continued in a deep, troubled voice. "I thought you were a nurse."

The color ebbed from Jo Marie's face. She'd looked for him, too. Although she'd never known his name, she had included him in her thoughts every day. He was her dream man, the stranger who had shared those enchanted moments of magic with her.

A GIFT BEYOND PRICE

"Erin ... you are like an angel
come to earth...."

The husky timbre of Mikhail's voice resonated through her, making her tremble. "I'm not...."

A faint smile curved the lips that were very close to her own. "Not what? Not beautiful, or not an angel?"

"N-neither... I'm just a woman...."

He laughed throatily. "Oh, yes...that you are. Warm and gentle and giving..." His head bent, and his arms drew her closer.

Mikhail's firm, seeking mouth tasted the smoothness of her brow, the curve of her cheek and the slender line of her throat before he at last gave in to her wordless plea and savored the sweetness of her lips.

Erin moaned softly, refusing to listen to the faint whispers of caution warning her that she was rushing into something beyond her control....

Dear Reader,

At this special season, we bring you our editors' choice of two full-length memorable holiday novels written by two of your favorite authors.

We hope your holiday season is as fulfilling and ultimately rewarding as it is for Jo Marie and Erin, the two women whose stories are captured in this volume.

Best wishes for a Happy New Year,

Candy Lee
Reader Service

Christmas Treasures

Harlequin Books

TORONTO • NEW YORK • LONDON
AMSTERDAM • PARIS • SYDNEY • HAMBURG
STOCKHOLM • ATHENS • TOKYO • MILAN

CHRISTMAS TREASURES © 1990 Harlequin Enterprises B. V.

This edition published 1992.

ISBN 0-373-83255-9

Christmas Masquerade © 1985 Debbie Macomber
A Gift Beyond Price © 1983 Maura Seger

CONTENTS

DEBBIE
MACOMBER

Christmas Masquerade

For Tara
A woman of grace, charm and sensitivity.
Thank you.

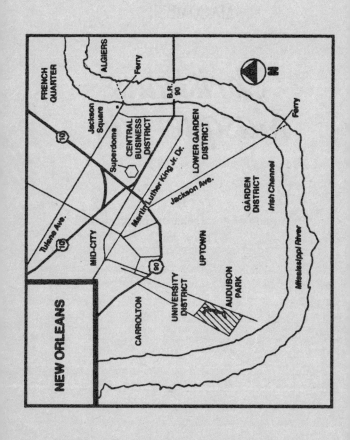

Prologue

The blast of a jazz saxophone that pierced the night was immediately followed by the jubilant sounds of a dixieland band. A shrieking whistle reverberated through the confusion. Singing, dancing, hooting and laughter surrounded Jo Marie Early as she painstakingly made her way down Tulane Avenue. Attracted by the parade, she'd arrived just in time to watch the flambeaux carriers light a golden arc of bouncing flames from one side of the street to the other. Now she was trapped in the milling mass of humanity when she had every intention of going in the opposite direction. The heavy Mardi Gras crowds hampered her progress to a slow crawl. The observation of the "Fat

Tuesday" had commenced two weeks earlier with a series of parades and festive balls. Tonight the celebrating culminated in a frenzy of singing, lively dancing and masqueraders who roamed the brilliant streets.

New Orleans went crazy at this time of year, throwing a city-wide party that attracted a million guests. After twenty-three years, Jo Marie thought she would be accustomed to the maniacal behavior in the city she loved. But how could she criticize when she was a participant herself? Tonight, if she ever made it out of this crowd, she was attending a private party dressed as Florence Nightingale. Not her most original costume idea, but the best she could do on such short notice. Just this morning she'd been in a snowstorm in Minnesota and had arrived back this afternoon to hear the news that her roommate, Kelly Beaumont, was in the hospital for a tonsillectomy. Concerned, Joe Marie had quickly donned one of Kelly's nurse's uniforms so she could go directly to the party after visiting Kelly in the hospital.

With a sigh of abject frustration, Jo Marie realized she was being pushed in the direction opposite the hospital.

"Please, let me through," she called, struggling against the swift current of the merrymaking crowd.

"Which way?" a gravelly, male voice asked in her ear. "Do you want to go this way?" He pointed away from the crowd.

"Yes...please."

The voice turned out to be one of three young men who cleared a path for Jo Marie and helped her onto a side street.

Laughing, she turned to find all three were dressed as cavaliers of old. They bowed in gentlemanly fashion, tucking their arms at their waists and sweeping their plumed hats before them.

"The Three Musketeers at your disposal, fair lady."

"Your rescue is most welcome, kind sirs," Jo Marie shouted to be heard above the sound of the boisterous celebration.

"Your destination?"

Rather than try to be heard, Jo Marie pointed toward the hospital.

"Then allow us to escort you," the second offered gallantly.

Jo Marie wasn't sure she should trust three young men wearing red tights. But after all, it was Mardi Gras and the tale was sure to cause Kelly to smile. And that was something her roommate hadn't been doing much of lately.

The three young men formed a protective circle around Jo Marie and led the way down a less crowded side street, weaving in and out of the throng when necessary.

Glancing above to the cast iron balcony railing that marked the outer limits of the French Quarter, Jo Marie realized her heroes were heading for the heart of the partying, apparently more interested in capturing her for themselves than in delivering her to the hospital. "We're headed the wrong way," she shouted.

"This is a short cut," the tallest of the trio explained humorously. "We know of several people this way in need of nursing."

Unwilling to be trapped in their game, Jo Marie broke away from her gallant cavaliers and walked as quickly as her starched white uniform would allow. Dark tendrils of her hair escaped the carefully coiled chignon and framed her small face. Her fingers pushed them aside, uncaring for the moment.

Heavy footsteps behind her assured Jo Marie that the Three Musketeers weren't giving up on her so easily. Increasing her pace, she ran across the street and was within a half block of the hospital parking lot when she collided full speed into a solid object.

Stunned, it took Jo Marie a minute to recover and recognize that whatever she'd hit was warm and lean. Jo Marie raised startled brown eyes to meet the intense gray eyes of the most striking man she had ever seen. His hands reached for her shoulder to steady her.

"Are you hurt?" he asked in a deep voice that was low and resonant, oddly sensuous.

Jo Marie shook her head. "Are you?" There was some quality so mesmerizing about this man that she couldn't move her eyes. Although she was self-consciously staring, Jo Marie was powerless to break eye contact. He wasn't tall—under six feet so that she had only to tip her head back slightly to meet his look.

Nor dark. His hair was brown, but a shade no deeper than her own soft chestnut curls. And he wasn't handsome. Not in the urbane sense. Although his look and his clothes spoke of wealth and breeding, Jo Marie knew intuitively that this man worked, played and loved hard. His brow was creased in what looked like a permanent frown and his mouth was a fraction too full.

Not tall, not dark, not handsome, but the embodiment of every fantasy Jo Marie had ever dreamed.

Neither of them moved for a long, drawn-out moment. Jo Marie felt as if she'd turned to stone. All those silly, schoolgirl dreams she'd shelved in the back of her mind as products of a whimsical imagination stood before her. He was the swashbuckling pirate to her captured maiden, Rhett Butler to her Scarlett O'Hara, Heathcliff to her Catherine....

"Are you hurt?" He broke into her thoughts. Eyes as gray as a winter sea narrowed with concern.

"No." She assured him with a shake of her head and forced her attention over her shoulder. Her three gallant heroes had discovered another female attraction and had directed their attention elsewhere, no longer interested in following her.

His hands continued to hold her shoulder. "You're a nurse?" he asked softly.

"Florence Nightingale," she corrected with a soft smile.

His finger was under her chin. Lifting her eyes, she saw his softly quizzical gaze. "Have we met?"

"No." It was on the tip of her tongue to tell him that yes they had met once, a long time ago in her romantic daydreams. But he'd probably laugh. Who wouldn't? Jo Marie wasn't a star-struck teenager, but a woman who had long since abandoned the practice of reading fairy tales.

His eyes were intent as they roamed her face, memorizing every detail, seeking something he couldn't define. He seemed as caught up in this moment as she.

"You remind me of a painting I once saw," he said, then blinked, apparently surprised that he'd spoken out loud.

"No one's ever done my portrait," Jo Marie murmured, frozen into immobility by the breathless bewilderment that lingered between them.

His eyes skidded past her briefly to rest on the fun-seeking Musketeers. "You were running from them?"

The spellbinding moment continued.

"Yes."

"Then I rescued you."

Jo Marie confirmed his statement as a large group of merrymakers crossed the street toward them. But she barely noticed. What captured her attention was the way in which this dream man was studying her.

"Every hero deserves a reward," he said.

Jo Marie watched him with uncertainty. "What do you mean?"

"This." The bright light of the streetlamp dimmed as he lowered his head, blocking out the golden rays. His warm mouth settled over hers, holding her prisoner, kissing her with a hunger as deep as the sea.

In the dark recesses of her mind, Jo Marie realized she should pull away. A man she didn't know was kissing her deeply, passionately. And the sensations he aroused were far beyond anything she'd ever felt. A dream that had become reality.

Singing voices surrounded her and before she could recognize the source the kiss was abruptly broken.

The Three Musketeers and a long line of others were doing a gay rendition of the rumba. Before she could protest, before she was even aware of what was happening, Jo Marie was grabbed from behind by the waist and forced to join in the rambunctious song and dance.

Her dark eyes sought the dream man only to discover that he was frantically searching the crowd for her, pushing people aside. Desperately, Jo Marie fought to break free, but couldn't. She called out, but to no avail, her voice drowned out by the song of the others. The long line of singing pranksters turned the corner, forcing Jo Marie to go with them. Her last sight of the dream man was of him pushing his way through the crowd to find her, but by then it was too late. She, too, had lost him.

Chapter One

Y ou've got that look in your eye again," pixie-faced Kelly Beaumont complained. "I swear every time you pick me up at the hospital something strange comes over you."

Jo Marie forced a smile, but her soft mouth trembled with the effort. "You're imagining things."

Kelly's narrowed look denied that, but she said nothing.

If Jo Marie had felt like being honest, she would have recognized the truth of what her friend was saying. Every visit to the hospital produced a deluge of memories. In the months that had passed, she was certain that the meeting with the dream man had blossomed and grown out of proportion in her memory. Every word, every action had been relived a thousand times until her mind had memorized the smallest detail, down to the musky, spicy scent of him. Jo Marie had never told anyone about that night of the Mardi Gras. A couple of times she'd wanted to confide in Kelly, but the words wouldn't come. Late in the evenings after she'd prepared for bed, it was the dream man's face that drifted into her consciousness as she fell asleep. Jo Marie couldn't understand why this man who had invaded her life so briefly would have such an overwhelming effect. And yet those few minutes had lingered all these months. Maybe in every woman's life there was a man who was meant to fulfill her dreams. And, in that brief five-minute interlude during Mardi Gras, Jo Marie had found hers.

"...Thanksgiving's tomorrow and Christmas is just around the corner." Kelly interrupted Jo Marie's thoughts. The blaring horn of an irritated motorist caused them both to grimace. Whenever possible, they preferred taking the bus, but both wanted an early start on the holiday weekend.

"Where has the year gone?" Jo Marie commented absently. She was paying close attention to the heavy traffic as she merged with the late evening flow that led Interstate 10 through the downtown district. The freeway would deliver them to the two-bedroom apartment they shared.

"I saw Mark today," Kelly said casually.

Something about the way Kelly spoke caused Jo Marie to turn her head. "Oh." It wasn't unnatural that her brother, a resident doctor at Tulane, would run into Kelly. After all, they both worked in the same hospital. "Did World War Three break out?" Jo Marie had never known any two people who could find more things to argue about. After three years, she'd given up trying to figure out why Mark and Kelly couldn't get along. Saying that they rubbed each other the wrong way seemed too trite an explanation. Antagonistic behavior wasn't characteristic of either of them. Kelly was a dedicated nurse and Mark a struggling resident doctor. But when the two were together, the lightning arced between them like a turbulent electrical storm. At one time Jo Marie had thought Kelly and Mark might be interested in each other. But after months of constant bickering she was forced to believe that the only thing between them was her overactive imagination.

"What did Mark have to say?"

Pointedly, Kelly turned her head away and stared out the window. "Oh, the usual."

The low, forced cheerfulness in her roommate's voice didn't fool Jo Marie. Where Kelly was concerned, Mark was merciless. He didn't mean to be cruel or insulting, but he loved to tease Kelly about her family's wealth. Not that money or position was that important to Kelly. "You mean he was kidding you about playing at being a nurse again.'' That was Mark's favorite crack.

One delicate shoulder jerked in response. ''Sometimes I think he must hate me,'' she whispered, pretending a keen interest in the view outside the car window.

The soft catch in Kelly's voice brought Jo Marie's attention from the freeway to her friend. ''Don't mind Mark. He doesn't mean anything by it. He loves to tease. You should hear some of the things he says about my job—you'd think a travel agent did nothing but hand out brochures for the tropics.''

Kelly's abrupt nod was unconvincing.

Mentally, Jo Marie decided to have a talk with her big brother. He shouldn't tease Kelly as if she were his sister. Kelly didn't know how to react to it. As the youngest daughter of a large southern candy manufacturer, Kelly had been sheltered and pampered most of her life. Her only brother was years older and apparently the age difference didn't allow for many sibling conflicts. With four brothers, Jo Marie was no stranger to family squabbles and could stand her own against any one of them.

The apartment was a welcome sight after the twenty-minute freeway drive. Jo Marie and Kelly thought of it as their port in the storm. The two-floor apartment buidling resembled the historic mansion from *Gone With the Wind*. It maintained the flavor of

the Old South without the problem of constant repairs typical of many older buildings.

The minute they were in the door, Kelly headed for
her room. "If you don't mind I think I'll pack."

"Sure. Go ahead." Carelessly, Jo Marie kicked off
her low-heeled shoes. Slouching on the love seat, she
leaned her head back and closed her eyes. The strain
of the hectic rush hour traffic and the tension of a
busy day ebbed away with every relaxing breath.

The sound of running bathwater didn't surprise Jo
Marie. Kelly wanted to get an early start. Her family
lived in an ultramodern home along Lakeshore Drive.
The house bordered Lake Pontchartrain. Jo Marie
had been inside the Beaumont home only once. That
had been enough for her to realize just how good the
candy business was.

Jo Marie was sure that Charles Beaumont may have
disapproved of his only daughter moving into an
apartment with a "nobody" like her, but once he'd
learned that she was the great-great granddaughter of
Jubal Anderson Early, a Confederate Army colonel,
he'd sanctioned the move. Sometime during the Civil
War, Colonel Early had been instrumental in saving
the life of a young Beaumont. Hence, a-hundred-and-
some-odd years later, Early was a name to respect.

Humming Christmas music softly to herself, Jo
Marie wandered into the kitchen and pulled the orange
juice from the refrigerator shelf.

"Want a glass?" She held up the pitcher to Kelly who stepped from the bathroom, dressed in a short terry-cloth robe, with a thick towel securing her bouncy blond curls. One look at her friend and Jo Marie set the ceramic container on the kitchen counter.

"You've been crying." They'd lived together for three years, and apart from one sad, sentimental movie, Jo Marie had never seen Kelly cry.

"No, something's in my eye," she said and sniffled.

"Then why's your nose so red?"

"Maybe I'm catching a cold." She offered the weak explanation and turned sharply toward her room.

Jo Marie's smooth brow narrowed. This was Mark's doing. She was convinced he was the cause of Kelly's uncharacteristic display of emotion.

Something rang untrue about the whole situation between Kelly and Mark. Kelly wasn't a soft, southern belle who fainted at the least provocation. That was another teasing comment Mark enjoyed hurling at her. Kelly was a lady, but no shrinking violet. Jo Marie had witnessed Kelly in action, fighting for her patients and several political causes. The girl didn't back down often. After Thanksgiving, Jo Marie would help Kelly fine-tune a few witty comebacks. As Mark's sister, Jo Marie was well acquainted with her brother's weak spots. The only way to fight fire was with fire she mused humorously. Together, Jo Marie and Kelly would teach Mark a lesson.

"You want me to fix something to eat before you head for your parents?" Jo Marie shouted from the kitchen. She was standing in front of the cupboard, scanning its meager contents. "How does soup and a sandwich sound?"

"Boring," Kelly returned. "I'm not really hungry."

"Eight hours of back-breaking work on the surgical ward and you're not interested in food? Are you having problems with your tonsils again?"

"I had them out, remember?"

Slowly, Jo Marie straightened. Yes, she remembered. All too well. It had been outside the hospital that she'd literally run into the dream man. Unbidden thoughts of him crowded her mind and forcefully she shook her head to free herself of his image.

Jo Marie had fixed herself dinner and was sitting in front of the television watching the evening news by the time Kelly reappeared.

"I'm leaving now."

"Okay." Jo Marie didn't take her eyes off the television. "Have a happy Thanksgiving; don't eat too much turkey and trimmings."

"Don't throw any wild parties while I'm away." That was a small joke between them. Jo Marie rarely dated these days. Not since—Mardi Gras. Kelly couldn't understand this change in her friend and affectionately teased Jo Marie about her sudden lack of an interesting social life.

"Oh, Kelly, before I forget—" Jo Marie gave her a wicked smile "—bring back some pralines, would you? After all, it's the holidays, so we can splurge."

At any other time Kelly would rant that she'd grown up with candy all her life and detested the sugary sweet concoction. Pralines were Jo Marie's weakness, but the candy would rot before Kelly would eat any of it.

"Sure, I'll be happy to," she agreed lifelessly and was gone before Jo Marie realized her friend had slipped away. Returning her attention to the news, Jo Marie was more determined than ever to have a talk with her brother.

The doorbell chimed at seven. Jo Marie was spreading a bright red polish on her toenails. She grumbled under her breath and screwed on the top of the bottle. But before she could answer the door, her brother strolled into the apartment and flopped down on the sofa that sat at right angles to the matching love seat.

"Come in and make yourself at home," Jo Marie commented dryly.

"I don't suppose you've got anything to eat around here." Dark brown eyes glanced expectantly into the kitchen. All five of the Early children shared the same dusty, dark eyes.

"This isn't a restaurant, you know."

"I know. By the way, where's money bags?"

"Who?" Confused, Jo Marie glanced up from her toes.

"Kelly."

Jo Marie didn't like the reference to Kelly's family wealth, but decided now wasn't the time to comment. Her brother worked long hours and had been out of sorts lately. "She's left for her parents' home already."

A soft snicker followed Jo Marie's announcement.

"Damn it, Mark, I wish you'd lay off Kelly. She's not used to being teased. It really bothers her."

"I'm only joking," Mark defended himself. "Kell knows that."

"I don't think she does. She was crying tonight and I'm sure it's your fault."

"Kelly crying?" He straightened and leaned forward, linking his hands. "But I was only kidding."

"That's the problem. You can't seem to let up on her. You're always putting her down one way or another."

Mark reached for a magazine, but not before Jo Marie saw that his mouth was pinched and hard. "She asks for it."

Rolling her eyes, Jo Marie continued adding the fire-engine-red color to her toes. It wouldn't do any good for her to argue with Mark. Kelly and Mark had to come to an agreement on their own. But that didn't mean Jo Marie couldn't hand Kelly ammunition now and again. Her brother had his vulnerable points, and

Jo Marie would just make certain Kelly was aware of them. Then she could sit back and watch the sparks fly.

Busy with her polish, Jo Marie didn't notice for several minutes how quiet her brother had become. When she lifted her gaze to him, she saw that he had a pained, troubled look. His brow was furrowed in thought.

"I lost a child today," he announced tightly. "I couldn't understand it either. Not medically, I don't mean that. Anything can happen. She'd been brought in last week with a ruptured appendix. We knew from the beginning it was going to be touch and go." He paused and breathed in sharply. "But you know, deep down inside I believed she'd make it. She was their only daughter. The apple of her parents' eye. If all the love in that mother's heart couldn't hold back death's hand, then what good is medical science? What good am I?"

Mark had raised these questions before and Jo Marie had no answers. "I don't know," she admitted solemnly and reached out to touch his hand in reassurance. Mark didn't want to hear the pat answers. He couldn't see that now. Not when he felt like he'd failed this little girl and her parents in some obscure way. At times like these, she'd look at her brother who was a strong, committed doctor and see the doubt in his eyes. She had no answers. Sometimes she wasn't even sure she completely understood his questions.

After wiping his hand across his tired face, Mark stood. "I'm on duty tomorrow morning so I probably won't be at the folks' place until late afternoon. Tell Mom I'll try to make it on time. If I can't, the least you can do is to be sure and save a plate for me."

Knowing Mark, he was likely to go without eating until tomorrow if left to his own devices. "Let me fix you something now," Jo Marie offered. From his unnatural pallor, Jo Marie surmised that Mark couldn't even remember when he'd eaten his last decent meal, coffee and a doughnut on the run excluded.

He glanced at his watch. "I haven't got time. Thanks anyway." Before she could object, he was at the door.

Why had he come? Jo Marie wondered absently. He'd done a lot of that lately—stopping in for a few minutes without notice. And it wasn't as if her apartment were close to the hospital. Mark had to go out of his way to visit her. With a bemused shrug, she followed him to the front door and watched as he sped away in that run-down old car he was so fond of driving. As he left, Jo Marie mentally questioned if her instincts had been on target all along and Kelly and Mark did hold some deep affection for each other. Mark hadn't come tonight for any specific reason. His first question had been about Kelly. Only later had he mentioned losing the child.

"Jo Marie," her mother called from the kitchen. "Would you mind mashing the potatoes?"

The large family kitchen was bustling with activity. The long white counter top was filled with serving bowls ready to be placed on the linen-covered dining room table. Sweet potato and pecan pies were cooling on the smaller kitchen table and the aroma of spice and turkey filled the house.

"Smells mighty good in here," Franklin Early proclaimed, sniffing appreciatively as he strolled into the kitchen and placed a loving arm around his wife's waist.

"Scat," Jo Marie's mother cried with a dismissive wave of her hand. "I won't have you in here sticking your fingers in the pies and blaming it on the boys. Dinner will be ready in ten minutes."

Mark arrived, red faced and slightly breathless. He kissed his mother on the cheek and when she wasn't looking, popped a sweet pickle into his mouth. "I hope I'm not too late."

"I'd say you had perfect timing," Jo Marie teased and handed him the electric mixer. "Here, mash these potatoes while I finish setting the table."

"No way, little sister." His mouth was twisted mockingly as he gave her back the appliance. "I'll set the table. No one wants lumpy potatoes."

The three younger boys, all in their teens, sat in front of the television watching a football game. The Early family enjoyed sports, especially football. Jo

Marie's mother had despaired long ago that her only daughter would ever grow up properly. Instead of playing with dolls, her toys had been cowboy boots and little green army men. Touch football was as much a part of her life as ballet was for some girls.

With Mark out of the kitchen, Jo Marie's mother turned to her. "Have you been feeling all right lately?"

"Me?" The question caught her off guard. "I'm feeling fine. Why shouldn't I be?"

Ruth Early lifted one shoulder in a delicate shrug. "You've had a look in your eye lately." She turned and leaned her hip against the counter, her head tilted at a thoughtful angle. "The last time I saw that look was in your Aunt Bessie's eye before she was married. Tell me, Jo Marie, are you in love?"

Jo Marie hesitated, not knowing how to explain her feelings for a man she had met so briefly. He was more illusion than reality. Her own private fantasy. Those few moments with the dream man were beyond explaining, even to her own mother.

"No," she answered finally, making busy work by placing the serving spoons in the bowls.

"Is he married? Is that it? Save yourself a lot of grief, Jo Marie, and stay away from him if he is. You understand?"

"Yes," she murmured, her eyes avoiding her mother's. For all she knew he could well be married.

Not until late that night did Jo Marie let herself into her apartment. The day had been full. After the huge family dinner, they'd played cards until Mark trapped Jo Marie into playing a game of touch football for old times' sake. Jo Marie agreed and proved that she hadn't lost her "touch."

The apartment looked large and empty. Kelly stayed with her parents over any major holidays. Kelly's family seemed to feel that Kelly still belonged at home and always would, no matter what her age. Although Kelly was twenty-four, the apartment she shared with Jo Marie was more for convenience sake than any need to separate herself from her family.

With her mother's words echoing in her ear, Jo Marie sauntered into her bedroom and dressed for bed. Friday was a work day for her as it was for both Mark and Kelly. The downtown area of New Orleans would be hectic with Christmas shoppers hoping to pick up their gifts from the multitude of sales.

As a travel agent, Jo Marie didn't have many walk-in customers to deal with, but her phone rang continuously. Several people wanted to book holiday vacations, but there was little available that she could offer. The most popular vacation spots had been booked months in advance. Several times her information was accepted with an irritated grumble as if she were to blame. By the time she stepped off the bus outside her apartment, Jo Marie wasn't in any mood for company.

No sooner had the thought formed than she caught sight of her brother. He was parked in the lot outside the apartment building. Hungry and probably looking for a hot meal, she guessed. He knew that their mother had sent a good portion of the turkey and stuffing home with Jo Marie so Mark's appearance wasn't any real surprise.

"Hi," she said and knocked on his car window. The faraway look in his eyes convinced her that after all these years Mark had finally learned to sleep with his eyes open. He was so engrossed in his thoughts that Jo Marie was forced to tap on his window a second time.

"Paging Dr. Early," she mimicked in a high-pitched hospital voice. "Paging Dr. Mark Early."

Mark turned and stared at her blankly. "Oh, hi." He sat up and climbed out of the car.

"I suppose you want something to eat." Her greeting wasn't the least bit cordial, but she was tired and irritable.

The edge of Mark's mouth curled into a sheepish grin. "If it isn't too much trouble."

"No," she offered him an apologetic smile. "It's just been a rough day and my feet hurt."

"My sister sits in an office all day, files her nails, reads books and then complains that her feet hurt."

Jo Marie was too weary to rise to the bait. "Not even your acid tongue is going to get a rise out of me tonight."

"I know something that will," Mark returned smugly.

"Ha." From force of habit, Jo Marie kicked off her shoes and strolled into the kitchen.

"Wanna bet?"

"I'm not a betting person, especially after playing cards with you yesterday, but if you care to impress me, fire away." Crossing her arms, she leaned against the refrigerator door and waited.

"Kelly's engaged."

Jo Marie slowly shook her head in disbelief. "I didn't think you'd stoop to fabrications."

That familiar angry, hurt look stole into Mark's eyes. "It's true, I heard it from the horse's own mouth."

Lightly shaking her head from side to side to clear her thoughts, Jo Marie still came up with a blank. "But who?" Kelly wasn't going out with anyone seriously.

"Some cousin. Rich, no doubt," Mark said and straddled a kitchen chair. "She's got a diamond as big as a baseball. Must be hard for her to work with a rock that size weighing down her hand."

"A cousin?" New Orleans was full of Beaumonts, but none that Kelly had mentioned in particular. "I can't believe it," Jo Marie gasped. "She'd have said something to me."

"From what I understand, she tried to phone last night, but we were still at the folks' house. Just as well,'' Mark mumbled under his breath. "I'm not about to toast this engagement. First she plays at being nurse and now she wants to play at being a wife."

Mark's bitterness didn't register past the jolt of surprise that Jo Marie felt. "Kelly engaged," she repeated.

"You don't need to keep saying it," Mark snapped.

"Saying what?" A jubilant Kelly walked in the front door.

"Never mind," Mark said and slowly stood. "It's time for me to be going, I'll talk to you later."

"What about dinner?"

"There's someone I'd like you both to meet," Kelly announced.

Ignoring her, Mark turned to Jo Marie. "I've suddenly lost my appetite."

"Jo Marie, I'd like to introduce you to my fiancé, Andrew Beaumont."

Jo Marie's gaze swung from the frustrated look on her brother's face to an intense pair of gray eyes. There was only one man on earth with eyes the shade of a winter sea. The dream man.

Chapter Two

Stunned into speechlessness, Jo Marie struggled to maintain her composure. She took in a deep breath to calm her frantic heartbeat and forced a look of pleasant surprise. Andrew Beaumont apparently didn't even remember her. Jo Marie couldn't see so much as a flicker of recognition in the depth of his eyes. In the last nine months it was unlikely that he had given her more than a passing thought, if she'd been worthy of even that. And yet, she vividly remembered every detail of him, down to the crisp dark hair, the broad, muscular shoulders and faint twist of his mouth.

With an effort that was just short of superhuman,

Jo Marie smiled. "Congratulations, you two. But what a surprise."

Kelly hurried across the room and hugged her tightly. "It was to us, too. Look." She held out her hand for Jo Marie to admire the flashing diamond. Mark hadn't been exaggerating. The flawless gem mounted in an antique setting was the largest Jo Marie had ever seen.

"What did I tell you," Mark whispered in her ear.

Confused, Kelly glanced from sister to brother. "Drew and I are celebrating tonight. We'd love it if you came. Both of you."

"No," Jo Marie and Mark declared in unison.

"I'm bushed," Jo Marie begged off.

"...and tired," Mark finished lamely.

For the first time, Andrew spoke. "We insist." The deep, resonant voice was exactly as Jo Marie remembered. But tonight there was something faintly arrogant in the way he spoke that dared Jo Marie and Mark to put up an argument.

Brother and sister exchanged questioning glances, neither willing to be drawn into the celebration. Each for their own reasons, Jo Marie mused.

"Well—" Mark cleared his throat, clearly ill at ease with the formidable fiancé "—perhaps another time."

"You're Jo Marie's brother?" Andrew asked with a mocking note.

"How'd you know?"

Kelly stuck her arm through Andrew's. "Family resemblance, silly. No one can look at the two of you and not know you're related."

"I can't say the same thing about you two. I thought it was against the law to marry a cousin." Mark didn't bother to disguise his contempt.

"We're distant cousins," Kelly explained brightly. Her eyes looked adoringly into Andrew's and Jo Marie felt her stomach tighten. Jealousy. This sickening feeling in the pit of her stomach was the green-eyed monster. Jo Marie had only experienced brief tastes of the emotion; now it filled her mouth until she thought she would choke on it.

"I...had a horribly busy day." Jo Marie sought frantically for an excuse to stay home.

"And I'd have to go home and change," Mark added, looking down over his pale gray cords and sport shirt.

"No, you wouldn't," Kelly contradicted with a provocative smile. "We're going to K-Paul's."

"Sure, and wait in line half the night." A muscle twitched in Mark's jaw.

K-Paul's was a renowned restaurant that was ranked sixth in the world. Famous, but not elegant. The small establishment served creole cooking at its best.

"No," Kelly supplied, and the dip in her voice revealed how much she wanted to share this night with her friends. "Andrew's a friend of Paul's."

Mark looked at Jo Marie and rolled his eyes. "I should have known," he muttered sarcastically.

"What time did you say we'd be there, darling?"

Jo Marie closed her eyes to the sharp flash of pain at the affectionate term Kelly used so freely. These jealous sensations were crazy. She had no right to feel this way. This man...Andrew Beaumont, was a blown-up figment of her imagination. The brief moments they shared should have been forgotten long ago. Kelly was her friend. Her best friend. And Kelly deserved every happiness.

With a determined jut to her chin, Jo Marie flashed her roommate a warm smile. "Mark and I would be honored to join you tonight."

"We would?" Mark didn't sound pleased. Irritation rounded his dark eyes and he flashed Jo Marie a look that openly contradicted her agreement. Jo Marie wanted to tell him that he owed Kelly this much for all the teasing he'd given her. In addition, her look pleaded with him to understand how much she needed his support tonight. Saying as much was impossible, but she hoped her eyes conveyed the message.

Jo Marie turned slightly so that she faced the tall figure standing only a few inches from her. "It's generous of you to include us," she murmured, but discovered that she was incapable of meeting Andrew's penetrating gaze.

"Give us a minute to freshen up and we'll be on our way," Kelly's effervescent enthusiasm filled the room. "Come on, Jo Marie."

The two men remained in the compact living room. Jo Marie glanced back to note that Mark looked like a jaguar trapped in an iron cage. When he wasn't pacing, he stood restlessly shifting his weight repeatedly from one foot to the other. His look was weary and there was an uncharacteristic tightness to his mouth that narrowed his eyes.

"What do you think," Kelly whispered, and gave a long sigh. "Isn't he fantastic? I think I'm the luckiest girl in the world. Of course, we'll have to wait until after the holidays to make our announcement official. But isn't Drew wonderful?"

Jo Marie forced a noncommittal nod. The raw disappointment left an aching void in her heart. Andrew should have been hers. "He's wonderful." The words came out sounding more like a tortured whisper than a compliment.

Kelly paused, lowering the brush. "Jo, are you all right? You sound like you're going to cry."

"Maybe I am." Tears burned for release, but not for the reason Kelly assumed. "It's not every day I lose my best friend."

"But you're not losing me."

Jo Marie's fingers curved around the cold bathroom sink. "But you are planning to get married?"

"Oh yes, we'll make an official announcement in January, but we haven't set a definite date for the wedding."

That surprised Jo Marie. Andrew didn't look like the kind of man who would encourage a long engagement. She would have thought that once he'd made a decision, he'd move on it. But then, she didn't know Andrew Beaumont. Not really.

A glance in the mirror confirmed that her cheeks were pale, her dark eyes haunted with a wounded, perplexed look. A quick application of blush added color to her bloodless face, but there was little she could do to disguise the troubled look in her eyes. She could only pray that no one would notice.

"Ready?" Kelly stood just outside the open door.

Jo Marie's returning smile was frail as she mentally braced herself for the coming ordeal. She paused long enough to dab perfume to the pulse points at the hollow of her neck and at her wrists.

"I, for one, am starved," Kelly announced as they returned to the living room. "And from what I remember of K-Paul's, eating is an experience we won't forget."

Jo Marie was confident that every part of this evening would be indelibly marked in her memory, but not for the reasons Kelly assumed.

Andrew's deep blue Mercedes was parked beside Mark's old clunker. The differences between the two men were as obvious as the vehicles they drove.

Clearly ill at ease, Mark stood on the sidewalk in front of his car. "Why don't Jo Marie and I follow you?"

"Nonsense," Kelly returned, "there's plenty of room in Drew's car for everyone. You know what the traffic is like. We could get separated. I wouldn't want that to happen."

Mark's twisted mouth said that he would have given a weeks' pay to suddenly disappear. Jo Marie studied her brother carefully from her position in the back seat. His displeasure at being included in this evening's celebration was confusing. There was far more than reluctance in his attitude. He might not get along with Kelly, but she would have thought that Mark would wish Kelly every happiness. But he didn't. Not by the stiff, unnatural behavior she'd witnessed from him tonight.

Mark's attitude didn't change any at the restaurant. Paul, the robust chef, came out from the kitchen and greeted the party himself.

After they'd ordered, the small party sat facing one another in stony silence. Kelly made a couple of attempts to start up the conversation, but her efforts were to no avail. The two men eyed each other, looking as if they were ready to do battle at the slightest provocation.

Several times while they ate their succulent Shrimp Remoulade, Jo Marie found her gaze drawn to Andrew. In many ways he was exactly as she remembered. In others, he was completely different. His voice was low pitched and had a faint drawl. And he wasn't a talker. His expression was sober almost to the point of being somber, which was unusual for a man celebrating his engagement. Another word that her mind tossed out was disillusioned. Andrew Beaumont looked as though he was disenchanted with life. From everything she'd learned he was wealthy and successful. He owned a land development firm. Delta Development, Inc. had been in the Beaumont family for three generations. According to Kelly, the firm had expanded extensively under Andrew's direction.

But if Jo Marie was paying attention to Andrew, he was nothing more than polite to her. He didn't acknowledge her with anything more than an occasional look. And since she hadn't directed any questions to him, he hadn't spoken either. At least not to her.

Paul's special touch for creole cooking made the meal memorable. And although her thoughts were troubled and her heart perplexed, when the waitress took Jo Marie's plate away she had done justice to the meal. Even Mark, who had sat uncommunicative and sullen through most of the dinner, had left little on his plate.

After K-Paul's, Kelly insisted they visit the French Quarter. The others were not as enthusiastic. After an hour of walking around and sampling some of the best jazz sounds New Orleans had to offer, they returned to the apartment.

"I'll make the coffee," Kelly proposed as they climbed from the luxury car.

Mark made a show of glancing at his watch. "I think I'll skip the chicory," he remarked in a flippant tone. "Tomorrow's a busy day."

"Come on, Mark—" Kelly pouted prettily "—don't be a spoil sport."

Mark's face darkened with a scowl. "If you insist."

"It isn't every day I celebrate my engagement. And, Mark, have you noticed that we haven't fought once all night? That must be some kind of a record."

A poor facsimile of a smile lifted one corner of his mouth. "It must be," he agreed wryly. He lagged behind as they climbed the stairs to the second-story apartment.

Jo Marie knew her brother well enough to know he'd have the coffee and leave as soon as it was polite to do so.

They sat in stilted silence, drinking their coffee.

"Do you two work together?" Andrew directed his question to Jo Marie.

Flustered she raised her palm to her breast. "Me?"

"Yes. Did you and Kelly meet at Tulane Hospital?"

"No, I'm a travel agent. Mark's the one in the family with the brains." She heard the breathlessness in her voice and hoped that he hadn't.

"Don't put yourself down," Kelly objected. "You're no dummy. Did you know that Jo Marie is actively involved in saving our wetlands? She volunteers her time as an office worker for the Land For The Future organization."

"That doesn't require intelligence, only time," Jo Marie murmured self-consciously and congratulated herself for keeping her voice even.

For the first time that evening, Andrew directed his attention to her and smiled. The effect it had on Jo Marie's pulse was devastating. To disguise her reaction, she raised the delicate china cup to her lips and took a tentative sip of the steaming coffee.

"And all these years I thought the LFTF was for little old ladies."

"No." Jo Marie was able to manage only the one word.

"At one time Jo Marie wanted to be a biologist," Kelly supplied.

Andrew arched two thick brows. "What stopped you?"

"Me," Mark cut in defensively. "The schooling she required was extensive and our parents couldn't afford to pay for us both to attend university at the same time. Jo Marie decided to drop out."

"That's not altogether true." Mark was making her sound noble and self-sacrificing. "It wasn't like that. If I'd wanted to continue my schooling there were lots of ways I could have done so."

"And you didn't?" Again Andrew's attention was focused on her.

She moistened her dry lips before continuing. "No. I plan to go back to school someday. Until then I'm staying active in the causes that mean the most to me and to the future of New Orleans."

"Jo Marie's our neighborhood scientist," Kelly added proudly. "She has a science club for children every other Saturday morning. I swear she's a natural with those kids. She's always taking them on hikes and planning field trips for them."

"You must like children." Again Andrew's gaze slid to Jo Marie.

"Yes," she answered self-consciously and lowered her eyes. She was grateful when the topic of conversation drifted to other subjects. When she chanced a look at Andrew, she discovered that his gaze centered on her lips. It took a great deal of restraint not to moisten them. And even more to force the memory of his kiss from her mind.

Once again, Mark made a show of looking at his watch and standing. "The evening's been—" he faltered looking for an adequate description "—interesting. Nice meeting you, Beaumont. Best wishes to you and Florence Nightingale."

The sip of coffee stuck in Jo Marie's throat, causing a moment of intense pain until her muscles relaxed enough to allow her to swallow. Grateful that no one had noticed, Jo Marie set her cup aside and walked with her brother to the front door. "I'll talk to you later," she said in farewell.

Mark wiped a hand across his eyes. He looked more tired than Jo Marie could remember seeing him in a long time. "I've been dying to ask you all night. Isn't Kelly's rich friend the one who filled in the swampland for that housing development you fought so hard against?"

"And lost." Jo Marie groaned inwardly. She had been a staunch supporter of the environmentalists and had helped gather signatures against the project. But to no avail. "Then he's also the one who bought out Rose's," she murmured thoughtfully as a feeling of dread washed over her. Rose's Hotel was in the French Quarter and was one of the landmarks of Louisiana. In addition to being a part of New Orleans' history, the hotel was used to house transients. It was true that Rose's was badly in need of repairs, but Jo Marie hated to see the wonderful old building destroyed in the name of progress. If annihilating the breeding habitat of a hundred different species of birds hadn't troubled Andrew Beaumont, then she doubted that an old hotel in ill-repair would matter to him either.

Rubbing her temple to relieve an unexpected and throbbing headache, Jo Marie nodded. "I remember

Kelly saying something about a cousin being responsible for Rose's. But I hadn't put the two together."

"He has," Mark countered disdainfully. "And come up with megabucks. Our little Kelly has reeled in quite a catch, if you like the cold, heartless sort."

Jo Marie's mind immediately rejected that thought. Andrew Beaumont may be the man responsible for several controversial land acquisitions, but he wasn't heartless. Five minutes with him at the Mardi Gras had proven otherwise.

Mark's amused chuckle carried into the living room. "You've got that battle look in your eye. What are you thinking?"

"Nothing," she returned absently. But already her mind was racing furiously. "I'll talk to you tomorrow."

"I'll give you a call," Mark promised and was gone.

When Jo Marie returned to the living room, she found Kelly and Andrew chatting companionably. They paused and glanced at her as she rejoined them.

"You've known each other for a long time, haven't you?" Jo Marie lifted the half-full china cup, making an excuse to linger. She sat on the arm of the love seat, unable to decide if she should stay and speak her mind or repress her tongue.

"We've known each other since childhood." Kelly answered for the pair.

"And Andrew is the distant cousin you said had bought Rose's."

Kelly's sigh was uncomfortable. "I was hoping you wouldn't put two and two together."

"To be honest, I didn't. Mark figured it out."

A frustrated look tightened Kelly's once happy features.

"Will someone kindly tell me what you two are talking about?" Andrew asked.

"Rose's," they chimed in unison.

"Rose's," he repeated slowly and a frown appeared between his gray eyes.

Apparently Andrew Beaumont had so much land one small hotel didn't matter.

"The hotel."

The unexpected sharpness in his voice caused Jo Marie to square her shoulders. "It may seem like a little thing to you."

"Not for what that piece of land cost me," he countered in a hard voice.

"I don't think Drew likes to mix business with pleasure," Kelly warned, but Jo Marie disregarded the well-intended advice.

"But the men living in Rose's will have nowhere to go."

"They're bums."

A sadness filled her at the insensitive way he referred to these men. "Rose's had housed homeless men for twenty years. These men need someplace where they can get a hot meal and can sleep."

"It's a prime location for luxury condominiums," he said cynically.

"But what about the transients? What will become of them?"

"That, Miss Early, is no concern of mine."

Unbelievably Jo Marie felt tears burn behind her eyes. She blinked them back. Andrew Beaumont wasn't the dream man she'd fantasized over all these months. He was cold and cynical. The only love he had in his life was profit. A sadness settled over her with a weight she thought would be crippling.

"I feel very sorry for you, Mr. Beaumont," she said smoothly, belying her turbulent emotions. "You may be very rich, but there's no man poorer than one who has no tolerance for the weakness of others."

Kelly gasped softly and groaned. "I knew this was going to happen."

"Are you always so opinionated, Miss Early?" There was no disguising the icy tones.

"No, but there are times when things are so wrong that I can't remain silent." She turned to Kelly. "I apologize if I've ruined your evening. If you'll excuse me now, I think I'll go to bed. Good night, Mr. Beaumont. May you and Kelly have many years of happiness together." The words nearly stuck in her throat but she managed to get them out before walking from the room.

"If this offends you in any way I won't do it." Jo Marie studied her roommate carefully. The demonstration in front of Rose's had been planned weeks ago. Jo Marie's wooden picket sign felt heavy in her hand. For the first time in her life, her convictions conflicted with her feelings. She didn't want to march against Andrew. It didn't matter what he'd done, but she couldn't stand by and see those poor men turned into the streets, either. Not in the name of progress. Not when progress was at the cost of the less fortunate and the fate of a once lovely hotel.

"This picket line was arranged long before you met Drew."

"That hasn't got anything to do with this. Drew is important to you. I wouldn't want to do something that will place your relationship with him in jeopardy."

"It won't."

Kelly sounded far more confident than Jo Marie felt.

"In fact," she continued, "I doubt that Drew even knows anything about the demonstration. Those things usually do nothing to sway his decision. In fact, I'd say they do more harm than good as far as he's concerned."

Jo Marie had figured that much out herself, but she couldn't stand by doing nothing. Rose's was scheduled to be shut down the following week...a short month before Christmas. Jo Marie didn't know how anyone could be so heartless. The hotel was to be torn down a week later and new construction was scheduled to begin right after the first of the year.

Kelly paused at the front door while Jo Marie picked up her picket sign and tossed the long strap of her purse over her shoulder.

"You do understand why I can't join you?" she asked hesitatingly.

"Of course," Jo Marie said and exhaled softly. She'd never expected Kelly to participate. This fight couldn't include her friend without causing bitter feelings.

"Be careful." Her arms wrapped around her waist to chase away a chill, Kelly walked down to the parking lot with Jo Marie.

"Don't worry. This is a peaceful demonstration. The only wounds I intend to get are from carrying this sign. It's heavy."

Cocking her head sideways, Kelly read the sign for the tenth time. Save Rose's Hotel. A Piece Of New Orleans History. Kelly chuckled and slowly shook her head. "I should get a picture of you. Drew would get a real kick out of that."

The offer of a picture was a subtle reminder that Drew wouldn't so much as see the sign. He probably wasn't even aware of the protest rally.

Friends of Rose's and several others from the Land For The Future headquarters were gathered outside the hotel when Jo Marie arrived. Several people who knew Jo Marie raised their hands in welcome.

"Have the television and radio stations been notified?" the organizer asked a tall man Jo Marie didn't recognize.

"I notified them, but most weren't all that interested. I doubt that we'll be given air time."

A feeling of gloom settled over the group. An unexpected cloudburst did little to brighten their mood. Jo Marie hadn't brought her umbrella and was drenched in minutes. A chill caused her teeth to chatter and no matter how hard she tried, she couldn't stop shivering. Uncaring, the rain fell indiscriminately over the small group of protesters.

"You little fool," Mark said when he found her an hour later. "Are you crazy, walking around wet and cold like that?" His voice was a mixture of exasperation and pride.

"I'm making a statement," Jo Marie argued.

"You're right. You're telling the world what a fool you are. Don't you have any better sense than this?"

Jo Marie ignored him, placing one foot in front of the other as she circled the sidewalk in front of Rose's Hotel.

"Do you think Beaumont cares?"

Jo Marie refused to be drawn into his argument. "Instead of arguing with me, why don't you go inside and see what's holding up the coffee?"

"You're going to need more than a hot drink to prevent you from getting pneumonia. Listen to reason for once in your life."

"No!" Emphatically Jo Marie stamped her foot. "This is too important."

"And your health isn't?"

"Not now." The protest group had dwindled down to less than ten. "I'll be all right." She shifted the sign from one shoulder to the other and flexed her stiff fingers. Her back ached from the burden of her message. And with every step the rain water in her shoes squished noisily. "I'm sure we'll be finished in another hour."

"If you aren't, I'm carting you off myself," Mark shouted angrily and returned to his car. He shook his finger at her in warning as he drove past.

True to his word, Mark returned an hour later and followed her back to the apartment.

Jo Marie could hardly drive she was shivering so violently. Her long chestnut hair fell in limp tendrils over her face. Rivulets of cold water ran down her neck and she bit into her bottom lip at the pain caused by gripping the steering wheel. Carrying the sign had formed painful blisters in the palms of her hands. This was one protest rally she wouldn't soon forget.

Mark seemed to blame Andrew Beaumont for the fact that she was cold, wet and miserable. But it wasn't Andrew's fault that it had rained. Not a single forecaster had predicted it would. She'd lived in New Orleans long enough to know she should carry an umbrella with her. Mark was looking for an excuse to dislike Andrew. Any excuse. In her heart, Jo Marie couldn't. No matter what he'd done, there was something deep within her that wouldn't allow any bitterness inside. In some ways she was disillusioned and hurt that her dream man wasn't all she'd thought. But that was as deep as her resentments went.

"Little fool," Mark repeated tenderly as he helped her out of the car. "Let's get you upstairs and into a hot bath."

"As long as I don't have to listen to you lecture all night," she said, her teeth chattering as she climbed the stairs to the second-story apartment. Although she was thoroughly miserable, there was a spark of humor in her eyes as she opened the door and stepped inside the apartment.

"Jo Marie," Kelly cried in alarm. "Good grief, what happened?"

A light laugh couldn't disguise her shivering. "Haven't you looked out the window lately? It's raining cats and dogs."

"This is your fault, Beaumont," Mark accused harshly and Jo Marie sucked in a surprised breath. In her misery, she hadn't noticed Andrew, who was casually sitting on the love seat.

He rose to a standing position and glared at Mark as if her brother were a mad man. "Explain yourself," he demanded curtly.

Kelly intervened, crossing the room and placing a hand on Andrew's arm. "Jo Marie was marching in that rally I was telling you about."

"In front of Rose's Hotel," Mark added, his fists tightly clenched at his side. He looked as if he wanted to get physical. Consciously, Jo Marie moved closer to her brother's side. Fist fighting was so unlike Mark. He was a healer, not a boxer. One look told Jo Marie that in a physical exchange, Mark would lose.

Andrew's mouth twisted scornfully. "You, my dear Miss Early, are a fool."

Jo Marie dipped her head mockingly. "And you, Mr. Beaumont, are heartless."

"But rich," Mark intervened. "And money goes a long way in making a man attractive. Isn't that right, Kelly?"

Kelly went visibly pale, her blue eyes filling with tears. "That's not true," she cried, her words jerky as she struggled for control.

"You will apologize for that remark, Early." Andrew's low voice held a threat that was undeniable.

Mark knotted and unknotted his fists. "I won't apologize for the truth. If you want to step outside, maybe you'd like to make something of it."

"Mark!" Both Jo Marie and Kelly gasped in shocked disbelief.

Jo Marie moved first. "Get out of here before you cause trouble." Roughly she opened the door and shoved him outside.

"You heard what I said," Mark growled on his way out the door.

"I've never seen Mark behave like that," Jo Marie murmured, her eyes lowered to the carpet where a small pool of water had formed. "I can only apologize." She paused and inhaled deeply. "And, Kelly, I'm sure you know he didn't mean what he said to you. He's upset because of the rally." Her voice was deep with emotion as she excused herself and headed for the bathroom.

A hot bath went a long way toward making her more comfortable. Mercifully, Andrew was gone by the time she had finished. She didn't feel up to another confrontation with him.

"Call on line three."

Automatically Jo Marie punched in the button and reached for her phone. "Jo Marie Early, may I help you?"

"You won."

"Mark?" He seldom phoned her at work.

"Did you hear me?" he asked excitedly.

"What did I win?" she asked humoring him.

"Beaumont."

Jo Marie's hand tightened around the receiver. "What do you mean?"

"It just came over the radio. Delta Development, Inc. is donating Rose's Hotel to the city," Mark announced with a short laugh. "Can you believe it?"

"Yes," Jo Marie closed her eyes to the onrush of emotion. Her dream man hadn't let her down. "I can believe it."

Chapter Three

But you must come,'' Kelly insisted, sitting across from Jo Marie. "It'll be miserable without you."

"Kell, I don't know.'' Jo Marie looked up from the magazine she was reading and nibbled on her lower lip.

"It's just a Christmas party with a bunch of stuffy people I don't know. You know how uncomfortable I am meeting new people. I hate parties."

"Then why attend?''

"Drew says we must. I'm sure he doesn't enjoy the party scene any more than I do, but he's got to go or offend a lot of business acquaintances."

"But I wasn't included in the invitation," Jo Marie argued. She'd always liked people and usually did well at social functions.

"Of course you were included. Both you and Mark," Kelly insisted. "Drew saw to that."

Thoughtfully, Jo Marie considered her roommate's request. As much as she objected, she really would like to go, if for no more reason than to thank Andrew for his generosity regarding Rose's. Although she'd seen him briefly a couple of times since, the opportunity hadn't presented itself to express her appreciation. The party was one way she could do that. New Orleans was famous for its festive balls and holiday parties. Without Kelly's invitation, Jo Marie doubted that there would ever be the chance for her to attend such an elaborate affair.

"All right," she conceded, "but I doubt that Mark will come." Mark and Andrew hadn't spoken since the last confrontation in the girls' living room. The air had hung heavy between them then and Jo Marie doubted that Andrew's decision regarding Rose's Hotel would change her brother's attitude.

"Leave Mark to me," Kelly said confidently. "Just promise me that you'll be there."

"I'll need a dress." Mentally Jo Marie scanned the contents of her closet and came up with zero. Nothing she owned would be suitable for such an elaborate affair.

"Don't worry, you can borrow something of mine," Kelly offered with a generosity that was innate to her personality.

Jo Marie nearly choked on her laughter. "I'm three inches taller than you." And several pounds heavier, but she preferred not to mention that. Only once before had Jo Marie worn Kelly's clothes. The night she'd met Andrew.

Kelly giggled and the bubbly sound was pleasant to the ears. "I heard miniskirts were coming back into style."

"Perhaps, but I doubt that the fashion will arrive in time for Christmas. Don't worry about me, I'll go out this afternoon and pick up some material for a dress."

"But will you have enough time between now and the party to sew it?" Kelly's blue eyes rounded with doubt.

"I'll make time." Jo Marie was an excellent seamstress. She had her mother to thank for that. Ruth Early had insisted that her only daughter learn to sew. Jo Marie had balked in the beginning. Her interests were anything but domestic. But now, as she had been several times in the past, she was grateful for the skill.

She found a pattern of a three-quarter-length dress with a matching jacket. The simplicity of the design made the outfit all the more appealing. Jo Marie could dress it either up or down, depending on the occasion. The silky, midnight blue material she purchased was perfect for the holiday, and Jo Marie knew that shade to be one of her better colors.

When she returned to the apartment, Kelly was gone. A note propped on the kitchen table explained that she wouldn't be back until dinner time.

After washing, drying, and carefully pressing the material, Jo Marie laid it out on the table for cutting. Intent on her task, she had pulled her hair away from her face and had tied it at the base of her neck with a rubber band. Straight pins were pressed between her lips when the doorbell chimed. The neighborhood children often stopped in for a visit. Usually Jo Marie welcomed their company, but she was busy now and interruptions could result in an irreparable mistake. She toyed with the idea of not answering.

The impatient buzz told her that her company was irritated at being kept waiting.

"Damn, damn, damn," she grumbled beneath her breath as she made her way across the room. Extracting the straight pins from her mouth, she stuck them in the small cushion she wore around her wrist.

"Andrew!" Secretly she thanked God the pins were out of her mouth or she would have swallowed them in her surprise.

"Is Kelly here?"

"No, but come in." Her heart was racing madly as he walked into the room. Nervous fingers tugged the rubber band from her chestnut hair in a futile attempt to look more presentable. She shook her hair free, then wished she'd kept it neatly in place. For days Jo Marie would have welcomed the opportunity to thank Andrew, but she discovered as she followed him into the living room that her tongue was tied and her mouth felt gritty and dry. "I'm glad you're here...I wanted to thank you for your decision about Rose's...the hotel."

He interrupted her curtly. "My dear Miss Early, don't be misled. My decision wasn't—"

Her hand stopped him. "I know," she said softly. He didn't need to tell her his reasoning. She was already aware it wasn't because of the rally or anything that she'd done or said. "I just wanted to thank you for whatever may have been your reason."

Their eyes met and held from across the room. Countless moments passed in which neither spoke. The air was electric between them and the urge to reach out and touch Andrew was almost overwhelming. The same breathlessness that had attacked her the night of the Mardi Gras returned. Andrew had to remember, he had to. Yet he gave no indication that he did.

Jo Marie broke eye contact first, lowering her gaze to the wool carpet. "I'm not sure where Kelly is, but she said she'd be back by dinner time." Her hand shook as she handed him the note off the kitchen counter.

"Kelly mentioned the party?"

Jo Marie nodded.

"You'll come?"

She nodded her head in agreement. "If I finish sewing this dress in time." She spoke so he wouldn't think she'd suddenly lost the ability to talk. Never had she been more aware of a man. Her heart was hammering at his nearness. He was so close all she had to do was reach out and touch him. But insurmountable barriers stood between them. At last, after all these months she was alone with her dream man. So many times a similar scene had played in her mind. But Andrew didn't remember her. The realization produced an indescribable ache in her heart. What had been the most profound moment in her life had been nothing to him.

"Would you like to sit down?" she offered, remembering her manners. "There's coffee on if you'd like a cup."

He shook his head. "No, thanks." He ran his hand along the top of the blue cloth that was stretched across the kitchen table. His eyes narrowed and he looked as if his thoughts were a thousand miles away.

"Why don't you buy a dress?"

A smile trembled at the edge of her mouth. To a man who had always had money, buying something as simple as a dress would seem the most logical solution.

"I sew most of my own things," she explained softly, rather than enlightening him with a lecture on economics.

"Did you make this?" His fingers touched the short sleeve of her cotton blouse and brushed against the sensitive skin of her upper arm.

Immediately a warmth spread where his fingers had come into contact with her flesh. Jo Marie's pale cheeks instantly flushed with a crimson flood of color. "Yes," she admitted hoarsely, hating the way her body, her voice, everything about her, was affected by this man.

"You do beautiful work."

She kept her eyes lowered and drew in a steadying breath. "Thank you."

"Next weekend I'll be having a Christmas party at my home for the employees of my company. I would be honored if both you and your brother attended."

Already her heart was racing with excitement; she'd love to visit his home. But seeing where he lived was only an excuse. She'd do anything to see more of him. "I can't speak for Mark," she answered after several moments, feeling guilty for her thoughts.

"But you'll come?"

"I'd be happy to. Thank you." Her only concern was that no one from Delta Development would recognize her as the same woman who was active in the protest against the housing development and in saving Rose's Hotel.

"Good," he said gruffly.

The curve of her mouth softened into a smile. "I'll tell Kelly that you were by. Would you like her to phone you?"

"No, I'll be seeing her later. Goodbye, Jo Marie."

She walked with him to the door, holding onto the knob longer than necessary. "Goodbye, Andrew," she murmured.

Jo Marie leaned against the door and covered her face with both hands. She shouldn't be feeling this eager excitement, this breathless bewilderment, this softness inside at the mere thought of him. Andrew Beaumont was her roommate's fiancé. She had to remember that. But somehow, Jo Marie recognized that her conscience could repeat the information all day, but it would have little effect on her restless heart.

The sewing machine was set up at the table when Kelly walked into the apartment a couple of hours later.

"I'm back," Kelly murmured happily as she hung her sweater in the closet.

"Where'd you go?"

"To see a friend."

Jo Marie thought she detected a note of hesitancy in her roommate's voice and glanced up momentarily from her task. She paused herself, then said, "Andrew was by."

A look of surprise worked its way across Kelly's pixie face. "Really? Did he say what he wanted?"

"Not really. He didn't leave a message." Jo Marie strove for nonchalance, but her fingers shook slightly and she hoped that her friend didn't notice the telltale mannerism.

"You like Drew, don't you?"

For some reason, Jo Marie's mind had always referred to him as Andrew. "Yes." She continued with the mechanics of sewing, but she could feel Kelly's eyes roam over her face as she studied her. Immediately a guilty flush reddened her cheeks. Somehow, some way, Kelly had detected how strongly Jo Marie felt about Andrew.

"I'm glad," Kelly said at last. "I'd like it if you two would fall in..." She hesitated before concluding with, "Never mind."

The two words were repeated in her mind like the dwindling sounds of an echo off canyon walls.

The following afternoon, Jo Marie arrived home from work and took a crisp apple from the bottom shelf of the refrigerator. She wanted a snack before pulling out her sewing machine again. Kelly was working late and had phoned her at the office so Jo Marie wouldn't worry. Holding the apple between her teeth, she lugged the heavy sewing machine out of the bedroom. No sooner had she set the case on top of the table than the doorbell chimed.

Releasing a frustrated sigh, she swallowed the bite of apple.

"Sign here, please." A clipboard was shoved under her nose.

"I beg your pardon," Jo Marie asked.

"I'm making a delivery, lady. Sign here."

"Oh." Maybe Kelly had ordered something without telling her. Quickly, she penned her name along the bottom line.

"Wait here," was the next abrupt instruction.

Shrugging her shoulder, Jo Marie leaned against the door jamb as the brusque man returned to the brown truck parked below and brought up two large boxes.

"Merry Christmas, Miss Early," he said with a sheepish grin as he handed her the delivery.

"Thank you." The silver box was the trademark of New Orleans' most expensive boutique. Gilded lettering wrote out the name of the proprietor, Madame Renaux Marceau, across the top. Funny, Jo Marie couldn't recall Kelly saying she'd bought something there. But with the party coming, Kelly had apparently opted for the expensive boutique.

Dutifully Jo Marie carried the boxes into Kelly's room and set them on the bed. As she did so the shipping order attached to the smaller box, caught her eye. The statement was addressed to her, not Kelly.

Inhaling a jagged breath, Jo Marie searched the order blank to find out who would be sending her anything. Her parents could never have afforded something from Madame Renaux Marceau.

The air was sucked from her lungs as Jo Marie discovered Andrew Beaumont's name. She fumbled with the lids, peeled back sheer paper and gasped at the beauty of what lay before her. The full-length blue dress was the same midnight shade as the one she was sewing. But this gown was unlike anything Jo Marie had ever seen. A picture of Christmas, a picture of elegance. She held it up and felt tears prickle the back of her eyes. The bodice was layered with intricate rows of tiny pearls that formed a V at the waist. The gown was breathtakingly beautiful. Never had Jo Marie thought to own anything so perfect or so lovely. The second box contained a matching cape with an ornate display of tiny pearls.

Very carefully, Jo Marie folded the dress and cape and placed them back into the boxes. An ache inside her heart erupted into a broken sob. She wasn't a charity case. Did Andrew assume that because she sewed her own clothes that what she was making for the party would be unpresentable?

The telephone book revealed the information she needed. Following her instincts, Jo Marie grabbed a sweater and rushed out the door. She didn't stop until she pulled up in front of the large brick building with the gold plaque in the front that announced that this was the headquarters for Delta Development, Inc.

A listing of offices in the foyer told her where Andrew's was located. Jo Marie rode the elevator to the third floor. Most of the building was deserted, only a few employees remained. Those that did gave her curious stares, but no one questioned her presence.

The office door that had Andrew's name lettered on it was closed, but that didn't dissuade Jo Marie. His receptionist was placing the cover over her typewriter when Jo Marie barged inside.

"I'd like to see Mr. Beaumont," she demanded in a breathless voice.

The gray-haired receptionist glanced at the boxes under Jo Marie's arms and shook her head. "I'm sorry, but the office is closed for the day."

Jo Marie caught the subtle difference. "I didn't ask about the office. I said I wanted to see Mr. Beaumont." Her voice rose with her frustration.

A connecting door between two rooms opened. "Is there a problem, Mrs. Stewart?"

"I was just telling..."

"Jo Marie." Andrew's voice was an odd mixture of surprise and gruffness, yet gentle. His narrowed look centered on the boxes clasped under each arm. "Is there a problem?"

"As a matter of fact there is," she said, fighting to disguise the anger that was building within her to volcanic proportions.

Andrew stepped aside to admit her into his office.

"Will you be needing me further?" Jo Marie heard his secretary ask.

"No, thank you, Mrs. Stewart. I'll see you in the morning."

No sooner had Andrew stepped in the door than Jo Marie whirled on him. The silver boxes from the boutique sat squarely in the middle of Andrew's huge oak desk.

"I think you should understand something right now, Mr. Beaumont," she began heatedly, not bothering to hold back her annoyance. "I am not Cinderella and you most definitely are not my fairy godfather."

"Would I be amiss to guess that my gift displeases you?"

Jo Marie wanted to scream at him for being so calm. She cut her long nails into her palms in an effort to disguise her irritation. "If I am an embarrassment to you wearing a dress I've sewn myself, then I'll simply not attend your precious party."

He looked shocked.

"And furthermore, I am no one's poor relation."

An angry frown deepened three lines across his wide forehead. "What makes you suggest such stupidity?"

"I may be many things, but stupid isn't one of them."

"A lot of things?" He stood behind his desk and leaned forward, pressing his weight on his palms. "You mean like opinionated, headstrong, and impatient."

"Yes," she cried and shot her index finger into the air. "But not stupid."

The tight grip Andrew held on his temper was visible by the way his mouth was pinched until the grooves stood out tense and white. "Maybe not stupid, but incredibly inane."

Her mouth was trembling and Jo Marie knew that if she didn't get away soon, she'd cry. "Let's not argue over definitions. Stated simply, the gesture of buying me a presentable dress was not appreciated. Not in the least."

"I gathered that much, Miss Early. Now if you'll excuse me, I have a dinner engagement."

"Gladly." She pivoted and stormed across the floor ready to jerk open the office door. To her dismay, the door stuck and wouldn't open, ruining her haughty exit.

"Allow me," Andrew offered bitterly.

The damn door! It would have to ruin her proud retreat.

By the time she was in the parking lot, most of her anger had dissipated. Second thoughts crowded her mind on the drive back to the apartment. She could have at least been more gracious about it. Second thoughts quickly evolved into constant recriminations so that by the time she walked through the doorway of the apartment, Jo Marie was thoroughly miserable.

"Hi." Kelly was mixing raw hamburger for meatloaf with her hands. "Did the dress arrive?"

Kelly knew! "Dress?"

"Yes. Andrew and I went shopping for you yesterday afternoon and found the most incredibly lovely party dress. It was perfect for you."

Involuntarily, Jo Marie stiffened. "What made you think I needed a dress?"

Kelly's smile was filled with humor. "You were sewing one, weren't you? Drew said that you were really attending this function as a favor to me. And since this is such a busy time of year he didn't want you spending your nights slaving over a sewing machine."

"Oh." A sickening feeling attacked the pit of her stomach.

"Drew can be the most thoughtful person," Kelly commented as she continued to blend the ground meat. Her attention was more on her task than on Jo Marie. "You can understand why it's so easy to love him."

A strangled sound made its way past the tightness in Jo Marie's throat.

"I'm surprised the dress hasn't arrived. Drew gave specific instructions that it was to be delivered today in case any alterations were needed."

"It did come," Jo Marie announced, more miserable than she could ever remember being.

"It did?" Excitement elevated Kelly's voice. "Why didn't you say something? Isn't it the most beautiful dress you've ever seen? You're going to be gorgeous." Kelly's enthusiasm waned as she turned around. "Jo, what's wrong? You look like you're ready to burst into tears."

"That's...that's because I am," she managed and covering her face with her hands, she sat on the edge of the sofa and wept.

Kelly's soft laugh only made everything seem worse. "I expected gratitude," Kelly said with a sigh and handed Jo Marie a tissue. "But certainly not tears. You don't cry that often."

Noisily Jo Marie blew her nose. "I...I thought I was an embarrassment...to you two...that...you didn't want me...at the party...because I didn't have...the proper clothes...and..."

"You thought what?" Kelly interrupted, a shocked, hurt look crowding her face. "I can't believe you'd even think anything so crazy."

"That's not all. I..." She swallowed. "I took the dress to...Andrew's office and practically...threw it in his face."

"Oh, Jo Marie." Kelly lowered herself onto the sofa beside her friend. "How could you?"

"I don't know. Maybe it sounds ridiculous, but I really believed that you and Andrew would be ashamed to be seen with me in an outfit I'd made myself."

"How could you come up with something so dumb? Especially since I've always complimented you on the things you've sewn."

Miserably, Jo Marie bowed her head. "I know."

"You've really done it, but good, my friend. I can just imagine Drew's reaction to your visit." At the thought Kelly's face grew tight. "Now what are you going to do?"

"Nothing. From this moment on I'll be conveniently tucked in my room when he comes for you..."

"What about the party?" Kelly's blue eyes were rounded with childlike fright and Jo Marie could only speculate whether it was feigned or real. "It's only two days away."

"I can't go, certainly you can understand that."

"But you've got to come," Kelly returned adamantly. "Mark said he'd go if you were there and I need you both. Everything will be ruined if you back out now."

"Mark's coming?" Jo Marie had a difficult time believing her brother would agree to this party idea. She'd have thought Mark would do anything to avoid another confrontation with Andrew.

"Yes. And it wasn't easy to get him to agree."

"I can imagine," Jo Marie returned dryly.

"Jo Marie, please. Your being there means so much to me. More than you'll ever know. Do this one thing and I promise I won't ask another thing of you as long as I live."

Kelly was serious. Something about this party was terribly important to her. Jo Marie couldn't understand what. In order to attend the party she would need to apologize to Andrew. If it had been her choice she would have waited a week or two before approaching him, giving him the necessary time to cool off. As it was, she'd be forced to do it before the party while tempers continued to run hot. Damn! She should have waited until Kelly was home tonight before jumping to conclusions about the dress. Any half-wit would have known her roommate was involved.

"Well?" Kelly regarded her hopefully.

"I'll go, but first I've got to talk to Andrew and explain."

Kelly released a rush of air, obviously relieved. "Take my advice, don't explain a thing. Just tell him you're sorry."

Jo Marie brushed her dark curls from her forehead. She was in no position to argue. Kelly obviously knew Andrew far better than she. The realization produced a rush of painful regrets. "I'll go to his office first thing tomorrow morning," she said with far more conviction in her voice than what she was feeling.

"You won't regret it," Kelly breathed and squeezed Jo Marie's numb fingers. "I promise you won't."

If that was the case, Jo Marie wanted to know why she regretted it already.

To say that she slept restlessly would be an understatement. By morning, dark shadows had formed under her eyes that even cosmetics couldn't completely disguise. The silky blue dress was finished and hanging from a hook on her cloest door. Compared to the lovely creation Andrew had purchased, her simple gown looked drab. Plain. Unsophisticated. Swallowing her pride had always left a bitter aftertaste, and she didn't expect it to be any different today.

"Good luck," Kelly murmured her condolences to Jo Marie on her way out the door.

"Thanks, I'll need that and more." The knot in her stomach grew tighter every minute. Jo Marie didn't know what she was going to say or even where to begin.

Mrs. Stewart, the gray-haired guardian, was at her station when Jo Marie stepped inside Andrew's office.

"Good morning."

The secretary was too well trained to reveal any surprise.

"Would it be possible to talk to Mr. Beaumont for a few minutes?"

"Do you have an appointment?" The older woman flipped through the calendar pages.

"No," Jo Marie tightened her fists. "I'm afraid I don't."

"Mr. Beaumont will be out of the office until this afternoon."

"Oh." Discouragement nearly defeated her. "Could I make an appointment to see him then?"

The paragon of virtue studied the appointment calendar. "I'm afraid not. Mr. Beaumont has meetings scheduled all week. But if you'd like, I could give him a message."

"Yes, please," she returned and scribbled out a note that said she needed to talk to him as soon as it was convenient. Handing the note back to Mrs. Stewart, Jo Marie offered the woman a feeble smile. "Thank you."

"I'll see to it that Mr. Beaumont gets your message," the efficient woman promised.

Jo Marie didn't doubt that the woman would. What she did question was whether Andrew would respond.

By the time Jo Marie readied for bed that evening, she realized that he wouldn't. Now she'd be faced with attending the party with the tension between them so thick it would resemble an English fog.

Mark was the first one to arrive the following evening. Dressed in a pin-stripe suit and a silk tie he looked exceptionally handsome. And Jo Marie didn't mind telling him so.

"Wow." She took a step in retreat and studied him thoughtfully. "Wow," she repeated.

"I could say the same thing. You look terrific."

Self-consciously, Jo Marie smoothed out an imaginary wrinkle from the skirt of her dress. "You're sure?"

"Of course, I am. And I like your hair like that."

Automatically a hand investigated the rhinestone combs that held the bouncy curls away from her face and gave an air of sophistication to her appearance.

"When will money bags be out?" Mark's gaze drifted toward Kelly's bedroom as he took a seat.

"Any minute."

Mark stuck a finger in the collar of his shirt and ran it around his neck. "I can't believe I agreed to this fiasco."

Jo Marie couldn't believe it either. "Why did you?"

Her brother's shrug was filled with self-derision. "I don't know. It seemed to mean so much to Kelly. And to be honest, I guess I owe it to her for all the times I've teased her."

"How do you feel about Beaumont?"

Mark's eyes narrowed fractionally. "I'm trying not to feel anything."

The door opened and Kelly appeared in a red frothy creation that reminded Jo Marie of Christmas and Santa and happy elves. She had seen the dress, but on Kelly the full-length gown came to life. With a lissome grace Jo Marie envied, Kelly sauntered into the room. Mark couldn't take his eyes off her as he slowly rose to a standing position.

"Kelly." He seemed to have difficulty speaking. "You...you're lovely."

Kelly's delighted laughter was filled with pleasure. "Don't sound so shocked. You've just never seen me dressed up is all."

For a fleeting moment Jo Marie wondered if Mark had ever really seen her roommate.

The doorbell chimed and three pairs of eyes glared at the front door accusingly. Jo Marie felt her stomach tighten with nervous apprehension. For two days she'd dreaded this moment. Andrew Beaumont had arrived.

Kelly broke away from the small group and answered the door. Jo Marie watched her brother's eyes narrow as Kelly stood on her tiptoes and lightly brushed her lips across Andrew's cheek. The involuntary reaction stirred a multitude of questions in Jo Marie about Mark's attitude toward Kelly. And her own toward Andrew.

When her gaze drifted from her brother, Jo Marie discovered that Andrew had centered his attention on her.

"You look exceedingly lovely, Miss Early."

"Thank you. I'm afraid the dress I should have worn was mistakenly returned." She prayed he understood her message.

"Let's have a drink before we leave," Kelly suggested. She'd been in the kitchen earlier mixing a concoction of coconut milk, rum, pineapple and several spices.

The cool drink helped relieve some of the tightness in Jo Marie's throat. She sat beside her brother, across from Andrew. The silence in the room was interrupted only by Kelly, who seemed oblivious to the terrible tension. She chattered all the way out to the car.

Again Mark and Jo Marie were relegated to the back seat of Andrew's plush sedan. Jo Marie knew that Mark hated this, but he submitted to the suggestion without comment. Only the stiff way he held himself revealed his discontent. The party was being given by an associate of Andrew's, a builder. The minute Jo Marie heard the name of the firm she recognized it as the one that had worked on the wetlands project.

Mark cast Jo Marie a curious glance and she shook her head indicating that she wouldn't say a word. In some ways, Jo Marie felt that she was fraternizing with the enemy.

Introductions were made and a flurry of names and faces blurred themselves in her mind. Jo Marie recognized several prominent people, and spoke to a few. Mark stayed close by her side and she knew without asking that this whole party scene made him uncomfortable.

In spite of being so adamant about needing her, Kelly was now nowhere to be seen. A half hour later, Jo Marie noticed that Kelly was sitting in a chair against the wall, looking hopelessly lost. She watched amazed as Mark delivered a glass of punch to her and claimed the chair beside her roommate. Kelly brightened immediately and soon the two were smiling and chatting.

Scanning the crowded room, Jo Marie noticed that Andrew was busy talking to a group of men. The room suddenly felt stuffy. An open glass door that led to a balcony invited her outside and into the cool evening air.

Standing with her gloved hands against the railing, Jo Marie glanced up at the starlit heavens. The night was clear and the black sky was adorned with a thousand glittering stars.

"I received a message that you wanted to speak to me." The husky male voice spoke from behind her.

Jo Marie's heart leaped to her throat and she struggled not to reveal her discomfort. "Yes," she said with a relaxing breath.

Andrew joined her at the wrought-iron railing. His nearness was so overwhelming that Jo Marie closed her eyes to the powerful attraction. Her long fingers tightened their grip.

"I owe you an apology. I sincerely regret jumping to conclusions about the dress. You were only being kind."

An eternity passed before Andrew spoke. "Were you afraid I was going to demand a reward, Florence Nightingale?"

Chapter Four

Jo Marie's heart went still as she turned to Andrew with wide, astonished eyes. "You do remember." They'd spent a single, golden moment together so many months ago. Not once since Kelly had introduced Andrew as her fiancé had he given her the slightest inkling that he remembered.

"Did you imagine I could forget?" he asked quietly.

Tightly squeezing her eyes shut, Jo Marie turned back to the railing, her fingers gripping the wrought iron with a strength she didn't know she possessed.

"I came back every day for a month," he continued in a deep, troubled voice. "I thought you were a nurse."

The color ebbed from Jo Marie's face, leaving her pale. She'd looked for him, too. In all the months since the Mardi Gras she'd never stopped looking. Every time she'd left her apartment, she had silently searched through a sea of faces. Although she'd never known his name, she had included him in her thoughts every day since their meeting. He was her dream man, the stranger who had shared those enchanted moments of magic with her.

"It was Mardi Gras," she explained in a quavering voice. "I'd borrowed Kelly's uniform for a party."

Andrew stood beside her and his wintry eyes narrowed. "I should have recognized you then," he said with faint self-derision.

"Recognized me?" Jo Marie didn't understand. In the short time before they were separated, Andrew had said she reminded him of a painting he'd once seen.

"I should have known you from your picture in the newspaper. You were the girl who so strongly protested the housing development for the wetlands."

"I...I didn't know it was your company. I had no idea." A stray tendril of soft chestnut hair fell forward as she bowed her head. "But I can't apologize for demonstrating against something which I believe is very wrong."

"To thine own self be true, Jo Marie Early." He spoke without malice and when their eyes met, she discovered to her amazement that he was smiling.

Jo Marie responded with a smile of her own. "And you were there that night because of Kelly."

"I'd just left her."

"And I was on my way in." Another few minutes and they could have passed each other in the hospital corridor without ever knowing. In some ways Jo Marie wished they had. If she hadn't met Andrew that night, then she could have shared in her friend's joy at the coming marriage. As it was now, Jo Marie was forced to fight back emotions she had no right to feel. Andrew belonged to Kelly and the diamond ring on her finger declared as much.

"And...and now you've found Kelly," she stammered, backing away. "I want to wish you both a life filled with much happiness." Afraid of what her expressive eyes would reveal, Jo Marie lowered her lashes which were dark against her pale cheek. "I should be going inside."

"Jo Marie."

He said her name so softly that for a moment she wasn't sure he'd spoken. "Yes?"

Andrew arched both brows and lightly shook his head. His finger lightly touched her smooth cheek, following the line of her delicate jaw. Briefly his gaze darkened as if this was torture in the purest sense.

"Nothing. Enjoy yourself tonight." With that he turned back to the railing.

Jo Marie entered the huge reception room and mingled with those attending the lavish affair. Not once did she allow herself to look over her shoulder toward the balcony. Toward Andrew, her dream man, because he wasn't hers, would never be hers. Her mouth ached with the effort to appear happy. By the time she made it to the punch bowl her smile felt brittle and was decidedly forced. All these months she'd hoped to find the dream man because her heart couldn't forget him. And now that she had, nothing had ever been more difficult. If she didn't learn to curb the strong sensual pull she felt toward him, she could ruin his and Kelly's happiness.

Soft Christmas music filled the room as Jo Marie found a plush velvet chair against the wall and sat down, a friendly observer to the party around her. Forcing herself to relax, her toe tapped lightly against the floor with an innate rhythm. Christmas was her favorite time of year—no, she amended, Mardi Gras was. Her smile became less forced.

"You look like you're having the time of your life," Mark announced casually as he took the seat beside her.

"It is a nice party."

"So you enjoy observing the life-style of the rich and famous." The sarcastic edge to Mark's voice was less sharp than normal.

Taking a sip of punch, Jo Marie nodded. "Who wouldn't?"

"To be honest I'm surprised at how friendly everyone's been," Mark commented sheepishly. "Obviously no one suspects that you and I are two of the less privileged."

"Mark," she admonished sharply. "That's a rotten thing to say."

Her brother had the good grace to look ashamed. "To be truthful, Kelly introduced me to several of her friends and I must admit I couldn't find anything to dislike about them."

"Surprise, surprise." Jo Marie hummed the Christmas music softly to herself. "I suppose the next thing I know, you'll be playing golf with Kelly's father."

Mark snorted derisively. "Hardly."

"What have you got against the Beaumonts anyway? Kelly's a wonderful girl."

"Kelly's the exception," Mark argued and stiffened.

"But you just finished telling me that you liked several of her friends that you were introduced to tonight."

"Yes. Well, that was on short acquaintance."

Standing, Jo Marie set her empty punch glass aside. "I think you've got a problem, brother dearest."

A dark look crowded Mark's face, and his brow was furrowed with a curious frown. "You're right, I do."

With an agitated movement he stood and made his way across the room.

Jo Marie mingled, talking with a few women who were planning a charity benefit after the first of the year. When they asked her opinion on an important point, Jo Marie was both surprised and pleased. Although she spent a good portion of the next hour with these older ladies, she drifted away as they moved toward the heart of the party. If Andrew had recognized her as the girl involved in the protest against the wetlands development, others might too. And she didn't want to do anything that would cause him and Kelly embarrassment.

Kelly, with her blue eyes sparkling like sapphires, rushed up to Jo Marie. "Here you are!" she exclaimed. "Drew and I have been looking for you."

"Is it time to leave?" Jo Marie was more than ready, uncomfortably aware that she could be recognized at any moment.

"No...no, we just wanted to be certain some handsome young man didn't cart you away."

"Me?" Jo Marie's soft laugh was filled with incredulity. Few men would pay much attention to her, especially since she'd gone out of her way to remain unobtrusively in the background.

"It's more of a possibility than you realize," Andrew spoke from behind her, his voice a gentle rasp against her ear. "You're very beautiful tonight."

"Don't blush, Jo Marie," Kelly teased. "You really are lovely and if you'd given anyone half a chance, they'd have told you so."

Mark joined them and murmured something to Kelly. As he did so, Andrew turned his head toward Jo Marie and spoke so that the other two couldn't hear him. "Only Florence Nightingale could be more beautiful."

A tingling sensation raced down Jo Marie's spine and she turned so their eyes could meet, surprised that he would say something like that to her with Kelly present. Silently, she pleaded with him not to make this any more difficult for her. Those enchanted moments they had shared were long past and best forgotten for both their sakes.

Jo Marie woke to the buzz of the alarm early the next morning. She sat on the side of the bed and raised her arms high above her head and yawned. The day promised to be a busy one. She was scheduled to work in the office that Saturday morning and then catch a bus to LFTF headquarters on the other side of the French Quarter. She was hoping to talk to Jim Rowden, the director and manager of the conservationists' group. Jim had asked for additional volunteers during the Christmas season. And after thoughtful consideration, Jo Marie decided to accept the challenge. Christmas was such a busy time of year that many of the other volunteers wanted time off.

The events of the previous night filled her mind. Lowering her arms, Jo Marie beat back the unexpected rush of sadness that threatened to overcome her. Andrew hadn't understood any of the things she'd tried to tell him last night. Several times she found him watching her, his look brooding and thoughtful as if she'd displeased him. No matter where she went during the course of the evening, when she looked up she found Andrew studying her. Once their eyes had met and held and everyone between them had seemed to disappear. The music had faded and it was as if only the two of them existed in the party-filled crowd. Jo Marie had lowered her gaze first, frightened and angry with them both.

Andrew and Mark had been sullen on the drive home. Mark had left the apartment almost immediately and Jo Marie had fled to the privacy of her room, unwilling to witness Andrew kissing Kelly goodnight. She couldn't have borne it.

Now, in the light of the new day, she discovered that her feelings for Andrew were growing stronger. She wanted to banish him to a special area of her life, long past. But he wouldn't allow that. It had been in his eyes last night as he studied her. Those moments at the Mardi Gras were not to be forgotten by either of them.

At least when she was at the office, she didn't have to think about Andrew or Kelly or Mark. The phone buzzed continually. And because they were short-staffed on the weekends, Jo Marie hardly had time to think about anything but airline fares, bus routes and train schedules the entire morning.

She replaced the telephone receiver after talking with the Costa Lines about booking a spring Caribbean cruise for a retired couple. Her head was bowed as she filled out the necessary forms. Jo Marie didn't hear Paula Shriver, the only other girl in the office on Saturday, move to her desk.

"Mr. Beaumont's been waiting to talk to you," Paula announced. "Lucky you," she added under her breath as Andrew took the seat beside Jo Marie's desk.

"Hello, Jo Marie."

"Andrew." Her hand clenched the ballpoint pen she was holding. "What can I do for you?"

He crossed his legs and draped an arm over the back of the chair giving the picture of a man completely at ease. "I was hoping you could give me some suggestions for an ideal honeymoon."

"Of course. What did you have in mind?" Inwardly she wanted to shout at him not to do this to her, but she forced herself to smile and look attentive.

"What would you suggest?"

She lowered her gaze. "Kelly's mentioned Hawaii several times. I know that's the only place she'd enjoy visiting."

He dismissed her suggestion with a short shake of his head. "I've been there several times. I was hoping for something less touristy."

"Maybe a cruise then. There are several excellent lines operating in the Caribbean, the Mediterranean or perhaps the inside passage to Alaska along the Canadian west coast."

"No." Again he shook his head. "Where would *you* choose to go on a honeymoon?"

Jo Marie ignored his question, not wanting to answer him. "I have several brochures I can give you that could spark an idea. I'm confident that any one of these places would thrill Kelly." As she pulled out her bottom desk drawer, Jo Marie was acutely conscious of Andrew studying her. She'd tried to come across with a strict business attitude, but her defenses were crumbling.

Reluctantly, he accepted the brochures she gave him. "You didn't answer my question. Shall I ask it again?"

Slowly, Jo Marie shook her head. "I'm not sure I'd want to go anywhere," she explained simply. "Not on my honeymoon. Not when the most beautiful city in the world is at my doorstep. I'd want to spend that time alone with my husband. We could travel later." Briefly their eyes met and held for a long, breathless moment. "But I'm not Kelly, and she's the one you should consider while planning this trip."

Paula stood and turned the sign in the glass door, indicating that the office was no longer open. Andrew's gaze followed her movements. "You're closing."

Jo Marie's nod was filled with relief. She was uncomfortable with Andrew. Being this close to him was a test of her friendship to Kelly. And at this moment, Kelly was losing...they both were. "Yes. We're only open during the morning on Saturdays."

He stood and placed the pamphlets on the corner of her desk. "Then let's continue our discussion over lunch."

"Oh, no, really that isn't necessary. We'll be finished in a few minutes and Paula doesn't mind waiting."

"But I have several ideas I want to discuss with you and it could well be an hour or so."

"Perhaps you could return another day."

"Now is the more convenient time for me," he countered smoothly.

Everything within Jo Marie wanted to refuse. Surely he realized how difficult this was for her. He was well aware of her feelings and was deliberately ignoring them.

"Is it so difficult to accept anything from me, Jo Marie?" he asked softly. "Even lunch?"

"All right," she agreed ungraciously, angry with him and angrier with herself. "But only an hour. I've got things to do."

A half smile turned up one corner of his mouth. "As you wish," he said as he escorted her to his Mercedes.

Jo Marie was stiff and uncommunicative as Andrew drove through the thick traffic. He parked on a narrow street outside the French Quarter and came around to her side of the car to open the door for her.

"I have reservations at Chez Lorraine's."

"Chez Lorraine's?" Jo Marie's surprised gaze flew to him. The elegant French restaurant was one of New Orlean's most famous. The food was rumored to be exquisite, and expensive. Jo Marie had always dreamed of dining there, but never had.

"Is it as good as everyone says?" she asked, unable to disguise the excitement in her voice.

"You'll have to judge for yourself," he answered, smiling down on her.

Once inside, they were seated almost immediately and handed huge oblong menus featuring a wide variety of French cuisine. Not having sampled several of the more traditional French dishes, Jo Marie toyed with the idea of ordering the calf's sweetbread.

"What would you like?" Andrew prompted after several minutes.

"I don't know. It all sounds so good." Closing the menu she set it aside and lightly shook her head. "I think you may regret having brought me here when I'm so hungry." She'd skipped breakfast, and discovered now that she was famished.

Andrew didn't look up from his menu. "Where you're concerned, there's very little I regret." As if he'd made a casual comment about the weather, he continued. "Have you decided?"

"Yes...yes," she managed, fighting down the dizzying effect of his words. "I think I'll try the salmon, but I don't think I should try the French pronunciation."

"Don't worry, I'll order for you."

As if by intuition, the waiter reappeared when they were ready to place their order. "The lady would like *les mouilles à la crème de saumon fumé,* and I'll have the *le canard de rouen braise.*"

With a nod of approval the red-jacketed waiter departed.

Self-consciously, Jo Marie smoothed out the linen napkin on her lap. "I'm impressed," she murmured, studying the old world French provincial decor of the room. "It's everything I thought it would be."

The meal was fabulous. After a few awkward moments Jo Marie was amazed that she could talk as freely to Andrew. She discovered he was a good listener and she enjoyed telling him about her family.

"So you were the only girl."

"It had its advantages. I play a mean game of touch football."

"I hope you'll play with me someday. I've always enjoyed a rousing game of touch football."

The fork was raised halfway to her mouth and Jo Marie paused, her heart beating double time. "I...I only play with my brothers."

Andrew chuckled. "Speaking of your family, I find it difficult to tell that you and Mark are related. Oh, I can see the family resemblance, but Mark's a serious young man. Does he ever laugh?"

Not lately, Jo Marie mused, but she didn't admit as much. "He works hard, long hours. Mark's come a long way through medical school." She hated making excuses for her brother. "He doesn't mean to be rude."

Andrew accepted the apology with a wry grin. "The chip on his shoulder's as big as a California redwood. What's he got against wealth and position?"

"I don't know," she answered honestly. "He teases Kelly unmercifully about her family. I think Kelly's money makes him feel insecure. There's no reason for it; Kelly's never done anything to give him that attitude. I never have understood it."

Pushing her clean plate aside, Jo Marie couldn't recall when she'd enjoyed a meal more—except the dinner they'd shared at K-Paul's the night Kelly and Andrew had announced their engagement. Some of the contentment faded from her eyes. Numbly, she folded her hands in her lap. Being here with Andrew, sharing this meal, laughing and talking with him wasn't right. Kelly should be the one sitting across the table from him. Jo Marie had no right to enjoy his company this way. Not when he was engaged to her best friend. Pointedly, she glanced at her watch.

"What's wrong?"

"Nothing." She shook her head slightly, avoiding his eyes, knowing his look had the ability to penetrate her soul.

"Would you care for some dessert?"

Placing her hand on her stomach, she declined with a smile. "I couldn't," she declared, but her gaze fell with regret on the large table display of delicate French pastries.

The waiter reappeared and a flurry of French flew over her head. Like everything else Andrew did, his French was flawless.

Almost immediately the waiter returned with a plate covered with samples of several desserts which he set in front of Jo Marie.

"Andrew," she objected, sighing his name, "I'll get fat."

"I saw you eyeing those goodies. Indulge. You deserve it."

"But I don't. I can't possibly eat all that."

"You can afford to put on a few pounds." His voice deepened as his gaze skimmed her lithe form.

"Are you suggesting I'm skinny?"

"My, my," he said, slowly shaking his head from side to side. "You do like to argue. Here, give me the plate. I'll be the one to indulge."

"Not on your life," she countered laughingly, and dipped her fork into the thin slice of chocolate cheesecake. After sampling three of the scrumptious desserts, Jo Marie pushed her plate aside. "Thank you, Andrew," she murmured as her fingers toyed with the starched, linen napkin. "I enjoyed the meal and...and the company, but we can't do this again." Her eyes were riveted to the tabletop.

"Jo Marie—"

"No. Let me finish," she interrupted on a rushed breath. "It...it would be so easy...to hurt Kelly and I won't do that. I can't. Please, don't make this so difficult for me." With every word her voice grew weaker and shakier. It shouldn't be this hard, her heart cried, but it was. Every womanly instinct was reaching out to him until she wanted to cry with it.

"Indulge me, Jo Marie," he said tenderly. "It's my birthday and there's no one else I'd rather share it with."

No one else...his words reverberated through her mind. They were on treacherous ground and Jo Marie felt herself sinking fast.

"Happy birthday," she whispered.

"Thank you."

They stood and Andrew cupped her elbow, leading her to the street.

"Would you like me to drop you off at the apartment?" Andrew asked several minutes later as they walked toward his parked car.

"No. I'm on my way to the LFTF headquarters." She stuck both hands deep within her sweater pockets.

"Land For The Future?"

She nodded. "They need extra volunteers during the Christmas season."

His wide brow knitted with a deep frown. "As I recall, that building is in a bad part of town. Is it safe for you to—"

"Perfectly safe." She took a step in retreat. "Thank you again for lunch. I hope you have a wonderful birthday," she called just before turning and hurrying along the narrow sidewalk.

Jo Marie's pace was brisk as she kept one eye on the darkening sky. Angry gray thunderclouds were rolling in and a cloud burst was imminent. Everything looked as if it was against her. With the sky the color of Andrew's eyes, it seemed as though he was watching her every move. Fleetingly she wondered if she'd ever escape him...and worse, if she'd ever want to.

The LFTF headquarters were near the docks. Andrew's apprehensions were well founded. This was a high crime area. Jo Marie planned her arrival and departure times in daylight.

"Can I help you?" The stocky man with crisp ebony hair spoke from behind the desk. There was a speculative arch to his bushy brows as he regarded her.

"Hello." She extended her hand. "I'm Jo Marie Early. You're Jim Rowden, aren't you?" Jim had recently arrived from the Boston area and was taking over the manager's position of the nonprofit organization.

Jim stepped around the large oak desk. "Yes, I remember now. You marched in the demonstration, didn't you?"

"Yes, I was there."

"One of the few who stuck it out in the rain, as I recall."

"My brother insisted that it wasn't out of any sense of purpose, but from a pure streak of stubbornness." Laughter riddled her voice. "I'm back because you mentioned needing extra volunteers this month."

"Do you type?"

"Reasonably well. I'm a travel agent."

"Don't worry I won't give you a time test."

Jo Marie laughed. "I appreciate that more than you know."

The majority of the afternoon was spent typing personal replies to letters the group had received after the demonstration in front of Rose's. In addition, the group had been spurred on by their success, and was planning other campaigns for future projects. At four-thirty, Jo Marie slipped the cover over the typewriter and placed the letters on Jim's desk for his signature.

"If you could come three times a week," Jim asked, "it would be greatly appreciated."

She left forty minutes later feeling assured that she was doing the right thing by offering her time. Lending a hand at Christmas seemed such a small thing to do. Admittedly, her motives weren't pure. If she could keep herself occupied, she wouldn't have to deal with her feelings for Andrew.

A lot of her major Christmas shopping was completed, but on her way to the bus stop, Jo Marie stopped in at a used-book store. Although she fought it all afternoon, her thoughts had been continually on Andrew. Today was his special day and she desperately wanted to give him something that would relay her feelings. Her heart was filled with gratitude. Without him, she may never have known that sometimes dreams can come true and that fairy tales aren't always for the young.

She found the book she was seeking. A large leather-bound volume of the history of New Orleans. Few cities had a more romantic background. Included in the book were hundreds of rare photographs of the city's architecture, courtyards, patios, ironwork and cemeteries. He'd love the book as much as she. Jo Marie had come by for weeks, paying a little bit each pay day. Not only was this book rare, but extremely expensive. Because the proprietor knew Jo Marie, he had made special arrangements for her to have this volume. But Jo Marie couldn't think of anything else Andrew would cherish more. She wrote out a check for the balance and realized that she would probably be short on cash by the end of the month, but that seemed a small sacrifice.

Clenching the book to her breast, Jo Marie hurried home. She had not right to be giving Andrew gifts, but this was more for her sake than his. It was her thank you for all that he'd given her.

The torrential downpour assaulted the pavement just as Jo Marie stepped off the bus. Breathlessly, while holding the paper-wrapped leather volume to her stomach, she ran to the apartment and inserted her key into the dead bolt. Once again she had barely escaped a thorough drenching.

Hanging her Irish knit cardigan in the hall closet, Jo Marie kicked off her shoes and slid her feet into fuzzy, worn slippers.

Kelly should arrive any minute and Jo Marie rehearsed what she was going to say to Kelly. She had to have some kind of explanation to be giving her friend's fiancé a birthday present. Her thoughts came back empty as she paced the floor, wringing her hands. It was important that Kelly understand, but finding a plausible reason without revealing herself was difficult. Jo Marie didn't want any ill feelings between them.

When her roommate hadn't returned from the hospital by six, Jo Marie made herself a light meal and turned on the evening news. Kelly usually phoned if she was going to be late. Not having heard from her friend caused Jo Marie to wonder. Maybe Andrew had picked her up after work and had taken her out to dinner. It was, after all, his birthday; celebrating with his fiancé would only be natural. Unbidden, a surge of resentment rose within her and caused a lump of painful hoarseness to tighten her throat. Mentally she gave herself a hard shake. *Stop it,* her mind shouted. *You have no right to feel these things. Andrew belongs to Kelly, not you.*

A mixture of pain and confusion moved across her smooth brow when the doorbell chimed. It was probably Mark, but for the first time in recent memory, Jo Marie wasn't up to a sparring match with her older brother. Tonight she wanted to be left to her own thoughts.

But it wasn't Mark.

"Andrew." Quickly she lowered her gaze, praying he couldn't read her startled expression.

"Is Kelly ready?" he asked as he stepped inside the entryway. "We're having dinner with my mother."

"She isn't home from work yet. If you'd like I could call the hospital and see what's holding her up." So they were going out tonight. Jo Marie successfully managed to rein in her feelings of jealousy, having dealt with them earlier.

"No need, I'm early. If you don't mind, I'll just wait."

"Please, sit down." Self-consciously she gestured toward the love seat. "I'm sure Kelly will be here any minute."

Impeccably dressed in a charcoal-gray suit that emphasized the width of his muscular shoulders, Andrew took a seat.

With her hands linked in front of her, Jo Marie fought for control of her hammering heart. "Would you like a cup of coffee?"

"Please."

Relieved to be out of the living room, Jo Marie hurried into the kitchen and brought down a cup and saucer. Spending part of the afternoon with Andrew was difficult enough. But being alone in the apartment with him was impossible. The tension between them was unbearable as it was. But to be separated by only a thin wall was much worse. She yearned to touch him. To hold him in her arms. To feel again, just this once, his mouth over hers. She had to know if what had happened all those months ago was real.

"Jo Marie," Andrew spoke softly from behind her.

Her pounding heart leaped to her throat. Had he read her thoughts and come to her? Her fingers dug unmercifully into the kitchen counter top. Nothing would induce her to turn around.

"What's this?" he questioned softly.

A glance over her shoulder revealed Andrew holding the book she'd purchased earlier. Her hand shook as she poured the coffee. "It's a book about the early history of New Orleans. I found it in a used-book store and..." Her voice wobbled as badly as her hand.

"There was a card on top of it that was addressed to me."

Jo Marie set the glass coffeepot down. "Yes...I knew you'd love it and I wanted you to have it as a birthday present." She stopped just before admitting that she wanted him to remember her. "I also heard on the news tonight that...that Rose's Hotel is undergoing some expensive and badly needed repairs, thanks to you." Slowly she turned, keeping her hands behind her. "I realize there isn't anything that I could ever buy for you that you couldn't purchase a hundred times over. But I thought this book might be the one thing I could give you...." She let her voice fade in midsentence.

A slow faint smile touched his mouth as he opened the card and read her inscription. "To Andrew, in appreciation for everything." Respectfully he opened the book, then laid it aside. "Everything, Jo Marie?"

"For your generosity toward the hotel, and your thoughtfulness in giving me the party dress and..."

"The Mardi Gras?" He inched his way toward her.

Jo Marie could feel the color seep up her neck and tinge her cheeks. "Yes, that too." She wouldn't deny how speical those few moments had been to her. Nor could she deny the hunger in his hard gaze as he concentrated on her lips. Amazed, Jo Marie watched as Andrew's gray eyes darkened to the shade of a stormy Arctic sea.

No pretense existed between them now, only a shared hunger that could no longer be repressed. A surge of intense longing seared through her so that when Andrew drew her into his embrace she gave a small cry and went willingly.

"Haven't you ever wondered if what we shared that night was real?" he breathed the question into her hair.

"Yes, a thousand times since, I've wondered." She gloried in the feel of his muscular body pressing against the length of hers. Freely her hands roamed his back. His index finger under her chin lifted her face and her heart soared at the look in his eyes.

"Jo Marie," he whispered achingly and his thumb leisurely caressed the full curve of her mouth.

Her soft lips trembled in anticipation. Slowly, deliberately, Andrew lowered his head as his mouth sought hers. Her eyelids drifted closed and her arms reached up and clung to him. The kiss was one of hunger and demand as his mouth feasted on hers.

The feel of him, the touch, the taste of his lips filled her senses until Jo Marie felt his muscles strain as he brought her to him, riveting her soft form to him so tightly that she could no longer breathe. Not that she cared.

Gradually the kiss mellowed and the intensity eased until he buried his face in the gentle slope of her neck. "It was real," he whispered huskily. "Oh, my sweet

Florence Nightingale, it was even better than I remembered.''

''I was afraid it would be.'' Tears burned her eyes and she gave a sad little laugh. Life was filled with ironies and finding Andrew now was the most painful.

Tenderly he reached up and wiped the moisture from her face. ''I shouldn't have let this happen.''

''It wasn't your fault.'' Jo Marie felt she had to accept part of the blame. She'd wanted him to kiss her so badly. ''I...I won't let it happen again.'' If one of them had to be strong, then it would be her. After years of friendship with Kelly she owed her roommate her loyalty.

Reluctantly they broke apart, but his hands rested on either side of her neck as though he couldn't bear to let her go completely. ''Thank you for the book,'' he said in a raw voice. ''I'll treasure it always.''

The sound of the front door opening caused Jo Marie's eyes to widen with a rush of guilt. Kelly would take one look at her and realize what had happened. Hot color blazed in her cheeks.

''Jo Marie!'' Kelly's eager voice vibrated through the apartment.

Andrew stepped out of the kitchen, granting Jo Marie precious seconds to compose herself.

''Oh, heavens, you're here already, Drew. I'm sorry I'm so late. But I've got so much to tell you.''

With her hand covering her mouth to smother the sound of her tears, Jo Marie leaned against the kitchen counter, suddenly needing its support.

Chapter Five

"Are you all right?" Andrew stepped back into the kitchen and brushed his hand over his temples. He resembled a man driven to the end of his endurance, standing with one foot in heaven and the other in hell. His fingers were clenched at his side as if he couldn't decide if he should haul her back into his arms or leave her alone. But the tortured look in his eyes told Jo Marie how difficult it was not to hold and reassure her.

"I'm fine." Her voice was eggshell fragile. "Just leave. Please. I don't want Kelly to see me." Not like this, with tears streaming down her pale cheeks and her eyes full of confusion. Once glance at Jo Marie and the astute Kelly would know exactly what had happened.

"I'll get her out of here as soon as she changes clothes," Andrew whispered urgently, his stormy gray eyes pleading with hers. "I didn't mean for this to happen."

"I know." With an agitated brush of her hand she dismissed him. "Please, just go."

"I'll talk to you tomorrow."

"No." Dark emotion flickered across her face. She didn't want to see him. Everything about today had been wrong. She should have avoided Andrew, feeling as she did. But in some ways, Jo Marie realized that the kiss had been inevitable. Those brief magical moments at the Mardi Gras demanded an exploration of the sensation they'd shared. Both had hoped to dismiss that February night as whimsy—a result of the craziness of the season. Instead, they had discovered how real it had been. From now on, Jo Marie vowed, she would shun Andrew. Her only defense was to avoid him completely.

"I'm sorry to keep you waiting." Kelly's happy voice drifted in from the other room. "Do I look okay?"

"You're lovely as always."

Jo Marie hoped that Kelly wouldn't catch the detached note in Andrew's gruff voice.

"You'll never guess who I spent the last hour talking to."

"Perhaps you could tell me on the way to mother's?" Andrew responded dryly.

"Drew." Some of the enthusiasm drained from Kelly's happy voice. "Are you feeling ill? You're quite pale."

"I'm fine."

"Maybe we should cancel this dinner. Really, I wouldn't mind."

"There's no reason to disappoint my mother."

"Drew?" Kelly seemed hesitant.

"Are you ready?" His firm voice brooked no disagreement.

"But I wanted to talk to Jo Marie."

"You can call her after dinner," Andrew responded shortly, his voice fading as they moved toward the entryway.

The door clicked a minute later and Jo Marie's fingers loosened their death grip against the counter. Weakly, she wiped a hand over her face and eyes. Andrew and Kelly were engaged to be married. Tonight was his birthday and he was taking Kelly to dine with his family. And Jo Marie had been stealing a kiss from him in the kitchen. Self-reproach grew in her breast with every breath until she wanted to scream and lash out with it.

Maybe she could have justified her actions if Kelly hadn't been so excited and happy. Her roommate had come into the apartment bursting with enthusiasm for life, eager to see and talk to Andrew.

The evening seemed interminable and Jo Marie had a terrible time falling asleep, tossing and turning long past the time Kelly returned. Finally at the darkest part of the night, she flipped on the beside lamp and threw aside the blankets. Pouring herself a glass of milk, Jo Marie leaned against the kitchen counter and drank it with small sips, her thoughts deep and dark. She couldn't ask Kelly to forgive her for what had happened without hurting her roommate and perhaps ruining their friendship. The only person there was to confront and condemn was herself.

Once she returned to bed, Jo Marie lay on her back, her head clasped in her hands. Moon shadows fluttered against the bare walls like the flickering scenes of a silent movie.

Unhappy beyond words, Jo Marie avoided her roommate, kept busy and occupied her time with other friends. But she was never at peace and always conscious that her thoughts never strayed from Kelly and Andrew. The episode with Andrew wouldn't happen again. She had to be strong.

Jo Marie didn't see her roommate until the following Monday morning. They met in the kitchen where Jo Marie was pouring herself a small glass of grapefruit juice.

"Morning." Jo Marie's stiff smile was only slightly forced.

"Howdy, stranger. I've missed you the past couple of days."

Jo Marie's hand tightened around the juice glass as she silently prayed Kelly wouldn't ask her about Saturday night. Her roommate must have known Jo Marie was in the apartment, otherwise Andrew wouldn't have been inside.

"I've missed you," Kelly continued. "It seems we hardly have time to talk anymore. And now that you're going to be doing volunteer work for the foundation, we'll have even less time together. You're spreading yourself too thin."

"There's always something going on this time of year." A chill seemed to settle around the area of Jo Marie's heart and she avoided her friend's look.

"I know, that's why I'm looking forward to this weekend and the party for Drew's company. By the way, he suggested that both of us stay the night on Saturday."

"Spend the night?" Jo Marie repeated like a recording and inhaled a shaky breath. That was the last thing she wanted.

"It makes sense, don't you think? We can lay awake until dawn the way we used to and talk all night." A distant look came over Kelly as she buttered the hot toast and poured herself a cup of coffee. "Drew's going to have enough to worry about without dragging us back and forth. From what I understand, he goes all out for his company's Christmas party."

Hoping to hide her discomfort, Jo Marie rinsed out her glass and deposited it in the dishwasher, but a gnawing sensation attacked the pit of her stomach. Although she'd promised Kelly she would attend the lavish affair, she had to find a way of excusing herself without arousing suspicion. "I've been thinking about Andrew's party and honestly feel I shouldn't go—"

"Don't say it. You're going!" Kelly interrupted hastily. "There's no way I'd go without you. You're my best friend, Jo Marie Early, and as such I want you with me. Besides, you know how I hate these things."

"But as Drew's wife you'll be expected to attend a lot of these functions. I won't always be around."

A secret smile stole over her friend's pert face. "I know, that's why it's so important that you're there now."

"You didn't seem to need me Friday night."

Round blue eyes flashed Jo Marie a look of disbelief. "Are you crazy? I would have been embarrassingly uncomfortable without you."

It seemed to Jo Marie that Mark had spent nearly as much time with Kelly as she had. In fact, her brother had spent most of the evening with Kelly at his side. It was Mark whom Kelly really wanted, not her. But convincing her roommate of that was a different matter. Jo Marie doubted that Kelly had even admitted as much to herself.

"I'll think about going," Jo Marie promised. "But I can't honestly see that my being there or not would do any good."

"You've got to come," Kelly muttered, looking around unhappily. "I'd be miserable meeting and talking to all those people on my own." Silently, Kelly's bottomless blue eyes pleaded with Jo Marie. "I promise never to ask anything from you again. Say you'll come. Oh, please, Jo Marie, do this one last thing for me."

An awkward silence stretched between them and a feeling of dread settled over Jo Marie. Kelly seemed so genuinely distraught that it wasn't in Jo Marie's heart to refuse her. As Kelly had pointedly reminded her, she was Kelly's best friend. "All right, all right," she agreed reluctantly. "But I don't like it."

"You won't be sorry, I promise." A mischievous gleam lightened Kelly's features.

Jo Marie mumbled disdainfully under her breath as she moved out of the kitchen. Pausing at the closet, she took her trusted cardigan from the hanger. "Say, Kell, don't forget this is the week I'm flying to Mazatlán." Jo Marie was scheduled to take a familiarization tour of the Mexican resort town. She'd be flying with ten other travel agents from the city and staying at the Riviera Del Sol's expense. The luxury hotel was sponsoring the group in hopes of having the agents book their facilities for their clients. Jo Marie usually took the "fam" tours only once or twice a year. This one had been planned months before and she mused that it couldn't have come at a better time. Escaping from Andrew and Kelly was just the thing she needed.

By the time she returned, she prayed, her life could be back to normal.

"This is the week?" Kelly stuck her head around the kitchen doorway. "Already?"

"You can still drive me to the airport, can't you?"

"Sure," Kelly answered absently. "But if I can't, Drew will."

Jo Marie's heart throbbed painfully. "No," she returned forcefully.

"He doesn't mind."

But I do, Jo Marie's heart cried as she fumbled with the buttons of her sweater. If Kelly wasn't home when it came time to leave for the airport, she would either call Mark or take a cab.

"I'm sure Drew wouldn't mind," Kelly repeated.

"I'll be late tonight," she answered, ignoring her friend's offer. She couldn't understand why Kelly would want her to spend time with Andrew. But so many things didn't make sense lately. Without a backward glance, Jo Marie went out the front door.

Joining several others at the bus stop outside the apartment building en route to the office, Jo Marie fought down feelings of guilt. She'd honestly thought she could get out of attending the party with Kelly. But there was little to be done, short of offending her friend. These constant recriminations regarding Kelly and Andrew were disrupting her neatly ordered life, and Jo Marie hated it.

Two of the other girls were in the office by the time Jo Marie arrived.

"There's a message for you," Paula announced. "I think it was the same guy who stopped in Saturday morning. You know, I'm beginning to think you've been holding out on me. Where'd you ever meet a hunk like that?"

"He's engaged," she quipped, seeking a light tone.

"He is?" Paula rolled her office chair over to Jo Marie's desk and handed her the pink slip. "You could have fooled me. He looked on the prowl, if you want my opinion. In fact, he was eyeing you like a starving man looking at a cream puff."

"Paula!" Jo Marie tried to toss off her co-worker's observation with a forced laugh. "He's engaged to my roommate."

Paula lifted one shoulder in a half shrug and scooted the chair back to her desk. "If you say so." But both her tone and her look were disbelieving.

Jo Marie read the message, which listed Andrew's office number and asked that she call him at her earliest convenience. Crumbling up the pink slip, she tossed it in the green metal wastebasket beside her desk. She might be attending this party, but it was under duress. And as far as Andrew was concerned, she had every intention of avoiding him.

Rather than rush back to the apartment after work, Jo Marie had dinner in a small café near her office.

From there she walked to the Land For The Future headquarters.

She was embarrassingly early when she arrived outside of the office door. The foundation's headquarters were on the second floor of an older brick building in a bad part of town. Jo Marie decided to arrive earlier than she'd planned rather than kill time by walking around outside. From the time she'd left the travel agency, she'd wandered around with little else to do. Her greatest fear was that Andrew would be waiting for her at the apartment. She hadn't returned his call and he'd want to know why.

Jim Rowden, the office manager and spokesman, was busy on the telephone when Jo Marie arrived. Quietly she slipped into the chair at the desk opposite him and glanced over the letters and other notices that needed to be typed. As she pulled the cover from the top of the typewriter, Jo Marie noticed a shadowy movement from the other side of the milky white glass inset of the office door.

She stood to investigate and found a dark-haired man with a worn felt hat that fit loosely on top of his head. His clothes were ragged and the faint odor of cheap wine permeated the air. He was curling up in the doorway of an office nearest theirs.

His eyes met hers briefly and he tugged his thin sweater around his shoulders. "Are you going to throw me out of here?" The words were issued in subtle challenge.

Jo Marie teetered with indecision. If she did tell him to leave he'd either spend the night shivering in the cold or find another open building. On the other hand if she were to give him money, she was confident it wouldn't be a bed he'd spend it on.

"Well?" he challenged again.

"I won't say anything," she answered finally. "Just go down to the end of the hall so no one else will find you."

He gave her a look of mild surprise, stood and gathered his coat before turning and ambling down the long hall in an uneven gait. Jo Marie waited until he was curled up in another doorway. It was difficult to see that he was there without looking for him. A soft smile of satisfaction stole across her face as she closed the door and returned to her desk.

Jim replaced the receiver and smiled a welcome at Jo Marie. "How'd you like to attend a lecture with me tonight?"

"I'd like it fine," she agreed eagerly.

Jim's lecture was to a group of concerned city businessmen. He relayed the facts about the dangers of thoughtless and haphazard land development. He presented his case in a simple, straightforward fashion without emotionalism or sensationalism. In addition, he confidently answered their questions, defining the difference between building for the future and preserving a link with the past. Jo Marie was impressed and from the looks on the faces of his audience, the businessmen had been equally affected.

"I'll walk you to the bus stop," Jim told her hours later after they'd returned from the meeting. "I don't like the idea of you waiting at the bus stop alone. I'll go with you."

Jo Marie hadn't been that thrilled with the prospect herself. "Thanks, I'd appreciate that."

Jim's hand cupped her elbow as they leisurely strolled down the narrow street, chatting as they went. Jim's voice was drawling and smooth and Jo Marie mused that she could listen to him all night. The lamplight illuminated little in the descending fog and would have created an eerie feeling if Jim hadn't been at her side. But walking with him, she barely noticed the weather and instead found herself laughing at his subtle humor.

"How'd you ever get into this business?" she queried. Jim Rowden was an intelligent, warm human being who would be a success in any field he chose to pursue. He could be making twice and three times the money in the business world that he collected from the foundation.

At first introduction, Jim wasn't the kind of man who would bowl women over with his striking good looks or his suave manners. But he was a rare, dedicated man of conscience. Jo Marie had never known anyone like him and admired him greatly.

"I'm fairly new with the foundation," he admitted, "and it certainly wasn't what I'd been expecting to do with my life, especially since I struggled through college for a degree in biology. Afterward I went to work for the state, but this job gives me the opportunity to work first hand with saving some of the—well, you heard my speech."

"Yes, I did, and it was wonderful."

"You're good for my ego, Jo Marie. I hope you'll stick around."

Jo Marie's eyes glanced up the street, wondering how long they'd have to wait for a bus. She didn't want their discussion to end. As she did, a flash of midnight blue captured her attention and her heart dropped to her knees as the Mercedes pulled to a stop alongside the curb in front of them.

Andrew practically leaped from the driver's side. "Just what do you think you're doing?" The harsh anger in his voice shocked her.

"I beg your pardon?" Jim answered on Jo Marie's behalf, taking a step forward.

Andrew ignored Jim, his eyes cold and piercing as he glanced over her. "I've spent the good part of an hour looking for you."

"Why?" Jo Marie demanded, tilting her chin in an act of defiance. "What business is it of yours where I am or who I'm with?"

"I'm making it my business."

"Is there a problem here, Jo Marie?" Jim questioned as he stepped forward.

"None whatsoever," she responded dryly and crossed her arms in front of her.

"Kelly's worried sick," Andrew hissed. "Now I suggest you get in the car and let me take you home before...." He let the rest of what he was saying die. He paused for several tense moments and exhaled a sharp breath. "I apologize, I had no right to come at you like that." He closed the car door and moved around the front of the Mercedes. "I'm Andrew Beaumont," he introduced himself and extended his hand to Jim.

"From Delta Development?" Jim's eyes widened appreciatively. "Jim Rowden. I've been wanting to meet you so that I could thank you personally for what you did for Rose's Hotel."

"I'm pleased I could help."

When Andrew decided to put on the charm it was like falling into a jar of pure honey, Jo Marie thought. She didn't know of a man, woman or child who couldn't be swayed by his beguiling showmanship. Having been under his spell in the past made it all the more recognizable now. But somehow, she realized, this was different. Andrew hadn't been acting the night of the Mardi Gras, she was convinced of that.

"Jo Marie was late coming home and luckily I remembered her saying something about volunteering for the foundation. Kelly asked that I come and get her. We were understandably worried about her taking the bus alone at this time of night.''

"I'll admit I was a bit concerned myself," Jim returned, taking a step closer to Jo Marie. "That's why I'm here."

As Andrew opened the passenger's side of the car, Jo Marie turned her head to meet his gaze, her eyes fiery as she slid into the plush velvet seat.

"I'll see you Friday," she said to Jim.

"Enjoy Mexico," he responded and waved before turning and walking back toward the office building. A fine mist filled the evening air and Jim pulled up his collar as he hurried along the sidewalk.

Andrew didn't say a word as he turned the key in the ignition, checked the rearview mirror and pulled back onto the street.

"You didn't return my call." He stopped at a red light and the full force of his magnetic gray eyes was turned on her.

"No," she answered in a whisper, struggling not to reveal how easily he could affect her.

"Can't you see how important it is that we talk?"

"No." She wanted to shout the word. When their eyes met, Jo Marie was startled to find that only a few inches separated them. Andrew's look was centered on her mouth and with a determined effort she averted her gaze and stared out the side window. "I don't want to talk to you." Her fingers fumbled with the clasp of her purse in nervous agitation. "There's nothing more we can say." She hated the husky emotion-filled way her voice sounded.

"Jo Marie." He said her name so softly that she wasn't entirely sure he'd spoken.

She turned back to him, knowing she should pull away from the hypnotic darkness of his eyes, but doing so was impossible.

"You'll come to my party?"

She wanted to explain her decision to attend—she hadn't wanted to go—but one glance at Andrew said that he understood. Words were unnecessary.

"It's going to be difficult for us both for a while."

He seemed to imply things would grow easier with time. Jo Marie sincerely doubted that they ever would.

"You'll come?" he prompted softly.

Slowly she nodded. Jo Marie hadn't realized how tense she was until she exhaled and felt some of the coiled tightness leave her body. "Yes, I'll...be at the party." Her breathy stammer spoke volumes.

"And wear the dress I gave you?"

She ended up nodding again, her tongue unable to form words.

"I've dreamed of you walking into my arms wearing that dress," he added on a husky tremor, then shook his head as if he regretted having spoken.

Being alone with him in the close confines of the car was torture. Her once restless fingers lay limp in her lap. Jo Marie didn't know how she was going to avoid Andrew when Kelly seemed to be constantly throwing them together. But she must for her own peace of mind...she must.

All too quickly the brief respite of her trip to Mazatlán was over. Saturday arrived and Kelly and Jo Marie were brought to Andrew's home, which was a faithful reproduction of an antebellum mansion.

The dress he'd purchased was hanging in the closet of the bedroom she was to share with Kelly. Her friend threw herself across the canopy bed and exhaled on a happy sigh.

"Isn't this place something?"

Jo Marie didn't answer for a moment, her gaze falling on the dress that hung alone in the closet. "It's magnificent." There was little else that would describe this palace. The house was a three-story structure with huge white pillars and dark shutters. It faced the Mississippi River and had a huge garden in the back. Jo Marie learned that it was his mother who took an avid interest in the wide variety of flowers that grew in abundance there.

The rooms were large, their walls adorned with paintings and works of art. If Jo Marie was ever to doubt Andrew's wealth and position, his home would prove to be a constant reminder.

"Drew built it himself," Kelly explained with a proud lilt to her voice. "I don't mean he pounded in every nail, but he was here every day while it was being constructed. It took months."

"I can imagine." And no expense had been spared from the look of things.

"I suppose we should think about getting ready," Kelly continued. "I don't mind telling you that I've had a queasy stomach all day dreading this thing."

Kelly had! Jo Marie nearly laughed aloud. This party had haunted her all week. Even Mazatlán hadn't been far enough away to dispel the feeling of dread.

Jo Marie could hear the music drifting in from the reception hall by the time she had put on the finishing touches of her makeup. Kelly had already joined Andrew. A quick survey in the full-length mirror assured her that the beautiful gown was the most elegant thing she would ever own. The reflection that came back to her of a tall, regal woman was barely recognizable as herself. The dark crown of curls was styled on top of her head with a few stray tendrils curling about her ears. A lone strand of pearls graced her neck.

Self-consciously she moved from the room, closing the door. From the top of the winding stairway, she looked down on a milling crowd of arriving guests. Holding in her breath, she placed her gloved hand on the polished bannister, exhaled, and made her descent. Keeping her eyes on her feet for fear of tripping, Jo Marie was surprised when she glanced down to find Andrew waiting for her at the bottom of the staircase.

As he gave her his hand, their eyes met and held in a tender exchange. "You're beautiful."

The deep husky tone in his voice took her breath away and Jo Marie could do nothing more than smile in return.

Taking her hand, Andrew tucked it securely in the crook of his elbow and led her into the room where the other guests were mingling. Everyone was meeting for drinks in the huge living room and once the party was complete they would be moving up to the ballroom on the third floor. The evening was to culminate in a midnight buffet.

With Andrew holding her close by his side, Jo Marie had little option but to follow where he led. Moving from one end of the room to the other, he introduced her to so many people that her head swam trying to remember their names. Fortunately, Kelly and Andrew's engagement hadn't been officially announced and Jo Marie wasn't forced to make repeated explanations. Nonetheless, she was uncomfortable with the way he was linking the two of them together.

"Where's Kelly?" Jo Marie asked under her breath. "She should be the one with you. Not me."

"Kelly's with Mark on the other side of the room."

Jo Marie faltered in midstep and Andrew's hold tightened as he dropped his arm and slipped it around her slim waist. "With Mark?" She couldn't imagine her brother attending this party. Not feeling the way he did about Andrew.

Not until they were upstairs and the music was playing did Jo Marie have an opportunity to talk to her brother. He was sitting against the wall in a high-backed mahogany chair with a velvet cushion. Kelly was at his side. Jo Marie couldn't recall a time she'd seen her brother dress so formally or look more handsome. He'd had his hair trimmed and was clean shaven. She'd never dreamed she'd see Mark in a tuxedo.

"Hello, Mark."

Her brother looked up, guilt etched on his face. "Jo Marie." Briefly he exchanged looks with Kelly and stood, offering Jo Marie his seat.

"Thanks," she said as she sat and slipped the high-heeled sandals from her toes. "My feet could use a few moments' rest."

"You certainly haven't lacked for partners," Kelly observed happily. "You're a hit, Jo Marie. Even Mark was saying he couldn't believe you were his sister."

"I've never seen you look more attractive," Mark added. "But then I bet you didn't buy that dress out of petty cash either."

If there was a note of censure in her brother's voice, Jo Marie didn't hear it. "No." Absently her hand smoothed the silk skirt. "It was a gift from Andrew...and Kelly." Hastily she added her roommate's name. "I must admit though, I'm surprised to see you here."

"Andrew extended the invitation personally," Mark replied, holding his back ramrod stiff as he stared straight ahead.

Not understanding, Jo Marie glanced at her roommate. "Mark came for me," Kelly explained, her voice soft and vulnerable. "Because I...because I wanted him here."

"We're both here for you, Kelly," Jo Marie reminded her and punctuated her comment by arching her brows.

"I know, and I love you both for it."

"Would you care to dance?" Mark held out his hand to Kelly, taking her into his arms when they reached the boundary of the dance floor as if he never wanted to let her go.

Confused, Jo Marie watched their progress. Kelly was engaged to be married to Andrew, yet she was gazing into Mark's eyes as if he were her knight in shining armor who had come to slay dragons on her behalf. When she'd come upon them, they'd acted as if she had intruded on their very private party.

Jo Marie saw Andrew approach her, his brows lowered as if something had displeased him. His strides were quick and decisive as he wove his way through the throng of guests.

"I've been looking for you. In fact, I was beginning to wonder if I'd ever get a chance to dance with you." The pitch of his voice suggested that she'd been deliberately avoiding him. And she had.

Jo Marie couldn't bring herself to meet his gaze, afraid of what he could read in her eyes. All night she'd been pretending it was Andrew who was holding her and yet she'd known she wouldn't be satisfied until he did.

"I believe this dance is mine," he said, presenting her with his hand.

Peering up at him, a smile came and she paused to slip the strap of her high heel over her ankle before standing.

Once on the dance floor, his arms tightened around her waist, bringing her so close that there wasn't a hair's space between them. He held her securely as if challenging her to move. Jo Marie discovered that she couldn't. This inexplicable feeling was beyond argument. With her hands resting on his muscular shoulders, she leaned her head against his broad chest and sighed her contentment.

She spoke first. "It's a wonderful party."

"You're more comfortable now, aren't you?" His fingers moved up and down her back in a leisurely exercise, drugging her with his firm caress against her bare skin.

"What do you mean?" She wasn't sure she understood his question and slowly lifted her gaze.

"Last week, you stayed on the outskirts of the crowd afraid of joining in or being yourself."

"Last week I was terrified that someone would recognize me as the one who had once demonstrated against you. I didn't want to do anything that would embarrass you," she explained dryly. Her cheek was pressed against his starched shirt and she thrilled to the uneven thump of his heart.

"And this week?"

"Tonight anyone who looked at us would know that we've long since resolved our differences."

She sensed more than felt Andrew's soft touch. The moment was quickly becoming too intimate. Using her hands for leverage, Jo Marie straightened, creating a space between them. "Does it bother you to have my brother dance with Kelly?"

Andrew looked back at her blankly. "No. Should it?"

"She's your fiancée." To the best of Jo Marie's knowledge, Andrew hadn't said more than a few words to Kelly all evening.

A cloud of emotion darkened his face. "She's wearing my ring."

"And...and you care for her."

Andrew's hold tightened painfully around her waist. "Yes, I care for Kelly. We've always been close." His eyes darkened to the color of burnt silver. "Perhaps too close."

The applause was polite when the dance number finished.

Jo Marie couldn't escape fast enough. She made an excuse and headed for the powder room. Andrew wasn't pleased and it showed in the grim set of his mouth, but he didn't try to stop her. Things weren't right. Mark shouldn't be sitting like an avenging angel at Kelly's side and Andrew should at least show some sign of jealousy.

When she returned to the ballroom, Andrew was busy and Jo Marie decided to sort through her thoughts in the fresh night air. A curtained glass door that led to the balcony was open, and unnoticed she slipped silently into the dark. A flash of white captured her attention and Jo Marie realized she wasn't alone. Inadvertently, she had invaded the private world of two young lovers. With their arms wrapped around each other they were locked in a passionate embrace. Smiling softly to herself, she turned to escape as silently as she'd come. But something stopped her. A sickening knot tightened her stomach.

The couple so passionately embracing were Kelly and Mark.

Chapter Six

Jo Marie woke just as dawn broke over a cloudless horizon. Standing at the bedroom window, she pressed her palms against the sill and surveyed the beauty of the landscape before her. Turning, she glanced at Kelly's sleeping figure. Her hands fell limply to her side as her face darkened with uncertainty. Last night while they'd prepared for bed, Jo Marie had been determined to confront her friend with the kiss she'd unintentionally witnessed. But when they'd turned out the lights, Kelly had chatted happily about the success of the party and what a good time she'd had. And Jo Marie had lost her nerve. What Mark and Kelly did wasn't any of her business, she mused. In addition, she had no right to judge her brother and her friend when she and Andrew had done the same thing.

The memory of Andrew's kiss produce a breathlessness, and surrendering to the feeling, Jo Marie closed her eyes. The infinitely sweet touch of his mouth seemed to have branded her. Her fingers shook as she raised them to the gentle curve of her lips. Jo Marie doubted that she would ever feel the same overpowering rush of sensation at another man's touch. Andrew was special, her dream man. Whole lifetimes could pass and she'd never find anyone she'd love more. The powerful ache in her heart drove her to the closet where a change of clothes were hanging.

Dawn's light was creeping up the stairs, awaking a sleeping world, when Jo Marie softly clicked the bedroom door closed. Her overnight bag was clenched tightly in her hand. She hated to sneak out, but the thought of facing everyone over the breakfast table was more than she could bear. Andrew and Kelly needed to be alone. Time together was something they hadn't had much of lately. This morning would be the perfect opportunity for them to sit down and discuss their coming marriage. Jo Marie would only be an intruder.

Moving so softly that no one was likely to hear her, Jo Marie crept down the stairs to the wide entry hall. She was tiptoeing toward the front door when a voice behind her interrupted her quiet departure.

"What do you think you're doing?"

Releasing a tiny, startled cry, Jo Marie dropped the suitcase and held her hand to her breast.

"Andrew, you've frightened me to death."

"Just what are you up to?"

"I'm...I'm leaving."

"That's fairly easy to ascertain. What I want to know is why." His angry gaze locked with hers, refusing to allow her to turn away.

"I thought you and Kelly should spend some time together and...and I wanted to be gone this morning before everyone woke." Regret crept into her voice. Maybe sneaking out like this wasn't such a fabulous idea, after all.

He stared at her in the dim light as if he could examine her soul with his penetrating gaze. When he spoke again, his tone was lighter. "And just how did you expect to get to town. Walk?"

"Exactly."

"But it's miles."

"All the more reason to get an early start," she reasoned.

Andrew studied her as though he couldn't believe what he was hearing. "Is running away so important that you would sneak out of here like a cat burglar and not tell anyone where you're headed?"

How quickly her plan had backfired. By trying to leave unobtrusively she'd only managed to offend Andrew when she had every reason to thank him. "I didn't mean to be rude, although I can see now that I have been. I suppose this makes me look like an ungrateful house guest.''

His answer was to narrow his eyes fractionally.

''I want you to know I left a note that explained where I was going to both you and Kelly. It's on the nightstand.''

''And what did you say?''

''That I enjoyed the party immensely and that I've never felt more beautiful in any dress.''

A brief troubled look stole over Andrew's face. ''Once,'' he murmured absently. ''Only onece have you been more lovely.'' There was an unexpectedly gentle quality to his voice.

Her eyelashes fluttered closed. Andrew was reminding her of that February night. He too hadn't been able to forget the Mardi Gras. After all this time, after everything that had transpired since, neither of them could forget. The spell was as potent today as it had been those many months ago.

''Is that coffee I smell?'' The question sought an invitation to linger with Andrew. Her original intent had been to escape so that Kelly could have the opportunity to spend this time alone with him. Instead, Jo Marie was seeking it herself. To sit in the early light of dawn and savor a few solitary minutes alone with Andrew was too tempting to ignore.

''Come and I'll get you a cup.'' Andrew led her toward the back of the house and his den. The room held a faint scent of leather and tobacco that mingled with the aroma of musk and spice.

Three walls were lined with leather-bound books that reached from the floor to the ceiling. Two wing chairs were angled in front of a large fireplace.

"Go ahead and sit down. I'll be back in a moment with the coffee."

A contented smile brightened Jo Marie's eyes as she sat and noticed the leather volume she'd given him lying open on the ottoman. Apparently he'd been reading it when he heard the noise at the front of the house and had left to investigate.

Andrew returned and carefully handed her the steaming earthenware mug. His eyes followed her gaze which rested on the open book. "I've been reading it. This is a wonderful book. Where did you ever find something like this?"

"I've known about it for a long time, but there were only a few volumes available. I located this one about three months ago in a used-book store."

"It's very special to me because of the woman who bought it for me."

"No." Jo Marie's eyes widened as she lightly tossed her head from side to side. "Don't let that be the reason. Appreciate the book for all the interesting details it gives of New Orleans' colorful past. Or admire the pictures of the city architects' skill. But don't treasure it because of me."

Andrew looked for a moment as if he wanted to argue, but she spoke again.

"When you read this book ten, maybe twenty, years from now, I'll only be someone who briefly passed through your life. I imagine you'll have trouble remembering what I looked like."

"You'll never be anyone who flits in and out of my life."

He said it with such intensity that Jo Marie's fingers tightened around the thick handle of the mug. "All right," she agreed with a shaky laugh. "I'll admit I barged into your peaceful existence long before Kelly introduced us but—"

"But," Andrew interrupted on a short laugh, "it seems we were destined to meet. Do you honestly believe that either of us will ever forget that night?" A faint smile touched his eyes as he regarded her steadily.

Jo Marie knew that she never would. Andrew was her dream man. It had been far more than mere fate that had brought them together, something almost spiritual.

"No," she answered softly. "I'll never forget."

Regret moved across his features, creasing his wide brow and pinching his mouth. "Nor will I forget," he murmured in a husky voice that sounded very much like a vow.

The air between them was electric. For months she'd thought of Andrew as the dream man. But coming to know him these past weeks had proven that he wasn't an apparition, but real. Human, vulnerable, proud, intelligent, generous—and everything that she had ever hoped to find in a man. She lowered her gaze and studied the dark depths of the steaming coffee. Andrew might be everything she had ever wanted in a man, but Kelly wore his ring and her roommate's stake on him was far more tangible than her own romantic dreams.

Taking an exaggerated drink of her coffee, Jo Marie carefully set aside the rose-colored mug and stood. "I really should be leaving."

"Please stay," Andrew requested. "Just sit with me a few minutes longer. It's been in this room that I've sat and thought about you so often. I'd always hoped that someday you would join me here."

Jo Marie dipped her head, her heart singing with the beauty of his words. She'd fantasized about him too. Since their meeting, her mind had conjured up his image so often that it wouldn't hurt to steal a few more moments of innocent happiness. Kelly would have him for a lifetime. Jo Marie had only today.

"I'll stay," she agreed and her voice throbbed with the excited beat of her heart.

"And when the times comes, I'll drive you back to the city."

She nodded her acceptance and finished her coffee. "It's so peaceful in here. It feels like all I need to do is lean my head back, close my eyes and I'll be asleep."

"Go ahead," he urged in a whispered tone.

A smile touched her radiant features. She didn't want to fall asleep and miss these precious moments alone with him. "No." She shook her head. "Tell me about yourself. I want to know everything."

His returning smile was wry. "I'd hate to bore you."

"Bore me!" Her small laugh was incredulous. "There's no chance of that."

"All right, but lay back and close your eyes and let me start by telling you that I had a good childhood with parents who deeply loved each other."

As he requested, Jo Marie rested her head against the cushion and closed her eyes. "My parents are wonderful too."

"But being raised in an ideal family has its drawbacks," Andrew continued in a low, soothing voice. "When it came time for me to think about a wife and starting a family there was always a fear in the back of my mind that I would never find the happiness my parents shared. My father wasn't an easy man to love. And I won't be either."

In her mind, Jo Marie took exception to that, but she said nothing. The room was warm, and slipping off her shoes, she tucked her nylon-covered feet under her. Andrew continued speaking, his voice droning on as she tilted her head back.

"When I reached thirty without finding a wife, I became skeptical about the women I was meeting. There were some who never saw past the dollar signs and others who were interested only in themselves. I wanted a woman who could be soft and yielding, but one who wasn't afraid to fight for what she believes, even if it meant standing up against tough opposition. I wanted someone who would share my joys and divide my worries. A woman as beautiful on the inside as any outward beauty she may possess."

"Kelly's like that." The words nearly stuck in Jo Marie's throat. Kelly was everything Andrew was describing and more. As painful as it was to admit, Jo Marie understood why Andrew had asked her roommate to marry him. In addition to her fine personal qualities, Kelly had money of her own and Andrew need never think that she was marrying him for any financial gains.

"Yes, Kelly's like that." There was a doleful timbre to his voice that caused Jo Marie to open her eyes.

Fleetingly she wondered if Andrew had seen Mark and Kelly kissing on the terrace last night. If he had created the picture of a perfect woman in his mind, then finding Kelly in Mark's arms could destroy him. No matter how uncomfortable it became, Jo Marie realized she was going to have to confront Mark about his behavior. Having thoughtfully analyzed the situation, Jo Marie believed it would be far better for her to talk to her brother. She could speak more freely with him. It may be the hardest thing she'd ever do, but after listening to Andrew, Jo Marie realized that she must talk to Mark. The happiness of too many people was at stake.

Deciding to change the subject, Jo Marie shifted her position in the supple leather chair and looked to Andrew. "Kelly told me that you built the house yourself."

Grim amusement was carved in his features. "Yes, the work began on it this spring."

"Then you've only been living in it a few months?"

"Yes. The construction on the house kept me from going insane." He held her look, revealing nothing of his thoughts.

"Going insane?" Jo Marie didn't understand.

"You see, for a short time last February, only a matter of moments really, I felt my search for the right woman was over. And in those few, scant moments I thought I had met that special someone I could love for all time."

Jo Marie's heart was pounding so fast and loud that she wondered why it didn't burst right out of her chest. The thickening in her throat made swallowing painful. Each breath became labored as she turned her face away, unable to meet Andrew's gaze.

"But after those few minutes, I lost her," Andrew continued. "Ironically, I'd searched a lifetime for that special woman, and within a matter of minutes, she was gone. God knows I tried to find her again. For a month I went back to the spot where I'd last seen her and waited. When it seemed that all was lost I discovered I couldn't get the memory of her out of my mind. I even hired a detective to find her for me. For months he checked every hospital in the city, searching for her. But you see, at the time I thought she was a nurse."

Jo Marie felt moisture gathering in the corner of her eyes. Never had she believed that Andrew had looked for her to the extent that he hired someone.

"For a time I was convinced I was going insane. This woman, whose name I didn't even know, filled my every waking moment and haunted my sleep. Building the house was something I've always wanted to do. It helped fill the time until I could find her again. Every room was constructed with her in mind."

Andrew was explaining that he'd built the house for her. Jo Marie had thought she'd be uncomfortable in such a magnificent home. But she'd immediately felt the welcome in the walls. Little had she dreamed the reason why.

"Sometimes," Jo Marie began awkwardly, "people build things up in their minds and when they're confronted with reality they're inevitably disappointed." Andrew was making her out to be wearing angel's wings. So much time had passed that he no longer saw her as flesh and bone, but a wonderful fantasy his mind had created.

"Not this time," he countered smoothly.

"I wondered where I'd find the two of you." A sleepy-eyed Kelly stood poised in the doorway of the den. There wasn't any censure in her voice, only her usual morning brightness. "Isn't it a marvelous morning? The sun's up and there's a bright new day just waiting for us.''

Self-consciously, Jo Marie unwound her feet from beneath her and reached for her shoes. ''What time is it?''

''A quarter to eight.'' Andrew supplied the information.

Jo Marie was amazed to realize that she'd spent the better part of two hours talking to him. But it would be time she'd treasure all her life.

''If you have no objections,'' Kelly murmured and paused to take a wide yawn, ''I thought I'd go to the hospital this morning. There's a special...patient I'd like to stop in and visit.''

A patient or Mark, Jo Marie wanted to ask. Her brother had mentioned last night that he was going to be on duty in the morning. Jo Marie turned to Andrew, waiting for a reaction from him. Surely he would say or do something to stop her. Kelly was his fiancée and both of them seemed to be regarding their commitment to each other lightly.

''No problem.'' Andrew spoke at last. ''In fact I thought I'd go into the city myself this morning. It is a beautiful day and there's no better way to spend a portion of it than in the most beautiful city in the world. You don't mind if I tag along with you, do you, Jo Marie?''

Half of her wanted to cry out in exaltation. If there was anything she wished to give of herself to Andrew it was her love of New Orleans. But at the same time she wanted to shake both Andrew and Kelly for the careless attitude they had toward their relationship.

"I'd like you to come." Jo Marie spoke finally, answering Andrew.

It didn't take Kelly more than a few moments to pack her things and be ready to leave. In her rush, she'd obviously missed the two sealed envelopes Jo Marie had left propped against the lamp on Kelly's nightstand. Or if she had discovered them, Kelly chose not to mention it. Not that it mattered, Jo Marie decided as Andrew started the car. But Kelly's actions revealed what a rush she was in to see Mark. If it was Mark that she was indeed seeing. Confused emotions flooded Jo Marie's face, pinching lines around her nose and mouth. She could feel Andrew's caressing gaze as they drove toward the hospital.

"Is something troubling you?" Andrew questioned after they'd dropped Kelly off in front of Tulane Hospital. Amid protests from Jo Marie, Kelly had assured them that she would find her own way home. Standing on the sidewalk, she'd given Jo Marie a happy wave, before turning and walking toward the double glass doors that led to the lobby of the hospital.

"I think Kelly's going to see Mark," Jo Marie ventured in a short, rueful voice.

"I think she is too."

Jo Marie sat up sharply. "And that doesn't bother you?"

"Should it?" Andrew gave her a bemused look.

"Yes," she said and nodded emphatically. She would never have believed that Andrew could be so blind. "Yes, it should make you furious."

He turned and smiled briefly. "But it doesn't. Now tell me where you'd like to eat breakfast. Brennan's?"

Jo Marie felt trapped in a labyrinth in which no route made sense and from which she could see no escape. She was thoroughly confused by the actions of the three people she loved.

"I don't understand any of this," she cried in frustration. "You should be livid that Kelly and Mark are together."

A furrow of absent concentration darkened Andrew's brow as he drove. Briefly he glanced in her direction. "The time will come when you do understand," he explained cryptically.

Rubbing the side of her neck in agitation, Jo Marie studied Andrew as he drove. His answer made no sense, but little about anyone's behavior this last month had made sense. She hadn't pictured herself as being obtuse, but obviously she was.

Breakfast at Brennan's was a treat known throughout the south. The restaurant was built in the classic Vieux Carre style complete with courtyard. Because they didn't have a reservation, they were put on a waiting list and told it would be another hour before there would be a table available. Andrew eyed Jo Marie, who nodded eagerly. For all she'd heard, the breakfast was worth the wait.

Taking her hand in his, they strolled down the quiet streets that comprised the French Quarter. Most of the stores were closed, the streets deserted.

"I was reading just this morning that the French established New Orleans in 1718. The Spanish took over the 3,000 French inhabitants in 1762, although there were so few Spaniards that barely anyone noticed until 1768. The French Quarter is like a city within a city."

Jo Marie smiled contentedly and looped her hand through his arm. "You mean to tell me that it takes a birthday present for you to know about your own fair city?"

Andrew chuckled and drew her closer by circling his arm around her shoulders. "Are you always snobbish or is this act for my benefit?"

They strolled for what seemed far longer than a mere hour, visiting Jackson Square and feeding the pigeons. Strolling back, with Andrew at her side, Jo Marie felt she would never be closer to heaven. Never would she want for anything more than today, this minute, with this man. Jo Marie felt tears mist her dusty eyes. A tremulous smile touched her mouth. Andrew was here with her. Within a short time he would be married to Kelly and she must accept that, but for now, he was hers.

The meal was everything they'd been promised. Ham, soft breads fresh from the bakery, eggs and a fabulous chicory coffee. A couple of times Jo Marie found herself glancing at Andrew. His expression revealed little and she wondered if he regretted having decided to spend this time with her. She prayed that wasn't the case.

When they stood to leave, Andrew reached for her hand and smiled down on her with shining gray eyes.

Jo Marie's heart throbbed with love. The radiant light of her happiness shone through when Andrew's arm slipped naturally around her shoulder as if branding her with his seal of protection.

"I enjoy being with you," he said and she couldn't doubt the sincerity in his voice. "You're the kind of woman who would be as much at ease at a formal ball as you would fishing from the riverside with rolled-up jeans."

"I'm not Huck Finn," she teased.

"No," he smiled, joining in her game. "Just my Florence Nightingale, the woman who has haunted me for the last nine months."

Self-consciously, Jo Marie eased the strap of her leather purse over her shoulder. "It's always been my belief that dreams have a way of fading, especially when faced with the bright light of the sun and reality."

"Normally, I'd agree with you," Andrew responded thoughtfully, "but not this time. There are moments so rare in one's life that recognizing what they are can sometimes be doubted. Of you, of that night, of us, I have no doubts."

"None?" Jo Marie barely recognized her own voice.

"None," he confirmed.

If that were so, then why did Kelly continue to wear his ring? How could he look at her with so much emotion and then ask another woman to share his life?

The ride to Jo Marie's apartment was accomplished in a companionable silence. Andrew pulled into the parking space and turned off the ignition. Jo Marie's gaze centered on the dashboard. Silently she'd hoped that he wouldn't come inside with her. The atmosphere when they were alone was volatile. And with everything that Andrew had told her this morning, Jo Marie doubted that she'd have the strength to stay out of his arms if he reached for her.

"I can see myself inside." Gallantly, she made an effort to avoid temptation.

"Nonsense," Andrew returned, and opening the car door, he removed her overnight case from the back seat.

Jo Marie opened her side and climbed out, not waiting for him to come around. A feeling of doom settled around her heart.

Her hand was steady as she inserted the key into the apartment lock, but that was the only thing that was. Her knees felt like rubber as the door swung open and she stepped inside the room, standing in the entryway. The drapes were pulled, blocking out the sunlight, making the apartment's surroundings all the more intimate.

"I have so much to thank you for," she began and nervously tugged a strand of dark hair behind her ear. "A simple thank you seems like so little." She hoped Andrew understood that she didn't want him to come any farther into the apartment.

The door clicked closed and her heart sank. "Where would you like me to put your suitcase?"

Determined not to make this situation any worse for them, Jo Marie didn't move. "Just leave it here."

A smoldering light of amused anger burned in his eyes as he set the suitcase down. "There's no help for this," he whispered as his hand slid slowly, almost unwillingly along the back of her waist. "Be angry with me later."

Any protests died the moment his mouth met hers in a demanding kiss. An immediate answering hunger seared through her veins, melting all resistance until she was molded against the solid wall of his chest. His caressing fingers explored the curve of her neck and shoulders and his mouth followed, blazing a trail that led back to her waiting lips.

Jo Marie rotated her head, giving him access to any part of her face that his hungry mouth desired. She offered no protest when his hands sought the fullness of her breast, then sighed with the way her body responded to the gentleness of his fingers. He kissed her expertly, his mobile mouth moving insistently over hers, teasing her with light, biting nips that made her yearn for more and more. Then he'd change his tactics and kiss her with a hungry demand. Lost in a mindless haze, she clung to him as the tears filled her eyes and ran unheeded down her cheeks. Everything she feared was happening. And worse, she was powerless to stop him. Her throat felt dry and scratchy and she uttered a soft sob in a effort to abate the flow of emotion.

Andrew went still. He cupped her face in his hands and examined her tear-streaked cheeks. His troubled expression swam in and out of her vision.

"Jo Marie," he whispered, his voice tortured. "Don't cry, darling, please don't cry." With an infinite tenderness he kissed away each tear and when he reached her trembling mouth, the taste of salt was on his lips. A series of long, drugging kisses only confused her more. It didn't seem possible she could want him so much and yet that it should be so wrong.

"Please." With every ounce of strength she possessed Jo Marie broke from his embrace. "I promised myself this wouldn't happen again," she whispered feeling miserable. Standing with her back to him, her hands cradled her waist to ward off a sudden chill.

Gently he pressed his hand to her shoulder and Jo Marie couldn't bring herself to brush it away. Even his touch had the power to disarm her.

"Jo Marie." His husky tone betrayed the depths of his turmoil. "Listen to me."

"No, what good would it do?" she asked on a quavering sob. "You're engaged to be married to my best friend. I can't help the way I feel about you. What I feel, what you feel, is wrong as long as Kelly's wearing your ring." With a determined effort she turned to face him, tears blurring her sad eyes. "It would be better if we didn't see each other again...at least until you're sure of what you want..or who you want."

Andrew jerked his hand through his hair. "You're right. I've got to get this mess straightened out."

"Promise me, Andrew, please promise me that you won't make an effort to see me until you know in your own mind what you want. I can't take much more of this." She wiped the moisture from her cheekbones with the tips of her fingers. "When I get up in the morning I want to look at myself in the mirror. I don't want to hate myself."

Andrew's mouth tightened with grim displeasure. He looked as if he wanted to argue. Tense moments passed before he slowly shook his head. "You deserve to be treated so much better than this. Someday, my love, you'll understand. Just trust me for now."

"I'm only asking one thing of you," she said unable to meet his gaze. "Don't touch me or make an effort to see me as long as Kelly's wearing your ring. It's not fair to any one of us." Her lashes fell to veil the hurt in her eyes. Andrew couldn't help but know that she was in love with him. She would have staked her life that her feelings were returned full measure. Fresh tears misted her eyes.

"I don't want to leave you like this."

"I'll be all right," she murmured miserably. "There's nothing that I can do. Everything rests with you, Andrew. Everything."

Dejected, he nodded and added a promise. "I'll take care of it today."

Again Jo Marie wiped the wetness from her face and forced a smile, but the effort was almost more than she could bear.

The door clicked, indicating that Andrew had gone and Jo Marie released a long sigh of pent-up emotion. Her reflection in the bathroom mirror showed that her lips were parted and trembling from the hungry possession of his mouth. Her eyes had darkened from the strength of her physical response.

Andrew had asked that she trust him and she would, with all her heart. He loved her, she was sure of it. He wouldn't have hired a detective to find her or built a huge home with her in mind if he didn't feel some-

thing strong toward her. Nor could he have held her
and kissed her the way he had today without loving
and needing her.

While she unpacked the small overnight bag a sense
of peace came over her. Andrew would explain everything to Kelly, and she needn't worry. Kelly's interests
seemed to be centered more on Mark lately, and
maybe…just maybe, she wouldn't be hurt or upset and
would accept that neither Andrew nor Jo Marie had
planned for this to happen.

Time hung heavily on her hands and Jo Marie toyed
with the idea of visiting her parents. But her mother
knew her so well that she'd take one look at Jo Marie
and want to know what was bothering her daughter.
And today Jo Marie wasn't up to explanations.

A flip of the radio dial and Christmas music drifted
into the room, surrounding her with its message of
peace and love. Humming the words softly to herself,
Jo Marie felt infinitely better. Everything was going to
be fine, she felt confident.

A thick Sunday paper held her attention for the
better part of an hour, but at the slightest noise, Jo
Marie's attention wandered from the printed page and
she glanced up expecting Kelly. One look at her friend
would be enough to tell Jo Marie everything she
needed to know.

Setting the paper aside, Jo Marie felt her nerves
tingle with expectancy. She felt weighted with a terrible guilt. Kelly obviously loved Andrew enough to

agree to be his wife, but she showed all the signs of falling in love with Mark. Kelly wasn't the kind of girl who would purposely hurt or lead a man on. She was too sensitive for that. And to add to the complications were Andrew and Jo Marie who had discovered each other again just when they had given up all hope. Jo Marie loved Andrew, but she wouldn't find her own happiness at her friend's expense. But Andrew was going to ask for his ring back, Jo Marie was sure of it. He'd said he'd clear things up today.

The door opened and inhaling a calming breath, Jo Marie stood.

Kelly came into the apartment, her face lowered as her gaze avoided her friend's.

"Hi," Jo Marie ventured hesitantly.

Kelly's face was red and blotchy; tears glistened in her eyes.

"Is something wrong?" Her voice faltered slightly.

"Drew and I had a fight, that's all." Kelly raised her hand to push back her hair and as she did so the engagement ring Andrew had given her sparkled in the sunlight.

Jo Marie felt the knot tighten in her stomach. Andrew had made his decision.

Chapter Seven

Somehow Jo Marie made it through the following days. She didn't see Andrew and made excuses to avoid Kelly. Her efforts consisted of trying to get through each day. Once she left the office, she often went to the LFTF headquarters, spending long hours helping Jim. Their friendship had grown. Jim helped her laugh when it would have been so easy to cry. A couple of times they had coffee together and talked. But Jim did most of the talking. This pain was so all-consuming that Jo Marie felt like a newly fallen leaf tossed at will by a fickle wind.

Jim asked her to accompany him on another speaking engagement which Jo Marie did willingly.

The talk was on a stretch of wetlands Jim wanted preserved and it had been well received. Silently, Jo Marie mocked herself for not being attracted to someone as wonderful as Jim Rowden. He was everything a woman could want. In addition, she was convinced that he was interested in her. But it was Andrew who continued to fill her thoughts, Andrew who haunted her dreams, Andrew whose soft whisper she heard in the wind.

Lost in the meandering trail of her musing, Jo Marie didn't hear Jim's words as they sauntered into the empty office. Her blank look prompted him to repeat himself. "I thought it went rather well tonight, didn't you?" he asked, grinning boyishly. He brushed the hair from his forehead and pulled out the chair opposite hers.

"Yes," Jo Marie agreed with an absent shake of her head. "It did go well. You're a wonderful speaker." She could feel Jim's gaze watching her and in an effort to avoid any questions, she stood and reached for her purse. "I'd better think about getting home."

"Want some company while you walk to the bus stop?"

"I brought the car tonight." She almost wished she was taking the bus. Jim was a friendly face in a world that had taken on ragged, pain-filled edges.

Kelly had been somber and sullen all week. Half the time she looked as if she were ready to burst into tears at the slightest provocation. Until this last week, Jo

Marie had always viewed her roommate as an emotionally strong woman, but recently Jo Marie wondered if she really knew Kelly. Although her friend didn't enjoy large parties, she'd never known Kelly to be intimidated by them. Lately, Kelly had been playing the role of a damsel in distress to the hilt.

Mark had stopped by the apartment only once and he'd resembled a volcano about to explode. He'd left after fifteen minutes of pacing the living-room carpet when Kelly didn't show.

And Andrew—yes, Andrew—by heaven's grace she'd been able to avoid a confrontation with him. She'd seen him only once in the last five days and the look in his eyes had seared her heart. He desperately wanted to talk to her. The tormented message was clear in his eyes, but she'd gently shaken her head, indicating that she intended to hold him to his word.

"Something's bothering you, Jo Marie. Do you want to talk about it?" Dimples edged into Jim's round face. Funny how she'd never noticed them before tonight.

Sadness touched the depths of her eyes and she gently shook her head. "Thanks, but no. Not tonight."

"Venturing a guess, I'd say it had something to do with Mr. Delta Development."

"Oh?" Clenching her purse under her arm, Jo Marie feigned ignorance. "What makes you say that?"

Jim shook his head. "A number of things." He rose and tucked both hands in his pants pockets. "Let me walk you to your car. The least I can do is see that you get safely outside."

"The weather's been exceptionally cold lately, hasn't it?"

Jim's smile was inviting as he turned the lock in the office door. "Avoiding my questions, aren't you?"

"Yes." Jo Marie couldn't see any reason to lie.

"When you're ready to talk, I'll be happy to listen." Tucking the keys in his pocket, Jim reached for Jo Marie's hand, placing it at his elbow and patting it gently.

"Thanks, I'll remember that."

"Tell me something more about you," Jo Marie queried in a blatant effort to change the subject. Briefly Jim looked at her, his expression thoughtful.

They ventured onto the sidewalk. The full moon was out, its silver rays clearing a path in the night as they strolled toward her car.

"I'm afraid I'd bore you. Most everything you already know. I've only been with the foundation a month."

"LFTF needs people like you, dedicated, passionate, caring."

"I wasn't the one who gave permission for a transient to sleep in a doorway."

Jo Marie softly sucked in her breath. "How'd you know?"

"He came back the second night looking for a handout. The guy knew a soft touch when he saw one."

"What happened?"

Jim shrugged his shoulder and Jo Marie stopped walking in mid-stride. "You gave him some money!" she declared righteously. "And you call me a soft touch."

"As a matter of fact, I didn't. We both knew what he'd spend it on."

"So what did you do?"

"Took him to dinner."

A gentle smile stole across her features at the picture that must have made. Jim dressed impeccably in his business suit and the alcoholic in tattered, ragged clothes.

"It's sad to think about." Slowly, Jo Marie shook her head.

"I got in touch with a friend of mine from a mission. He came for him afterward so that he'll have a place to sleep at least. To witness, close at hand like that, a man wasting his life is far worse to me than..." he paused and held her gaze for a long moment, looking deep into her brown eyes. Then he smiled faintly and shook his head. "Sorry, I didn't mean to get so serious."

"You weren't," Jo Marie replied, taking the car keys from her purse. "I'll be back Monday and maybe we could have a cup of coffee."

The deep blue eyes brightened perceptively. "I'd like that and listen, maybe we could have dinner one night soon."

Jo Marie nodded, revealing that she'd enjoy that as well. Jim was her friend and she doubted that her feelings would ever go beyond that, but the way she felt lately, she needed someone to lift her from the doldrums of self-pity.

The drive home was accomplished in a matter of minutes. Standing otuside her apartment building, Jo Marie heaved a steadying breath. She dreaded walking into her own home—what a sad commentary on her life! Tonight, she promised herself, she'd make an effort to clear the air between herself and Kelly. Not knowing what Andrew had said to her roommate about his feelings for her, if anything, or the details of the argument, had put Jo Marie in a precarious position. The air between Jo Marie and her best friend was like the stillness before an electrical storm. The problem was that Jo Marie didn't know what to say to Kelly or how to go about making things right.

She made a quick survey of the cars in the parking lot to assure herself that Andrew wasn't inside. Relieved, she tucked her hands inside the pockets of her cardigan and hoped to give a nonchalant appearance when she walked through the front door.

Kelly glanced up from the book she was reading when Jo Marie walked inside. The red, puffy eyes were a testimony of tears, but Kelly didn't explain and Jo Marie didn't pry.

"I hope there's something left over from dinner," she began on a forced note of cheerfulness. "I'm starved."

"I didn't fix anything," Kelly explained in an ominously quiet voice. "In fact I think I'm coming down with something. I've got a terrible stomachache."

Jo Marie had to bite her lip to keep from shouting that she knew what was wrong with the both of them. Their lives were beginning to resemble a three-ring circus. Where once Jo Marie and Kelly had been best friends, now they rarely spoke.

"What I think I'll do is take a long, leisurely bath and go to bed."

Jo Marie nodded, thinking Kelly's sudden urge for a hot soak was just an excuse to leave the room and avoid the problems that faced them.

While Kelly ran her bathwater, Jo Marie searched through the fridge looking for something appetizing. Normally this was the time of the year that she had to watch her weight. This Christmas she'd probably end up losing a few pounds.

The radio was playing a series of spirited Christmas carols and Jo Marie started humming along. She took out bread and cheese slices from the fridge. The cupboard offered a can of tomato soup.

By the time Kelly came out of the bathroom, Jo Marie had set two places at the table and was pouring hot soup into deep bowls.

"Dinner is served," she called.

Kelly surveyed the table and gave her friend a weak, trembling smile. "I appreciate the effort, but I'm really not up to eating."

Exhaling a dejected sigh, Jo Marie turned to her friend. "How long are we going to continue pretending like this? We need to talk, Kell."

"Not tonight, please, not tonight."

The doorbell rang and a stricken look came over Kelly's pale features. "I don't want to see anyone," she announced and hurried into the bedroom, leaving Jo Marie to deal with whoever was calling.

Resentment burned in her dark eyes as Jo Marie crossed the room. If it was Andrew, she would simply explain that Kelly was ill and not invite him inside.

"Merry Christmas." A tired-looking Mark greeted Jo Marie sarcastically from the other side of the door.

"Hi." Jo Marie watched him carefully. Her brother looked terrible. Tiny lines etched about his eyes revealed lack of sleep. He looked as though he was suffering from both mental and physical exhaustion.

"Is Kelly around?" He walked into the living room, sat on the sofa and leaned forward, roughly rubbing his hands across his face as if that would keep him awake.

"No, she's gone to bed. I don't think she's feeling well."

Briefly, Mark stared at the closed bedroom door and as he did, his shoulder hunched in a gesture of defeat.

"How about something to eat? You look like you haven't had a decent meal in days."

"I haven't." He moved lackadaisically to the kitchen and pulled out a chair.

Lifting the steaming bowls of soup from the counter, Jo Marie brought them to the table and sat opposite her brother.

As Mark took the soup spoon, his tired eyes held a distant, unhappy look. Kelly's eyes had revealed the same light of despair. "We had an argument," he murmured.

"You and Kell?"

"I said some terrible things to her." He braced his elbow against the table and pinched the bridge of his nose. "I don't know what made me do it. The whole time I was shouting at her I felt as if it was some stranger doing this. I know it sounds crazy but it was almost as if I were standing outside myself watching, and hating myself for what I was doing."

"Was the fight over something important?"

Defensively, Mark straightened. "Yeah, but that's between Kelly and me." He attacked the toasted cheese sandwich with a vengeance.

"You're in love with Kelly, aren't you?" Jo Marie had yet to touch her meal, more concerned about what was happening between her brother and her best friend than about her soup and sandwich.

Mark hesitated thoughtfully and a faint grimness closed off his expression. "In love with Kelly? I am?"

"You obviously care for her."

"I care for my cat, too," he returned coldly and his expression hardened. "She's got what she wants— money. Just look at who she's marrying. It isn't enough that she's wealthy in her own right. No, she sets her sights on J. Paul Getty."

Jo Marie's chin trembled in a supreme effort not to reveal her reaction to his words. "You know Kelly better than that." Averting her gaze, Jo Marie struggled to hold back the emotion that tightly constricted her throat.

"Does either one of us really know Kelly?" Mark's voice was taut as a hunter's bow. Cyncism drove deep grooved lines around his nose and mouth. "Did she tell you that she and Drew have set their wedding date?" Mark's voice dipped with contempt.

A pain seared all the way through Jo Marie's soul. "No, she didn't say." With her gaze lowered, she struggled to keep her hands from shaking.

"Apparently they're going to make it official after the first of the year. They're planning on a spring wedding."

"How...nice." Jo Marie nearly choked on the words.

"Well, all I can say is that those two deserve each other." He tossed the melted cheese sandwich back on the plate and stood. "I guess I'm not very hungry, after all."

Jo Marie rose with him and glanced at the table. Neither one of them had done more than shred their sandwiches and stir their soup. "Neither am I," she said, and swallowed at the tightness gripping her throat.

Standing in the living room, Mark stared for a second time at the closed bedroom door.

"I'll tell Kelly you were by." For a second it seemed that Mark hadn't heard.

"No," he murmured after a long moment. "Maybe it's best to leave things as they are. Good night, sis, thanks for dinner." Resembling a man carrying the weight of the world on his shoulders, Mark left.

Leaning against the front door, Jo Marie released a bitter, pain-filled sigh and turned the dead bolt. Tears burned for release. So Andrew and Kelly were going to make a public announcement of their engagement after Christmas. It shouldn't shock her. Kelly had told her from the beginning that they were. The wedding plans were already in the making. Wiping the salty dampness from her cheek, Jo Marie bit into the tender skin inside her cheek to hold back a sob.

"There's a call for you on line one," Paula called to Jo Marie from her desk.

"Thanks." With an efficiency born of years of experience, Jo Marie punched in the telephone tab and lifted the receiver to her ear. "This is Jo Marie Early, may I help you?"

"Jo Marie, this is Jim. I hope you don't mind me calling you at work."

"No problem."

"Good. Listen, you, ah, mentioned something the other night about us having coffee together and I said something about having dinner."

If she hadn't known any better, Jo Marie would have guessed that Jim was uneasy. He was a gentle man with enough sensitivity to campaign for the future. His hesitancy surprised her now. "I remember."

"How would you feel about this Wednesday?" he continued. "We could make a night of it."

Jo Marie didn't need to think it over. "I'd like that very much." After Mark's revelation, she'd realized the best thing to do was to put the past and Andrew behind her and build a new life for herself.

"Good." Jim sounded pleased. "We can go Wednesday night...or would you prefer Friday?"

"Wednesday's fine." Jo Marie doubted that she could ever feel again the deep, passionate attraction she'd experienced with Andrew, but Jim's appeal wasn't built on fantasy.

"I'll see you then. Goodbye, Jo Marie."

"Goodbye Jim, and thanks."

The mental uplifting of their short conversation was enough to see Jo Marie through a hectic afternoon. An airline lost her customer's reservations and the tickets didn't arrive in time. In addition the phone rang repeatedly.

By the time she walked into the apartment, her feet hurt and there was a nagging ache in the small of her back.

"I thought I heard you." Kelly sauntered into the kitchen and stood in the doorway dressed in a robe and slippers.

"How are you feeling?"

She lifted one shoulder in a weak shrug. "Better."

"You stayed home?" Kelly had still been in bed when Jo Marie left for work. Apparently her friend had phoned in sick.

"Yeah." She moved into the living room and sat on the sofa.

"Mark was by last night." Jo Marie mentioned the fact casually, waiting for a response from her roommate. Kelly didn't give her one. "He said that the two of you had a big fight," she continued.

"That's all we do anymore—argue."

"I don't know what he said to you, but he felt bad about it afterward."

A sad glimmer touched Kelly's eyes and her mouth formed a brittle line that Jo Marie supposed was meant to be a smile. "I know he didn't mean it. He's exhausted. I swear he's trying to work himself to death.''

Now that her friend mentioned it, Jo Marie realized that she hadn't seen much of her brother lately. It used to be that he had an excuse to show up two or three times a week. Except for last night, he had been to the apartment only twice since Thanksgiving.

"I don't think he's eaten a decent meal in days," Kelly continued. "He's such a good doctor, Jo Marie, because he cares so much about his patients. Even the ones he knows he's going to lose. I'm a nurse, I've seen the way the other doctors close themselves off from any emotional involvement. But Mark's there, always giving.'' Her voice shook uncontrollably and she paused to bite into her lip until she regained her composure. "I wanted to talk to him the other night, and do you know where I found him? In pediatrics holding a little boy who's suffering with terminal cancer. He was rocking this child, holding him in his arms and telling him the pain wouldn't last too much longer. From the hallway, I heard Mark talk about heaven and how there wouldn't be any pain for him there. Mark's a wonderful man and wonderful doctor.''

And he loves you so much it's tearing him apart, Jo Marie added silently.

"Yesterday he was frustrated and angry and he took it out on me. I'm not going to lie and say it didn't hurt. For a time I was devastated, but I'm over that now.''

"But you didn't go to work today." They both knew why she'd chosen to stay home.

"No, I felt Mark and I needed a day away from each other."

"That's probably a good idea." There was so much she wanted to say to Kelly, but everything sounded so inadequate. At least they were talking, which was a major improvement over the previous five days.

The teakettle whistled sharply and Jo Marie returned to the kitchen bringing them both back a steaming cup of hot coffee.

"Thanks." Kelly's eyes brightened.

"Would you like me to talk to Mark?" Jo Marie's offer was sincere, but she wasn't exactly sure what she'd say. And in some ways it could make matters worse.

"No. We'll sort this out on our own."

The doorbell chimed and the two exchanged glances. "I'm not expecting anyone," Kelly murmured and glanced down self-consciously at her attire. "In fact I'd rather not be seen, so if you don't mind I'll vanish inside my room."

The last person Jo Marie expected to find on the other side of the door was Andrew. The welcome died in her eyes as their gazes met and clashed. Jo Marie quickly lowered hers. Her throat went dry and a rush of emotion brought a flood of color to her suddenly pale cheeks. A tense air of silence surrounded them. Andrew raised his hand as though he wanted to reach out and touch her. Instead he clenched his fist and lowered it to his side, apparently having changed his mind.

"Is Kelly ready?" he asked after a breathless moment. Jo Marie didn't move, her body blocking the front door, refusing him admittance.

She stared up at him blankly. "Ready?" she repeated.

"Yes, we're attending the opera tonight. Bizet's *Carmen*," he added as if in an afterthought.

"Oh, dear." Jo Marie's eyes widened. Kelly had obviously forgotten their date. The tickets for the elaborate opera had been sold out for weeks. Her roommate would have to go. "Come in, I'll check with Kelly."

"Andrew's here," Jo Marie announced and leaned against the wooden door inside the bedroom, her hands folded behind her.

"Drew?"

"Andrew to me, Drew to you," she responded cattily. "You have a date to see *Carmen*."

Kelly's hand flew to her forehead. "Oh, my goodness, I completely forgot."

"What are you going to do?"

"Explain, what else is there to do?" she snapped.

Jo Marie followed her friend into the living room. Andrew's gray eyes widened at the sight of Kelly dressed in her robe and slippers.

"You're ill?"

"Actually, I'm feeling better. Drew, I apologize, I completely forgot about tonight."

As Andrew glanced at his gold wristwatch, a frown marred his handsome face.

"Kelly can shower and dress in a matter of a few minutes," Jo Marie said sharply, guessing what Kelly was about to suggest.

"I couldn't possibly be ready in forty-five minutes," she denied. "There's only one thing to do. Jo Marie, you'll have to go in my place."

Andrew's level gaze crossed the width of the room to capture Jo Marie's. Little emotion was revealed in the impassive male features, but his gray eyes glinted with challenge.

"I can't." Her voice was level with hard determination.

"Why not?" Two sets of eyes studied her.

"I'm...." Her mind searched wildly for an excuse. "I'm baking cookies for the Science Club. We're meeting Saturday and this will be our last time before Christmas."

"I thought you worked Saturdays," Andrew cut in sharply.

"Every other Saturday." Calmly she met this gaze. Over the past couple of weeks, Kelly had purposely brought Jo Marie and Andrew together, but Jo Marie wouldn't fall prey to that game any longer. She'd made an agreement with him and refused to back down. As long as he was engaged to another woman she wouldn't...couldn't be with him. "I won't go," she explained in a steady voice which belied the inner turmoil that churned her stomach.

"There's plenty of time before the opening curtain if you'd care to change your mind."

Kelly tossed Jo Marie an odd look. "It looks like I'll have to go," she said with an exaggerated sigh. "I'll be as fast as I can." Kelly rushed back inside the bedroom leaving Jo Marie and Andrew separated by only a few feet.

"How have you been?" he asked, his eyes devouring her.

"Fine," she responded on a stiff note. The lie was only a little one. The width of the room stood between them, but it might as well have been whole lightyears.

Bowing her head, she stared at the pattern in the carpet. When she suggested Kelly hurry and dress, she hadn't counted on being left alone with Andrew. "If you'll excuse me, I'll get started on those cookies."

To her dismay Andrew followed her into the kitchen.

"What are my chances of getting a cup of coffee?" He sounded pleased with himself, his smile was smug.

Wordlessly Jo Marie stood on her tiptoes and brought down a mug from the cupboard. She poured in the dark granules, stirred in hot water and walked past him to carry the mug into the living room. All the while her mind was screaming with him to leave her alone.

Andrew picked up the mug and followed her back into the kitchen. "I've wanted to talk to you for days."

"You agreed."

"Jo Marie, believe me, talking to Kelly isn't as easy as it seems. There are some things I'm not at liberty to explain that would resolve this whole mess."

"I'll just bet there are." The bitter taste of anger filled her mouth.

"Can't you trust me?" The words were barely audible and for an instant Jo Marie wasn't certain he'd spoken.

Everything within her yearned to reach out to him and be assured that the glorious times they'd shared had been as real for him as they'd been for her. Desperately she wanted to turn and tell him that she would trust him with her life, but not her heart. She couldn't, not when Kelly was wearing his engagement ring.

"Jo Marie." A faint pleading quality entered his voice. "I know how all this looks. At least give me a chance to explain. Have dinner with me tomorrow. I swear I won't so much as touch you. I'll leave everything up to you. Place. Time. You name it."

"No." Frantically she shook her head, her voice throbbing with the desire to do as he asked. "I can't."

"Jo Marie." He took a step toward her, then another, until he was so close his husky voice breathed against her dark hair.

Forcing herself into action, Jo Marie whirled around and backed out of the kitchen. "Don't talk to me like that. I realized last week that whatever you feel for Kelly is stronger than any love you have for me. I've tried to accept that as best I can."

Andrew's knuckles were clenched so tightly that they went white. He looked like an innocent man facing a firing squad, his eyes resigned, the line of his jaw tense, anger and disbelief etched in every rugged mark of his face.

"Just be patient, that's all I'm asking. In due time you'll understand everything."

"Will you stop?" she demanded angrily. "You're talking in puzzles and I've always hated those. All I know is that there are four people who—"

"I guess this will have to do," Kelly interrupted as she walked into the room. She had showered, dressed and dried her hair in record time.

Jo Marie swallowed the taste of jealousy as she watched the dark, troubled look dissolve from Andrew's eyes. "You look great," was all she could manage.

"We won't be too late," Kelly said on her way out.

"Don't worry," Jo Marie murmured and breathed in a sharp breath. "I won't be up; I'm exhausted."

Who was she trying to kid? Not until the key turned in the front door lock five hours later did Jo Marie so much as yawn. As much as she hated herself for being so weak, the entire time Kelly had been with Andrew, Jo Marie had been utterly miserable.

The dinner date with Jim the next evening was the only bright spot in a day that stretched out like an empty void. She dressed carefully and applied her makeup with extra care, hoping to camouflage the effects of a sleepless night.

"Don't fix dinner for me, I've got a date," was all she said to Kelly on her way out the door to the office.

As she knew it would, being with Jim was like stumbling upon an oasis in the middle of a sand-tossed desert. He made her laugh, teasing her affectionately. His humor was subtle and light and just the antidote for a broken heart. She'd known from the moment they'd met that she was going to like Jim Rowden. With him she could relax and be herself. And not once did she have to look over her shoulder.

"Are you going to tell me what's been troubling you?" he probed gently over their dessert.

"What? And cry all over my lime-chiffon pie?"

Jim's returning smile was one of understanding and encouragement. Again she noted the twin dimples that formed in his cheeks. "Whenever you're ready, I'm available to listen."

"Thanks." She shook her head, fighting back an unexpected swell of emotion. "Now what's this surprise you've been taunting me with most of the evening?'' she questioned, averting the subject from herself.

''It's about the wetlands we've been crusading for during the last month. Well, I talked to a state senator today and he's going to introduce a bill that would make the land into a state park.'' Lacing his hands together, Jim leaned toward the linen-covered table. ''From everything he's heard, George claims from there it should be a piece of cake.''

''Jim, that's wonderful.'' This was his first success and he beamed with pride over the accomplishment.

''Of course, nothing's definite yet, and I'm not even sure I should have told you, but you've heard me give two speeches on the wetlands and I wanted you to know.''

''I'm honored that you did.''

He acknowledged her statement with a short nod. ''I should know better than to get my hopes up like this, but George—my friend—sounded so confident.''

''Then you should be too. We both should.''

Jim reached for her hand and squeezed it gently. ''It would be very easy to share things with you, Jo Marie. You're quite a woman.''

Flattery had always made her uncomfortable, but Jim sounded so sincere. It cost her a great deal of effort to simply smile and murmur her thanks.

Jim's arm rested across her shoulder as they walked back toward the office. He held open her car door for her and paused before lightly brushing his mouth over hers. The kiss was both gentle and reassuring. But it wasn't Andrew's kiss and Jim hadn't the power to evoke the same passionate response Andrew seemed to draw so easily from her.

On the ride home, Jo Marie silently berated herself for continuing to compare the two men. It was unfair to them both to even think in that mode.

The apartment was unlocked when Jo Marie let herself inside. She was hanging up her sweater-coat when she noticed Andrew. He was standing in the middle of the living room carpet, regarding her with stone cold eyes.

One glance and Jo Marie realized that she'd never seen a man look so angry.

"It's about time you got home." His eyes were flashing gray fire.

"What right is it of yours to demand what time I get in?"

"I have every right." His voice was like a whip lashing out at her. "I suppose you think you're playing a game. Every time I go out with Kelly, you'll pay me back by dating Jim?"

Stunned into speechlessness, Jo Marie felt her voice die in her throat.

"And if you insist on letting him kiss you the least you can do is look for someplace more private than the street.'' The white line about his mouth became more pronounced as his eyes filled with bitter contempt. "You surprise me, Jo Marie, I thought you had more class than that."

Chapter Eight

How dare you...how dare you say such things to me!'' Jo Marie's quavering voice became breathless with rage. Her eyes were dark and stormy as she turned around and jerked the front door open.

"What do you expect me to believe?" Andrew rammed his hand through his hair, ruffling the dark hair that grew at his temple.

"I expected a lot of things from you, but not that you'd follow me or spy on me. And then...then to have the audacity to confront and insult me." The fury in her faded to be replaced with a deep, emotional pain that pierced her heart.

Andrew's face was bloodless as he walked past her and out the door. As soon as he was through the portal, she slammed it closed with a sweeping arc of her hand.

Jo Marie was so furious that the room wasn't large enough to contain her anger. Her shoulders rose and sagged with her every breath. At one time Andrew had been her dream man. Quickly she was learning to separate the fantasy from the reality.

Pacing the carpet helped relieve some of the terrible tension building within her. Andrew's behavior was nothing short of odious. She should hate him for saying those kinds of things to her. Tears burned for release, but deep, concentrated breaths held them at bay. Andrew Beaumont wasn't worth the emotion. Staring sightlessly at the ceiling, her damp lashes pressed against her cheek.

The sound of the doorbell caused her to whirl around. Andrew. She'd stake a week's salary on the fact. In an act of defiance, she folded her arms across her waist and stared determinedly at the closed door. He could rot in the rain before she'd open that door.

Again the chimes rang in short, staccato raps. "Come on, Jo Marie, answer the damn door."

"No," she shouted from the other side.

"Fine, we'll carry on a conversation by shouting at each other. That should amuse your neighbors."

"Go away." Jo Marie was too upset to talk things out. Andrew had hurt her with his actions and words.

"Jo Marie." The appealing quality in his voice couldn't be ignored. "Please, open the door. All I want is to apologize."

Hating herself for being so weak, Jo Marie turned the lock and threw open the solid wood door. "You have one minute."

"I think I went a little crazy when I saw Jim kiss you," he said pacing the area in front of the door. "Jo Marie, promise me that you won't see him again. I don't think I can stand the thought of any man touching you."

"This is supposed to be an apology?" she asked sarcastically. "Get this, Mr. Beaumont," she said, fighting to keep from shouting at him as her finger punctuated the air. "You have no right to dictate anything to me."

His tight features darkened. "I can make your life miserable."

"And you think you haven't already?" she cried. "Just leave me alone. I don't need your threats. I don't want to see you again. Ever." To her horror, her voice cracked. Shaking her head, unable to talk any longer, she shut the door and clicked the lock.

Almost immediately the doorbell chimed, followed by continued knocking. Neither of them were in any mood to discuss things rationally. And perhaps it was better all the way around to simply leave things as they were. It hurt, more than Jo Marie wanted to admit, but she'd recover. She'd go on with her life and put Andrew, the dream man and all of it behind her.

Without glancing over her shoulder, she ignored the sound and moved into her bedroom.

The restaurant was crowded, the luncheon crowd filling it to capacity. With Christmas only a few days away the rush of last-minute shoppers filled the downtown area and flowed into the restaurants at lunch time.

Seeing Mark come through the doors, Jo Marie raised her hand and waved in an effort to attract her brother's attention. He looked less fatigued than the last time she'd seen him. A brief smile momentarily brightened his eyes, but faded quickly.

"I must admit this is a surprise," Jo Marie said as her brother slid into the upholstered booth opposite her. "I can't remember the last time we met for lunch."

"I can't remember either." Mark picked up the menu, decided and closed it after only a minute.

"That was quick."

"I haven't got a lot of time."

Same old Mark, always in a rush, hurrying from one place to another. "You called me, remember?" she taunted softly.

"Yeah, I remember." His gaze was focused on the paper napkin which he proceeded to fold into an intricate pattern. "This is going to sound a little crazy so promise me you won't laugh."

The edge of her mouth was already twitching. "I promise."

"I want you to attend the hospital Christmas party with me Saturday night."

"Me?"

"I don't have time to go out looking for a date and I don't think I can get out of it without offending half the staff."

In the past three weeks, Jo Marie had endured enough parties to last her a lifetime. "I guess I could go."

"Don't sound so enthusiastic."

"I'm beginning to feel the same way about parties as you do."

"I doubt that," he said forcefully and shredded the napkin in half.

The waitress came for their order and delivered steaming mugs of coffee almost immediately afterward.

Jo Marie lifted her own napkin, toying with the pressed paper edge. "Will Kelly and...Drew be there?"

"I doubt it. Why should they? There won't be any ballroom dancing or a midnight buffet. It's a pot luck. Can you picture old 'money bags' sitting on a folding chair and balancing a paper plate on her lap? No.

Kelly goes more for the two-hundred-dollar-a-place-setting affairs.''

Jo Marie opened her mouth to argue, but decided it would do little good. Discussing Andrew—Drew, her mind corrected—or Kelly with Mark would be pointless.

"I suppose Kelly's told you?"

"Told me what?" Jo Marie glanced up curious and half-afraid. The last time Mark had relayed any information about Drew and Kelly it had been that they were going to publicly announce their engagement.

"She's given her two-week notice."

"No," Jo Marie gasped. "She wouldn't do that. Kelly loves nursing; she's a natural." Even more surprising was the fact that Kelly hadn't said a word to Jo Marie about leaving Tulane Hospital.

"I imagine with the wedding plans and all that she's decided to take any early retirement. Who can blame her, right?"

But it sounded very much like Mark was doing exactly that. His mouth was tight and his dark eyes were filled with something akin to pain. What a mess this Christmas was turning out to be.

"Let's not talk about Kelly or Drew or anyone for the moment, okay. It's Christmas next week." She forced a bit of yuletide cheer into her voice.

"Right," Mark returned with a short sigh. "It's almost Christmas." But for all the enthusiasm in his voice he could have been discussing German measles.

Their soup and sandwiches arrived and they ate in strained silence. "Well, are you coming or not?" Mark asked, pushing his empty plate aside.

"I guess." No need to force any enthusiasm into her voice. They both felt the same way about the party.

"Thanks, sis."

"Just consider it your Christmas present."

Mark reached for the white slip the waitress had placed on their table, examining it. "And consider this lunch yours," he announced and scooted from his seat. "See you Saturday night."

"Mark said you've given the hospital your two-week notice?" Jo Marie confronted her roommate first thing that evening.

"Yes," Kelly replied lifelessly.

"I suppose the wedding will fill your time from now on."

"The wedding?" Kelly gave her an absent look. "No," she shook her head and an aura of dejected defeat hung over her, dulling her responses. "I've got my application in at a couple of other hospitals."

"So you're going to continue working after you're married."

For a moment it didn't look as if Kelly had heard her. "Kell?" Jo Marie prompted.

"I'd hoped to."

Berating herself for caring how Kelly and Andrew lived their lives, Jo Marie picked up the evening paper and pretended an interest in the front page. But if Kelly had asked her so much as what the headline read she couldn't have answered.

Saturday night Jo Marie dressed in the blue dress that she'd sewn after Thanksgiving. It fit her well and revealed a subtle grace in her movements. Although she took extra time with her hair and cosmetics, her heart wasn't up to attending the party.

Jo Marie had casually draped a lace shawl over her shoulder when the front door opened and Kelly entered with Andrew at her side.

"You're going out," Kelly announced, stopping abruptly inside the living room. "You...you didn't say anything."

Jo Marie could feel Andrew's gaze scorching her in a slow, heated perusal, but she didn't look his way. "Yes, I'm going out; don't wait up for me."

"Drew and I have plans too."

Reaching for her evening bag, Jo Marie's mouth curved slightly upward in a poor imitation of a smile. "Have a good time."

Kelly said something more, but Jo Marie was already out the door, grateful to have escaped without another confrontation with Andrew.

Mark had given her the address of the party and asked that she meet him there. He didn't give any particular reason he couldn't pick her up. He didn't need an excuse. It was obvious he wanted to avoid Kelly.

She located the house without a problem and was greeted by loud music and a smoke-filled room. Making her way between the dancing couples, Jo Marie delivered the salad she had prepared on her brother's behalf to the kitchen. After exchanging pleasantries with the guests in the kitchen, Jo Marie went back to the main room to search for Mark.

For all the noisy commotion the party was an orderly one and Jo Marie spotted her brother almost immediately. He was sitting on the opposite side of the room talking to a group of other young men, who she assumed were fellow doctors. Making her way across the carpet, she was waylaid once by a nurse friend of Kelly's that she'd met a couple of times. They chatted for a few minutes about the weather.

"I suppose you've heard that Kelly's given her notice," Julie Frazier said with a hint of impatience. "It's a shame, if you ask me."

"I agree," Jo Marie murmured.

"Sometimes I'd like to knock those two over the head." Julie motioned toward Mark with the slight tilt of her head. "Your brother's one stubborn male."

"You don't need to tell me. I'm his sister."

"You know," Julie said and glanced down at the cold drink she was holding in her hand. "After Kelly had her tonsils out I could have sworn those two were headed for the altar. No one was more surprised than me when Kell turns up engaged to this mystery character."

"What do you mean about Kelly and Mark?" Kelly's tonsils had come out months ago during the Mardi Gras. No matter how much time passed, it wasn't likely that Jo Marie would forget that.

"Kelly was miserable—adult tonsillectomies are seldom painless—anyway, Kelly didn't want anyone around, not even her family. Mark was the only one who could get close to her. He spent hours with her, coaxing her to eat, spoon-feeding her. He even read her to sleep and then curled up in the chair beside her bed so he'd be there when she woke."

Jo Marie stared back in open disbelief. "Mark did that?" All these months Mark had been in love with Kelly and he hadn't said a word. Her gaze sought him now and she groaned inwardly at her own stupidity. For months she'd been so caught up in the fantasy of those few precious moments with Andrew that she'd been blind to what was right in front of her own eyes.

"Well, speaking of our friend, look who's just arrived."

Jo Marie's gaze turned toward the front door just as Kelly and Andrew came inside. From across the length of the room, her eyes clashed with Andrew's. She watched as the hard line of his mouth relaxed and he smiled. The effect on her was devastating; her heart somersaulted and color rushed up her neck, invading her face. These were all the emotions she had struggled against from the beginning. She hated herself for being so vulnerable when it came to this one man. She didn't want to feel any of these emotions toward him.

"Excuse me—" Julie interrupted Jo Marie's musings "—there's someone I wanted to see."

"Sure." Mentally, Jo Marie shook herself and joined Mark, knowing she would be safe at his side.

"Did you see who just arrived?" Jo Marie whispered in her brother's ear.

Mark's dusty dark eyes studied Kelly's arrival and Jo Marie witnessed an unconscious softening in his gaze. Kelly did look lovely tonight, and begrudgingly Jo Marie admitted that Andrew and Kelly were the most striking couple in the room. They belonged together—both were people of wealth and position. Two of a kind.

"I'm surprised that she came," Mark admitted slowly and turned his back to the pair. "But she's got as much right to be here as anyone."

"Of course she does."

One of Mark's friends appointed himself as disc jockey and put on another series of records for slow dancing. Jo Marie and Mark stood against the wall and watched as several couples began dancing on the makeshift dance floor. When Andrew turned Kelly into his arms, Jo Marie diverted her gaze to another section of the room, unable to look at them without being affected.

"You don't want to dance, do you?" Mark mumbled indifferently.

"With you?"

"No, I'd get one of my friends to do the honors. It's bad enough having to invite my sister to a party. I'm not about to dance with you, too."

Jo Marie couldn't prevent a short laugh. "You really know how to sweet talk a woman don't you, brother dearest?"

"I try," he murmured and his eyes narrowed on Kelly whose arms were draped around Andrew's neck as she whispered in his ear. "But obviously not hard enough," he finished.

Standing on the outskirts of the dancing couples made Jo Marie uncomfortable. "I think I'll see what I can do to help in the kitchen," she said as an excuse to leave.

Julie Frazier was there, placing cold cuts on a round platter with the precision of a mathematician.

"Can I help?" Jo Marie offered, looking around for something that needed to be done.

Julie turned and smiled her appreciation. "Sure. Would you put the serving spoons in the salads and set them out on the dining room table?"

"Glad to." She located the spoons in the silverware drawer and carried out a large glass bowl of potato salad. The Formica table was covered with a vinyl cloth decorated with green holly and red berries.

"And now ladies and gentleman—" the disc jockey demanded the attention of the room "—this next number is a ladies' choice."

With her back to the table, Jo Marie watched as Kelly whispered something to Andrew. To her surprise, he nodded and stepped aside as Kelly made her way to the other side of the room. Her destination was clear—Kelly was heading directly to Mark. Jo Marie's pulse fluttered wildly. If Mark said or did anything cruel to her friend, Jo Marie would never forgive him.

Her heart was in her eyes as Kelly tentatively tapped Mark on the shoulder. Engrossed in a conversation, Mark apparently wasn't aware he was being touched. Kelly tried again and Mark turned, surprise rounding his eyes when he saw her roommate.

Jo Marie was far enough to the side so that she couldn't be seen by Mark and Kelly, but close enough to hear their conversation.

"May I have this dance?" Kelly questioned, her voice firm and low.

"I thought it was the man's prerogative to ask." The edge of Mark's mouth curled up sarcastically. "And if you've noticed, I haven't asked."

"This number is ladies' choice."

Mark tensed visibly as he glared across the room, eyeing Andrew. "And what about Rockefeller over there?"

Slowly, Kelly shook her head, her inviting gaze resting on Mark. "I'm asking you. Don't turn me down, Mark, not tonight. I'll be leaving the hospital in a little while and then you'll never be bothered with me again.''

Jo Marie doubted that her brother could have refused Kelly anything in that moment. Wordlessly he approached the dance floor and took Kelly in his arms. A slow ballad was playing and the soft, melodic sounds of Billy Joel filled the room. Kelly fit her body to Mark's. Her arms slid around his neck as she pressed her temple against his jaw. Mark reacted to the contact by closing his eyes and inhaling as his eyes drifted closed. His hold, which had been loose, tightened as he knotted his hands at the small of Kelly's back, arching her body closer.

For the first time that night, her brother looked completely at ease. Kelly belonged with Mark. Jo Marie had been wrong to think that Andrew and Kelly were meant for each other. They weren't, and their engagement didn't make sense.

Her eyes sought out the subject of her thoughts. Andrew was leaning against the wall only a few feet from her. His eyes locked with hers, refusing to release her. He wanted her to come to him. She couldn't. His gaze seemed to drink her in as it had the night of the Mardi Gras. She could almost feel him reaching out to her, imploring her to come, urging her to cross the room so he could take her in his arms.

With unconscious thought Jo Marie took one step forward and stopped. No. Being with Andrew would only cause her more pain. With a determined effort she lightly shook her head, effectively breaking the spell. Her heart was beating so hard that breathing was difficult. Her steps were marked with decision as she returned to the kitchen.

A sliding glass door led to a lighted patio. A need to escape for a few moments overtook her and silently she slipped past the others and escaped into the darkness of the night.

A chill ran up her arms and she rubbed her hands over her forearms in an effort to warm her blood. The stars were out in a dazzling display and Jo Marie tilted her face toward the heavens, gazing at the lovely sight.

Jo Marie stiffened as she felt more than heard someone join her. She didn't need to turn around to realize that it was Andrew.

He came and stood beside her, but he made no effort to speak, instead focusing his attention on the dark sky.

Whole eternities seemed to pass before Andrew spoke. "I came to ask your forgiveness."

All the pain of his accusation burned in her breast. "You hurt me," she said on a breathless note after a long pause.

"I know, my love, I know." Slowly he removed his suit jacket and with extraordinary concern, draped it over her shoulders, taking care not to touch her.

"I'd give anything to have those thoughtless words back. Seeing Jim take you in his arms was like waving a red flag in front of an angry bull. I lashed out at you, when it was circumstances that were at fault.''

Something about the way he spoke, the emotion that coated his words, the regret that filled his voice made her feel that her heart was ready to burst right out of her breast. She didn't want to look at him, but somehow it was impossible to keep her eyes away. With an infinite tenderness, he brushed a stray curl from her cheek.

"Can you forgive me?"

"Oh, Andrew." She felt herself weakening.

"I'd go on my knees if it would help."

The tears felt locked in her throat. "No, that isn't necessary."

He relaxed as if a great burden had been lifted from his shoulders. "Thank you."

Neither moved, wanting to prolong this tender moment. When Andrew spoke it was like the whisper of a gentle breeze and she had to strain to hear him.

"When I first came out here you looked like a blue sapphire silhouetted in the moonlight. And I was thinking that if it were in my power, I'd weave golden moonbeams into your hair."

"Have you always been so poetic?"

His mouth curved upward in a slow, sensuous smile. "No." His eyes were filled with an undisguised hunger as he studied her. Ever so slowly, he raised his hand and placed it at the side of her neck.

The tender touch of his fingers against her soft skin caused a tingling sensation to race down her spine. The feeling was akin to pain. Jo Marie loved this man as she would never love again and he was promised to another woman.

"Jo Marie," he whispered and his warm breath fanned her mouth. "There's mistletoe here. Let me kiss you."

There wasn't, of course, but Jo Marie was unable to pull away. She nodded her acquiescence. "One last time." She hadn't meant to verbalize her thoughts.

He brought her into his arms and she moistened her lips anticipating the hungry exploration of his mouth over hers. But she was to be disappointed. Andrew's lips lightly moved over hers like the gentle brush of the spring sun on a hungry earth. Gradually the kiss deepened as he worked his way from one corner of her mouth to another—again like the earth long starved from summer's absence.

"I always knew it would be like this for us, Florence Nightingale," he whispered against her hair. "Even when I couldn't find you, I felt a part of myself would never be the same."

"I did too. I nearly gave up dating."

"I thought I'd go crazy. You were so close all these months and yet I couldn't find you."

"But you did." Pressing her hands against the strong cushion of his chest she created a space between them. "And now it's too late."

Andrew's eyes darkened as he seemed to struggle within himself. "Jo Marie." A thick frown marred his face.

"Shh." She pressed her fingertips against his lips. "Don't try to explain. I understand and I've accepted it. For a long time it hurt so much that I didn't think I'd be able to bear it. But I can and I will."

His hand circled her wrist and he closed his eyes before kissing the tips of her fingers. "There's so much I want to explain and can't."

"I know." With his arm holding her close, Jo Marie felt a deep sense of peace surround her. "I'd never be the kind of wife you need. Your position demands a woman with culture and class. I'm proud to be an Early and proud of my family, but I'm not right for you."

The grip on her wrist tightened. "Is that what you think?" The frustrated anger in his voice was barely suppressed. "Do you honestly believe that?"

"Yes," she answered him boldly. "I'm at peace within myself. I have no regrets. You've touched my heart and a part of me will never be the same. How can I regret having loved you? It's not within me."

He dropped her hand and turned from her, his look a mixture of angry torment. "You honestly think I should marry Kelly."

It would devastate Mark, but her brother would need to find his own peace. "Or someone like her." She removed his suit jacket from her shoulders and handed it back to him, taking care to avoid touching him. "Thank you," she whispered with a small catch to her soft voice. Unable to resist any longer, she raised her hand and traced his jaw. Very lightly, she brushed her mouth over his. "Goodbye, Andrew."

He reached out his hand in an effort to stop her, but she slipped past him. It took her only a moment to collect her shawl. Within a matter of minutes, she was out the front door and on her way back to the apartment. Mark would never miss her.

Jo Marie spent Sunday with her family, returning late that evening when she was assured Kelly was asleep. Lying in bed, studying the darkness around her, Jo Marie realized that she'd said her final goodbye to Andrew. Continuing to see him would only make it difficult for them both. Avoiding him had never succeeded, not when she yearned for every opportunity to be with him. The best solution would be to leave completely. Kelly would be moving out soon and Jo Marie couldn't afford to pay the rent on her own. The excuse would be a convenient one although Kelly was sure to recognize it for what it was.

After work Monday afternoon, before she headed for the LFTF office, Jo Marie stopped off at the hospital, hoping to talk to Mark. With luck, she might be able to convince her brother to let her move in with him. But only until she could find another apartment and another roommate.

Julie Frazier, the nurse who worked with both Kelly and Mark, was at the nurses' station on the surgical floor when Jo Marie arrived.

"Hi," she greeted cheerfully. "I don't suppose you know where Mark is?"

Julie glanced up from a chart she was reading. "He's in the doctors' lounge having a cup of coffee."

"Great. I'll talk to you later." With her shoes making clicking sounds against the polished floor, Jo Marie mused that her timing couldn't have been more perfect. Now all she needed was to find her brother in a good mood.

The doctors' lounge was at the end of the hall and was divided into two sections. The front part contained a sofa and a couple of chairs. A small kitchen area was behind that. The sound of Mark's and Kelly's voices stopped Jo Marie just inside the lounge.

"You can leave," Mark was saying in a tight, pained voice. "Believe me I have no intention of crying on your shoulder."

"I didn't come here for that," Kelly argued softly.

Jo Marie hesitated, unsure of what she should do. She didn't want to interrupt their conversation which seemed intense, nor did she wish to intentionally stay and listen in either.

"That case with the Randolph girl is still bothering you, isn't it?" Kelly demanded.

"No, I did everything I could. You know that."

"But it wasn't enough, was it?"

Jo Marie had to bite her tongue not to interrupt Kelly. It wasn't like her roommate to be unnecessarily cruel. Jo Marie vividly recalled her brother's doubts after the young child's death. It had been just before Thanksgiving and Mark had agonized that he had lost her.

"No," Mark shouted, "it wasn't enough."

"And now you're going to lose the Rickard boy." Kelly's voice softened perceptively.

Fleetingly Jo Marie wondered if this child was the one Kelly had mentioned who was dying of cancer.

"I've known that from the first." Mark's tone contained the steel edge of anger.

"Yes, but it hasn't gotten any easier, has it?"

"Listen, Kelly, I know what you're trying to do, but it isn't going to work."

"Mark," Kelly murmured his name on a sigh, "sometimes you are so blind."

"Maybe it's because I feel so inadequate. Maybe it's because I'm haunted with the fact that there might have been something more I could have done."

"But there isn't, don't you see?" Kelly's voice had softened as if her pain was Mark's. "Now won't you tell me what's really bothering you?"

"Maybe it's because I don't like the odds with Tommy. His endless struggle against pain. The deck was stacked against him from the beginning and now he hasn't got a bettor's edge. In the end, death will win."

''And you'll have lost, and every loss is a personal one.''

Jo Marie didn't feel that she could eavesdrop any longer. Silently she slipped from the room.

The conversation between Mark and Kelly played back in her mind as she drove toward the office and Jim. Mark would have serious problems as a doctor unless he came to terms with these feelings. Kelly had recognized that and had set personal relationships aside to help Mark settle these doubts within himself. He'd been angry with her and would probably continue to be until he fully understood what she was doing.

Luckily Jo Marie found a parking space within sight of the office. With Christmas just a few days away the area had become more crowded and finding parking was almost impossible.

Her thoughts were heavy as she climbed from the passenger's side and locked her door. Just as she turned to look both ways before crossing the street she caught a glimpse of the dark blue Mercedes. A cold chill raced up her spine. Andrew was inside talking to Jim.

Chapter Nine

Is everything all right?'' Wearily Jo Marie eyed Jim, looking for a telltale mannerism that would reveal the reason for Andrew's visit. She'd avoided bumping into him by waiting in a small antique shop across the street from the foundation. After he'd gone, she sauntered around for several additional minutes to be certain he was out of the neighborhood. Once assured it was safe, she crossed the street to the foundation's office.

"Should anything be wrong?'' Jim lifted two thick brows in question.

"You tell me. I saw Andrew Beaumont's car parked outside.''

"Ah, yes." Jim paused and smiled fleetingly. "And that concerns you?"

"No." She shook her head determinedly. "All right, yes!" She wasn't going to be able to fool Jim, who was an excellent judge of human nature.

A smile worked its way across his round face. "He came to meet the rest of the staff at my invitation. The LFTF Foundation is deeply indebted to your friend."

"My friend?"

Jim chuckled. "Neither one of you has been successful at hiding your feelings. Yes, my dear, sweet, Jo Marie, *your* friend."

Any argument died on her tongue.

"Would you care for a cup of coffee?" Jim asked, walking across the room and filling a Styrofoam cup for her.

Jo Marie smiled her appreciation as he handed it to her and sat on the edge of her desk, crossing his arms. "Beaumont and I had quite a discussion."

"And?" Jo Marie didn't bother to disguise her curiosity.

The phone rang before Jim could answer her. Jim reached for it and spent the next ten minutes in conversation. Jo Marie did her best to keep occupied, but her thoughts were doing a crazy tailspin. Andrew was here on business. She wouldn't believe it.

"Well?" Jo Marie questioned the minute Jim replaced the receiver.

His expression was empty for a moment. "Are we back to Beaumont again?"

"I don't mean to pry," Jo Marie said with a rueful smile, "but I'd really like to know why he was here."

Jim was just as straightforward. "Are you in love with him?"

Miserably, Jo Marie nodded. "A lot of good it's done either of us. Did he mention me?"

A wry grin twisted Jim's mouth. "Not directly, but he wanted to know my intentions."

"He didn't!" Jo Marie was aghast at such audacity.

Chuckling, Jim shook his head. "No, he came to ask me about the foundation and pick up some of our literature. He's a good man, Jo Marie."

She studied the top of the desk and typewriter keys. "I know."

"He didn't mention you directly, but I think he would have liked to. I had the feeling he was frustrated and concerned about you working here so many nights, especially in this neighborhood."

"He needn't worry, you escort me to my car or wait at the bus stop until the bus arrives."

Jim made busy work with his hands. "I had the impression that Beaumont is deeply in love with you. If anything happened to you while under my protection, he wouldn't take it lightly."

Even hours later when Jo Marie stepped into the apartment the echo of Jim's words hadn't faded. Andrew was concerned for her safety and was deeply in love with her. But it was all so useless that she refused to be comforted.

Kelly was sitting up, a blanket wrapped around her legs and torso as she paid close attention to a television Christmas special.

"Hi, how'd it go tonight?" Kelly greeted, briefly glancing from the screen.

Her roommate looked pale and slightly drawn, but Jo Marie attributed that to the conversation she'd overheard between her brother and her roommate. She wanted to ask how everything was at the hospital, but doubted that she could adequately disguise her interest.

"Tonight...oh, everything went as it usually does...fine."

"Good." Kelly's answer was absentminded, her look pinched.

"Are you feeling all right, Kell?"

Softly, she shook her head. "I've got another stomachache."

"Fever?"

"None to speak of. I think I might be coming down with the flu."

Tilting her head to one side, Jo Marie mused that Kelly had been unnaturally pale lately. But again she had attributed that to painfully tense times they'd all been through in the past few weeks.

"You know, one advantage of having a brother in the medical profession is that he's willing to make house calls."

Kelly glanced her way, then turned back to the television. "No, it's nothing to call Mark about."

But Kelly didn't sound as convincing as Jo Marie would have liked. With a shrug, she went into the kitchen and poured herself a glass of milk.

"Want one?" She raised her glass to Kelly for inspection.

"No thanks," Kelly murmured and unsuccessfully tried to disguise a wince. "In fact, I think I'll head for bed. I'll be fine in the morning, so don't worry about me."

But Jo Marie couldn't help doing just that. Little things about Kelly hadn't made sense in a long time—like staying home because of an argument with Mark. Kelly wasn't a shy, fledgling nurse. She'd stood her ground with Mark more than once. Even her behavior at the Christmas parties had been peculiar. Nor was Kelly a shrinking violet, yet she'd behaved like one. Obviously it was all an act. But her reasons remained unclear.

In the morning, Kelly announced that she was going to take a day of sick leave. Jo Marie studied her friend with worried eyes. Twice during the morning she phoned to see how Kelly was doing.

"Fine," Kelly answered impatiently the second time. "Listen, I'd probably be able to get some decent rest if I didn't have to get up and answer the phone every fifteen minutes."

In spite of her friend's testiness, Jo Marie chuckled. "I'll try to restrain myself for the rest of the day."

"That would be greatly appreciated."

"Do you want me to bring you something back for dinner?"

"No," she answered emphatically. "Food sounds awful."

Mark breezed into the office around noon, surprising Jo Marie. Sitting on the corner of her desk, he dangled one foot as she finished a telephone conversation.

"Business must be slow if you've got time to be dropping in here," she said, replacing the receiver.

"I come to take you to lunch and you're complaining?"

"You've come to ask about Kelly?" She wouldn't hedge. The time for playing games had long passed.

"Oh?" Briefly he arched a brow in question. "Is that so?"

"She's got the flu. There, I just saved you the price of lunch." Jo Marie couldn't disguise her irritation.

"You didn't save me the price of anything," Mark returned lazily. "I was going to let you treat."

Unable to remain angry with her brother for long, Jo Marie joined him in a nearby café a few minutes later, but neither of them mentioned Kelly again. By unspoken agreement, Kelly, Andrew, and Kelly's unexpected resignation were never mentioned.

Jo Marie's minestrone soup and turkey sandwich arrived and she unwrapped the silverware from the paper napkin. "How would you feel about a roommate for a while?" Jo Marie broached the subject tentatively.

"Male or female?" Dusky dark eyes so like her own twinkled with mischief.

"This may surprise you—female."

Mark laid his sandwich aside. "I'll admit my interest has been piqued."

"You may not be as keen once you find out that it's me."

"You?"

"Well I'm going to have to find someplace else to move sooner or later and—"

"And you're interested in the sooner," he interrupted.

"Yes." She wouldn't mention her reasons, but Mark was astute enough to figure it out for himself.

Peeling open his sandwich, Mark removed a thin slice of tomato and set it on the beige plate. "As long as you do the laundry, clean, and do all the cooking I won't object."

A smile hovered at the edges of her mouth. "Your generosity overwhelms me, brother dearest."

"Let me know when you're ready and I'll help you cart your things over."

"Thanks, Mark."

Briefly he looked up from his meal and grinned. "What are big brothers for?"

Andrew's car was in the apartment parking lot when Jo Marie stepped off the bus that evening after work. The darkening sky convinced her that waiting outside for him to leave would likely result in a drenching. Putting aside her fears, she squared her shoulders and tucked her hands deep within her pockets. When Kelly was home she usually didn't keep the door locked so Jo Marie was surprised to discover that it was. While digging through her purse, she was even more surprised to hear loud voices from the other side of the door.

"This has to stop," Andrew was arguing. "And soon."

"I know," Kelly cried softly. "And I agree. I don't want to ruin anyone's life."

"Three days."

"All right—just until Friday."

Jo Marie made unnecessary noise as she came through the door. "I'm home," she announced as she stepped into the living room. Kelly was dressed in her robe and slippers, slouched on the sofa. Andrew had apparently been pacing the carpet. She could feel his gaze seek her out. But she managed to avoid it, diverting her attention instead to the picture on the wall behind him. "If you'll excuse me I think I'll take a hot shower."

"Friday," Andrew repeated in a low, impatient tone.

"Thank you, Drew," Kelly murmured and sighed softly.

Kelly was in the same position on the sofa when Jo Marie returned, having showered and changed clothes. "How are you feeling?"

"Not good."

For Kelly to admit to as much meant that she'd had a miserable day. "Is there anything I can do?"

Limply, Kelly laid her head back against the back of the couch and closed her eyes. "No, I'm fine. But this is the worst case of stomach flu I can ever remember?"

"You're sure it's the flu?"

Slowly Kelly opened her eyes. "I'm the nurse here."

"Yes, your majesty." With a dramatic twist to her chin, Jo Marie bowed in mock servitude. "Now would you like me to fix you something for dinner?"

"No."

"How about something cool to drink?"

Kelly nodded, but her look wasn't enthusiastic. "Fine."

As the evening progressed, Jo Marie studied her friend carefully. It could be just a bad case of the stomach flu, but Jo Marie couldn't help but be concerned. Kelly had always been so healthy and full of life. When a long series of cramps doubled Kelly over in pain, Jo Marie reached for the phone.

"Mark, can you come over?" She tried to keep the urgency from her voice.

"What's up?"

"It's Kelly. She's sick." Jo Marie attempted to keep her voice low enough so her roommate wouldn't hear. "She keeps insisting it's the flu, but I don't know. She's in a lot of pain for a simple intestinal virus."

Mark didn't hesitate. "I'll be right there."

Ten minutes later he was at the door. He didn't bother to knock, letting himself in. "Where's the patient?"

"Jo Marie." Kelly's round eyes tossed her a look of burning resentment. "You called Mark?"

"Guilty as charged, but I wouldn't have if I didn't think it was necessary."

Tears blurred the blue gaze. "I wish you hadn't," she murmured dejectedly. "It's just the flu."

"Let me be the judge of that." Mark spoke in a crisp professional tone, kneeling at her side. He opened the small black bag and took out the stethoscope.

Not knowing what else to do, Jo Marie hovered at his side for instructions. "Should I boil water or something?"

"Call Drew," Kelly insisted. "He at least won't overreact to a simple case of the flu."

Mark's mouth went taut, but he didn't rise to the intended gibe.

Reluctantly Jo Marie did as she was asked. Andrew answered on the third ring. "Beaumont here."

"Andrew, this is—"

"Jo Marie," he finished for her, his voice carrying a soft rush of pleasure.

"Hi," she began awkwardly and bit into the corner of her bottom lip. "Mark's here. Kelly's not feeling well and I think she may have something serious. She wanted to know if you could come over."

"I'll be there in ten minutes." He didn't take a breath's hesitation.

As it was, he arrived in eight and probably set several speed records in the process. Jo Marie answered his hard knock. "What's wrong with Kelly? She seemed fine this afternoon." He directed his question to Mark.

"I'd like to take Kelly over to the hospital for a couple of tests."

Jo Marie noted the way her brother's jaw had tightened as if being in the same room with Andrew was a test of his endurance. Dislike exuded from every pore.

"No," Kelly protested emphatically. "It's just the stomach flu."

"With the amount of tenderness in the cecum?" Mark argued, shaking his head slowly from side to side in a mocking gesture.

"Mark's the doctor," Andrew inserted and Jo Marie could have kissed him for being the voice of reason in a room where little evidence of it existed.

"You think it's my appendix?" Kelly said with shocked disbelief.

"It isn't going to hurt to run a couple of tests," Mark countered, again avoiding answering a direct question.

"Why should you care?" Kelly's soft voice wavered uncontrollably. "After yesterday I would have thought..."

"After yesterday," Mark cut in sharply, "I realized that you were right and that I owe you an apology." His eyes looked directly into Kelly's and the softness Jo Marie had witnessed in his gaze at the hospital Christmas party returned. He reached for Kelly's hand, folding it in his own. "Will you accept my apology? What you said yesterday made a lot of sense, but at the time I was angry at the world and took it out on you. Forgive me?"

With a trembling smile, Kelly nodded. "Yes, of course I do."

The look they shared was both poignant and tender, causing Jo Marie to feel like an intruder. Briefly, she wondered what Andrew was thinking.

"If it does turn out that I need surgery would you be the one to do it for me?"

Immediately Mark lowered his gaze. "No."

His stark response was cutting and Kelly flinched. "There's no one else I'd trust as much as you."

"I said I wouldn't." Mark pulled the stethoscope from his neck and placed it inside his bag.

"Instead of fighting about it now, why don't we see what happens?" Jo Marie attempted to reason. "There's no need to argue."

"There's every reason," Andrw intervened. "Tell us, Mark, why wouldn't you be Kelly's surgeon if she needed one?"

Jo Marie stared at Andrew, her dark eyes filled with irritation. Backing Mark into a corner wouldn't help the situation. She wanted to step forward and defend her brother, but Andrew stopped her with an abrupt motion of his hand, apparently having read her intent.

"Who I chose as my patients is my business." Mark's tone was dipped in acid.

"Isn't Kelly one of your patients?" Andrew questioned calmly. "You did hurry over here when you heard she was sick."

Coming to a standing position, Mark ignored the question and the man. "Maybe you'd like to change clothes." He directed his comment to Kelly.

Shaking her head she said, "No, I'm not going anywhere."

"Those tests are important." Mark's control on his anger was a fragile thread. "You're going to the hospital."

Again, Kelly shook her head. "No, I'm not."

"You're being unreasonable." Standing with his feet braced apart, Mark looked as if he was willing to take her to the hospital by force if necessary.

"Why not make an agreement," Andrew suggested with cool-headed resolve. "Kelly will agree to the tests, if you agree to be her doctor."

Tiredly, Mark rubbed a hand over his jaw and chin. "I can't do that."

"Why not?" Kelly implored.

"Yes, Mark, why not?" Andrew taunted.

Her brother's mouth thinned grimly as he turned aside and clenched his fists. "Because it isn't good practice to work on the people you're involved with emotionally."

The corners of Kelly's mouth lifted in a sad smile. "We're not emotionally involved. You've gone out of your way to prove that to me. If you have any emotion for me it would be hate."

Mark's face went white and it looked for an instant as if Kelly had physically struck him. "Hate you?" he repeated incredulously. "Maybe," he replied in brutal honesty. "You're able to bring out every other emotion in me. I've taken out a lot of anger on you recently. Most of which you didn't deserve and I apologize for that." He paused and ran a hand through his hair, mussing it. "No, Kelly," he corrected, "I can't hate you. It would be impossible when

I love you so much,'' he announced with an impassive expression and pivoted sharply.

A tense silence engulfed the room until Kelly let out a small cry. ''You love me? All these months you've put me through this torment and you love me?'' She threw back the blanket and stood, placing her hands defiantly on her hips.

''A lot of good it did me.'' Mark's angry gaze crossed the width of the room to hold hers. ''You're engaged to Daddy Warbucks over there so what good would it do to let you know?''

Jo Marie couldn't believe what she was hearing and gave a nervous glance to Andrew. Casually standing to the side of the room, he didn't look the least disturbed by what was happening. If anything, his features were relaxed as if he were greatly relieved.

''And if you cared for me then why didn't you say something before now?'' Kelly challenged.

Calmly he met her fiery gaze. ''Because he's got money, you've got money. Tell me what can I offer you that could even come close to the things he can give you.''

''And you relate love and happiness with things?'' Her low words were scathing. ''Let me tell you exactly what you can offer me, Mark Jubal Early. You have it in your power to give me the things that matter most in my life: your love, your friendship, your respect. And...and...if you turn around and walk out that door, by heaven I'll never forgive you.''

"I have no intention of leaving," Mark snapped in return. "But I can't very well ask you to marry me when you're wearing another man's ring."

"Fine." Without hesitating Kelly slipped Andrew's diamond from her ring finger and handed it back to him. Lightly she brushed her mouth over his cheeks. "Thanks, Drew."

His hands cupped her shoulders as he kissed her back. "Much happiness, Kelly," he whispered.

Brother and sister observed the scene with open-mouthed astonishment.

Turning, Kelly moved to Mark's side. "Now," she breathed in happily, "if that was a proposal, I accept."

Mark was apprently too stunned to answer.

"Don't tell me you've already changed your mind?" Kelly muttered.

"No, I haven't changed my mind. What about the hospital tests?" he managed finally, his voice slightly raw as his eyes devoured her.

"Give me a minute to change." Kelly left the room and the three were left standing, Jo Marie and Mark staring blankly at each other. Everything was happening so fast that it was like a dream with dark shades of unreality.

Kelly reappeared and Mark tucked her arm in his. "We should be back in an hour," Mark murmured, but he only had eyes for the pert-faced woman on his arm. Kelly's gaze was filled with a happy radiance that brought tears of shared happiness to Jo Marie's eyes.

"Take your time and call if you need us," Andrew said as the happy couple walked toward the door.

Jo Marie doubted that either Kelly or Mark heard him. When she turned her attention to Andrew she discovered that he was already walking toward her. With eager strides he eliminated the distance separating them.

"As I recall, our agreement was that I wouldn't try to see you or contact you again while Kelly wore my engagement ring."

Her dark eyes smiled happily into his. "That's right."

"Then let's be rid of this thing once and for all." He led her into the kitchen where he carelessly tossed the diamond ring into the garbage.

Jo Marie gasped. Andrew was literally throwing away thousands of dollars. The diamond was the largest she had ever seen.

"The ring is as phony as the engagement."

Still unable to comprehend what he was saying, she shook her head to clear her thoughts. "What?"

"The engagement isn't any more real than that so-called diamond."

"Why?" Reason had escaped her completely.

His hands brought Jo Marie into the loving circle of his arms. "By Thanksgiving I'd given up every hope of ever finding you again. I'd convinced myself that those golden moments were just a figment of my imagination and that some quirk of fate had brought us together, only to pull us apart."

It seemed the most natural thing in the world to have his arms around her. Her eyes had filled with moisture so that his features swam in and out of her vision. "I'd given up hope of finding you, too," she admitted in an achingly soft voice. "But I couldn't stop thinking about you."

Tenderly he kissed her, briefly tasting the sweetness of her lips. As if it was difficult to stop, he drew in an uneven breath and rubbed his jaw over the top of her head, mussing her hair. "I saw Kelly at her parents' house over the Thanksgiving holiday and she was miserable. We've always been close for second cousins and we had a long talk. She told me that she'd been in love with Mark for months. The worst part was that she was convinced that he shared her feelings, but his pride was holding him back. Apparently your brother has some strange ideas about wealth and position."

"He's learning," Jo Marie murmured, still caught in the rapture of being in Andrew's arms. "Give him time." She said this knowing that Kelly was willing to devote the rest of her life to Mark.

"I told Kelly she should give him a little competition and if someone showed an interested in her, then Mark would step forward. But apparently she'd already tried that."

"My brother can be as stubborn as ten men."

"I'm afraid I walked into this phony engagement with my eyes wide open. I said that if Mark was worth his salt, he wouldn't stand by and let her marry another man. If he loved her, really loved her, he'd step in."

"But he nearly didn't."

"No," Andrew admitted. "I was wrong. Mark loved Kelly enough to sacrifice his own desires to give her what he thought she needed. I realized that the night of my Christmas party. By that time I was getting desperate. I'd found you and every minute of this engagement was agony. In desperation, I tried to talk to Mark. But that didn't work. He assumed I was warning him off Kelly and told me to make her happy or I'd pay the consequences."

The irony of the situation was almost comical. "You were already suffering the consequences. Why didn't you say something? Why didn't you explain?"

"Oh, love, if you'd been anyone but Mark's sister I would have." Again his mouth sought hers as if he couldn't get enough of her kisses. "Here I was trapped in the worst set of circumstances I've ever imagined. The woman who had haunted me for months was within my grasp and I was caught in a steel web."

"I love you, Andrew. I've loved you from the moment you held me all those months ago. I knew then that you were meant to be someone special in my life."

"This has taught me the most valuable lesson of my life." He arched her close. So close it was impossible to breath normally. "I'll never let you out of my arms again. I'm yours for life, Jo Marie, whether you want me or not. I've had to trust again every instinct that you would wait for me. Dear Lord, I had visions of you falling in love with Jim Rowden, and the worst part was I couldn't blame you if you did. I can only imagine what kind of man you thought me."

Lovingly, Jo Marie spread kisses over his face. "It's going to take me a lifetime to tell you."

"Oh, love." His grip tightened against the back of her waist, arching her closer until it was almost painful to breathe. Not that Jo Marie cared. Andrew was holding her and had promised never to let her go again.

"I knew something was wrong with you and Kelly from the beginning," she murmured between soft, exploring kisses. Jo Marie couldn't have helped but notice.

"I've learned so much from this," Andrew confessed. "I think I was going slowly mad. I want more than to share my life with you, Jo Marie. I want to see our children in your arms. I want to grow old with you at my side."

"Oh, Andrew." Her arms locked around his neck and the tears of happiness streamed down her face.

"I love you, Florence Nightingale."

"And you, Andrew Beaumont, will always be my dream man."

"Forever?" His look was skeptical.

She lifted her mouth to his. "For all eternity," she whispered in promise.

"An ulcer?" Jo Marie shook her head slowly.

"Well, with all the stress I was under in the past few weeks, it's little wonder," Kelly defended herself.

The four sat in the living room sipping hot cocoa. Kelly was obediently drinking plain heated milk and hating it. But her eyes were warm and happy as they rested on Mark who was beside her with an arm draped over her shoulders.

"I've felt terrible about all this, Jo Marie," Kelly continued. "Guilt is a horrible companion. I didn't know exactly what was going on with you and Andrew. But he let it be known that he was in love with you and wanted this masquerade over quickly."

"You felt guilty?" Mark snorted. "How do you think I felt kissing another man's fiancée?"

"About the same way Jo Marie and I felt," Andrew returned with a chuckle.

"You know, Beaumont. Now that you're marrying my sister, I don't think you're such a bad character after all."

"That's encouraging."

"I certainly hope you get along since you're both going to be standing at the altar at the same time."

Three pairs of blank eyes stared at Kelly. "Double wedding, silly. It makes sense, doesn't it? The four of us have been through a lot together. It's only fitting we start our new lives at the same time.''

''But soon,'' Mark said emphatically. ''Sometime in January.''

Everything was moving so fast, Jo Marie barely had time to assimilate the fact that Andrew loved her and she was going to share his life.

''Why not?'' she agreed with a small laugh. ''We've yet to do anything else conventionally.''

Her eyes met Andrew's. They'd come a long way, all four of them, but they'd stuck it out through the doubts and the hurts. Now their whole lives stretched before them filled with promise.

* * * * *

MAURA
SEGER

A Gift Beyond Price

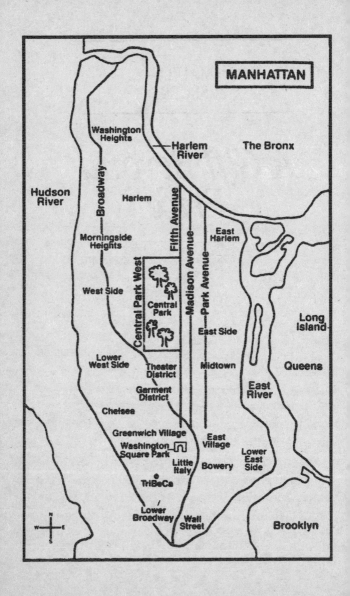

Chapter One

"What'sa matter, lady? Waitin' fer a color ye like?"

Erin Hennessey glared at the driver behind her. The traffic light guarding one of Kennedy Airport's overcrowded parking lots had just turned green, but harassed motorists were already blaring their horns.

She sighed resignedly. After five years in New York she should be used to the frenetic pace. A rueful smile curved her generous mouth as she reflected that the City's high-pressure environment was a large part of its attraction.

There were times when she missed the gentler, more natural rhythms of life on her parents' Wyoming ranch, but she wouldn't have traded her life in New York and her career with *Focus*—the national news magazine that made almost as many headlines as it reported—for anything.

Squeezing into a spot between a behemoth convertible and a garishly painted panel truck, Erin glanced at her watch. Ten minutes to four. The Air France jet carrying Mikhail Demertov from Paris to New York would be making its final approach.

Outside the International Arrivals Building a tall, gaily decorated Christmas tree added an unusually joyful touch. Erin's large green eyes widened slightly as she noticed it. The events of the last few days had banished all thoughts of the coming holidays from her mind.

Since learning that Mikhail Demertov was coming to the United States, she had found it impossible to concentrate on anything else. Even as she entered the cavernous terminal she could hardly believe that in just a short time she would be meeting the man whose writing she had admired for years and whose freedom from an East European prison she had worked to accomplish. In the end, it had been the extraordinary events following the collapse of the Iron Curtain that led to his release but she still felt a profound sense of satisfaction

The flashing arrivals monitor indicated that the Air France flight was on time. Standing at one of the wide plate-glass windows overlooking the runways, Erin watched the jet taxi to its gate. It would take at least half an hour for the passengers to leave the plane and begin clearing customs. Her stomach tightened with impatience, but no outward sign ruffled the cool, calm exterior she presented to the world.

Her shoulder-length auburn hair was swept into a neat twist at the back of her well-shaped head. The dank December wind had loosened a few feathery tendrils that did nothing to detract from the elegance of smooth, apricot-tinted skin, slender yet strong features set off by expressive emerald eyes, and her surprisingly sensual mouth hinting at facets of her character usually kept under rigorous control.

She was simply dressed in a camel's-hair pantsuit whose austerely elegant lines were lightened by a soft moss-green turtleneck. The well-tailored outfit set off the long, slim line of her body, while not quite concealing the gentle swell of high, firm breasts.

At twenty-eight, Erin had come a long way from the naïve girl who had arrived in New York with a head full of dreams and very little practical grasp of how to achieve them, but she had lost none of the vibrant intelligence and warm good nature that first won her an entry into journalism. Though on the outside she might appear strictly professional, concerned only with getting the job done, on the inside she could still feel as deeply as ever about the injustices of the world and their victims.

It was that ability to care about other people less fortunate than herself that was responsible for her being at Kennedy Airport on a blustery December day, waiting for a man she had never met but nonetheless felt she knew well.

Too tense to sit down, Erin prowled the corridor outside the customs area thinking about Mikhail Demertov. Few men knew as much about injustice or were as willing to speak out against it, regardless of personal danger.

At thirty-two the brilliant East European writer already had a worldwide reputation. Published secretly in his homeland, his books were a clarion call to freedom. The "Demertov Papers," as they had come to be known, were heralded around the world as a testimony to human courage and determination.

He had paid a heavy price for his convictions. Hunted for years by his country's secret police, he had lived in basements and attics while keeping constantly on the move. Despite desperate efforts to protect him, his whereabouts had finally been betrayed. For several years Mikhail had been in a labor camp near the Arctic Circle, suffering deprivations few could even imagine.

The Western news media had covered the Demertov story in depth, but it was Erin's acutely sensitive, moving articles for *Focus* that transformed an international celebrity into a person millions of people felt they knew as well as the members of their own families.

In her brown leather shoulder bag was a photo of the man Erin was waiting to meet. Taken nine years before it showed a young, handsome intellectual with aristocratic features beneath his short blond hair and a tall, rangy body that looked as though it had not quite grown into itself.

Glancing toward the doors of the customs area, Erin wondered how much of that young man remained. After the hardships and brutality he had endured, Mikhail could be expected to have lost the confident enthusiasm she sensed in the photo. If his years as a fugitive hadn't done so, then his experiences in the labor camp must surely have made him hard and embittered.

She bit her lip as she wondered, not for the first time, just how well equipped she was to help such a man carry out his vital and delicate mission.

But if she didn't do it, who would? Some anonymous functionary from the State Department, concerned only with looking good to his superiors? Or well-meaning but self-centered political groups, who would see Mikhail as a useful rallying point? Or media stars, who wouldn't hesitate to exploit his newsworthy appeal?

Granted, her own motives weren't completely selfless. Erin hoped to round off her coverage of the Demertov story with a personal, exclusive interview. But she was most concerned with helping Mikhail make the case for increased financial support to his country's new and still very fragile democracy.

A stream of people began to exit the customs area to be welcomed by eager friends and relatives. Standing a little apart from the busy scene, Erin craned her neck to get a look inside the huge room, where a few unlucky travelers were unpacking their belongings at low tables while most were waved through with just a few questions.

Erin breathed a silent prayer that Mikhail would not be detained. What an introduction it would be to the United States if he were held back by overeager officials anxious to rifle through his belongings.

She needn't have worried. The man who stepped through the automatic doors a moment later looked far too tired to be concerned with anything other than putting one foot in front of the other.

It took her an instant to realize who he was, because Mikhail Demertov bore little resemblance to his photograph. In one sense his experiences had dealt harshly with him, etching deep lines into his face and adding a grim set to his mouth. But in another, far more potent way, they had magnified his innate strength and masculinity to a remarkable degree.

Her breath caught in her throat. Struck by the sheer impact of male grace and power unlike anything she had ever before experienced, she struggled vainly to achieve her usual reporter's objectivity.

The years had widened the broad sweep of his shoulders and chest and toughened the long, sinewy lines of his legs. Not an ounce of fat marred his lean, hard body or softened his features.

Beneath tousled blond hair shot through with silver, his gray eyes were deeply set. Chiseled cheekbones emphasized the ruggedness of his features and highlighted the bronze of his skin. He wore a full beard that, coupled with his casual dress and the duffel bag slung over his shoulder, gave him the look of another, simpler age. He might have been a Viking home from the sea instead of a man recently released from hell.

Only the shuttered blankness of his gaze hinted at what he had suffered. Studying him, Erin was reminded of a dangerous animal brought to bay but nonetheless ready to turn on its hunters and exact full measure from them.

That impression was strengthened as she approached him. Mikhail's back stiffened, further accentuating the vast difference in their heights. Erin was tall for a woman, but he towered over her. Slowly, giving him plenty of time to see it as a gesture of friendship, she held out her hand.

"I'm Erin Hennessey, Mr. Demertov. I'm very glad to meet you at last."

For a moment he continued to stare at her guardedly. Then some flicker of recognition lightened his eyes. A big, callused hand accepted hers.

"Forgive me, Miss Hennessey. Of course, I knew you were planning to be here, but I didn't expect anyone so young or so... striking."

The deep timbre of his voice seemed to resonate within Erin. A faint blush stained her cheeks. Whatever she had expected from this man, it wasn't courtly compliments. She was acutely aware of the warmth of his hand, which was still holding hers. Forced to look up at him, she was struck by the intensity of the smoky gray eyes moving over her with undisguised interest.

Recalling herself with difficulty, Erin freed her hand. "I—I'm sure you're anxious to get some rest. My car is just outside...."

Still staring at her, Mikhail nodded. He shifted the duffel bag more comfortably on his shoulder as they made their way through the milling crowd.

Erin was silent until they reached her car. All the careful, reassuring things she had meant to say were now beyond her. A swift readjustment in her thinking was clearly essential.

When she was approached about taking charge of Mikhail Demertov and guiding him through his first difficult weeks in her country, Erin hadn't hesitated to agree. The suggestion from her editor at *Focus* had made perfect sense, and the thought of helping a man whose work she intensely admired had banished any small doubt she might have had.

Now, barely five minutes after meeting him, Erin understood the ridiculousness of thinking anyone could "take charge" of Mikhail. He had come through an experience that would have destroyed most men, and with his self-command and virility vividly intact. The situation suddenly had ramifications she had not even begun to consider.

Mikhail dropped his bag into the trunk of the car, then paused before settling into the passenger seat. He stood, tall and agile, looking out over the lighted ribbons of highway leading toward the city's diamond-splattered skyline. Again Erin had the impression of an immensely powerful, proud animal, this time surveying its new territory before taking possession. She even thought she heard a low growl of satisfaction as he slid into the car.

Within the confines of the compact car his presence became even more overwhelming. Maneuvering into traffic, she glanced at him surreptitiously. He was leaning back against the headrest, his eyes half closed. Long legs stretched out in front of him, the worn denim emphasizing the taut muscles of his thighs. Despite his relaxed pose he was clearly attentive to everything going on around her.

Realizing that he did not intend to sleep, Erin asked, "Were there any problems with customs?"

Mikhail smiled faintly. "None at all. They were the soul of courtesy."

Erin suspected that was an exaggeration but she was still grateful to the anonymous functionaries who, in the finest tradition of New Yorkers, considered it a matter of honor never to express surprise at anything.

"As far as the next few days go," she went on tentatively, "I thought you'd just want to rest and get your bearings. Perhaps have a checkup...."

She broke off, not anxious to dwell on the possible aftereffects of his experience. Having envisioned all sorts of physical problems that might limit his abilities, she was greatly relieved to find Mikhail apparently healthy, but she didn't underestimate the emotional scars he must bear. No one could endure so much without paying some price.

"I don't need a doctor," he informed her flatly. If I had been in the camp a few more months it might have been a different story, but, as it is, I am very fortunate."

He didn't elaborate, and Erin made no effort to draw him out. She knew few survived the prison camps with their bodies and spirits intact. When Mikhail had been only a distant figure in her mind, the thought of what he was suffering had been painful enough. But now that she saw him as a real, flesh-and-blood man, she instinctively shied away from images of his past.

"This is a new experience for me," she admitted softly. "Normally our State Department would be in charge. They're good at their job, but they're also very...impersonal. Since *Focus* helped to secure your visa my editor got the government to agree that we would also assist with your activities here. However, if you would prefer a different arrangement...?"

She unconsciously held her breath as she waited for his reply, then let it go when he said, "Not at all. I have every confidence that you will take excellent care of me, Miss Hennessey."

What was it about this man that gave him the ability to make her blush more in the last hour than she had in years? His drawing pronunciation of her name hinted at the extent of the "care" he might be anticipating. As she glanced at him worriedly, Erin was surprised by his unbridled grin. With a start she realized that this man, who had endured suffering most people couldn't even imagine, was still strong and secure enough to be teasing her.

Relieved, she matched his smile with her own. "And I have every confidence you won't hesitate to let me know if I make a mistake, Mr. Demertov."

He laughed softly. "Since neither of us has been through anything like this before, I suppose we will work it out together. For my part, I have no immediate plans beyond getting some sleep and finding my bearings. After that I will have to think about finding a place to stay and begin the work I want to do. But, for the moment, I wish only to put my thoughts in order."

The fact that he was able to give any consideration at all to the future, and particularly to his writing, strengthened Erin's already considerable admiration for him. "About your work," she said softly, "I realize your primary purpose in being here is to raise money but I hope that won't prevent you from writing."

He glanced at her quizzically. "Do you imagine I have a choice? The need to write is a living force inside me. For that reason alone I have been able to survive what would otherwise have certainly destroyed me."

He shook his head firmly. "It would be the greatest irony if freedom accomplished what all the repressions of my former government could not. As soon as I am able, I will begin again to tell the story of my people and their suffering. But this time there will be no secret police to hide from, no government-controlled press to deny my words."

His big body moved slightly in the passenger seat, as though he were already rising to the challenge. "I will be truly free to think . . . to write . . . and, most importantly, to publish. That is as necessary to me as air and water."

Listening to him, Erin felt oddly humbled. On the surface she and the man beside her had a great deal in common. They were both writers who faced the injustices of the world with clarity and courage. Both wrote from deeply rooted convictions and an often unbearable sense of outrage.

But there the similarities ended. While Erin observed the sufferings of others with insight and compassion, Mikhail had actually lived them. For him, freedom was not some abstract ideal but a concrete force without which he could not endure. He might have enjoyed a comfortable, even luxurious existence in his own country if he had been willing to use his talents in the service of its repressive government. Instead, he had chosen to risk everything rather than give up his beliefs.

Curiosity about what motivated such a man surged through Erin, but she knew her questions should wait until he had a chance to regain his equilibrium. She turned her mind to easier thoughts. "I know before you began writing you did quite a lot of traveling. Did you get to New York?"

"No, this is one Western city I missed. In recent years my travel has been very restricted," Mikhail reminded her gently. "I have not been outside my own country since I was a teenager."

Yet he wrote with an understanding of human nature that transcended any single time or place. Keeping her tone light, Erin said, "Then perhaps, once you've rested, you'd like to play tourist. I'll be happy to show you around."

Mikhail nodded gravely. "Thank you. I would like that. If you will give me your phone number...?"

"Actually, that won't be necessary. I thought...that is...if I were you, I wouldn't want to be staying in a hotel right now. My apartment is quite large.... You're welcome to use the guest room.... That is, unless you'd rather not."

She was putting it clumsily. What had seemed so simple when she had thought of Mikhail only as a highly intelligent, talented writer in need of help now appeared far more complex. Never had she imagined that she would be opening her home to such a potently male stranger.

"Your apartment will be fine," he said quietly. "I really wasn't looking forward to staying in a hotel."

He sounded so matter-of-fact that some of the tension eased from her. Surely there was no reason why two sensible adults couldn't share the same accommodations for a short time without becoming anything more than friends. Her neighbors wouldn't think twice about the arrangement unless they became aware of Mikhail's identity, and then they would only be excited to have such a renowned figure in their midst. That was one good thing about New York, she thought wryly. No one cared about what anyone else did so long as they weren't too noisy about it.

Keeping her eyes on the road, Erin fought against a growing sense of unease. Her life so far had been relatively uncomplicated, with hard work leading to achievement and satisfaction. She had long ago grown accustomed to feeling very much in control of her own destiny.

Now that feeling was abruptly gone. The man beside her was an unknown quantity with the power to affect her in ways she couldn't begin to imagine. Created by experiences that were utterly alien to her, he had needs and objectives different from those of any other man she knew. His relentless strength of both body and will had already proven him capable of surmounting even the greatest obstacles. Already she sensed the potential for a clash between them growing out of the age-old confrontation between men and women. If that happened, she would have very little chance of emerging unscathed.

That knowledge at once frightened and excited her. She was shivering slightly as she pulled into the garage beneath her apartment house.

Chapter Two

"Do all American writers live like this?" Mikhail asked, making no effort to hide his astonishment. He stood in the center of the large entry hall, staring ahead to the large windows overlooking the City's skyline. Below, the winter-bare expanse of Central Park stretched far into the distance. Through the caverns of residential and office buildings framing it on the other side, the East River gleamed dully.

"Very few," Erin admitted. "I was extremely lucky to find this co-op."

That was putting it mildly. She could still hardly believe her good fortune at being able to buy a home

in one of the city's loveliest buildings. Only the determined generosity of an old-time reporter, who saw in
Erin the daughter she'd never had, had made it possible. "I've got all the money I'll ever need," the
woman had insisted shortly before she retired to live
in the Caribbean. "But I'd like to know my home is
being enjoyed by someone I have something in common with."

And enjoy it Erin did. She took pride in the high-
ceilinged, airy rooms tastefully furnished with a per-
sonalized blend of antiques and contemporary pieces
and highlighted by her small but select collection of
pre-Colombian art. The style was uniquely her own,
and the result was a warm, homey atmosphere that
said a lot about the person who lived there.

Handwoven native American rugs were scattered
across the parquet floors. Their muted earth tones
complemented the polished veneers of the oak tables
and bookcases. Low-slung modular units covered in
unbleached cotton provided ample seating, even for
the large parties she occasionally liked to give. A
burled walnut desk stood in one corner of the living
room. On the wall opposite it hung a vivid, star-
pattern quilt. Large plants in wicker containers
brought a welcome touch of green.

"In my country," Mikhail said, still looking around
bemusedly, "this could only have belonged to a top
government official."

Erin took a step closer to him, noticing how the powerful sweep of his back and shoulders blotted out the view. "It's to be hoped that will change now."

He turned, flashing her a sharply perceptive look. "Not unless we manage to rescue the shambles that is our economy. Right now just feeding everyone is a problem."

As he continued to stand in the entry hall, Erin took his hand. Gently she guided him into the cheerful country kitchen and sat him down at the butcher-block table. "Speaking of feeding, I expect you're hungry. I'm not the world's greatest cook, but I can rustle up some steak and eggs. How does that sound?"

"Luxurious," Mikhail murmured dryly.

They spoke little as she prepared the meal, then not at all as he ate. His meticulous attention to the food brought home to her forcibly how much she had always taken for granted. He ate with the care usually reserved for gourmet feasts, but finished before the plate was empty.

"I'm sorry, but I'm full." A wry grin touched his mouth. "Perhaps in time I will be able to do justice to your cooking. It's better than you suggested."

Erin nodded silently. She should have realized he wouldn't be able to get through a regular meal until his stomach had a chance to adjust to such a relatively large quantity of food. As for her cooking, she considered him a less than discriminating audience, but hoped his palate would soon improve.

Stacking the dishwasher she said, "You must be tired. I'll get your bed ready."

After making use of the adjacent bath, Mikhail followed her into the guest room. He took in the large platform bed, well-stocked bookshelves and TV silently. After folding back the down-filled comforter, Erin turned to leave. However dazed and weary he might be, he was a grown man who definitely did not need tucking in.

At the door she paused. For all his unmistakable strength, Mikhail looked achingly vulnerable. His broad shoulders stooped slightly, and his eyes were shadowed with fatigue. Gently she said. "Sleep as late as you like. I'm taking the next few days off, so I'll be here to fix breakfast whenever you wake up."

So softly that she had to strain to hear him, he murmured, "Thank you, Erin. You are very kind."

She nodded mutely, closing the door before he could see the sudden sheen of tears in her emerald eyes.

Still too awake to consider sleeping, Erin wandered out to the living room. She selected a book at random and curled up on one of the couch units. For a few minutes she could hear faint sounds from the bedroom as Mikhail settled down. Then silence. She sighed faintly, hoping he would sleep well.

The book was a mystery she had wanted to read for some time, but not even its tense, fast-paced plot could hold her attention. Her thoughts remained on the man in the next room. In her years as a reporter she had met many different kinds of people in many different situations, but never had she reacted to anyone as strongly as she did to Mikhail. The near-awe she had felt for him as a writer was turning rapidly to admiration and attraction for what she saw in him as a man.

Telling herself it would be foolhardy to mistake natural sympathy for anything deeper, Erin tried again to concentrate on the book. She had gotten as far as the third page when the phone shrilled.

She dashed to answer it before it could ring again, disturbing Mikhail, and she wasn't surprised to find her editor on the other end. Derek Kent talked a lot about giving his reporters free rein and trusting them to function on their own, but in fact he liked to be kept constantly up to date on the progress of any assignment.

"Is he there?" Derek demanded without preamble.

"He's asleep," Erin answered, just as bluntly. "Or at least he was. Couldn't you have waited until tomorrow to call?"

"Sorry, honey," Derek soothed, "but you can't blame me for being anxious. Demertov's a big story."

Bristling at the inappropriate endearment, Erin wondered silently if she would ever be able to break him of such a noxious habit. On the whole Derek treated all his reporters—both male and female— equally. He would overwork and underpay anyone dumb enough to let him get away with it. Erin didn't.

She had long ago demanded fair assignments and decent pay. In the process she had earned Derek's grudging respect. But that didn't stop him from calling her by little pet names whenever he felt on the defensive.

"Right now," Erin said tightly, "he's a very tired man who needs some time to get used to his new surroundings without anyone putting more pressure on him."

Derek laughed mockingly. "I might have known the soulful, highbrow type would bring out your protective urges. Just don't get carried away. While you're mothering the great man, keep in mind that you're supposed to be putting together a personal interview to top off your coverage. Got it?"

"Got it," Erin repeated, too amused by his description of Mikhail to take offense at his highhandedness. The thought of what would happen when the two men met made her grin. Though she and Derek had never dated, she knew that her editor was interested in her in more than a strictly professional sense. Now that he had finally secured his second divorce, she sensed he was getting ready to make a move.

Discovering that an intensely virile, commanding man had taken up residence in her apartment—at his own urging—was going to have Derek chewing his nails.

With rare submissiveness that must have left him thoroughly puzzled, Erin promised that he had noth-

ing to worry about. She would complete the assignment to his absolute satisfaction. Still smiling, she
hung up, enjoying the image of her big, self-assured
editor frowning in bewilderment. Nothing in Derek's
experience as a pro football star or in his successful
transition to the top ranks of journalism could have
prepared him for her sudden amicability.

Convinced that their conversation had gone as well
as possible, for her at least, Erin switched off the living room lights and checked once more to make sure
the apartment door was secure before turning in.

Her room was just across the hall from Mikhail's.
She stopped for a moment, listening for any sound
that might indicate he was awake, but there was none.
Pleased, she closed her door and prepared for bed.

A warm shower helped her to relax enough to realize that she was more tired than she had thought. She
delayed only long enough to take down her gleaming
auburn hair and slip on a sea-green night-gown before dropping into bed.

But once there sleep eluded her. She lay awake,
staring at the ceiling. Her discontent puzzled her until
she realized that for the first time in years she felt
lonely. Mikhail's arrival had somehow made her uncomfortable with the solitude that she had more often
than not considered essential to her well-being.

It wasn't that she shunned company. During the day
she was constantly surrounded by people. Depending
on her work schedule and mood, she enjoyed social-

izing. Three or four men she knew made pleasant escorts, in part because they accepted her insistence on casual, friendly relationships that didn't demand more of her than she was willing to give. All the passion of her warm, generous nature went into her work, a fact that was at least partially responsible for her success.

Sometimes she worried over the lack of a deep, loving commitment in her life. But never before had she lain awake dwelling on it. Turning over restlessly, she punched her pillow into a more comfortable shape and closed her eyes determinedly.

Less than an hour later she emerged from the depths of sleep wondering hazily what had awakened her. The answer wasn't long in coming. Erin sat bolt upright as a tortured scream ripped the air.

She was out of bed in an instant, flinging open first her door and then Mikhail's. Moonlight flooded his room, illuminating the man caught in the throes of some unimaginable nightmare.

Low moans broke from him, punctuated by harsh snatches of words in his own language. His big, hard body twisted helplessly on the bed as he fought to free himself from whatever horror filled his mind.

Erin reached out to him instinctively. Without pausing to think, knowing only that she had to stop his pain, she knelt beside him. As she stroked his golden hair she drew him closer. "Mikhail, wake up! You're having a nightmare. Wake up!"

Rough hands grasped her. Even though he was asleep, his strength was formidable. Before she could begin to resist he had drawn her onto the bed, pressing her slender body into the mattress and trapping her flailing arms above her head.

"Mikhail! Don't! It's Erin!" Fear darted through her as she felt for the first time the full impact of his weight and power. He was unconscious, tormented and liable to do anything. Fighting now in earnest, Erin tried desperately to get free, but succeeded only in bruising herself.

Her breath was coming in low gasps that turned to a startled yelp as she realized abruptly that Mikhail was nude, and that some awareness of her womanly softness must have penetrated even his tortured sleep, because he was becoming unmistakably aroused.

In her frantic efforts to get away the thin silk of her nightgown had twisted up around her thighs. The hair-roughened length of his leg rasped against her smoothness as he shifted to hold her even closer. Still restraining both her arms in his massive grip, he slid one hand down to cup her breast.

In the shadowy light of the bedroom Erin could make out his features looming above her. His slightly uptilted gray eyes and high cheekbones gave him the look of a blond Mongol warrior. A pulse beat in his firm jaw, and his mouth was drawn in a grim, determined line that not even his silken beard could hide. The thick hair of his chest brushed against her as the corded muscles of his broad shoulders tensed. The warm, musky scent of him filled her breath.

He was the epitome of a rampaging male who had snapped the bonds of civilization and was intent only on satisfying his most primitive desires. Erin should have felt nothing but terror. Yet as his callused fingers stroked her breast through the fragile nightgown, bringing the nipple achingly alive, a fierce dart of pleasure stabbed through her.

Appalled at her responsiveness, she moaned softly. That tiny, desperate sound reached Mikhail as nothing else had been able to. For just a moment his eyes focused on her terrified features.

"Erin! My God! I'm sorry...." He moved far enough away to enable her to slip a leg out from under him. But before he could fully free her, exhaustion claimed him once again, and he slumped unconscious over her body.

Trapped by his sheer size and weight, Erin had no choice but to remain where she was. She managed to wiggle into a slightly more comfortable position, only to find that her movement encouraged him to draw her even more closely against his hair-roughened torso.

Snuggled into his warmth, she gave up her efforts to put some distance between them. With a soft sigh Erin drifted off to sleep, oddly comforted by Mikhail's now gentle embrace.

That comfort lasted until just after sunrise, when she slowly became aware of someone staring at her. So intense was the scrutiny that it reached her even through the mist of her dreams. She stirred uneasily, coming awake to find Mikhail, propped up on one elbow, looking down at her.

The furious passion she had glimpsed the night before was gone. In its place was a cutting cynicism that made her wince. Mikhail caught the motion. His face hardened derisively. "Is this part of the usual hospitality?"

Erin stared at him blankly for a moment before the meaning of his words reached her. Then she blushed furiously. "How dare you! You think I'm here because . . . ?" She broke off, her face reddening even more as she followed his scathing gaze down her scantily clad body. The covers had slipped back, revealing the beauty of high, firm breasts whose contours were clearly visible through the delicate sea-green silk.

Mikhail shrugged dismissively. "Why the pretended outrage? We're both adults." His eyes were cold as he added, "I only hope you weren't disappointed. Don't take it personally, but frankly, I can't remember a thing."

Despite his callous advice, Erin took it very personally indeed. Straightening, she dragged the covers up to her shoulders and glared at him. "You admit you can't remember what happened, but you're still willing to believe I came in here on my own and crawled into bed with you to . . ."

"... to have sex," Mikhail finished for her. Heedless of his nudity, he sat up, running a hand through his rumpled hair. "Don't misunderstand me. You're a beautiful woman. I'm happy to oblige, even though I would have preferred to be fully conscious."

"You're unbelievable!" Erin gasped. "Whatever else has happened to you, your ego is in perfect shape! I've never met a more arrogant, presumptuous man! You're an absolute b—"

"That's enough!" Hard fingers dug into her shoulders as Mikhail shook her angrily. "I can appreciate a wanton in my bed, but not a fishwife!"

Staring at him in dumb amazement, Erin was unaware of how lovely and vulnerable she looked. Her long, glistening hair was in disarray, the auburn curls tumbling past her fine-boned shoulders. Her lips, bitten in her fury, pouted softly. Outrage lent a luminous glow to her skin and eyes that, under other circumstances, might have been mistaken for sensual satisfaction.

"I cannot understand how you manage to look so unsullied when you're willing to sleep with a man you hardly know," Mikhail groaned. He turned away suddenly, as though unable to bear the sight of her.

Part of Erin was tempted to take advantage of his withdrawal to escape, but her pride wouldn't let him get away with his unfounded accusations. Clutching the blanket in one hand, she indignantly raised the other. "Take a look, Mikhail. Is that what a *willing* woman has to show for a night in bed with you?"

Reluctantly, he focused his gaze on her wrist. As Erin watched, all the color drained from his face. Beneath his beard and rugged tan he turned a sickly gray. The faint bruises he had left on her pale skin stunned him.

His unmistakable distress made Erin ashamed of her own hasty action. Granted, he had behaved abominably, but allowances had to be made for his recent experiences. How had she so quickly forgotten the horror he had just passed through and that still haunted his dreams?

"The truth is," she began gently, "I bruise rather easily. When I came in here last night you were having a nightmare. You had cried out in your sleep. I tried to wake you, but couldn't. You...pulled me onto the bed with you. Then you seemed to settle down, though you wouldn't let me go. I didn't want to disturb you further, so I just stayed here."

Sensing that he didn't fully believe her, she added, "Nothing else happened, Mikhail. You've been through a terrible experience. It's natural that there will be some aftereffects. So let's just forget it and—"

"You do not need to make excuses for me," he broke in huskily. "I can see that I hurt you. An apology is utterly inadequate, but please believe me, I am very sorry. Not only for last night, but for what I said to you just now." Wearily, he shook himself. "I don't understand how I could have acted so basely. It is not like me to do such a thing.''

Erin swallowed hard. His profound remorse made her want to reach out and comfort him, but she sensed he would allow no such reassurance. Everything she knew about him from his writings indicated he was a man of rare decency and honor. The glimpse of raw pain she saw in his eyes made her understand how intensely he despised his own actions.

Sensitive to his need to be alone for a while to come to terms with what had happened, Erin slipped from the bed. She left the room quietly, looking back for just a moment at the man who refused to meet her gaze.

After a quick shower she dressed in warm corduroy slacks and a russet wool sweater. Leaving her hair down and dispensing with all but a minimum of makeup, she went out to the kitchen to start breakfast.

Mikhail had still not appeared when she slid the bacon onto a paper towel to drain and stuck four English muffins in the toaster. She heard the shower running in the guest bathroom, then muted sounds as he dressed.

He joined her in the kitchen just as she set the eggs out to scramble. Wearing jeans and a soft blue flannel shirt, he looked even bigger and more uncompromisingly male than he had the day before. But it wasn't his clothes that froze Erin's attention. His beard was gone. The square line of his jaw emphasized the strong, clean ruggedness of his features. With his face now fully bared to her, Erin could see just how much the events of the morning were affecting him. He was at once acutely regretful and strongly determined.

Compelled by some impulse she didn't fully understand, she spoke quickly. "Breakfast is almost ready. Would you like some coffee?"

Mikhail shook his head gravely. "No, thank you. I think it would be better if I left right away."

The whisk Erin was holding almost dropped from her fingers. "L-left?"

He moved away from the door slowly, his movements guarded, as though he were concerned he might frighten her. "We both know what almost happened last night, Erin. You can't believe that I would continue to subject you to such a threat."

He looked away from her, his eyes focusing on something she couldn't see. "It honestly never occurred to me that I might be a danger to you. Even when we met at the airport, and I realized at once that I found you very attractive, I didn't stop to think that there was any reason to be concerned. But it seems that I underestimated the effects of the last few years on me. It now appears that I'm all too likely to commit the very kinds of acts I have always despised."

"No!" Erin blurted, unable to bear the torment she saw as this proud, honorable man was confronted by a side of himself he had never before suspected.

"You're blowing this completely out of proportion. Please, couldn't you just sit down and let us talk about it sensibly?"

Mikhail hesitated. "I'm not sure there is anything more to say. This is your home. You have every right to be safe here."

Determinedly, Erin pulled out a chair and urged him into it. She didn't fully understand how what had begun as a purely professional relationship had turned so abruptly personal, but that didn't matter. She had to stop him. "And I have every right to speak my mind about something that concerns us both. If you don't want to talk, fine. But at least do me the courtesy of listening."

A frown creased his broad forehead. For a long moment she thought he was going to refuse. When he finally lowered himself into the chair, she smiled in relief.

"As long as we're going to talk, you might as well eat, too." She bustled over to the counter, where she quickly put his breakfast on a plate, then brought it back to him. Mikhail looked at the food doubtfully, but didn't refuse it.

As he ate, Erin spoke quietly but firmly. "Last night I came to you when you were in the midst of a nightmare. I won't ask you to tell me what you were dreaming about, because I suspect that I couldn't bear to hear it. But I have enough knowledge of what you've suffered to understand how you might be driven to do something absolutely foreign to your nature.''

Sitting across from him, she compelled his smoky gray gaze to meet her own. "I admit to having been frightened and to having a few bruises. But that's all. You stopped before doing anything irreparable. Despite the nightmare, despite everything that must have been in your mind at that moment, you stopped. On your own. I couldn't have prevented you from doing anything you chose. But all you did was hold me gently while we both slept. Where, then, is this great danger that you think I should fear?''

A long silence stretched out between them before Mikhail said huskily, "You are too forgiving. What about the things I said to you this morning?''

"What about them? You say you find me attractive, but I gather you prefer to be the one doing the pursuing rather than the other way around. So my presence took you by surprise and put you on the defensive. There's nothing unforgivable about that."

A rueful grin curved his sensuous mouth. "I can see now why you are such a good writer. You have an instinctive understanding of people that is enviable."

The compliment caught Erin by surprise, but she was getting used to blushing around him and hardly noticed that she did so yet again. "You should talk. Everything I've read of yours speaks of an immense sensitivity to human motivations and need. Can't you extend that same sympathy to yourself?''

"Are you quite certain," Mikhail drawled, "that you aren't with the State Department? You argue as well as any diplomat."

Uncertain how to take that, Erin stared at him worriedly. "I'm not trying to trick you, Mikhail. I just want you to stay, and I think you want that too."

Not until she said the words did Erin know how much she meant them. The thought that Mikhail would walk out of her home and her life brought a hard knot to her throat. Somehow this man whom she had met less than a day before was already very important to her. She wanted to be near him, to be warmed by his strength and gentleness. And she wanted to share herself with him, to do everything she could to make up in some small measure for his suffering.

But already she knew enough about Mikhail to understand that he would not be swayed by anyone. He couldn't have survived so long under such terrible conditions without possessing an extraordinary degree of self-will and discipline. Only he could make the decision whether to go or stay.

Toying nervously with her coffee cup, Erin waited for his verdict.

Chapter Three

"Are you absolutely certain," Mikhail asked slowly, "that you will not feel threatened in any way by me?"

Erin hesitated. In all honesty she couldn't deny being somewhat wary of him—but not for the reasons he meant. Mikhail set off yearnings within her that she had successfully repressed through all the years of her steady climb to the top of her profession. He made her aware of feelings and needs that, to say the least, confused her greatly.

Yet none of that was what he was concerned about. He had no inkling of the dizzying waves of pleasure that had washed over her when he had held her trapped in his bed. Nor did he apparently remember the traitorous response of her body that had longed to know his in the most intimate way possible. For both his sake and hers, Erin couldn't bring herself to give him any hint of the real reason why she remained concerned about what would happen if they both continued living in the same apartment.

She felt only the tiniest bit guilty as she said, "I'm sure you don't mean me any harm, Mikhail, and I think that, despite everything you've been through, you're not going to lose control of yourself and hurt me unintentionally. So I see no reason for you not to stay here."

Her answer seemed to satisfy him. He considered the situation for a while longer before at last inclining his head gravely. "Thank you, Erin. I will do everything in my power to be worthy of your trust."

A sigh of relief escaped her. Giving him a smile more dazzling than she could have suspected, she said, "I appreciate that, Mikhail. Now, suppose we give some thought to what you'd like to do today."

The warm look he sent her had its own effect, leaving Erin feeling as though the rest of the world were somehow fading away until there was no one but the two of them left. She was caught up in the sheer impact of his presence, whirling down a sun-washed path to an end she couldn't see.

Wrenching her gaze away, she forced herself to concentrate on the gray, drab landscape whose bareness never failed to dampen her spirits, only to discover that she might have been gazing at the soft green beginnings of spring for all the effect it had on her rather giddy mood. Not even the sight of stray bits of newspaper dancing up the avenue on sturdy gusts of wind could dent her happiness.

Despite the fact that the analytical part of her mind told her she was being absurdly silly, she couldn't resist the urge to indulge herself at least a little. While Mikhail was with her, she refused to let anything dim the pleasure she found in his company.

As though he too were slightly dazed by what was happening between them, Mikhail murmured, "It doesn't look like a very good day for sight-seeing, so perhaps you wouldn't mind helping me with a few errands I need to run?"

Erin agreed without even asking what he had in mind. Half an hour later she and Mikhail were finished tidying up the kitchen. He had insisted on helping, despite her assurances that she could manage alone.

"You must not think of me as a guest," he had informed her with an engaging smile. "But rather as a . . . what is the word? *Room-mate*?"

Why not? That might be the safest way to handle the situation. It certainly wasn't unheard of for men and women with purely platonic relationships to share apartments. But then, very little was unheard of in New York.

She closed her eyes for a moment, thinking of what her folks back in Wyoming would say about such an arrangement before firmly putting that concern out of her mind. Her parents were both sensible, level-headed people who trusted her to make her own decisions and live by the standards they had instilled in her. She had no doubt that they would understand perfectly about Mikhail, but she nonetheless couldn't help but be grateful that there was no reason for them to ever find out.

As she was getting into her warm winter coat Erin stopped, realizing that Mikhail had donned only the same thin jacket he had worn the evening before.

He caught her look of dismay and laughed gently. "Don't worry about me. I'm used to the cold."

Erin flinched, all too aware of exactly how accustomed he must be. In a prison camp near the Arctic Circle cold was a constant, relentless enemy. As strong and determined as he was, he must have fought a desperate battle against it every day he was there.

Seeing her expression, Mikhail was instantly contrite. He had spoken without thinking, never considering the images he would unlock in her fertile mind. He had just told her that he wouldn't hurt her, and already he had done so.

"I am sorry, Erin," he said softly, raising a hand to her ashen cheek. "You must not let your tender heart be upset so easily. Remember, I am a free man now. I do not intend to let the past torment me when I would do much better to concentrate on the present and future. Nor should you allow it to cause you pain.''

She nodded mutely, struck as much by his understanding as by the gentleness of his touch. With an effort she managed to smile. "Still, I think some additions to your wardrobe would be a good idea." Gently, she added, "I'll be happy to help out with that."

Praying that he wouldn't be stubborn about accepting the money, Erin was surprised when he merely shrugged dismissively. "That won't be necessary. I already have a bank account here that should be adequate to cover my needs."

Sensing his need to be outside, where he could absorb the reality of his presence in the city that had previously only existed in his imagination, she accepted his suggestion that they walk instead of taking a cab.

As they strolled down Central Park she pointed out the more interesting buildings dotting the sky-line. The day was overcast, but they could still make out the graceful stone residences that clustered around the Park, which gave way only grudgingly to the glass and steel towers of Midtown.

After exiting the park near Fifth Avenue, they walked along looking in the windows of the exclusive shops that crowded both sides of the street. Mikhail was fascinated by F.A.O. Schwartz, possibly the most elaborate and expensive toy shop in the world. He stared in amazement at a reproduction of an Alpine village, complete with a working railroad and ski lift. Above it, perched in a corner of the window, loomed a life-size baby giraffe carrying a multitude of other stuffed animals on its back. More teddy bears, koalas, rabbits and the like rode in a scale model of a sportscar that included a working engine, headlights and a CB radio.

"Do people actually buy such things for their children?" he asked.

"Apparently, but I suspect a lot of the toys sold here end up being enjoyed by grown-ups."

"You might be right. I seem to remember that when I was little I always had more fun with the boxes than the actual presents."

Erin glanced up at him, startled. She supposed she really shouldn't be surprised that a man who came from such a different background could have memories very similar to her own. But knowing that he did brought him a little closer to her in a way she couldn't help but appreciate.

After continuing on down Fifth Avenue for more than ten blocks, they turned east toward Madison and the relentlessly elegant bastion of male fashion known as Brooks Brothers. Erin had visited the store several times to buy presents for her father and brothers, but she had never before ventured above the first floor. As she and Mikhail exited the elevator she glanced around curiously.

There was an air of old-world grandeur about the polished wood tables and counters, the gleaming brass drawer handles and railings, the subtle scents of fine wool and linen. Even the salesmen, scattered unobtrusively about, bespoke an earlier, more graceful era. Despite his rough dress and somewhat uncouth appearance, Mikhail was approached by an older gentleman who politely inquired if he might be of any assistance.

Erin had to stifle a laugh as she remembered that an eccentric appearance often went hand in hand with great wealth. At least, they apparently thought so at Brooks Brothers, because the kindly man did not hesitate to direct Mikhail to the finest and, not coincidentally, the most expensive suits, as well as an assortment of casual clothes, ranging from a down-filled parka to sweaters, shirts and slacks.

She barely glanced at one of the discreet price tags before clamping her mouth down hard on a gasp of dismay. Trying to catch Mikhail's eye, she was astounded when he merely nodded and said, "I presume you can begin on the order today?"

"Certainly, sir. The tailor will be happy to take your measurements, if you will just come this way."

"Do you mind waiting a few minutes?" Mikhail asked her courteously.

"No, of course not, but . . ."

She never got a chance to finish. He merely nodded his thanks and disappeared after the salesman into the fitting rooms, leaving her to wonder if she had imagined the gleam of amusement in his silvery eyes.

Before she had a chance to become bored he was back, having concluded his business with the tailor. His conversation with the salesman, who kept jotting down items in a little notebook, indicated that he was purchasing everything he needed for a complete wardrobe.

Erin wondered dazedly if he had any idea how much he was spending. She needn't have worried. Not even Brooks Brothers was so discreet as to leave the matter of payment in doubt. When Mikhail produced a store credit card to pay for his purchases, her astonishment was complete.

Helpless to stop herself, she said. "I didn't realize it was possible to get those in your homeland."

Mikhail laughed. "It isn't. We have a way to go before we achieve such amenities. This and a number of similar essentials for life in the West were waiting for me in Paris, courtesy of an old friend who believes the old adage that the only people who can go around asking for money are those who look as though they don't need it." The old friend, whoever he—or she— happened to be, might have applied for the card, but it was in Mikhail's name, forcing Erin to rapidly reassess his financial status. That, at least, was one problem she didn't have to worry about. Somehow he was in possession of more than enough money to support what even she had to admit were his luxurious tastes.

As they left the store Erin felt driven to bring up a delicate subject. Tentatively she said, "Uh... Mikhail... I don't mean to pry, but if you're carrying a large amount of cash, you should know it isn't a good idea in this city. I mean, we have something of a crime problem."

"Oh, yes, so I have heard," he said lightly. "All the time the newspapers in my country ran articles about your terrible crime rates, riots, poverty, social upheaval, that sort of thing. Why, if I didn't know better from my travels in the West when I was a teenager, I would have stepped off the plane last night expecting to be bashed over the head and stripped of all my worldly possessions, such as they were."

Though she knew he was teasing her, Erin tried to remain serious. "Even so, you really do have to be careful...."

His steady gray eyes met hers intently. "Do you really think I have any cause to be afraid of your city and its people?"

Meeting his gaze, she realized what he meant. Mikhail was perfectly capable of taking care of himself in any situation. His instincts and reflexes had been toughened in the harshest circumstances. When it came to self-preservation, he was an expert. For a fleeting moment Erin actually felt sorry for any would-be mugger stupid enough to try to attack him.

"No...I guess you don't...."

"Good; however, just in case you continue to worry, I have also availed myself of a fine old institution: traveler's checks." An engaging grin slashed across his rugged features. "So you see, I am becoming rapidly Westernized. Why, in a few more months I will undoubtedly be a full-fledged capitalist lackey. Don't you think?"

"I think," Erin giggled, "that you have a wicked sense of humor. When you were little, didn't you have any sisters to tease?"

"Unfortunately not. I was an only child. What about you?"

"I have three older brothers, but there's a big difference in our ages, so in a way I was brought up on my own. Not that I minded. There was always plenty to do back in Wyoming."

"This 'Wyoming'—it's one of the states, yes?"

"That's the place. My folks own a ranch there."

Mikhail's eyes widened slightly. "A ranch? You mean with cowboys and broncos and things like that?"

"Well, no, not exactly...." Seeing his disappointment, she relented hastily. "I guess you could describe it that way. My father runs cattle and raises horses. He does a little planting on the side, but mostly his business is in livestock."

"Ah, now that is the life! A little piece of land, crops ripening in the sun, a few cows fattening in the fields."

"Uh...there aren't really many small farms left in this country. Mom and Dad's place is about five thousand acres."

Mikhail appeared to be truly stunned. He shook his head in amazement. "They own all that themselves?"

"Them and the bank. Even though Dad has borrowed a lot less money than some other ranchers, he grumbles about the interest rates."

"But it is still his land?"

"Very much so. It's been in our family for three generations, ever since my great-grandfather, Sean Hennessey, trekked west with one of the wagon trains and staked it out for himself."

"I have heard of such things," Mikhail murmured, "but I never actually met someone who lived in such a place. How did you bring yourself to leave?"

"I ask myself that, too, sometimes," Erin admitted. "I guess I just wanted to see more of the world, and then..." She hesitated, surprised at how close she had come to something she had never talked about before.

"Then...what?" Mikhail prodded gently. They had stopped at a street corner. The wind whistled along the caverns of steel and glass buildings, some sporting brave holiday decorations that looked stark and unappealing without the cloak of darkness. People hurried by, their bodies hunched against the cold. From far off in the distance Erin could hear the signal horns of the boats plying the rivers. One of the more evocative names for New York flashed through her mind: Oz on the Hudson. It was that, and more. But she didn't regret the steps that had led her down the yellow brick road, even though some had been more painful than others.

"My brothers will inherit the ranch," she said softly. "That's only fair, since they're the ones with both the interest and skills to keep it going. If I had stayed I'd naturally have wanted a home of my own. And to get that I'd probably have ended up married to some local boy."

"And you didn't wish such a marriage?"

"It wasn't a question of not wishing.... There was someone I would have liked to marry, but he...he preferred a cousin of mine."

She paused, expecting the usual platitudes that she'd heard all too often before. But Mikhail voiced none of them. Instead he asked, "Are they happy together?"

"Yes...I think so. They certainly seem happy." She smiled faintly. "Last time I was home Katie was expecting her third child. She was hoping for a girl, but it turned out to be another boy. Not that she minded, of course."

"Then, if this man you wanted is happy with your cousin, it's fortunate he did not marry you instead. He would have made you miserable."

"I wouldn't have done him any good, either." Erin laughed, surprised that she could do so. It was the first time she had ever joked about the fact that Frank hadn't loved her. "I think even then I had my heart set on seeing the world."

"And have you?" Mikhail asked, picking up on her lighter mood. He took her arm as they crossed the street and continued to hold it tucked against him as they strolled up Fifth Avenue.

"A fair portion of it. What about you? I remember reading that your father was a diplomat and that you grew up in several of the major European capitals."

"That's right. My father's rank was sufficient to allow him to bring his family with him. I lived in Paris, London and Rome while I was still very young. His last posting was in Washington, but we weren't there long enough for me to see much of your country."

"What happened to him?" Erin asked softly. She already knew part of the answer, but as was so often the case in such matters, there were big chunks missing.

"He was purged," Mikhail said matter-of-factly. "During the early 1960s there was a great deal of turmoil in my country, mostly behind the scenes. Many men lost their positions because they were no longer considered trustworthy. That was especially true with those who had lived in the West. Their loyalty was automatically suspect."

"Is your father still alive?"

"No, he died in a labor camp years ago. I'm not sure exactly when, because by that time I was also on the run from the authorities."

"And your mother . . . ?"

Mikhail's eyes hardened. All the life and warmth abruptly vanished from them. "She remarried a party official who could support her in the fashion to which she had become accustomed. The last I heard, she was telling people she had never been married before or had any children."

Erin couldn't hide the sympathy that she knew was written clearly on her face. When she contrasted such behavior with that of her own loving family . . .

"Do not pity me," Mikhail ordered harshly.

"I d-don't. . . ."

"Then what was that look I just saw? No, Erin, if you must pity anyone, let it be my mother. She sold herself no differently from the way any whore would."

"You shouldn't talk about your mother like that."

"Why not? I have only said the truth." His expression made it clear that far more determined people than she had tried—unsuccessfully—to stop him from speaking his mind.

Disheartened, Erin was silent as they walked several more blocks. They were nearing the majestic granite facade of St. Patrick's Cathedral when Mikhail suddenly sighed. "It's a good thing there weren't more people around to hear me say that. Some spokesman for the oppressed! I sounded like a hurt little boy."

"You sounded like a man who has suffered a great deal," Erin corrected gently.

"As I believe I have already commented, you are very understanding."

"No more so than you...." Catching herself, Erin laughed. "We could stand here all day and trade compliments, but it is a bit nippy. What do you say we go home and find out what's left in the refrigerator."

"I will gladly agree with the first part, but not the second. It's my turn to cook, so first we must stop off at a food store."

"Your turn? But you don't have to..."

"Isn't it only proper for good roommates to share the chores?"

"Well, yes, but..."

"But what? Ah, I see what is troubling you. You don't think I can cook. I will have you know, Miss Hennessey, that such lack of faith wounds me deeply. Admittedly it has been some time since I have—how do you say—slung hash? But I can still find my way around a kitchen."

"You may not have spent much time in Washington, but you sure picked up your share of Americanisms. Okay, you win. We'll go food shopping."

The shop they chose was Zabar's the gourmet delicatessen that was famous throughout New York and beyond. "I have heard of this place," Mikhail said as he looked around in fascination at the crowd of shoppers crammed between counters of cold cuts, cheeses, smoked fish, breads, pastries, coffees and every other manner of delicacy the mind of man had managed to dream up. "But I wouldn't have believed the stories if I hadn't actually been here. This is as far from any store in my country as it's humanly possible to get."

"Zabar's doesn't have much in common with other stores anywhere," Erin said dryly. "I would be willing to bet it's one of the few places in the world that's genuinely in a class by itself."

Despite the mass of people they had no difficulty getting waited on at any of the various counters. Erin listened silently as Mikhail debated the merit of various kinds of salmon with the knowledgeable deli man, selected herbs with the help of a little old lady swathed in black, who, it turned out, came from a village near his own hometown, and examined half-a-dozen types of coffee under the indulgent eye of a young lady who seemed willing to wait all afternoon for him to make his selection. Back outside, their arms laden with packages, they hailed a taxi and headed for Erin's apartment. Once there, Mikhail took charge.

Rolling up his sleeves, he frowned at the combination microwave and convection oven before dismissively pushing the food processor off to one side.

Under his patient direction Erin spent the next hour peeling, chopping and pounding as they concocted dishes she had never had but that, with each passing moment, began to smell more and more appetizing. The kitchen was filled with delectable aromas when she excused herself long enough to tidy her hair and slip into a fresh sweater, the one she had been wearing having acquired a decided scent of onions, paprika and sour cream.

Mikhail had promised her a sampling of all his favorite dishes, and he didn't disappoint. They started off with *kulebiaka*, light pastries stuffed with mushrooms and salmon, followed by a delectable chicken dish flavored with nutmeg, paprika and cognac, potatoes stuffed with caviar, and finally, for dessert, a *pasha* of cheese, sugar, candied fruits and almonds, washed down by the strong coffee that he admitted was the only non-traditional element of the dinner, but which he had missed far too much to do without.

Relaxed and replete, they settled in front of the living-room fireplace after sharing the tidying up chores. Erin had tried to convince him to let her take care of them alone, since he had done most of the cooking, but once again Mikhail had insisted.

Erin had given in bemusedly. She still had trouble believing that she was sharing her apartment with a tender giant of a man whose remarkable courage and spirit drew her as potently as his compellingly masculine strength and virility. It was a heady combination that sent her senses reeling. For the first time in her life she was becoming truly aware of her full potential as a woman. Mikhail's nearness alone was enough to wake forces within her that frightened even as they excited.

Settled in front of the fire with snifters of brandy, neither felt any need to speak. As the wind picked up outside droplets of snow splattered against the windows. But inside all was warm and secure. In the aftermath of a delicious meal, with a cheerful blaze holding the darkness at bay, they were more than content to simply enjoy each other's company.

Seated close together on the couch, they began to talk quietly of little things, small details of their lives, deliberately avoiding the vast issues that had brought them together. By tacit agreement they didn't speak of the concerns facing a patriotic writer and a journalist dedicated to helping him spread his message of freedom and hope. Instead they indulged some measure of the need they felt to learn about each other purely as a man and a woman.

Erin laughed as Mikhail described his childhood misadventures in the embassies to which his father had been posted. "I was what you call a holy terror," he admitted unrepentantly. "Being one of the few children in any of the places we lived, I tended to be rather spoiled. That and the fact that my father's rank made it impolitic for anyone to criticize me led to some pranks I blush to think of even now."

"I'll bet you weren't as badly behaved as I was," Erin claimed. "Being the only girl in the family, and the youngest child, I got into more trouble than I was worth. My poor parents despaired of my ever learning to behave myself."

A teasing gleam darkened Mikhail's silvery gaze. "And did you?"

"Oh, I finally accepted the fact that it wasn't nice to drop ice down ladies' dresses and put frogs in people's beds. But I never quite lost the urge to stir things up a bit. I guess that's why I became a reporter."

"Yes," he said softly, "I think every writer is spurred at least in part by a certain childlike enjoyment of the world, even when it is at its worst."

Erin stared up at him, fascinated by the play of the firelight against his burnished skin. Thick sun-tipped lashes hid his eyes, making it impossible for her to see his expression. But she was acutely conscious of the sensual fullness of his mouth, which softened as he studied her in turn.

His big hand moved slowly to cup the back of her head, his callused fingers tangling in the silken skeins of her auburn hair. "Erin...you are so beautiful...like an angel come to earth...."

The husky timbre of his voice resonated through her, making her tremble. "I'm not..."

A faint smile curved the lips that were very close to her own. "Not what? Not beautiful, or not an angel?"

"N-neither.... I'm just a woman...."

He laughed throatily. "Oh, yes...that you are...warm and gentle and giving...." His head bent, and his arms drew her closer. The warmth and strength of his big body reached out to engulf her.

Despite the power she sensed within him and the desire she knew he was holding tightly in check, Erin felt no hesitation. There was only a sense of rightness, of something long wished for, as her softness yielded to the velvet steel of his embrace.

Mikhail's firm, seeking mouth tasted the smoothness of her brow, the curve of her cheek and the slender line of her throat before he at last gave in to her wordless plea and savored the sweetness of her lips.

Slowly, without the slightest sense of haste or intrusion, his tongue probed the moist secrets of her mouth, meeting hers in an erotic duel that sent coils of fire spiraling through her.

Erin moaned softly, her arms tightening around him, needing to bring him closer yet. He was so strong and gentle, so attuned to her every need and response.... And she wanted him with a fierce hunger that shocked her even as she welcomed it joyfully.

For the moment, at least, she refused to listen to the faint whispers of caution warning her that she was rushing into something vastly beyond her control, something that might turn out very differently from anything she could envision.

Chapter Four

"There's a staff meeting this afternoon at three o'clock," Jenny Stewart said, "and the proofs of the article you're doing are on your desk, along with a stack of phone messages. Oh, and Mr. Kent wants to see you right away."

Erin nodded glumly. She had only been out for a couple of days and already her small office looked as though a tornado had hit it. Despite Jenny's best efforts, there was only so much the young secretary could do, especially with three other reporters to look after.

Mail, research material, drafts of pending articles, photos and all sorts of effluvia littered every available surface. Stacks of books were precariously balanced on the shelves and floor. A lone plant somehow managed to flourish in the midst of the mess, but Erin doubted that she would be able to cope as well.

Jenny smiled sympathetically. "It really isn't much worse than usual. You've just been away long enough to forget."

"The human brain blocks out scenes like this. It's part of our instinctive self-defense mechanism."

"Why don't you sit down, relax, and take a few minutes to tell me all the news?"

"What news?" Erin muttered, still faintly dazed by what she was going to have to wade through in the next few hours.

"About *him*, of course! Mikhail Demertov. He did get here, didn't he?"

A dull flush crept up Erin's cheeks. She ducked her head slightly, pretending great interest in a memo. The soft apricot wool dress she wore suddenly seemed too warm, despite the chilly day.

"Oh, sure, he got here. Everything's fine. Uh . . . didn't you say Derek wanted to see me?"

Jenny waved that aside. Her honey-blond curls practically wiggled with excitement as she demanded, "How can you be so calm about it? Mikhail Demertov! If he's anything like his books, he's positively dreamy!"

"He writes about the brutal oppression of people longing for freedom. What's *dreamy* about that?"

"The way he does it, of course. He's so . . . sensitive and . . . deep."

A soft sigh escaped Erin. She supposed comments like that were inevitable from a nineteen-year-old, even one as sensible as Jenny. But they were still a little hard to take first thing in the morning. Trying to persuade herself that her reluctance to talk about Mikhail had nothing to do with what had happened between them the previous night, she said, "I'll tell him you said so, but right now I think I'd better see what Derek wants."

Jenny's china blue eyes darkened. With one of those remarkable shifts from silliness to maturity that occurred at her age, she said, "Erin, is anything wrong? I mean . . . you seem sort of upset. . . ."

Embarrassed at not being able to hide her feelings more successfully, Erin shook her head. "No, I'm fine. . . . I didn't mean to sound so abrupt. I have a lot on my mind, but that's no excuse." Smiling slightly, she added, "I'm sure Mikhail will be coming by here eventually. If you like, I'll introduce you."

"*Like?* I'd love it. But . . . you won't really tell him I said he was dreamy, will you?"

"No, of course not. Although—" her smile broadened as her usual good humor began to assert itself "—between the two of us, he really is!"

Jenny's eyes opened wider, along with her mouth. But before she could launch into the stream of questions that comment had inspired, Erin was gone, hurrying down the corridor to the managing editor's office.

Derek Kent was behind the huge marble-topped table that served as his desk. His big linebacker's body was comfortably ensconced in a burnished leather chair that some of the less-reverent members of his staff claimed bore an intentional resemblance to a throne.

His thick chestnut hair was neatly trimmed around his powerful head. A stray lock fell across his broad forehead, above coal-black eyes that had long ago mastered the art of the intimidating look. As usual his suit jacket was hung over the back of the chair, his shirt sleeves were rolled up to his bare sinewy forearms and his tie was undone to reveal the tanned column of his throat.

At forty-two Derek Kent was a man long accustomed to getting exactly what he wanted in both his business and private lives. He was intelligent, clever, determined and not overly burdened by scruples. Men took to him instantly, enjoying the virile sense of camaraderie he exuded. Women needed only one look to guess that he would be a highly proficient, demanding lover. More than a few had found out they were right.

Erin regarded him warily. She wasn't at all immune to his attractions, but had no intention of ever doing anything about them. Very simply, she didn't trust Derek Kent an inch. For all the surface charm, he had a tendency to use people for his own benefit.

Winter sunlight poured in through the ceiling-high windows behind him. During other times of the year, when the sun was more intense, the glare striking anyone sitting in the visitors' chairs could be blinding. That was deliberate. Just as when he'd been a football player, Derek wasn't above taking any advantage to get what he wanted from those unfortunate enough to wander into his den.

During their first meeting, when she had been applying for the job at *Focus*, Erin had thrown him by simply getting up and moving her chair out of the sun's path. Four years later she was still convinced that simple action had won her the position. Certainly Derek had never forgotten it, as his first words when he spotted her confirmed.

"Come on in, honey. Take a seat. Sun's not in your eyes, is it?"

"I'd let you know if it were," she said, smiling sweetly. Smoothing her apricot wool skirt, she crossed her legs while ignoring his appreciative glance.

Several moments passed before he asked, "How's your house guest this morning?"

"Still asleep when I left, but I'm sure he's doing fine. He's making a remarkable adjustment."

"Oh, yeah? Tell me about it."

Sighing, Erin filled him in on the shopping expedition of the day before while omitting all the more personal details. When she finished Derek looked far more interested than he had before. "So the guy isn't hurting for bucks. That's a twist I didn't expect. Where's the money coming from?"

"I have no idea."

"Why haven't you asked?"

Good question. Normally she wouldn't have hesitated to probe every aspect of a story, but somewhere along the line she had stopped thinking about Mikhail in purely professional terms.

"It's too soon," she hedged. "He needs to settle in more before I start pestering him."

"I thought you said he was making a remarkable adjustment."

"He is, but why press our luck?"

Derek frowned. "This doesn't sound like you, Erin. You're always the first one out of the starting gate at the mere hint of a good story. What's going on?"

Carefully keeping her gaze locked on his so as not to give the appearance of being evasive, she said quietly, "You've got to realize we're not dealing with some reclusive pop star or uncooperative politician. This man spent several years in a place that can probably be best described as hell on earth. As soon as he got out, he was plunged in to the efforts to rebuild his country. Now's he's realized he can best do that by coming here. He's been through one change after another and he's had to cope with a steady stream of dangers and challenges. He deserves a chance to catch his breath.''

Leaning back in his chair, Derek folded both arms behind his head and sneered. ''*Intellectuals.* They're all the same. Sensitive, tortured souls who have to be protected and coddled. They wouldn't last ten seconds out on the football field.''

''And how long would you have lasted in that prison camp where Mikhail was held?'' Erin snapped. For once she had run out of patience with her boss's macho bias. ''Your survival skills may be fine on a hundred yards of Astroturf and in the corporate jungle, but believe it or not, there are more demanding arenas. I've just spent the weekend with a man who survived what most of us can't even imagine. If you're as smart as you like to think, you'll take my advice and give him room to breathe. Otherwise you're liable to find yourself up against a brand of toughness you never even knew existed.''

Long, strained moments of silence followed her pronouncement. A pulse began to beat in Derek's square jaw. He had made a career of never being outclassed by anyone and wasn't about to change that.

Irately he growled, ''What lit your fire, lady? Or do I have to ask? Sounds like it didn't take this guy very long to get to you. Of course, after all that time up near the Arctic, I guess he wouldn't be turned off by the threat of a little frostbite."

"Is that little innuendo supposed to upset me?" Erin shot back. "Nothing you say changes the fact that I can only cover this story my way. And that means not pushing him."

Implicit in her words was the suggestion that Mikhail wasn't the only one who shouldn't be pushed. Derek should know her well enough by now to realize that she didn't respond any better to that sort of treatment than he would himself.

For a moment they glared at each other stubbornly, neither wanting to be the first to give in. Finally he whistled softly. "It's a good thing I could never stand the mealy-mouthed type."

Erin almost sighed with relief, but she was still wary enough to ask, "Does that mean I can handle the story my way?"

Derek groaned. "You don't give an inch, do you? I almost feel sorry for Demertov. The guy will never know what hit him."

Since that was as close to a vote of confidence as she was likely to get, Erin opted to overlook the implicit suggestion that she was merely setting Mikhail up for a fall. Little did Derek know, she thought glumly as they went on to chat of other things. She was the one precariously balanced on an emotional edge, and she might well have tumbled off the night before if Mikhail hadn't pulled her back.

The memory of how his kiss had made her feel was still powerful enough to send shivers of warmth radiating through her. How Derek would laugh if he knew that the woman he regarded as a formidable challenge to his masculine charms had so easily succumbed to a man she barely knew.

And yet, was that really the case? In a sense she had known Mikhail for years through his writing. Their minds and spirits had been attuned long before she'd experienced the shock of their mutual physical attraction. And that it was mutual she had no doubt. Mikhail had made it eminently clear that he desired her every bit as much as she did him. But he was also unwilling to plunge into a relationship that might end up hurting them both.

In the bright light of morning she was grateful for the conscientiousness and concern that had enabled him to gently but firmly end the passionate encounter before either was irrevocably set on a course that might lead only to pain.

"It is too soon, beautiful Erin," he had murmured shakily. "What we feel is very powerful...almost frighteningly so.... We must go carefully to make this everything it can be for both of us."

He was right, of course, but that hadn't made it any easier for her to sleep after he had left her at her bedroom door with a tenderly chaste kiss on her forehead. She suspected that he had found it every bit as hard to put the fiery passion of their bodies' responses from his mind. When she had peered into his room that morning to tell him she was leaving for the office, she had found him asleep in a tumbled bed that looked as though it had been the scene of considerable tossing and turning.

An undeniable sense of satisfaction curved her mouth as she remembered how, even in the midst of her confusion and disappointment, she had felt infinitely cared for and protected.

The smile faded when Derek suddenly interrupted her thoughts. "I'm not keeping you from something more important, am I?" His tone made it clear that absolutely nothing was more important than a meeting with her managing editor and that she would be well advised to remember that.

"Oh, no, of course not. Uh...it's just that I am a little concerned about Mikhail. Being on his own for the first time today and all."

"I asked you to take the guy home with you so you could interview him, not turn into a surrogate mother." Derek sighed exasperatedly. "If you want someone to coddle, how about a harassed managing editor?"

Erin couldn't help but laugh. Even though she knew that the lost little boy look he was sending her was only one more attempt in his on-again, off-again campaign to maneuver her into seeing him on a social basis, she couldn't help but be impressed.

"I'd have to get in line," she said coolly. "Between that rugged he-man attitude you usually project and the poor-little-me pout you can put on at a second's notice, you must have to beat the women off with a club." Standing up swiftly, she added, "And while you're doing that, I'll see about clearing away the mess that's accumulated on my desk."

"If you weren't such a damn good reporter..." Derek was muttering as she departed. His secretary, a ravishingly gorgeous blonde whom he had hired to be decorative, only to discover that she could both type up a storm and had a husband as big as Derek himself, winked as Erin passed through the outer office.

Erin had no doubt that by afternoon the grapevine would know that she had once again gone head to head with her boss and emerged unscathed. Now, if only she could continue to keep him away from Mikhail long enough to straighten out her own bewildering feelings and make some progress on the story....

"How did it go?" Jenny asked as Erin passed by on her way back to her office. Jenny was almost as fascinated by their managing editor as she was by Mikhail, but fortunately that didn't get in the way of her work.

She kept right on typing as Erin said, "Okay, I guess. I don't suppose the elves shoveled off my desk while I was gone?"

"Nope, but Joe Caniglio dropped by to ask if you could cover for him on Christmas. Can you believe he drew holiday duty for the fourth time this year?"

"That's because he's the junior man on staff. But since I'll be in town anyway, I'll be glad to stay by my phone in case anything comes up. He's got several kids, doesn't he?"

Jenny nodded. "Three, all under the age of six, so you can imagine what a big deal Christmas must be at his house." She hesitated a moment before asking, "Are you really disappointed about not being able to go home to Wyoming?"

"A little, but when I explained to my folks about Mikhail they understood perfectly. Anyway, I've always wanted to see New York during Christmas, so now's my chance."

"You sure do roll with the punches," Jenny said admiringly. "If I were in your shoes I'd probably be all upset about missing the holiday with my folks, plus a nervous wreck about how to cope with Mikhail."

From the lofty position of her twenty-eight years Erin murmured, "You don't cope with men like him."

Jenny finally stopped typing. She looked up with definite interest, hoping to learn something far more useful than how to get ahead in journalism. "What do you do?"

"You..." Erin shrugged, shaking her head ruefully. "Darned if I know. I've never met anyone like him before."

The younger girl laughed. Her innocent blue eyes held a definitely devilish gleam as she said, "Then maybe you'd better just hang on and hope for the best. It could be a heck of a ride."

Erin had the sneaky suspicion it would be just that, but she wasn't about to say so. Back in her own office, she plunked herself down in front of her overloaded desk with every intention of putting the previous night behind her and getting on with what might well be one of the most important stories of her career.

Chapter Five

But when she got home that evening there was no sign of her "story." The apartment was dark and quiet, the winter chill permeating even its normally cheerful corners.

Erin stood in the entry hall, glancing around apprehensively. Once again she was struck by the emptiness of the place. What had always been a warm, cheerful home suddenly seemed almost unbearably lonely.

Taking a deep breath to calm the unaccustomed racing of her heart, she called, "Mikhail...I'm home."

No answer. Maybe he had fallen asleep. Not bothering to take off her coat, she stuck her head in the guest room. It was empty. The bed was neatly made, and there were no stray clothes or other items left scattered about. If it weren't for the book lying open on the bedside table she might have thought she had imagined the events of the previous few days.

Where had he gone? Erin returned to the living room and paced back and forth nervously. It didn't seem likely that he would have gone out for a walk on such a gloomy afternoon, with snow threatening. But then, she really had very little idea of what he was or was not inclined to do. Perhaps, after all those months of confinement, he hadn't been able to resist the urge to get out and roam around.

That must be it, she told herself as she finally took off her coat and put her briefcase away. Fixing herself a cup of tea, she stared at the clock. It really wasn't all that late. She had no reason to be worried, especially since Mikhail was far better equipped than the vast majority of New Yorkers to handle any difficulty he might encounter.

But what about unforeseen dangers which might threaten him specifically? There were rumors that members of the old, repressive regimes in Eastern Europe had survived and that they still dreamt of reclaiming power. It wasn't impossible that they would see a man of Mikhail's courage and eloquence as a threat to them.

You're being ridiculous, she told herself sternly, imagining conspiracies where there are none. Yet her doubts persisted. Had it even occurred to Mikhail that he should be especially cautious? Or was he so exuberant about his freedom that he might forget even the most basic rules for survival instilled in him over the years?

A long, trying hour passed during which her vivid imagination conjured up all sorts of distressing visions. She grew steadily more upset, despite her best efforts to reason with herself. It wasn't like her to be overly protective of anyone, much less a man she had only met a couple of days before. But then, nothing seemed to be the same since Mikhail had walked into her life.

Within the space of a few dozen hours she had come close to forgetting her deeply held conviction that physical intimacy belonged only in a relationship where there was already firm emotional commitment, and she had lost sight of her professional responsibility to get the story without regard to personal considerations. So why should she be surprised that her usually calm, rational facade was also crumbling?

Determined to distract herself, she changed into soft, well-worn jeans and a bulky mauve turtleneck that highlighted the delicate flush of her cheeks. Pulling out the pins that had held her hair in a neat chignon, she brushed it until it crackled.

She was just returning to the kitchen when she heard Mikhail letting himself in with the extra set of keys she had provided. Rushing to the door, she found him maneuvering a large and obviously heavy carton through the narrow entranceway.

A slashing smile lit his face. His gaze missed nothing of her slightly disheveled appearance. The thoroughly male gleam of appreciation made her self-conscious, but also pleased her. Their eyes met, hers drinking in the sheer size and strength of him. His golden mane of hair was tousled by the wind, which had also blown his jacket taut against his chest. His burnished skin was slightly flushed, making his silvery eyes look even more vivid by contrast.

The vigorous cold of the outdoors clung to him, but beneath it she could sense the warmth of his powerful body and sense the tensile steel that ran through him. Feeling inordinately foolish for having been so worried, she turned her attention firmly to the carton he carried.

"What's that?"

"A typewriter. An *electric* one."

As she followed him Mikhail took the box into the bedroom, opened it and placed the machine on the desk near the window. He looked so pleased that Erin didn't have the heart to mention anything about word processors. He could work up to that.

"I hope you don't mind," he said, "that I want to start writing before looking for other accommodations."

"Of course not!" Erin was genuinely appalled that such a thought would even have occurred to him. "Nothing's more important than your writing. If you feel able to work you shouldn't let anything distract you."

"Now, *that* may prove very difficult," he teased, caressing her with his gaze. Despite the bulky sweater and jeans, he seemed to have no trouble discerning the softly rounded body he had come so close to possessing the night before.

It amazed Erin how a single look from him could transform her back into an adolescent. More than a little flustered, she said, "W-whether it is or not, I'm delighted you want to write. If there's any way I can help..."

Mikhail took a step closer, his expression suddenly gentle as he murmured. "But you already have, more than you will ever know."

"You m-mean by trying to get you out? But lots of people were involved in that...."

"Not just that. Of late I have thought only of very big concepts—revolution, freedom. politics. In the upheaval of all that, I seemed to lose track of the smaller, more human dimension. Then I stepped off a plane and met you." A smile curved his hard mouth. " You have managed to remind me that life is not all grim struggle and desperate hope. Sometimes it can be simply tender and beautiful."

Deeply moved, Erin couldn't hide the effect his words had on her. She was at once immensely touched and relieved to know that he shared the belief that something extraordinary was happening between them. When his hand gently touched the curve of her cheek she made no effort to withdraw. Rather, she welcomed his touch with every fiber of her being. They came together as naturally as if they had known each other for a lifetime.

Drawn close against his body, she luxuriated in the sense of protective strength that reached out to enfold her. Her hands reached up along the hard, sinewy line of his back to stroke his broad shoulders. He was so near that she could clearly make out every shadowed plane and sculpted angle of his face. There was nothing gentle about his features. They had been carved by the harsh wind of experience. Yet his eyes were still capable of tenderness, and there was no roughness in his touch. He held her reverently, as though almost afraid she would break.

Breathing in deeply, she savored the crisp, clean scent of him. Her fingers tangled in the silken pelt of his hair as a soft moan escaped her. "Oh, Mikhail...please...I want..."

"So do I, sweet angel," he murmured in the instant before his mouth claimed hers.

Erin's eyes fluttered shut. Her body melted against his, no hint of resistance or doubt marring the perfection of a closeness sweeter and more profound than any she had ever known. She was vaguely aware of his powerful arms tightening around her, drawing her upward until she stood balanced on the tips of her toes. All her weight was thrown against him, but he took it easily. His big hands slipped down the slender line of her back, making her arch like a contented kitten. A low rumble of pleasure escaped him as he felt the quiver of desire that ran though her.

"Beautiful...." he muttered thickly before deepening the kiss to an intensity that made all her senses sing. The silken roughness of his hair beneath her fingers contrasted vividly with the velvet smoothness of his tongue gently tasting her with slow, savoring strokes. The fresh, natural scent of him filled her even as the surging rhythm of his heart echoed her own.

No thought of protest dimmed Erin's delight as his hands slipped up under her loose sweater to stroke the petal-soft skin of her waist before reaching upward to the fullness of her breasts. When he took them gently in his big, calloused palms, a low whimper of pleasure rippled from her. Slowly, tenderly, his thumbs rubbed over her throbbing nipples as he leaned forward, holding her within the arc of his body.

Although she could feel the full intensity of his own arousal, Erin never doubted that he was in complete control of himself. Knowing that enabled her to trust him absolutely and to abandon herself to caresses that might otherwise have alarmed her.

For endless moments they stood enraptured by each other. Far below on the street the usual rush-hour traffic rumbled and honked, but they didn't hear it. The world narrowed down to a single time and place, an interlude of utterly private discovery and communication.

When they at last drew away from each other, they were both dazed and exhilarated. Erin understood more than ever why Mikhail was determined that they not rush into an intimate relationship. She needed no great experience to tell her that when they did come together in that way, forces would be unleashed that, once freed, could never again be readily contained.

"I think," Mikhail murmured shakily, "that perhaps we should go out to dinner tonight."

Erin agreed immediately. They needed to put some distance between themselves and the wide, inviting bed that beckoned so seductively.

They chose a small Spanish restaurant less than a block from the apartment, which, though comfortably casual, served only the finest quality and variety of traditional dishes. Over a Catalonian shellfish stew that included lobster, shrimp, mussels and clams, they talked as easily as longtime friends.

A warm glow of contentment enveloped them by the time Erin said, "I have a favor to ask. I really would like your help with a very important project."

"Of course," Mikhail said readily. "What is it?"

Her smile broadened. "Christmas, of course. I haven't done a thing to get ready for it, and it's only a few days away."

"Christmas.... That was forbidden to us for so long that now we hardly know what to do. There are celebrations, of course, and special songs, what is the English word?"

"Caroling. You'll hear plenty of that this week, and the decorations are already up. I guess you were still too tired to notice them when we went shopping, but perhaps, if you'd like..." Breaking off, Erin looked at him uncertainly. She wasn't sure if he would share her enthusiasm.

"Perhaps what?" Mikhail encouraged gently. "Your eyes are all lit up, and for just a moment you looked as I imagine you must have when you were a little girl. Now you must finish what you were going to say so I will know what caused such an expression of happiness."

Self-consciously Erin complied. "Perhaps after we finish here you'd like to go for a walk and see all the decorations and hear the carolers. The city turns into such a magical place at Christmas that it would be a shame for you to miss it."

To her delight Mikhail agreed at once. The delicious orange caramel custard that concluded the meal prompted them to linger awhile longer, but they were soon out on the street, joining the eager crowd of strollers wandering along the avenues.

In a city aglow with a seemingly infinite sea of lights it was never truly dark, but a cloud-filled sky hovered over them like a thick, velvety blanket, against which the Christmas decorations stood out radiantly. The winter-bare branches of the trees were festooned with strands of tiny bulbs that looked like diamonds tossed into the air by a giant's hand. Every store window glittered with elaborate displays of angels and elves, wise men and reindeer. Wide-eyed children pressed their noses against the glass panes as their parents looked on, recapturing their own sense of awe at a season wrapped in magic.

Mikhail smiled down at her, clearly sharing her pleasure. Hand-in-hand they meandered along Fifth Avenue until at last they came to Rockefeller Center, where an immense Christmas tree towered above the people who had come to admire it. A group of Salvation Army carolers was singing nearby, their voices rising harmoniously to the night sky in a hymn for peace.

Catching Mikhail's puzzled look, Erin realized that he wasn't accustomed to seeing people in uniform behave in such a manner. Quietly she explained who they were and why they were standing patiently, hour after hour in the cold, to collect money for the less fortunate.

When she finished, and had made her own donation, Mikhail did the same. She had no idea how much he gave, but she guessed from the startled reaction of the young woman standing next to the kettle into which all contributions were dropped that it was substantial. She thanked him warmly, though only to the same sincere degree that she did everyone else, no matter what they gave.

As they walked forward for a closer look at the tree Mikhail suddenly asked, "It just occurred to me when you spoke of the people in the city who don't have families that you had probably planned to spend the holiday in Wyoming. Was that the case?''

"Not after I learned you were coming. Besides, a blizzard hit this morning. I spent one Christmas in an airport, and I don't intend to go through that again. We'll just have to make our own holiday right here in the city."

"I don't really know what that involves," Mikhail laughed. "but it sounds delightful. Where do we start?"

"Well... if we really wanted to do it up right, we'd get a tree."

His gaze shifted from her glowing face to the giant fir towering above them, rising up and up until at last it ended in a blazing star at the top. "Like that one?"

"Not quite as big, but you get the idea. Then we'd have to have decorations... a wreath for the door... Christmas music... all the traditional foods."

She couldn't quite keep a note of wistfulness out of her voice as she visualized past holidays at the ranch. Mikhail caught the fleeting emotion she tried to suppress. Plump flakes of snow began to drift gently out of the sky, glistening against her hair and lashes. Gently he put an arm around her shoulders and drew her more closely against the shelter of his body.

"Then we'd better get started right away, sweet angel," he teased. "It sounds as though we have a busy night ahead!"

Outside a delicatessen near the apartment they found a six-foot-tall fir tree that Erin tried to tell herself was too big, but which Mikhail rightly surmised she longed for and insisted on buying. Further down the street, at a tiny shop about to close for the evening, they selected lights, ornaments and several records of Christmas music.

After they staggered home under their burdens, Erin left Mikhail to get the tree up in its bright-red stand while she ran out to raid the nearest food store. She got back to find Handel's *Messiah* on the stereo, a fragrant log blazing away in the fireplace, and the fir already partially strung with lights.

Pausing at the door, she took in the scene as a warm sense of contentment stole over her. The feeling was similar to what she had always experienced at her parents' home, and yet different. Along with delight in the pleasures and sentiments of the holiday, she felt a deeply rooted sense of satisfaction in the fact that she was able to help create such a magical time and share it with another person.

As the scattered flakes of snow thickened into a steady stream, they decorated the tree in between sips of mulled wine, bites of fruit cake, and much laughter. By the time they'd finished, the harsh contours of the city lay buried under a billowing cloud of softness. Turning off all the lights but those on the tree, they stood close together at the window, gazing at the luminescent glow of the street lamps.

Mikhail's breath was warm against the top of her head as he murmured, "If anyone had told me I would actually come to like snow... But then, I could never have imagined being here with you, feeling as I do...." Tilting her head back, he stared at her for a long moment before gently touching his mouth to hers.

With their arms around each other, they settled down on the couch in front of the fire to sip more wine and talk. Exactly when the conversation petered out into contented silence Erin didn't know. Nor could she say when her head nestled against his broad chest or her eyes fluttered closed. Sometime during the night she was carried to bed, her outer clothing gently removed, and a warm quilt tucked around her. A soft smile curved her mouth as Mikhail dropped a tender kiss on her forehead. As though in a dream she heard the quiet murmur of his voice saying, "Sleep, sweet angel."

As she slipped away into a dream she missed his low masculine chuckle as he added, "While you can!"

Chapter Six

The warm, relaxed mood continued between them the next morning as they shared an early breakfast. Over the poached eggs Mikhail had prepared and Erin's best bran muffins, she felt comfortable enough to admit, "I was worried about you when I got home and found you weren't here. All sorts of crazy thoughts went through my mind."

Mikhail nodded apologetically. "I should have left a note, but, to be truthful, I'm so unaccustomed to someone being concerned about me that I didn't think of it."

"Oh, I understand that. When you walked in I felt foolish for having let my imagination get the better of me. But for a while there..."

"What worried you, Erin? Was there anything specific?"

"Yes, in a way.... Perhaps it will sound ridiculous to you, but I actually found myself wondering if your country's former regime might not regret the new openness and try to prevent someone like you from speaking out."

"That is not at all ridiculous," Mikhail said quietly, "but I had hoped it would not occur to you. It's unlikely they would even make an attempt; if I thought otherwise I would not be staying in your apartment. But the possibility does remain that something might be tried out on the street, where an assailant could quickly disappear into the crowds."

His calm acceptance that his life could be in jeopardy dismayed Erin. The mere thought of him being forced to suffer more pain than he already had, or perhaps even being killed, sickened her. "How can you speak of it so matter-of-factly? Don't you want to do something... get some sort of protection?"

He reached across the table to take her hand gently in his own, his touch comforting. "There is no protection, Erin. This above all I have learned over the last few years. If tyrannical, amoral people are determined to destroy you, there is nothing you can do to stop them. However, it *is* possible to make the cost of that destruction so high that the very pragmatic men who make such decisions will decide against it."

"How?"

"By speaking out. I realize that my arrival in this country has been kept very quiet in order to give me time to get my bearings and settle in a bit. I appreciate that, but I don't think I should delay any longer before making a public statement. Not only do I owe it to my homeland, but it is also the surest way of guaranteeing my own safety. Once I have put myself in the public eye, so to speak it, it will be far too risky for them to try to silence me."

"I see..." Erin murmured. What he said made sense. If holdovers from his former government did try to eliminate him after he had spoken out, they would only be lending added credibility to his charges. Once she understood how a press conference could enhance his safety, she was anxious for one to be arranged as quickly as possible. But when she suggested that the State Department would be the appropriate place to go for assistance in dealing with the media, Mikhail disagreed.

"I am going to be asking your government—as well as private businesses—for funding. I don't want to also ask them for protection. No, this must be done independently, with only representatives of the media and myself involved. That is why I am hoping you will agree to help me." He hesitated before adding, "But perhaps it would present a conflict of interest with your position on *Focus*.''

''Not at all,'' Erin assured him quickly. ''Since *Focus* is a weekly news magazine, rather than a daily, we concentrate on more in-depth coverage of the issues. That's what led to my series of articles about you; they really weren't the sort of thing a newspaper or TV station could have done. We're not in competition with them at all, so I don't see how anyone could object to my helping you arrange a meeting with their representatives.''

Privately, she wasn't as confident as she sounded. When Derek heard about Mikhail's plans he was going to be more than a little upset. It would take careful handling to make him see that any help they could give Mikhail would only improve the magazine's stature, but Erin told herself she could pull it off. After all, she had to. Mikhail's reasons for holding the press conference were far too important for her to let anything get in the way.

Unfortunately Derek didn't agree. ''Why would you want to help him with that?'' he demanded as they confronted each other across the wide expanse of his desk later in the day.

Erin smothered a sigh. She had just spent half an hour trying to explain how much they could benefit from assisting Mikhail, but so far she had made little progress toward convincing the managing editor. Derek was proving distressingly obstinate. He refused to see beyond the fact that she wanted to reveal a story that he regarded as exclusively the magazine's own to other reporters.

Although he understood perfectly well how Mikhail would increase his safety by putting himself in the public eye, he claimed not to consider that to be top priority, at least not when compared to the all-important goal of staying out in front of the competition.

Nor did the fact that Mikhail felt compelled to speak out against the enduring threat of renewed oppression particularly move him. The smart man didn't let sentiment get in the way of his own best interests.

Erin got the distinct impression that he wanted to be convinced, but only in some way that didn't undermine his tough-guy image. In desperation she resorted to her final argument. Remembering that Derek had long coveted the Editor of the Year award bestowed by his colleagues in the media, and that he had been nominated yet again that year, she said, "Of course, if you did agree to the press conference it would certainly take the air out of Ed MacElroy's sails."

At the mention of his nearest rival for the award Derek straightened slightly. "You think so?"

"Definitely. In fact you might even say it would be a really dirty trick to pull on him. After all, doesn't MacElroy try to present himself as the dean of editors, the statesman of the business and all that? What's more statesmanlike than helping a writer of Mikhail Demertov's stature speak out on an issue of international importance?''

Derek thought for a moment, his broad forehead furrowed in concentration. ''It might just work...." Catching the triumphant gleam in her eye, he quickly added, ''I know perfectly well that you're trying to manipulate me, Hennessey. Ordinarily I wouldn't let you get away with it, but this time you do have a point.''

''Does that mean we can hold the conference here?''

With the decisiveness that had marked his abrupt rise in the industry, he nodded. ''You damn well better, since I plan to be the one who introduces Demertov and sets the stage for whatever he has to say. Let's see..." Leaning back in his chair, he pictured the scene. ''The boardroom upstairs should be perfect. It's classy but low-key and will hold a good-size crowd. Check with building maintenance to make sure the wiring can support the TV lights and cameras. How long do you think he plans to talk before we open it up to questions and answers?''

''I don't know.''

''Will he come across well on camera?''

''I have no idea.''

''Can he field the questions a mob of reporters are likely to throw at him?''

''Beats me.''

Derek scowled. Ignoring the delectable vision she presented in a red wool suit with her umber hair hanging loose around her shoulders and her high-boned cheeks slightly flushed, he sent her his most intimidating look. His frown deepened as she returned his gaze imperturbably. "Has it occurred to you," he demanded, "that you are not particularly well prepared to cope with a major publicity event?"

"That's not how I think of it. We're talking about people's lives and freedoms, not the introduction of a new brand of corn flakes."

"Call it whatever you want, the fact remains that when Demertov gets up there our prestige is going to be on the line."

Erin translated that to mean that Derek's chances for the award, and quite possibly her job, would be at stake. She didn't care a fig for the first, but the second was important enough to make her refrain from giving vent to the anger his loused-up priorities provoked.

As calmly as she could she said. "Then I'll go ahead and make the arrangements. I've already suggested to Mikhail that tomorrow afternoon would be the best time to hold the conference. That will assure coverage in the morning and afternoon papers on Christmas Day, when the story should have maximum impact."

"Not bad," Derek drawled. "Ever think of a career in journalism?"

"Is that what this is? I thought we were just generating a little publicity to improve our image."

"Put a lid on that fine Irish temper, Hennessey, and keep your mind on business. That'll work out best for everyone involved, including the illustrious Mr. Demertov."

Though she hated to admit it, she knew he was right. Derek was far too astute to do more than subtly exploit the news conference. He knew full well that at the first sign of blatant self-promotion his colleagues in the media would turn on him with a vengeance and take great pleasure in shredding both his reputation and his career.

That being the case, she could count on him demonstrating precisely the right degree of sincere concern. What Mikhail would make of his presence, she couldn't guess, but she was certain that, after having come through so much, he wouldn't let one ambitious editor get in the way of what he planned to say.

After returning to her office she asked Jenny to put through a call to building maintenance while she began assembling a list of those who would be invited to attend. Derek's secretary, Sheila, had offered to do the telephoning, for which Erin was grateful. She wanted to concentrate on coming up with a series of probable questions to help Mikhail prepare his responses.

Though most of the newspeople were likely to treat him with more than the usual degree of respect and courtesy, there were bound to be some who would consider it a matter of honor to play devil's advocate. She was determined to do everything possible to minimize their verbal attacks and assure that the key points Mikhail wanted to get across would be fairly reported.

By noon she had made enough progress to return home. As she came in the door she was surprised to hear voices in the living room. Mikhail was seated on the bed wearing gray wool slacks that emphasized the long, hard line of his hips and thighs. A periwinkle blue sweater hugged the firm breadth of his chest. Beneath it a gray-and-blue plaid shirt was open at the collar, revealing the beginnings of the thick mat of golden curls that covered his torso. His hair was freshly trimmed; just enough had been taken off to bring out the rugged strength of his features more clearly. He looked so uncompromisingly male that Erin was helpless to prevent the sudden surge of excitement that darted through her. She barely noticed the earnest young man seated in a chair across from him who jumped up when she entered.

Mikhail rose also, but with none of the other's anxiousness. He beamed her a warm smile. "Ah, Erin, I have been wondering when you would get back. Let me introduce Mr. Chester Robeson, of the State Department."

Taking a steadying breath, she managed to nod politely. "I hope I'm not interrupting...?"

"Of course not," Mikhail assured her. "I was just explaining to Mr. Robeson that I am in excellent hands and that, much as I appreciate his interest, I really do not need any further assistance."

Erin frowned slightly. The State Department had already agreed to let Mikhail stay with her. There was no reason that she knew of for anyone from the government to be checking up on him.

"Is there some particular matter you came to discuss?" she asked the young man quietly.

Robeson's prominent Adam's apple bobbed up and down as he nodded. "Well, yes, in a manner of speaking, there is. But first let me say how delighted we are that Mr. Demertov is settling in so well. Frankly, some of us at the Department were a bit concerned about the idea of a civilian, so to speak, looking after him. But you seem to be doing a splendid job, Miss Hennessey. Just splendid."

Ordinarily the young man's pompousness would have amused her, but Erin was beginning to feel more than a bit uneasy. She was no stranger to public officials who tried to mask unpalatable suggestions in a mass of flowery compliments.

"I'm sure you're a very busy man, Mr. Robeson, and you *have* come all the way from Washington, so don't feel you have to stand on ceremony. Why don't you just explain why you're here?"

The words were said politely enough, but there was an undercurrent of firmness in her tone that made it clear that the explanation had better be good. Robeson frowned uneasily. "Actually, Miss Hennessey, this matter is between Mr. Demertov and myself. I don't quite see how you're involved...."

"She is involved because I say she is," Mikhail explained quietly. Taking Erin's arm, he led her over to the couch and sat down next to her. Robeson had no choice but to accede to her presence. Nonetheless he stubbornly directed his comments to Mikhail.

"As I was explaining when Miss Hennessey arrived, we at the Department are very anxious to assist you in any way we can. While we understand that you prefer to remain in New York, we would like to arrange some time with you to discuss your plans while you are in this country."

Mikhail raised an eyebrow. "Are you suggesting they require your approval?"

"Not at all. It's merely an accepted procedure. A courtesy, if you will."

Mikhail smiled wryly. "I'm all in favor of courtesy, Mr. Robeson. Naturally, I will provide all the information I can to help your government decide to increase the level of assistance to my country."

The State Department man's eyes narrowed. Leaning forward slightly, he said, "Let's be frank, Mr. Demertov. You were considered such a danger to the former regime of your country that they didn't even keep you in one of their own prisons. They shipped you off to the Arctic Circle and we all *know* who runs thē show up there. We just want you to be a little diplomatic, that's all.''

Erin muttered something rude under her breath, but Mikhail merely looked amused. ''Your concern for the sensibilities of the gentlemen in Moscow is very touching. But truth is truth. The Soviet Union must accept its part in the repression of millions of people. Guilt must not be laid exclusively at the door of governments that are now safely out of existence.''

Robeson frowned. ''Where I come from, Mr. Demertov, that's called just plain stupid.''

Erin opened her mouth to deliver the dressing down she was convinced he richly deserved, but Mikhail forestalled her. Quietly he asked, ''And where precisely do you come from, Mr. Robeson? That very impressive identification card you waved in front of me could have been printed up in any number of places.''

That was enough for Erin. She stood up quickly and headed for the phone. ''I'm calling a contact of mine at the State Department. If they didn't send this guy, we'll find out right away.''

''Hold it,'' Robeson muttered. He had slumped on the couch, staring at them with mingled frustration and annoyance. ''There's no reason to make a big thing out of this. I just told you I was from the State Department because that seemed the easiest way to get you to talk to me.''

Mikhail raised one eyebrow skeptically. "Wouldn't it be more accurate to say you knew that if you told the truth I wouldn't be inclined to let you into the apartment, much less talk to you?"

Sighing, Robeson nodded. "Look, it's not easy working for the C.I.A. We have a real image problem."

"C.I.A.?" Erin repeated. After just about deciding that he was either an agent for Mikhail's former government or a rival reporter, she had to do a rapid reordering of her thinking.

Mikhail had no such problem. He appeared completely unsurprised by the young man's disclosure. "I've been expecting you. Why did you wait this long to show up?"

Robeson shrugged. "We were trying to be discreet."

"You didn't succeed very well." Smiling cordially, he stood up. "I will explain this only once more. I have great respect for your country and everything it represents. But my first commitment is to the truth. I trust that I am making myself clear, Mr. Robeson?"

The young man nodded glumly. He picked up his briefcase and turned toward the door. "I'll put that in my report, Mr. Demertov. But don't expect my superiors to be happy about it."

After he had left Erin shook her head disbelieving. "I thought there wasn't much left that could surprise me, but that was incredible."

"Unfortunately it is also all too common. Mr. Robeson is a considerable cut above others in his line of work I have encountered, but he operates from a similar willingness to do whatever is considered expedient without regard to right or wrong."

"I hate to sound naïve, but there is a law against the C.I.A. operating inside the United States. What just happened here was strictly illegal."

"I'm glad to hear it. That means Mr. Robeson and his ilk will be very sensitive to the possibility of public exposure, so it becomes even more urgent for me to hold that press conference as quickly as possible. Were you able to make any progress on that?"

Erin nodded. Quickly she explained the arrangements. When she was through, she added, "Since you can expect to draw some of the top reporters in the country, it might be a good idea to hold a dress rehearsal, so to speak."

"Rehearsal? I don't understand. What is there to rehearse?"

"Whatever you hope to get across to the media and, through them, to the public. No one who can avoid it confronts reporters without first giving a lot of time and attention to predicting what they'll ask and preparing the best possible responses."

Mikhail still looked skeptical. "How can you anticipate the questions other reporters will ask? After all, aren't the members of a free press likely to pose any inquiry that occurs to them?"

"Certainly, but since I have some experience with such situations myself, it isn't especially hard to guess what questions will arise. Not all of them, of course, but a good number."

"The leaders of your country commonly do this? They prepare their answers in advance?"

"Absolutely. Everyone does it, and not because they're trying to hide anything, although that does sometimes come into it. More often it's because we all recognize that in the heat of the moment, when the television cameras are whirring, dozens of microphones are turned on and reporters are shouting questions from every side, it's very easy to forget an important point or put something in such a way that it might be misunderstood."

"Yes . . . I can see how that would be the case. . . ." Mikhail thought it over for another moment before nodding. "All right, if you think it's a good idea to have this 'rehearsal' then we will do so."

They were quickly settled in front of the Christmas tree, making short work of coffee and sandwiches as she described the arrangements for the conference.

Erin was careful not to mention the difficulties she had encountered with Derek, because she didn't want to add in any way to the tension she was certain Mikhail must already be feeling. But some measure of her impatience with the managing editor must have gotten through, because he said, "It sounds as though your boss presented some problems. Was that the case?''

''Yes,'' she admitted reluctantly, ''a few, but you shouldn't be concerned about that. Derek feels the conference is very important, and he'll do everything he can to help.'' She saw no reason to add that his cooperation stemmed in large measure from self-interest.

As they began to go through the questions and answers, she was relieved to note that for someone who had never before addressed the media, he showed a remarkable grasp of how to tailor words and ideas to get the most attention focused where he wanted it.

Long before they were finished, Erin had no doubt that the conference would make headlines. The full weight of public condemnation would be brought to bear on the suffering he had experienced. Great sympathy would be raised for his efforts to help rebuild his country.

She also learned far more than she had ever wanted to know about the human capacity for brutality. Even as she marveled at the extraordinary courage and spirit that had enabled him to triumph over seemingly insurmountable obstacles, she knew that the images his words unleashed would haunt her forever.

After they retired again to their separate bedrooms Erin lay awake far into the night. Not until shortly before dawn did she manage to slip into an uneasy sleep that did little to prepare her for the day ahead.

Chapter Seven

Fifteen minutes before the news conference was due to begin, Derek met them in the small waiting area behind the boardroom. Erin had to give him credit; he looked the epitome of the intelligent, committed executive.

The gray pin-striped suit and light-blue shirt he wore were perfectly suited to television and projected just the right image of conservative elegance. His thick chestnut hair was brushed back with a seeming casualness that was appropriate for a man far too busy to fuss over his appearance. The judicious use of the

tanning room at his health club had given his skin a
burnished glow.

As he strode into the room he exuded an air of utterly unshakable command that wavered only slightly
when he came face to face with Mikhail.

The understated luxury of the dark blue suit that
had arrived that morning from Brooks Brothers
should have made them no more than equals in appearance. But while the editor's sartorial elegance
caught the eye, Mikhail's did not. All such superficial
details were blocked out by the sheer impact of the
man himself.

His courage, sensitivity and determination were
obvious to even the least observant eye. As the two
men surveyed each other Derek's eyes narrowed spec-
ulatively. He glanced from the tall, powerful man who
was looking him over quietly to Erin, standing close
beside Mikhail's side. A slight frown furrowed his
brow. With a smile that made no pretense at warmth,
he offered his hand. "Mr. Demertov...welcome to the
United States. It's a pleasure to meet you."

Without giving Mikhail a chance to respond, he
turned to Erin. "Can he understand what I'm saying? His English is good enough for that, isn't it?"

Unperturbed, Mikhail said quietly, "My English is
more than adequate, Mr. Kent. You need not be concerned about that." Though he spoke with perfect
courtesy, he somehow managed to make it sound as

though Derek were unduly nervous and worrying over trifles.

Erin fought to hide a smile that she knew would only worsen an already tense situation. For reasons she didn't care to explore, her boss seemed bent on the hopeless task of trying to establish his superiority over a man he could never hope to best.

"Just checking," Derek muttered. "Once those old boys in there get going, you're not going to know what's coming at you. Try to stay cool, and don't say anything you don't want to hear spewing out of a TV tonight or read about in tomorrow's papers."

"I'll keep that in mind," Mikhail said dryly.

The level of noise reaching them from the boardroom might have dismayed a lesser man, but he showed no flicker of concern. Certain of both the importance of the information he intended to present and his ability to communicate it clearly, he said, "I understand you have offered to introduce me to the media, Mr. Kent. May I suggest we do that now, since from the sound of it they are, as you say, chomping at the bit?"

Derek's scowl deepened, though whether from annoyance with the other man's insurmountable confidence and ability, or simply because he didn't like having control of the situation taken from him, was impossible to say. Nodding curtly, he led the way into the boardroom.

As they entered, the cacophony momentarily lessened, only to surge back more powerfully than ever as the reporters bandied first impressions of Mikhail back and forth among themselves, while some of the more aggressive hurled questions which he politely ignored.

Derek took his place at the dais, straightening his tie. He gave the cameramen a few moments to adjust their lights and lenses, and photographers for various newspapers and magazines began snapping off what were likely to be the first of many rolls of film.

When the noise had subsided to a polite hush, he began. "Ladies and gentlemen, my colleagues in the news media, I am honored to welcome you here today, and I am gratified by your attention to a matter of truly worldwide importance. As many of you know, efforts have been under way for several years to secure the release of Mikhail Demertov, a highly respected dissident writer, from prison in the Communist bloc and to bring him safely to the United States. Events in Eastern Europe brought about what we had all been so eagerly seeking. Mr. Demertov is here now as a spokesman for his country's new government and to answer your questions. Mr. Demertov..."

After stepping away from the dais, Derek went to stand beside Erin. Relieved that none of his personal resentment of the other man had come through in his introduction, she was feeling more kindly disposed to

him. Together they watched as Mikhail stepped forward to the dais. Cameras clicked away furiously and
reporters pressed closer, anxious for a good look at a
fellow writer who exemplified the finest ideals of their
profession.

Removing a single page of notes from his pocket, he
glanced out over the audience as he said, "First, I wish
to express my thanks to both the United States government and the many private citizens of this country
and others who helped to bring about the collapse of
the Iron Curtain. But grateful as I am to be here with
you today, I cannot lose sight of the fact that democracy is still a very new and fragile phenomenon for
those like me who have previously known only
repression. It will be many years before we can be secure in our freedoms. The legacy of our past is a burden that must be understood before it can be put to
rest."

Quietly but firmly he went on to outline the conditions he had experienced as a victim of the repression
he still feared could return. Long periods of solitary
confinement were common; Mikhail himself had lived
completely alone in a tiny cell for six months.

Forced labor projects were the norm. After his
captors had decided that his spirit could not be broken by isolation, he had been moved into the general
prison population, where he toiled eighteen hours a
day in the frigid Arctic winter, building a pipeline that

was intended to deliver natural gas to customers in the western part of the country.

He had seen men die of exhaustion, starvation and exposure. Others had been crushed by the brutally dehumanizing conditions and became human automatons, no longer capable of thought or reason. But resistance had continued. The love of freedom was too great to be destroyed even by such ruthless oppression. Despite all the horrors he had described, he concluded on a note of optimism, with the hope that the struggle for human dignity would prevail against the most overwhelming odds.

The silence when he finished was an eloquent testimony to the impact of his words. Very little could impress a horde of reporters strongly enough to win even a few seconds of quiet, let alone the long, drawn-out hush that followed his statement.

The faces turned toward him were grim, each man and woman confronting the possibility that but for an accident of birth they might have been the ones to suffer such persecution. Implicit within each was the uncertainty whether or not they would have been among those who survived, or whether they would have joined the countless, nameless mass of victims who perished because of their ideals.

In that atmosphere of silent self-examination and empathy for those less fortunate than they, the questions began.

Mikhail paused for a moment to wipe away the perspiration caused by the intense heat of the television lights, Erin studied him closely. His composure was undented. Neither the strain of the rapid-fire interrogation of the reporters nor the painful memories he must be reliving showed on his chiseled features. He continued to look out at the audience calmly and determinedly. No one who saw and heard him could doubt that he was a man who believed absolutely in what he was doing.

But at least one person who watched him was determined to shake his confidence, for reasons that became clear as soon as the young man identified himself as a representative of *The People's Press*. "Isn't it true," he demanded stridently, "that far from being the freedom fighter you would like us to believe, you were in fact arrested for being an agent of the C.I.A. and that you are still in the pay of that organization?"

Instead of reacting angrily, as he might have been expected to, Mikhail simply laughed. "I would have thought that by now the people responsible for my imprisonment would have been able to come up with a better excuse for it. Speaking as one writer to another, you should know that charges of C.I.A. involvement are the worst sort of cliché. You would be well advised to freshen up your act if you expect to have any chance of undermining my credibility."

As the rest of the media representatives chuckled the young man flushed. Even more loudly he insisted, "Then how do you account for your obvious affluence? You're clearly getting money from somewhere."

Mikhail frowned slightly, and Erin knew that he was wondering exactly how many aspects of his personal affairs were known to the representatives of his former government and the people they chose to speak for them. Quietly he said, "There is a marvelous invention here in the free world called author royalties. For years my books have been smuggled out of my homeland to be published in the United States and elsewhere. Their sales have been gratifyingly large, and my publisher has been commendably conscientious about depositing my earnings in various bank accounts." He added humorously, "I know it's expected for writers to complain about being poorly paid, but in my case, I genuinely have no quarrel with either the reading public or my publisher. In fact, I owe them both my thanks."

Having neatly turned what might otherwise have been a serious threat to his credibility into a joke, Mikhail went on to answer several dozen other questions from reporters who had no axes to grind.

As he did so Derek leaned closer to Erin and muttered, "I should have figured that's where the money was coming from. Let's not have any more surprises like that. From now on I expect you to pin him down on every question and every lead. By next week I want one hell of a wrap-up story on my desk. Got it?''

Reluctantly Erin nodded. She sensed that she had pushed Derek as far as she could, and that he wouldn't give another inch, especially now that he had met Mikhail and seen for himself the other man's indomitable strength and determination. Unless she wanted to see the story turned over to another reporter, she had better produce it quickly.

Ordinarily that wouldn't have posed any problem, but with Mikhail, she knew that she would have to struggle to maintain the objectivity that was so vital to good journalism. Silently she wondered how she could manage it when each moment with him led her deeper into an emotional and sensual maelstrom from which she had not the slightest wish to escape.

Chapter Eight

"You did a bang-up job, Demertov," Derek announced grandly when the conference was over and they were all settled in his office with a round of drinks. "I can't remember the last time I saw a mob of reporters take to anyone like that. You can count on some very complimentary coverage."

"I appreciate that," Mikhail said quietly, "but I am not looking for compliments. If they simply relay the facts I will be more than satisfied."

"Sure, sure. But it doesn't hurt to know who's on your side and who isn't. That little creep from *The*

People's Press, for instance. I'd like to find out how he got in there.''

"It was an open conference," Erin reminded him. "We knew perfectly well that word of it was bound to spread beyond the people we actually invited, and if we had tried to bar journalists we thought would be unfriendly, we would have caused a storm of protest."

"I suppose," Derek muttered. "But he still came close to doing some damage with that C.I.A. charge. It's not quite the cliché we'd like to think."

Mikhail shrugged. "Perhaps.... But at any rate, there is nothing I can do about it. If my former government is determined to air such a ridiculous accusation, it will do so, no matter what I say."

"You should at least be prepared to go on denying it," Derek insisted.

"I do not agree. If I continue to protest my innocence I will only draw more attention to the charge itself. No, from now on I intend to concentrate on raising the funds my country needs and writing the truth about what happened there."

The managing editor frowned, not at all pleased to have his advice so summarily dismissed. He was accustomed to having his recommendations gratefully received, not rejected out of hand.

Perhaps because of that, or simply because he didn't like the warm looks that had been passing between Erin and Mikhail since the conclusion of the news conference, he said, "I hope that doesn't mean you don't want to give any more interviews, because Erin is counting on a big story from you."

Mikhail's silvery eyes widened slightly before becoming just a bit guarded. "Oh? I was not aware that *Focus* planned any further coverage of me."

Shaking his head ruefully, Derek laughed. "Well, now, I can't imagine how she forgot to mention that to you. Did it just slip your mind, Erin, honey?"

The angry disbelief that had seized her the moment she realized he intended to mention the story to Mikhail broke through to the surface. "No, Derek, *sweetheart*," she snapped. "It didn't slip my mind, as you know perfectly well, since we just talked about it again not ten minutes ago. Or did you forget that I promised to deliver the article next week? That is...if Mikhail agrees to give me the information I need."

Glancing over at him worriedly, she was half afraid of the displeasure she might see in his eyes. Considering his past experiences with betrayal and exploitation, he might be excused for wondering how much of her interest in him was genuinely motivated by personal feelings and how much stemmed from her determination to stay at the top of her profession.

A moment later Erin breathed a sigh of relief as he said, "I will be happy to provide any assistance I can with the story. In fact, since it is due next week, perhaps we should get started right away."

Telling herself that she should have realized Mikhail was far too perceptive and intelligent to fall for such an obvious attempt to cause trouble between them, she agreed at once. They left Derek's office a few minutes later.

Outside, Erin introduced Mikhail to the staff members who had gathered in the hope of meeting him. She had to bite back a laugh as Jenny gazed up at him adoringly, and even the usually cool Sheila did an excellent impression of starstruck awe. But the smile faded as she realized that their admiration was as much for the man himself as for the immense talent he possessed.

Having already felt the full force of Mikhail's potent attraction herself, she could hardly deny that he affected other women just as powerfully. From the most hard-boiled reporter to the most impressionable copy girl, no one was immune to his appeal. A tight knot of apprehension grew in her stomach as she wondered what the odds were that a man so long deprived of female companionship was likely to want to settle down contentedly with one woman when he could so easily sample many.

That thought remained with her as they finally left the building and started walking up Fifth Avenue. It was snowing again, and the street was crowded with last-minute shoppers. The City seemed to have called a brief truce with its residents. Even the traffic police were smiling as they worked to keep the endless flow of cars moving, if not quickly, at least smoothly. The pungent aroma of chestnuts roasting over open fires and the joyous pealing of church bells high up in the steeples of St. Patrick's filled the air.

Mikhail had taken her hand in his and shortened his long stride to match hers. They walked along in what would have been a contented silence if Erin hadn't been feeling the full force of her insecurities and doubts about herself as a woman.

It didn't take long for him to realize that something was wrong, although he wasn't sure what. Gently he asked, "Erin, that meeting with your editor...it didn't distress you, did it?"

"What? Oh, no, of course not. I was annoyed that he felt called upon to mention the story I want to do, but that's standard procedure for Derek. He always shoots from the hip."

"Shoots from the hip?" Mikhail repeated, savoring what was for him a new expression. "That's very good. I can figure out what it means without ever having heard it before. And yes, you are quite correct. He strikes me as the sort of man who would behave that way."

"Always," Erin said dryly. "He's an expert at bullying people verbally, or, at least, most people. I noticed he didn't seem to faze you."

"Did you think he would when he mentioned the story?"

"Yes...it did cross my mind."

Shaking his head, Mikhail smiled down at her. "We are both writers, so I have no difficulty understanding how important your work is to you. And even if I did not, I still would not presume that you should give up all professional interest in me just because we have become personally involved."

The slightly husky timbre of his voice and the warm look in his eyes made Erin's throat tighten. Hesitantly she said, "Are we . . . personally involved?"

"Oh, yes," Mikhail declared without the slightest doubt. "And we are going to be even more so." His gaze darkened as he added, "I think you already know that, regardless of your relationship with Kent, I intend to have you for myself."

This startling announcement, uttered with blatantly male confidence, stunned Erin. She was struck by both his misinterpretation of her involvement with the managing editor and his frankness about the role he meant to play in her life and opted to deal with the easier part first. "But I only work for Derek. There's nothing personal between us."

Mikhail frowned. "He called you 'honey', and you called him 'sweetheart'."

"And you thought that meant we were involved outside the office?"

"What else was I to think?"

Laughter bubbled up in Erin. "That was just sarcasm. Derek knows it bothers me to be called by pet names in such an inappropriate setting, so he does it whenever he's really annoyed. And I finally got so tired of it that I decided to do the same to him."

"I thought that might be it," Mikhail admitted, making no effort to hide his relief, "but with English not being my native language, I couldn't be sure. Not that it makes any difference," he added matter-of-factly. "You are a woman well worth fighting for."

Never having thought of herself in such a decidedly primitive way, Erin couldn't quite suppress a little shiver of feminine pleasure, but she felt compelled to struggle against it. "That doesn't sound very liberated. You wouldn't be a closet male chauvinist, would you?"

"Not at all. But neither am I so foolish as to believe that because men and women are equal, we are also identical. There are still very powerful forces at work in us that no amount of social change can alter."

As though to demonstrate the truth of what he had just said, Mikhail stopped suddenly and drew her into his arms. Before she could even begin to object his mouth claimed hers in a soul-searing kiss that drove out all thought of protest. Oblivious to the crowd of shoppers who smiled at them indulgently, he took her on a long, thorough exploration of the senses that didn't stop until they were both breathless.

When at last he lifted his head she was flushed and wide-eyed. The rapid rise and fall of her breasts was visible even under the heavy wool coat she wore.

Brushing a snowflake from her upturned nose, he laughed softly. "Beautiful Erin, you are as lovely as the island you were named for. Certainly your eyes are as green, and sometimes as sad. You must know I will not do anything to hurt you."

She nodded mutely. Not for a moment did she think Mikhail would ever intentionally harm her. But she also realized that when such overwhelming emotions were released, it wasn't always possible to predict what would happen. Even as she accepted the fact that she was set on a course she couldn't bear to abandon, she had to wonder where it would lead her.

As they covered the remaining few blocks home, the snow grew steadily heavier. By the time they reached the apartment house where Erin lived they could see only a couple of yards ahead. Traffic was thinning out rapidly as the last shoppers hurried home. There was a hushed, expectant quality to the crystalline air that Mikhail had no difficulty in sensing.

Pausing outside the ornate art-deco lobby, they knocked the snow from their boots as he asked, "Is it always like this at Christmas? As though you are all waiting for something important to happen?"

"I guess it is," Erin said slowly, entering the elevator. He had put into words something she had only been able to sense. "Even though we're commemorating an event that took place almost two thousand years ago, it retains such a sense of mystery and wonder that it's impossible to remember clearly from year to year. It has to be captured each time as though it had never been experienced before.''

''There are other experiences like that,'' he murmured, unlocking the apartment door.

She turned, gazing up into the quicksilver glimmer of his eyes. ''Like what?''

A burnished finger touched her cheek gently. ''Every time I feel the softness of your skin, hear your voice, smell the perfume you always wear, I think I will remember the sensation. But I cannot, at least not completely. Each time, I rediscover you all over again.'' He laughed softly as she dropped her gaze self-consciously. ''You are a remarkable collection of complexities. Today, at your office, I saw the calm, collected journalist and businesswoman, and she impressed me very much. But there is another part of you I have also seen, the soft, yielding part that has come to haunt my dreams.''

Unwilling to meet his eyes even when he tilted her head back, Erin laughed shakily. ''It's no wonder your books have such impact, Mikhail. You have the soul of a poet.''

''Thank you,'' he murmured, ''but I have no need of poetry to express what I feel for you. I have only to say the truth.'' Quietly he added, ''And you have only to accept it.''

Still Erin could not respond. Her thoughts were in too great a turmoil. The yearnings he set off in her body threatened to overwhelm her, but they were as nothing compared to the ache in her heart. Never would she have thought it possible for any man to so effortlessly undermine her defenses and make her want to completely disregard the teachings of a lifetime.

With Mikhail she forgot to be prudent, forgot to worry about the future, forgot even that she had never intended to know a man intimately without first being certain that they shared a mutual commitment to each other. All that mattered now was that they come closer and closer until at last even the barriers of physical separation would dissolve so they could be truly one.

Shaken by the force of her own emotions, Erin instinctively backed away from him. Correctly gauging the dismay in her eyes, Mikhail let her go, but only as far as the kitchen. While she started dinner he turned on the tree lights, pulled the curtains and got a fragrant log going in the fireplace. When she returned with a simple but delicious meal of steaks, salad, freshly baked French bread and a hearty red wine, the room had taken on a soft glow that relaxed her almost against her will.

They spoke little as they ate. Erin was caught up in her own thoughts, struggling to decipher feelings and actions that were so out of character for her that they might have belonged to a stranger. She had no doubt about where the intimate dinner in front of the fireplace was leading. Some new level of decisiveness that she sensed in Mikhail warned her that he had no intention of waiting much longer.

Nor did she try to fool herself into believing that she wanted to delay what she yearned for so irresistibly. Silently she acknowledged that she had reached the point where all the forethought, analysis and reason in the world had to be jettisoned in favor of the powerful inner voice that was telling her to yield to her most fundamental needs. The time had come to trust her instincts and her heart.

They cleared the dishes away together and returned to settle down once again in front of the fire. Mikhail took off his jacket before adding a fresh log to the blaze. Erin watched as the finely woven linen of his shirt stretched over the sculpted muscles of his arms and back. His movements were startlingly graceful for so large and powerful a man. His hands, lifting the heavy log as easily as though it were a matchstick, were big and lightly sprinkled with golden hair. The memory of their calloused but gentle touch shivered through her.

A pulse began to beat in the slender column of her throat. Her gaze was drawn irresistibly downward along the taut length of his tapered hips and sinewy legs. Without her being aware of it, her sea-green eyes grew soft and slumberous, giving her an alluringly seductive look.

As he turned back to her the firelight darkened his hair to burnished copper while emphasizing the hard lines and shadowy planes of his face. She couldn't make out his expression, but she did hear his sharply indrawn breath as he surveyed her sensual beauty.

While working in the kitchen she had discarded the jacket of her turquoise wool suit, leaving her in only the softly draped skirt and a delicate cream silk blouse trimmed at the collar with handmade lace. Her hair, which had begun the day in a neat chignon, had come undone to tumble around her shoulders. Her high-boned cheeks were faintly flushed from the heat of the fire, and from her thoughts.

He stopped, staring down at her from his great height. She thought she must have imagined the slight trembling of his hands when at last he moved toward her again. "Erin..." he breathed softly as he sat down beside her on the floor, close to the fire. "I can't quite convince myself that you aren't a dream."

Startled, she gazed back at him. "A dream? No, I'm not a dream.... You are...." She laughed shyly, unable to stop herself. "I used to dream about a man like you...strong, tender, intelligent.... I had almost given up hope that you really existed. But you do...and you're here...."

A tender smile curved his hard mouth as he raised a hand to gently cup the back of her head. His fingers tangled in the silken strands of her hair, drawing her closer. "Then, if we're both dreams, let us share the night, sweet Erin; I can't bear to be without you any longer."

A feather-light kiss touched her brow before his lips moved slowly down along the curve of her cheek to the lobe of her ear. She gasped as he nipped her gently, only to instantly soothe the tiny hurt with his tongue. Waves of pleasure undulated through her, washing over and drowning the last faint remnants of reason.

Moaning softly, she moved deeper into his embrace, giving herself up to his impassioned touch. Yet even as he took her mouth completely, his big hands stroking circles of pleasure along her silk-covered back, she was certain of the absolute control he maintained over himself. Though she no longer had any doubt that this time there would be no drawing back for either of them, she trusted Mikhail to go slowly and make the experience as perfect for her as she wanted to make it for him.

As he trailed a line of fire down her throat to the scented hollow at the base of her collarbone, he lowered her gently to the carpet. Stretched out beneath him, her body engulfed by the overwhelming size and strength of his, Erin knew for the first time in her life the sensation of being truly vulnerable. Yet the knowledge that he could easily overpower her brought no fear. Implicit in it was the realization that his strength would soon be joined to hers as together they found a union far beyond anything they could ever experience as individuals.

A heady sense of her own femininity coursed through her, prompting her to return his caresses in kind. As his mouth claimed hers again she met him in an erotic duel that presaged what was to come on an even more intimate level.

Mikhail groaned deep in his throat. Holding her firmly with one hand, he slid the other up to cup the fullness of her breast. Through the thin silk of her blouse, his mouth nuzzled the pouting nipple, his tongue rasping over it in a motion that ignited bursts of flame deep within her.

She cried out softly, kneading the taut muscles of his back. Knowing only that she couldn't bear to be separated from him by even the thin layers of their clothes, she pulled his shirt from the waistband of his slacks and slid her hands under it, savoring the unyielding warmth of skin over steely muscles.

The quiver of pleasure that coursed through him warned her that his need was every bit as great as her own. No thought of resistance remained in her when he pressed her back into the soft rug and determinedly unfastened the buttons of her blouse. It fell open to reveal her low-cut bra, little more than a scrap of lace that hid nothing from his eyes. They glowed like molten silver as he unclipped the front fastener, feasting on the beauty laid bare before him.

Erin shivered helplessly from the heady combination of passion and fear. She wanted so desperately to please him, but she was struck by doubt about her ability to do so. Seeing the uncertainty in her eyes, he murmured huskily, "Undress me, Erin. I need to feel your hands on me."

Tremulously she obeyed, pushing aside the smooth linen of his shirt to reveal the massive expanse of his chest. A soft gasp broke from her as she yielded to the compelling need to learn his body as thoroughly as he was learning hers.

Tentatively at first, then with growing confidence, she stroked the flat male nipples that hardened at her touch. Breathing in the heady scent of his sandal-wood after-shave combined with the potently male essence of his body, she smiled enticingly. Her lips caressed the velvety expanse of muscles covered by thick golden curls as her tongue darted out to taste him.

Mikhail shook with the impact of her touch. A deep rumble like the breaking of waves on a distant shore rose from his chest. All the carefully erected barriers that had sheltered his heart and spirit through the long, treacherous years were cracking wide open. Rays of golden light pierced him, making him almost cry out in exaltation.

Moving swiftly, yet with infinite gentleness, he unfastened her skirt and stripped it from her, along with the silken pantyhose and blouse. Her bra followed, leaving her in only a tiny fragment of lace guarding the juncture of her satiny thighs.

Modesty mingling with desire made her flush. Bending over her, savoring her exquisite loveliness, Mikhail laughed softly. "You are exquisite . . . so perfect in every way. Every inch of you is so beautiful...."

Driven close to mindlessness by hungers she had never even imagined, much less experienced, Erin moaned softly. "Please ... I need you so badly...."

Mikhail heard her plea and echoed it. Taking both her hands in one of his, he guided them to the buckle of his belt. "Then free me for you, Erin. Let there be nothing between us but our own flesh."

Her fingers fumbled with the supple leather, but she managed to undo it and to unfasten the button of his waistband. Beyond that she could not go. She had to endure his indulgent chuckle as he pulled down the zipper and swiftly tossed away all but his briefs.

Staring at him as he loomed over her in the firelight, Erin breathed in sharply. He was so uncompromisingly male that he unleased her most primeval feminine urges. When he came down beside her, stroking the silken smoothness of her body, she moaned softly. His hands moved slowly from the swelling fullness of her breasts down the incline of her waist to the flat expanse of her abdomen, where they tightened on her hips. Huskily, he murmured gentle words of desire and reassurance.

His deep, tender voice soothed her even as his touch excited her unbearably. Trembling, she reached out to stroke the hair-roughened length of his thigh as it eased between her slender legs. His skin was hot beneath her fingers, and she could feel the acute tension tightening his muscles.

When his fingers reached beneath the delicate rim of her panties she jerked slightly, but lay quietly as he removed them. The almost reverent admiration glowing in his silvery eyes touched her deeply. Without hesitation she opened her arms to him.

Mikhail gathered her into his embrace, cradling her against his massive length. Well aware of how easily he could hurt her if he went too quickly or roughly, he caressed her with slow, gentle strokes that made her quiver helplessly.

Slipping his hands beneath her, he squeezed her buttocks as he let her feel the full extent of his arousal. A soft gasp broke from her, followed instantly by a rippling purr of contentment as his mouth captured the taut peak of her breast to suckle her with gentle fierceness.

Launched headlong into an ecstatic flight toward some shimmering peak she could barely envision, Erin yielded utterly. She was barely aware when he lifted her high against his chest, capturing her lips with his as he carried her into his room. When he laid her on the bed she shivered in the sudden coolness that vanished the instant his body returned to hers.

No trace of the embarrassment she had felt earlier remained to dim her pleasure as she realized that the last barrier separating them was gone. Luxuriating in the ardent proof of his desire, she moved instinctively to bring them even closer.

As her legs fell open he slid between them with all the naturalness of a homecoming. His tongue plunged deeply within the moist cavern of her mouth, his hands gently kneading and stroking the aching fullness of her breasts.

Waves of sensation piled one upon the other until she thought she couldn't possibly bear anything more. But Mikhail had other ideas. Determined to savor every inch of her, he slid down her body, raining heated kisses along the delicate line of her ribs, into her dimpled navel, across the silken smoothness of her belly to the ultrasensitive skin of her inner thighs.

Overwhelmed by spiraling coils of pleasure that threatened to explode at any moment, Erin abandoned herself to his most daring caresses. Writhing beneath him, she became a wild thing, swept by repeating flashes of ecstasy that melded together into a firestorm of need.

When Mikhail moved away from her for a moment she cried out in protest. He soothed her with a gentle caress even as he held his own desire at bay long enough to protect her.

The realization that he could think of her well-being at such a time shattered her last thin hold on restraint. She welcomed him back joyously, an ecstatic cry breaking from her as he at last made them one.

Holding himself still within her, Mikhail waited until he was certain that she had adjusted to his intimate possession. Only then did he move slowly and gently to bring their pleasure to a shattering crescendo.

Swept by irresistible convulsions, Erin cried out his name. His features were tightly drawn, and his eyes glowed with the light of inner flames as their gazes locked. Mikhail was fully with her in that timeless instant, an instant torn out of all the rest of existence and made purely their own. Together they ascended to the furthest limits of ecstasy before shattering in an incandescent burst of release.

Consciousness slowly re-formed as they drifted back down to earth. Erin lay still, barely breathing, luxuriating in the sensation of his weight still holding her to the bed. When he thought to move, worried that he might be crushing her, she stopped him with a gentle touch. "Stay... please.... You feel so good."

His mouth curved in a smile against her silken skin. "I can't possibly feel any better to you than you do to me, my beautiful Erin." Raising his head enough to look into her eyes, he murmured, "I never knew it was possible to experience such joy."

Knowing that she was only telling him what he already knew, she couldn't resist the urge to whisper, "Neither did I. Nothing could have prepared me for this."

Mikhail laughed deep in his throat, an utterly male sound of satisfaction. "And I am very glad nothing did. You are mine now, Erin. Only mine."

His fierce possessiveness sent tiny echoes of remembered pleasure shimmering through her. Lovingly entwined in his arms, she slipped away into a sleep deeper and more content than any she had ever known.

Chapter Nine

Something was tickling Erin's nose. Refusing to open
her eyes, she eased a hand out from under the covers
and batted at it desultorily. Instead of going away, as
any self-respecting feather or whatever it was should
have done, it grew more persistent. A soft sigh escaped her as she was finally forced to admit that she
was awake.

Her eyelids fluttered once, twice, then snapped wide
open as she realized that Mikhail was gazing down at
her, teasing the tip of her nose with a strand of her
hair.

"Good morning," he murmured, smiling as he took in her confusion, which gave way almost instantly to memories that made her blush.

"Oh...uh...good morning...." Sitting up slightly, she clutched the covers to her breasts as she gazed at him in mingled disbelief and astonishment. Had the previous night really happened? Had she really lain in his arms and been transformed into the impassioned creature she remembered?

The intimacy of their bodies lying close together under the sheet and a lingering sense of languid well-being told her that it had been no dream. Nor could she summon the faintest hint of regret. Gazing into Mikhail's silvery eyes, drinking in the sight of his stubble-roughened cheeks, tousled hair and powerful chest visible above the covers filled her with delight.

Long moments passed before she realized that he was watching her closely, apparently searching for belated pangs of conscience or remorse. Instinctively she reached out to reassure him. "I'm so glad you're here," she murmured softly, "and so glad we're together."

His relief was complete and unfeigned. He smiled broadly and kissed her lightly on the nose before climbing calmly out of bed. "That calls for breakfast, or at least coffee. Are you hungry?"

Distracted by the sight of him standing naked in the dim light filtering through the curtains, she could only nod. Not for the world could she tear her eyes from

him as he shrugged into a terry-cloth robe, then held
out a large flannel shirt for her.

Realizing that he meant for her to leave the protection of the sheet she still clutched, Erin hesitated, but
only for a moment. The tenderly mocking grin he shot
her forced her to swallow the remnants of the modesty that had somehow managed to survive the unbridled passion of the night before. Stepping quickly
toward him, she reached for the shirt, only to have him
hold it just beyond her grasp as his powerful arm
wrapped around her and drew her close.

Breathing in the fresh scent of her hair, he said
softly, "You must not be shy around me. Your body
is exquisitely beautiful. It gives me great pleasure to
see you like this."

His words and the arousing touch of his body combined to send a thrill of pleasure through her. Standing on tiptoe, she gently touched her lips to his. The
caress conveyed appreciation for his reassurance, and
far more. As they stepped slightly apart, Mikhail
holding the shirt open for her, their eyes met in shared
agreement that they would soon be back in the big,
welcoming bed.

But first there was the ritual of Christmas morning
to enjoy. As he made coffee and slipped half a dozen
croissants into the oven, Erin quickly retrieved the
presents she had stashed in her closet and slipped them
under the tree. After turning on the lights she took a
peek out the window. The blizzard that had struck the

western states with such fury had descended on New York.

The city was having a truly white Christmas. Through the swirling clouds of snow she could barely make out the buildings across the street. Cars left parked along the curbs were already beginning to disappear. The branches of the trees were etched in white, and front stoops had vanished under fluffy, wind-tossed blankets. Nothing moved for as far as she could see. Nature had decreed a rare moment of tranquility where there was usually none. Erin meant to enjoy it to the fullest.

She turned back just as Mikhail came into the room. His eyes widened as he spied the presents that had appeared under the tree. "What is this?"

She shrugged teasingly. "Beats me. It looks as though Santa Claus dropped by."

"E-rin..." He tried to sound stern, but failed completely. The delighted, almost little-boy, look that lit his face was reward enough just by itself.

From across the width of the room he gazed at her tenderly, his expression so open and vulnerable that her throat tightened. "Just a moment," he said. "I'll be right back."

Puzzled, she wondered what he was up to. Her question was quickly answered when he returned with his arms laden with gaily wrapped packages.

Laughing, Erin shook her head ruefully. "Mikhail..."

"I had nothing to do with this," he claimed as he placed the presents under the tree. "A very large man in a red suit left them."

Sitting side by side on the couch sipping their coffee, they made an effort at decorum. But they kept glancing at the pile of gifts and at each other, until, like giddy children, they could wait no longer.

"You first," Erin insisted, holding out a package wrapped in silver paper and tied with a large red bow.

He began to open it eagerly, but slowed down when he realized what he was holding. Carefully he turned the large leather-bound book in his hands. "I have always wanted to read Thoreau, but his works were banned in my country. Now I will finally have the chance. Thank you, Erin."

It didn't seem possible that anything could make her feel happier at that moment, but she quickly discovered that her assumption was mistaken. The package Mikhail selected from under the tree and handed to her contained a delicate, intricately carved gold locket that she knew at first glance was an antique. It appealed to both her sense of beauty and her love of the past. Everything about it said that it had been chosen with special care, and that touched her as much as the gift itself.

"Thank you," she said softly. "I'll always treasure this."

His touch was gentle on the back of her neck as he lifted her hair away so he could secure the locket.

When it was in place he sat back slightly, studying her. Erin met his eyes calmly. A deep sense of contentment and purpose was growing in her. She hugged it to her, instinctively understanding that she might well need it later when the full enormity of what was happening to her sank in.

But for the moment, at least, there was only more laughter and enjoyment as the rest of the presents were unwrapped. Her guess that Mikhail would want books had proved correct. He was delighted with the works by John Steinbeck, Ernest Hemingway and Thomas Paine that she had selected. Added to the books she had already noticed accumulating around his desk, they made the beginnings of a good collection.

Just as she had chosen gifts that she knew would fulfill his yearning for knowledge he had been denied, his presents paid tribute to the utterly feminine part of her nature that was usually constrained by her high-pressured, professional world.

In addition to the locket there were a crystal flask of her favorite perfume, a jade comb for her hair and, last but hardly least, a white silk and lace peignoir that was at once intensely romantic and unmistakably sensual.

As she lifted it from the box Erin couldn't resist the impulse to ask, "When did you choose this?"

Mikhail's grin told her that he knew exactly what she was thinking. "Several days ago. You see, I was determined that you would be mine, and once I make up my mind about something, I am not easily deterred.''

"I can hardly claim to have led you much of a chase," she murmured, her eyes still on the gossamer fabric she held. It was so light that she could barely feel it. Against her body it would be little more than a tantalizing cloud, hiding almost nothing from his gaze.

"Does that distress you?" Perceptively he had guessed that the swiftness of her surrender might be an embarrassment to her.

Erin nodded reluctantly. She wasn't about to try to explain to him that what was happening between them challenged her most deeply held beliefs and values. She would never have thought it possible for her to become so intimately involved with any man on such short acquaintance. Whenever she had tried to imagine how the love she hoped for would come into her life, she had envisioned a slow progression from friendship to far greater commitment. Instead she had encountered an explosion of passion and desire for which she had been completely unprepared. It made her feel acutely vulnerable, but still she couldn't stop herself from responding with all the warmth in her generous nature.

"It shouldn't," he said quietly. "There are a few irresistible forces in this world that can never be controlled. We seem to have encountered one of them. To try to slow it down, to channel it in any particular direction, would be not only futile, but possibly destructive."

Erin heard the warning implicit in his words and understood it. He was a man who nurtured many ideals, but no illusions. He recognized the immense difficulty of trying to knit together two lives as disparate as their own, but he was also very clearly determined that they would overcome the challenges their relationship presented.

She took comfort from his resolve even as her own determination rose to match it. Smiling, she said, "All your gifts are beautiful, Mikhail, but last night was the most beautiful of all. Nothing will ever equal it."

Too late she realized that the words could be taken as a challenge. The utterly male gleam in his eyes told her he had chosen to interpret them as just that. Reaching for her, he murmured, "You think not? Then I shall have to convince you otherwise."

Flustered, she tried to draw back. "I was going to take a shower...."

Her tentative objection left him unperturbed. Rising, he lifted her effortlessly into his arms, then strode down the hallway toward the bathroom. "That's an excellent idea."

There was something deliciously exciting about being carried off like that, Erin decided. Her stomach fluttered softly in anticipation even as the wantonness of her imaginings brought a rosy glow to her skin. Seeing her blush, Mikhail laughed. "I hope you never try to bluff your way out of any situation. Your every thought shows on your face.''

''I always did have expressive features,'' she murmured, far more interested in the hard sweep of his chest beneath her cheek and the warmth of his gaze as he scrutinized her tenderly than in her own words.

After he had set her on her feet in the blue-and-white tile bathroom, Erin stood motionless as Mikhail turned on the shower. Her eyes never left his when he reached for the buttons of her shirt, undoing them and gently easing the covering from her. His own followed swiftly. She had barely a moment to admire the long, lean sweep of his body before he took her hand, and together they stepped under the stream of pleasantly hot water.

A world of new sensation opened for Erin. She had thought that she had experienced the ultimate in her body's capacity to feel, but she had been wrong. As the heated mist rose around them Mikhail led her on a rapturous voyage beyond anything she could ever have imagined.

His palms gently cupped her swelling breasts as he cropped feather-light kisses along the curve of her cheek, over the bridge of her upturned nose, down across the slender line of her throat. When at last he met her mouth with his, she moaned softly. Their tongues touched, stroking in a provocative rhythm that made her tremble.

The thick mat of golden hair covering his chest felt like silk beneath her fingers as she yielded to the need to touch him. Slowly, savoring every moment, she followed the sculpted hardness of his chest up to his massive shoulders, stroking the hollow at the base of his corded neck before reaching up to trace the rugged planes and angles of his face.

Her finger teased his mouth gently, only to be teased in turn as he suddenly drew it into the moist cavern, nipping gently.

"Mikhail..." The rush of water almost drowned out her voice, but it couldn't dim the ardent look in her emerald eyes. It was answered by his own as he drew her closer, the urgency of his need making her arch against him.

Bending his head, he slowly, tantalizingly, flicked his tongue across her taut nipples, teasing first one and then the other until she thought she would surely go mad from the sensation. When he finally drew one into his mouth to suckle her gently she trembled uncontrollably.

The sense of her own womanly power that he had awakened in her the night before demanded that she give pleasure as well as receive it. Tentatively at first, then with growing assurance, she let her hands and mouth wander over him until he groaned in delight.

"I was wrong, Erin," he muttered huskily as he gently put some slight distance between them. "You are not an angel, but a sorceress. Much more of your magic and I will be undone."

Elated by her ability to stir him so intensely, she laughed confidently. "Would that be so terrible?"

"No, but I prefer that it be in bed." A devilish gleam entered his eyes as he added, "Later, when we are more accustomed to each other, I will be happy to explore other alternatives with you. But just now..."

She didn't hear the rest of what he said. Her imagination had taken over, conjuring up visions that turned her face bright red. Mikhail laughed heartily at her reaction. "You are a delightful bundle of contradictions." Picking up the soap, he began to work up a lather between his hands. "How many women are both genuinely shy and gratifyingly eager?"

Erin could hardly deny that she was either. It was too much of an effort to even speak. She could only stand docilely before him as he gently but thoroughly bathed her. No spot on her body was missed by his careful, insistent touch. On the sensitive skin of her breasts and inner thighs he used his hands. Everywhere else he rubbed her vigorously with the rough-textured loofah until her body glowed.

When he was finished he handed the soap and cloth to her, and she hesitated for only a moment. The need to touch him overwhelmed all else. Tentatively at first, then with growing assurance, she explored his body as thoroughly as he had hers.

Framed by immense shoulders and arms, his back was a long sweep of powerful muscle and sinew leading down to the flat, hard planes of his buttocks. His skin might once have been pale, but long exposure to the elements had darkened it to a warm bronze that contrasted vividly with his golden hair.

Taking a deep breath, she murmured for him to turn. When he did so their eyes met for an instant. His were slumberous with a passion so intense as to send a shiver of anticipation through her, but she was still not yet ready to give up her enthralling explorations. This was her first opportunity to really see his body, and she intended to make the most of it.

The sculpted muscles of his chest fascinated her, as did the lean hardness of his flat belly and the tensile strength of his thighs. Golden hair covered his torso and tapered down past his narrow waist.

So enthralled was she by the enticing differences between them that she only gradually became aware of the scars that added a poignant note of vulnerability to his male beauty. Her face pale as she took in the mute reminders of experiences that she couldn't bear to contemplate. Trembling, she blinked hard in a futile effort to hold back the sudden rush of tears that turned her eyes to sea-washed pools.

"Erin..." Mikhail's voice was a husky whisper, barely audible above the cascade of water. "Do not cry...." He touched a gentle finger to her cheek, catching the diamond droplet.

"I can't help it.... It hurts to think of you being hurt."

Gathering her closer, he soothed her with a gentle caress. "That part of my life is over. From now on there is only freedom and a chance for happiness beyond anything I could have imagined. Think of that, Erin, not of what is done with."

She knew that he was right, but it was still difficult to forget all he had endured. Driven by an instinctive need to comfort him, she nuzzled her head into the breadth of his shoulder. The silken weight of her hair drifted through his hands and over the rippling muscles of his arms. Her breasts brushed against him gently, the taut peaks hardening further as they encountered the thick mat of hair covering his chest.

All thought, all reason, all doubt, slipped away from her, and she let them go without regret. The need that had driven her into his arms the night before was now even more intense. Later there might come a time to look back and regret, but just then she could do nothing but savor the wonder of what was happening between them.

Mikhail seemed to share her awe. Gently, as though he feared she might vanish from right between his hands, he lifted her out of the shower. After being wrapped in a big, fluffy towel she was carefully dried from the top of her glistening hair to the bottoms of her feet.

When he was done she returned the favor just as scrupulously. She could feel the tremors of desire racing through him even as he forced himself to remain quiet under her touch. The hard lines of his face were drawn almost painfully taut when at last she dropped the towel and stood before him, proud in her nudity and confident of the pleasure she could give.

Mikhail's silvery eyes swept over her, piercing her with the sheer male intensity of his approval. His look left no doubt that everything he saw delighted him. The low growl of demand he gave as he pulled her to him rumbled to the very core of Erin's being.

As he swept her up into his arms again she laughed softly. "I could get very used to being carried off like this."

He grinned down at her rakishly. "That's good, because I intend to keep right on doing it."

The implication that he considered their relationship to have a future wasn't the absolute declaration of intent she would have liked, but it still reassured her. There was no hint of restraint or doubt in her response when he laid her on the bed and came down beside her swiftly.

As their limbs lovingly entwined Erin surrendered to the overpowering sensations he unleashed within her. Their union of the night before had taught her much about her own body and his. Now she added to that knowledge. Not content to merely receive pleasure, she was determined to give it as well. His surprise when she pressed her hands against his shoulders, urging him onto his back, gave way instantly to wholehearted approval. Guided by instincts as old as humanity, and emboldened by Mikhail's obvious delight, she gently but persistently nourished his passion until at last he could bear nothing more.

Turning swiftly, he positioned her under him. His mouth and hands teased her to a level of pleasure so intense that it teetered on the edge of pain. Her head tossed wildly back and forth on the pillow, her hair streaming out in a silken fall around them. Every cell of her body was acutely sensitized, every nerve ending primed and ready. When he entered her at last she cried out in relief that gave way instantly to even more intense waves of desire.

Slowly, persistently, he drove her toward a shimmering explosion of fulfillment. The ecstatic denouement was almost upon her when he suddenly pulled back. Erin cried out in longing, reaching for him, only to have Mikhail elude her grasp.

"Be patient," he groaned into her mouth, the husky quality of his voice revealing his own acute arousal. "I want this to be perfect for you."

Gasping, she tried to tell him that it already was, but the words wouldn't come. She was beyond speech, beyond thought, capable only of responding to the electrifying sensations that were spreading through her in undulating waves that carried her higher and higher with each passing moment.

His return to her body was swift and even more forceful than before. Arching her hips, Erin moved with him, perfectly matching his rhythm. They soared together, coming ever closer to the final burst of ecstasy on which her consciousness now focused. But despite the completeness of their joining, she was still powerless to stop him when he withdrew yet again.

"Oh, no...please...."

Mikhail could answer her only with his eyes. His quicksilver gaze was on fire with unbridled passion and determination. His breath came in harsh gasps and his skin glistened with perspiration. The powerful muscles of his chest and arms were tightly clenched. Yet the hands that touched her were infinitely gentle, and the lips that claimed hers offered the promise that the enthralling torment would soon end.

Emboldened by passion so intense as to make even the thought of restraint unendurable, she stroked the broad sweep of his shoulders and chest, reaching down along the taut muscles of his hips and thighs. Mikhail groaned, and a hoarse gasp broke from him when at last she touched him intimately.

"Bring me to you, sweet Erin. Show me that your need is as great as mine."

No fragment of resistance hindered her as she moved to do his bidding. The utter rightness of their lovemaking banished all inhibition, and a joyful sigh escaped her as they came together in shattering completeness. Their flight reached beyond the boundaries of time and place to join them totally in exhilarating union. Their very souls seemed to meld in the instant when the world exploded around them and reality became only their two bodies locked together and their two hearts beating as one.

Chapter Ten

"Play in the snow?" Mikhail repeated dubiously. "Are you sure that's what you want to do?"

Erin smiled at him from across the breakfast table. They were enjoying a rather late brunch of blueberry pancakes with maple syrup, thick rashers of bacon and freshly squeezed orange juice. After a long, languorous morning spent in bed she was ravenously hungry.

"Absolutely. Not only is it a lot of fun, but I think it's time I got to introduce *you* to a new experience instead of the other way around"

Mikhail laughed gently. She watched him, thinking how she loved the way his eyes lightened when he was amused and how tender his mouth looked when he smiled. Sighing inwardly, she admitted to herself that there was no getting around the fact that she was deep in the throes of infatuation.

Everything about him beguiled her. Every word and gesture was a source of endless fascination. Moment to moment his impact on her grew. She could hardly believe that he was real, much less that he was sitting just across the table from her wearing only a terry-cloth robe that hid little of the lean, hard body that had so thoroughly enthralled hers throughout all the magical hours of the night and early morning.

The simple act of lifting a forkful of pancakes to her mouth was almost too much for her despite her hunger. The only consolation lay in the fact that Mikhail seemed equally bemused. In the midst of refilling their coffee cups he became distracted by the play of light across the curve of her cheek and let the hot liquid slosh onto the table. As they both scrambled for towels to mop up the spill their eyes met teasingly.

"We'd better go out," Mikhail said, "before we wreck this place."

"Why do you say that? Just because I burned the first batch of pancakes, we almost threw out the orange juice instead of the peels and the floor still smells of the maple syrup we spilled?"

"That and the fact that I could swear I saw steam rising from the bed." Laughing at her blush, he kissed her lightly. "Let's give it a few hours to cool off while you convince me there's something good about snow."

Half an hour later, warmly dressed in boots, ski pants and down-filled jackets, they left the apartment. The blizzard had stopped during the night after dumping more than a foot of snow on the city. Plows had cleared the major avenues, but the side streets were still heavy going. Erin was glad of Mikhail's help; he easily lifted her over drifts that came almost to her waist.

People were beginning to emerge from the buildings wearing the outwardly blasé but inwardly pleased air of adults temporarily catapulted back into childhood. With all the offices and stores that had planned to be open the day after Christmas suddenly shut down by the weather, there was no possibility of working or running errands. The only thing left to do was to go out and play.

Already enterprising street vendors were doing a brisk business in sleds. "We have to get a red one," Erin insisted as she and Mikhail stopped to look over the selection.

The wiry young man who was selling them sighed. "They're all the same, but no one wants to buy anything but red. Even these real nice silver jobs aren't moving too well." He looked at them hopefully, but Erin shook her head.

"It has to be red," she repeated. "All the sleds I've ever had were red. I'm not sure anything else would work."

Shrugging at the vagaries of fate, which made apparently intelligent people believe that gravity wouldn't function the same way when confronted by a blue or yellow or silver sled, the young man pulled a large red one out of his pile.

"It's kind of heavy," he warned, only to break off as Erin's very large companion tucked it effortlessly under one arm.

As they strolled toward Central Park Mikhail's slate-gray eyes lightened in the way Erin already knew meant that he was thinking of something pleasant. Seeing her quizzical look, he explained, "I had a sled just like this when I was about eight years old. My parents and I were living in Paris. We used to go to the Bois de Boulogne for sleigh rides." He smiled wryly. "I haven't thought of that in years. It was a very happy time."

Glad that she'd had some part in helping him to remember the enjoyable experiences that had been temporarily hidden beneath all the pain and treachery marring his adult years, Erin squeezed his hand gently. A sense of companionship too deep for words enveloped them as they walked farther into the park.

The oasis of natural beauty in the midst of Manhattan's glass and steel towers lay buried under a pristine blanket of white, transformed into a fantasy realm of magical shapes and otherworldly vistas. White-jacketed tree branches stood out clearly against the periwinkle sky. Sunshine reflecting off the crystalline banks filled the air with liquid light. A clean, crisp wind blew out of the north, reddening their cheeks.

Because he wore no hat, Mikhail's golden hair ruffled slightly in the breeze. His features were more relaxed than Erin had yet seen them. The last few days seemed to have stripped years from him, restoring a measure of the youthful exuberance and optimism that were a fitting accompaniment to his vast intelligence and courage. His resiliency amazed her, even as she understood that it was his ultimate gesture of defiance against the system that had tried to destroy him.

She had difficulty remembering that a relatively short time before he had been facing a life sentence in a brutalizing prison camp. Seeing him now, it was possible for her to believe that he had never confronted any problem greater than what normally occurred in the course of a talented, ambitious life. Only when she gazed into his eyes did she see the shadows that nothing would ever erase completely.

Following a path of beaten-down snow, they reached a large, gently sloping hill already dotted by brightly colored sleds. Mikhail shook his head ruefully as they watched the exuberant crowd of children and grown-ups. Laughing down at Erin, he said, "I have a feeling I'm about to experience a side of you I haven't encountered yet."

"You mean something other than the incredibly astute reporter and the seductive *femme fatale*?" she teased.

His eyes were softly indulgent as he nodded. "I can see the little girl you used to be. She's a charming sight."

Laughing self-consciously, Erin tugged at his hand. "Come on. Let's climb to the top."

They had to wait their turn before at last being able to position the sled at the edge of the slope. Erin nestled in front of Mikhail, whose arms wrapped around her while his long legs were stretched out on either side of hers. At her signal they both threw their combined weight forward. Their downward progress began slowly enough, but quickly picked up speed. Within seconds they were hurtling headlong toward the bottom of the hill, the air tearing at them and the ground careening up at full tilt. Landing in a snowbank, they tipped off the sled and rolled a few feet, ending up in a tangled heap.

Cushioned against Mikhail's big body, her eyes glowing and her whole being suffused by a radiant sense of well-being, Erin laughed delightedly. "That was great! Let's do it again."

He groaned and made a show of humoring her, even though it was clear that he was enjoying himself every bit as much as she was. Hand in hand they tromped back up the hill, only to come flying down it again moments later. That ride was followed by another and another, until they were both covered with snow, their faces red and their smiles as broad as any child's.

When they were at last briefly satiated, they left the sledders and joined a group building a snowman. Or at least Mikhail helped with it. Erin, the other women and a cluster of little girls insisted on making a snowwoman. Theirs turned out much better, to the chagrin of the men and boys, who promptly challenged them to a snowball fight.

Mikhail joined in with some reluctance, apparently concerned that the women might be hurt. He quickly discovered that their aims were every bit as good as the men's. When Erin hurled a snowball that hit him squarely in the chest he didn't hesitate to retaliate. His deft throw knocked the wool hat from her head. As she turned to retrieve it he tackled her from behind, sending them both rolling into a snowdrift.

"No fair!" she protested, unable to restrain her giggles. "Let me up!"

"Not until you pay a forfeit," he insisted with a menacing gleam in his eyes.

"What for? I hit you fair and square."

"No, you didn't. I would have ducked, but you're so beautiful that you distracted me. I claim a penalty."

Though she had a very clear idea of how much she would enjoy the punishment he intended to mete out, Erin continued to make a show of outrage. "Oh, no! I'm not giving an inch."

His powerful head bent toward her as he growled, "Then I will just have to take what I want."

For all his pretended fierceness, the lips that teased and coaxed her own were infinitely gentle. Lying beneath him in the snow, her breath coming fast and hard, Erin was helpless to deny her response. Like a flower opening to the sun, she strained toward him, meeting the proprietary thrust of his tongue with a fervor that matched his own.

The velvet roughness with which he stroked the tender inner flesh of her mouth sent waves of fire spiraling through her. She moaned softly deep in her throat, and his powerful arms slid beneath her to cradle her protectively even as he drew her further and further into an inexorable web of pleasure. The barriers of their clothing and the relative lack of privacy restrained them somewhat, but even so, all her senses were on fire with need by the time he reluctantly drew away.

"I think," Mikhail muttered thickly, "that we should go home."

Erin nodded, too dazed to speak. He helped her up and they dusted each other off beneath the indulgent glances of the opposing teams, who didn't have to be told that the snowball fight had just lost two participants. The sun was beginning to slant below the winter-bare branches etched against the western sky as they left the park, once again hand in hand.

They were barely inside the apartment with the door locked behind them when their clothes began to come off. Their boots and jackets were left in a pile in the entry hall, while the distance to the bedroom was littered with sweaters and shirts.

Her hands worked quickly at the buckle of his belt as Mikhail unzipped her slacks and pulled them from her. They tumbled across the bed, savoring the taste and touch of each other. After unfastening her bra he tossed it onto the floor, then gentle cupped her breasts in his big hands. His tongue flicked repeatedly over the nipples as Erin arched beneath him, moaning softly.

The arousal that had begun to build while they'd been in the park was increasing so swiftly that she couldn't bear sustained lovemaking. On fire with need for him, she stroked the hard length of his back as her slender legs entwined with his.

Sensing her urgency, which he fully shared, Mikhail quickly stripped the last garments from them. He waited only long enough to be sure that she could receive him before bringing them together in a shattering explosion of ecstasy that hurtled them both beyond the furthest limits of consciousness.

Only much later, when she had recovered sufficiently to speak, did Erin murmur, "If that's what playing in the snow does for us, I'm going to pray for a long winter."

Rolling over, Mikhail grinned down at her. "I'll join you. I had no idea a blizzard could result in such fun."

They lay together in a warm, contented heap until hunger of a different sort finally drove them to dress in dry clothes and make their way to the kitchen. Once dinner was started they settled down to read about Mikhail's press conference, which was prominently featured on the front pages of the major papers. The staid morning paper declared "East European Writer Charges Human Rights Violations" while the more brazen evening tabloid trumpeted "Author Blasts Commies."

The coverage was even more detailed than Erin had hoped. Sidebar stories accompanying the report on the conference described the history of oppression in the Eastern bloc and quoted the responses of other exiles living in the West. The consensus seemed to be that Mikhail had accurately described a brutal system of persecution that had existed for decades and was not yet fully laid to rest.

"Is it my imagination," Mikhail asked as they set the table, "or were the reports of what I said somewhat slanted in my favor?"

"There were a few paragraphs that went a bit beyond the usual standards of objective journalism," Erin admitted. "But that isn't surprising. Any writer listening to what you described is bound to feel intensely sympathetic. It's a real 'There but for the grace of God go I' situation."

"Is that how you feel?"

She hesitated, unsure of how completely she wanted to reveal the complex and almost frightening emotions he aroused in her. "I'm trying to follow your advice and not dwell on what you've been through," she said at last. "It's just too painful for me at this point. But before, when you were still in prison and no one could be certain that you'd be freed, I did sometimes wonder how well I would do in a similar situation. The only answer I came up with is that it's impossible to tell without actually experiencing it."

"I understand what you are saying," Mikhail told her gently, "but I think you are underrating yourself. You possess a rare sense of strength and courage that I believe would serve you well under any circumstances."

Deeply moved by his quiet words, Erin nonetheless felt compelled to ask. "How can you be really sure of anything about me when we've known each other such a short time?"

"Are you suggesting I should doubt you?" he shot back, the hint of a smile curving his mouth. "No, Erin, I will not accept that. Our acquaintance, brief though it has been, is too intense to allow for any of the usual pretenses people hide behind. Whether you are ready to admit it yet or not, we have come to each other honestly."

Biting her lip, she considered what he had just said. Was he fully aware of how quickly he had become a vital part of her life and of how vulnerable that made her feel? And if he was, could she also take his words to mean that the emotions she thought she saw in him, all the tenderness and understanding he had shown her, were completely genuine and unfeigned? Was it possible that he had really learned to care for her so greatly in such a short time?

Unwilling to voice the questions out loud, Erin had to be content with silent rumination. Caught up in an extraordinarily emotional and sensual experience, she understood that any attempt to make sense out of what was happening to her was bound to fail, but even so, the more reasoned part of her mind insisted that she try.

Throughout dinner, while they talked comfortably of books they had read, people they admired and other safe topics, she continued to examine her own feelings for some clue as to where her relationship with Mikhail might be headed.

Wryly, she remembered her father's teasing comment that she was the only one of his children who relished the careful analysis of a problem, pulling it apart into tiny pieces before meticulously arriving at a solution. That characteristic, which had sometimes made her seem slow and plodding compared to her more impulsive siblings, had stood her in a good stead in her career.

A large measure of her success as a journalist stemmed from her ability to thoroughly analyze complicated situations and report her finds in terms other people could readily understand. But now, as she attempted to do that to herself, she was discovering that some human experiences didn't yield easily to such dissection.

"You're very far away," Mikhail said gently. "What is on your mind?"

Disconcerted yet again by his perceptiveness, Erin tried to evade the question. "Oh, I was just thinking about my family back in Wyoming. We're so different in some ways, and yet we manage to be very close."

"Do you miss being with them?"

"A little.... Not as much as I expected." She smiled. "You make it very hard for me to miss anyone."

"Good, that is as it should be." He put down his wineglass and gazed at her over the flickering candles. "I see the worry in you, Erin, and I wish there was something I could say or do to soothe it. But I can't, because the future is as hidden to me as it is to you. We will have to discover it together."

His admission that he too was uncertain of where their relationship was heading should have worried her, but instead she was reassured to know that he wasn't playing some sort of sophisticated game in which she would ultimately be the loser. As he had said, they'd come to each other honestly. Whatever happened between them would at least have that much going for it.

She slept that night in his arms after long, exquisite lovemaking that left her at once completely drained and utterly fulfilled. She deliberately refused to think about what lay ahead of her the following morning when she had to begin work on the assignment from Derek. All her considerable skill as a journalist would be needed to write objectively about the man who enthralled her body and soul. Her commitment to her profession demanded that she at least try, even as she doubted what chance, if any, she had of succeeding.

Chapter Eleven

"So how's the article going?" Jenny asked as she dropped a stack of mail on Erin's desk.

Looking up from the pages of what was supposed to be a final draft, Erin grimaced. "Okay, I guess. I'm not really sure."

"That doesn't sound like you. Is something wrong?"

Something...everything...Erin wasn't clear which. But she did know that the article wasn't turning out as she had expected. It was supposed to be a straight news story providing in-depth details on Mikhail's experiences in the prison camp, his charges of oppression by the former authorities of his country and his concern that without substantial aid the fledgling democracies would fail. So far, so good. But other elements had crept in that added a level of perception that she couldn't help but recognize as intensely personal.

For almost a week she had wrestled with the problem of keeping her own feelings out of her writing, but the task had proved far more difficult than she could ever have envisioned. Over and over she thought she had finally gotten it right, only to go back and discover that what she believed was straightforward journalism was, on closer reading, nothing of the kind.

And yet the story was good. Better, perhaps, than anything else she had ever written. It had taken her a long time to come around to admitting that, principally because it meant that she should quit trying to make it into something it clearly wasn't going to be and send it through to Derek as it was.

Only the thought of how he would react made her hesitate. "Nothing's really wrong," she said slowly as Jenny continued to study her with concern. "It's just that the story has turned out to be less a clear-cut case of reporting and more a subjective look at how oppression can bring out extraordinary human characteristics."

"That sounds great," the younger girl insisted loyally. "Why should you be worried about it?"

"Because...the story should only be about Mikhail. But it isn't. Somehow a lot of myself got mixed in, and I don't know how to get it out."

"I'm not sure I understand. Isn't there bound to be something of yourself in anything you write?"

"Yes..." Erin admitted hesitantly. "But not like this." She couldn't quite go so far as to explain that what she heard in the words she had written was even more of a revelation to her than it would be to the general reader. It was as though a hitherto unacknowledged part of herself was speaking from the pages.

The days spent going over his experiences with Mikhail and the nights spent in his arms had coalesced into a single vision of him as a man in whom intrinsic human vulnerability coexited with incredible strength and intelligence.

Her work on the article had led her to review all the acclaimed "Demertov Papers," which had first spurred her interest in him. Mikhail's writing brought home to her more forcefully than ever the depth of his talent as a writer and his determination to redeem brutalizing experiences by giving them meaning.

What stood out most remarkably in both his own work and the vision of him her article revealed was his remarkable lack of hatred. Despite all that had happened to him, Mikhail nurtured a genuine love and sympathy for the rest of the human race. He didn't in any way attempt to excuse the oppression he had suffered, but he brought it down to a human scale, so that both the victim and the perpetrator were seen struggling with their own fears and inadequacies.

The result was that readers could not merely sympathize with the person who appeared to be on the side of good. They were also forced to understand the motivations of evil and to feel the capacity for similar abuses within themselves.

His sensitivity to subtleties of human behavior and thought was so great as to make her confront a similar, though not yet as well-defined, ability in herself. Through the long, difficult hours she had spent at her typewriter a single truth had emerged to stare at her from the pages of her article and ring in every word she had written: She was in love with Mikhail.

Not merely infatuated, not merely overcome by admiration or enveloped in physical rapture. Love, pure and undeniable, shone in every phrase and image she had created. It soared beyond the confines of her subject to add an astonishing degree of insight and wisdom to what was no longer simply a profile of a man, but an affirmation of the age-old struggle to discover and attain the furthest limits of human potential, no matter how perilous the task.

The revelation of her true feelings at once frightened and elated her. No longer could she puzzle over why she had cast off the teachings of a lifetime to rush into intimacy with him. The intensity of her love was such as to make it unthinkable that it should be denied so fundamental a form of expression. But neither could she find consolation in the thought that if they weren't able to weave a lasting relationship, she could resume her old life without more than lingering regret, because that simply wasn't true.

In fact, she was almost unbearably defenseless against a degree of pain she could hardly even imagine, and her vulnerability was growing more intense with each passing hour. Though it seemed impossible, her very ability to love appeared to be increasing. A vast reservoir of emotion was opening up within her—in which she might easily drown.

"Erin..." Jenny said softly, "are you all right? You're so pale and you look almost...scared."

"What? Oh, no, I'm fine." Jerking herself back from her painful thoughts, she managed to smile shakily. "I was just wondering how Derek will react when he reads this." She gestured toward the pile of pages covered with scribbled rewrites that more often than not were themselves crossed out as she decided that the original version was best. "After I retype it, of course."

"I'll do that for you, if you like," Jenny offered. "I'm not really busy right now."

Touched by the offer, since typing reporters's copy wasn't one of the younger woman's usual responsibilities, Erin nonetheless shook her head. "Thanks, but I'll bet you're anxious to get out of here. Going anywhere special for New Year's?"

Jenny smiled, her eyes bright with anticipation of the night ahead. "No, my boyfriend and I are just going to stay at his place and split a bottle of champagne. I know that doesn't sound very glamorous, but I'm really looking forward to it."

"I don't blame you. I've never liked going out on New Year's, and tonight's no exception."

"Even though you're invited to Mr. Kent's party?" Jenny asked, her eyes widening as she envisioned the dozens of well-known, glamorous socialites who would be gathering at the managing editor's Fifth Avenue apartment.

"Even though. I just hope Mikhail enjoys it."

"Oh, that's right, he's going with you." Jenny couldn't quite keep a note of envy out of her voice, though she quickly explained, "I'm crazy about my boyfriend, and I wouldn't trade him in for anyone, but I've got to admit, when Mr. Demertov was up here the other day he really wowed me. I never knew anybody could be so—" Words failing her, she fell back on a tried-and-truism. "—so dreamy. He actually gives me goosebumps!"

Erin knew the feeling, although she was careful not to say so. The speculative looks that had come her way recently hadn't escaped her notice. She was fully aware that those of her co-workers who knew where Mikhail was staying were curious about the exact nature of their relationship. So far, at least, she had managed to keep them guessing, but she had no confidence that such a state of affairs could be maintained, especially after her article began to circulate.

An hour later she had typed a clean version of it, tucked it into an envelope and dropped it off on Derek's desk. Firmly putting aside her doubts about the wisdom of what she had done, she headed home to dress for the party.

As she unlocked the door she could hear the steady tapping of Mikhail's typewriter, the same sound that had filled the apartment through every waking hour of the last week except for those times when they were talking, eating or otherwise engaged.

Her own awareness of the difficulties a writer faced when beginning a new project prevented her from asking what he was working on, but she couldn't deny her curiosity. The first book or article or whatever he did in the new atmosphere of freedom was bound to excite even greater interest than his work ordinarily received. Would he continue the type of writing he had done in the past, or would this new work signal a departure as radically different as the new life in which he found himself?

Mulling over those questions, she stripped off the mahogany slacks and yellow-gold sweater she had worn to work and stepped under the shower. Memories of certain passionate interludes spent in similar circumstances flashed through her mind as she soaped herself with jasmine-scented lather and shampooed her hair. Though she struggled to keep her mind on the present, she was nonetheless hard pressed not to give in to the temptation to climb out, wrap a towel around herself and go interrupt Mikhail in a way he would undoubtedly appreciate.

Only the knowledge that she had barely an hour to get ready for the party kept her from doing so. Sighing, she dried off, cleared the mist from the mirror and tackled the problem of what to do with her face.

Not that it was much of a challenge. She radiated the sense of a supremely satisfied woman. It could be seen in the fresh glow of her apricot-tinted skin, the bright gleam of her emerald eyes and the graceful carriage of her slender body. Even her hair seemed unusually cooperative. After it was dried, she had only to put it up on hot rollers for a few minutes before brushing it into a flatteringly soft style that framed her face before falling in an auburn cloud to her shoulders.

Checking the time, she wondered if she should remind Mikhail about the party. The sound of the shower running in the guest bathroom told her it wasn't necessary. She suspected that he was looking forward to the event more than he cared to admit and resolved to do her utmost to make it a success, if only for him.

In front of her closet, dressed only in delicate lace undergarments and silk stockings held up by a matching lace garter belt, she studied the gown she had bought especially for the occasion. Now that she had admitted the full extent of her love for Mikhail, she could recognize its powerful influence in many of her recent actions. The turquoise taffeta dress was a vast departure from the rest of her wardrobe. It was an unabashedly sensual and romantic creation that a woman would wear only for a man she wanted very much to attract.

After strapping on the delicate evening slippers that matched it, she stepped into the gown. The full, ankle-length skirt rustled luxuriously. Above the narrow waist, the low-cut bodice revealed the swell of her breasts, while the equally scanty back framed the delicate lines of her shoulder blades. Wide, puffed sleeves and a ruffled collar that framed her face gave the final touch to the utterly feminine confection.

She added a spray of perfume in which rare flowers and spices mingled provocatively, then carefully secured the locket that Mikhail had given her around her neck. Suspended on a thin gold chain, it nestled in the shadowy cleft between her breasts.

Staring at herself in the mirror, she battled a final moment of doubt. Granted, it was a gala evening when a woman could be expected to dress rather more flamboyantly than usual. But she would be mingling with at least a few of her co-workers, most notably Derek himself, who might well guess the reason for such a dramatic transformation.

Even as she debated the merits of sacrificing vanity to good sense, the opportunity to change disappeared. Mikhail stuck his head into the bedroom and started to say something, then stopped stock still as he took in her appearance. The sudden flare of desire in his silvery eyes was reward enough for all her efforts even before he whistled softly.

"You have always been beautiful, Erin, but tonight..." Taking her hand, he turned her so that he could take in the full effect of the gown and the slender but ripely curved body it more or less covered.

A blatantly proprietarial gleam sharpened his gaze. "You look like a glorious butterfly. Every man at the party tonight will be drawn to you. But don't get any ideas about flitting around, because I intend to keep you close beside me."

That was fine with Erin, who couldn't deny a tiny spurt of pleasure at his possessiveness. Granted, it wasn't exactly in keeping with her view of herself as an independent woman, but the truth was that it could still be quite pleasant.

"You should talk," she teased, letting her gaze wander over him. "I'll have to fight the other women off with a big stick."

Though the words were said jokingly, she was only half kidding. Dressed in a black velvet evening suit and white silk shirt, he looked at once utterly elegant and ruthlessly masculine.

The costly materials and meticulous tailoring in no way softened the hard sweep of his shoulders and chest or the sinewy line of his narrow hips and powerful thighs. His golden hair, still faintly damp from the shower he had just taken, was brushed back from his broad forehead. Beneath slanting brows his eyes glittered dangerously.

The burnished skin pulled tautly over the almost harsh planes and angles of his face only emphasized his faintly predatory air. He looked like exactly what he was: a supremely fit male animal made all the more formidable by acute intelligence and unshakable determination.

It was difficult to remember that he was the same man she had laughed and joked with over the last few days and in whose arms she had discovered ecstasy beyond imagining, a man whose every touch was enticingly gentle. A slight shiver ran through her as she considered what a formidable enemy he would make. Toughened by merciless circumstances, he would be unlikely to grant the least quarter to anyone he felt deserved his condemnation.

The thought faded almost the same instant that it occurred as Mikhail reached for her gently. The hands on her shoulders as he held her coat were warm and enticing. Not for the first time she wished they were staying home with the whole evening in which to indulge the passion she knew was fully awake in them both.

But duty called, along with a reluctance to deny Mikhail what might turn out to be a very enjoyable excursion into society. He was certain to be the center of attention, even at a party crowded by luminaries in politics, entertainment, business and the media. But when she said as much on the way into the elevator, he merely laughed.

"Why would those people be interested in me? Even if some of them have actually read my work, as opposed to simply buying it, I'm sure they have far more engrossing concerns."

"Perhaps, but I still think you should prepare to be mobbed. Frankly, I doubt Derek would have invited me to this shindig on my own. He only did it because he knew I'd bring you along. You're quite a social feather in his cap."

Holding the taxi door open for her, Mikhail shook his head bemusedly. "You lost me. What is a *shindig*?"

"Sorry. It's a fancy party where people tend to put on airs."

"Okay, now, about the feather in a cap. That's Yankee Doodle, right? And—what is it—macaroni?"

Suspecting that she was being teased, Erin laughed. "Well, no, not exactly."

"Oh, yes, that much I know. I even know how the song goes." To her delight and the enjoyment of the taxi driver, who promptly joined in, he launched into a rendition of all the choruses to "Yankee Doodle" that lasted until they pulled up in front of Derek Kent's luxurious East Side apartment house.

As they got out the driver leaned forward to grin at them both. "That was great, Mac, especially those last few stanzas. I never heard them before."

Mikhail leaned forward, a conspiratorial gleam in his eyes. "I made them up, but don't tell anyone." Adding a generous tip to the fare, he grinned at the bemused man, took Erin by the arm and informed her sternly, "Stop giggling. If you're going to be seen with a literary lion, you should at least endeavor to look properly impressed."

"Oh, but I am," she told him between chuckles. "And I'm sure everyone else will be, too, particularly if you have a few more songs, especially bawdy ones, in your repertoire."

"At least a dozen, but unfortunately, most of them are in various East European languages, and I doubt this evening's guests would be able to appreciate them. I could, of course, endeavor to translate, but somehow, that just isn't the same."

"Don't worry. By midnight everyone will be so plastered you could sing the originals and they'd think they understood every word."

"Getting plastered is a New Year's tradition, isn't it?"

"For some." She smiled up at him engagingly. "I however, have plans for a rather private celebration once we escape from this one. And for that, I intend to stay relatively sober."

Mikhail's answering grin made it clear that he was in full accord. They were still smiling at each other when a butler in black tie and tails opened the door to Derek's apartment.

Chapter Twelve

Her experience as a reporter had prepared Erin to mingle comfortably with all sorts of people, so she felt no self-consciousness as the butler took her coat and she and Mikhail strolled into the crowd of elegantly dressed men and women who exuded an almost palpable aura of wealth and power.

Her customary equanimity was quickly dented when she realized that not only was Mikhail an immediate source of interest and excitement, but that she was receiving a considerable share of attention herself.

The men's perusal was unmistakably appreciative, the women's less so. Whatever its origins, such scrutiny made her uncomfortable. She was glad for the solid strength of Mikhail's arm beneath her hand and the comfort of his nearness.

"What did I tell you?" he growled. "I'll be fighting off would-be interlopers all night."

The prospect didn't seem to particularly displease him. In fact, he might almost have been looking forward to it. A flicker of dismay coursed through her as she realized how much the man at her side relished a challenge.

She wasn't sure how she felt about inadvertently providing him with such a diversion, but she was certain that she was not going to stand by and let anything happen that she could prevent, so when Derek approached them there was a decidedly frosty gleam in her eyes, which the managing editor didn't miss.

"Erin, my dear," he murmured as he took her hand and coolly lifted it to his lips, "you should have warned me. Over the years I've managed to get used to the delectable vision you present in the office. But this—" his gaze ran over her body beneath the turquoise gown "—is quite another matter." Leaning closer, he added, "How is it that, after I've known you so long, you still manage to surprise me?"

Before she could respond, Mikhail interjected smoothly, "Is there any reason why she shouldn't? After all, I believe this is the first time you and Erin have had occasion to be in the same place outside of working hours."

Not quite masking the displeasure behind a jovial smile, Derek murmured, "Is that a fact? How remiss of me. I must make sure such a lapse isn't repeated." Taking advantage of the duties of a good host, he remained with them as other guests began to filter over, all eager to be introduced to Mikhail. The men were honest in their respect for his courage, but the women found other qualities to admire.

Erin had to stand by politely as he was positively fawned over by a bevy of blondes, brunettes and redheads whose numbers grew with each passing moment. Worse yet, Mikhail clearly enjoyed their attention. He was completely relaxed and at ease. The combination of his devastating good looks, obvious affluence and innate sensuality brought out the hunting instinct in more than a few of the young ladies clustered about him. Erin found herself maneuvered farther and farther away, until at last she could just make out the top of his head above the crowd.

A low chuckle made her turn abruptly. Derek was lounging against one of the French windows leading onto the terrace garden. His thick chestnut hair was slightly mussed and there was a dull flush in his cheeks.

"Feeling abandoned, my dear?"

"No, of course not. I was just...looking for somewhere to sit down."

"To the best of my knowledge the bedrooms are still unoccupied. But somehow I don't think you'd go for that."

Erin stared at him frostily. "You're right." She moved to pass him, only to find him blocking her way. Getting a firm grip on her temper, she murmured, "Excuse me."

Instead of stepping aside as she had hoped, Derek reached for her. Too late she realized that he had been drinking more than she had guessed, and also that the reflexes that had served him so well in professional football were still surprisingly intact. Holding her wrist, he drew her inexorably toward him. Short of making an all-out scene, Erin had no choice but to comply.

When they were standing so close that she could feel the warmth emanating from his body and smell the Scotch on his breath, he muttered, "Demertov's a fool to let anything distract him from you. But you can't blame the poor guy for having his head turned by all the attention. After what he's been through, he must think he's died and gone to heaven."

He chuckled humorlessly. The sound made her emerald eyes darken with worry. Not only was he perilously close to being drunk, he was also furiously angry. "I waited too long with you, didn't I?" he demanded. "I should have put more pressure on you to go out with me instead of letting you dart away every time I got too close."

A grim smile twisted his mouth. "You know what stopped me? Something really funny. You're too damned good at your job. I didn't want to lose you, and I couldn't help but respect your ability." Dully, he shook his head. "Respect and beautiful women don't mix. I should have forgotten all about that terrific brain you've got tucked under all that gorgeous hair and just followed my instincts. If I had, you'd be in my bed now instead of Demertov's."

Even as she felt the embarrassed flush staining her cheeks, Erin fought to keep her composure. Coolly she said, "You don't know anything about my relationship with Mikhail, so why pretend otherwise?"

Derek stared at her unblinkingly. "Don't I? Even if I hadn't suspected the two of you were lovers the day of the press conference, I would have realized it when I read your article. There's no mistaking how you feel about him, and you're not the kind of cold-blooded woman who could keep from expressing those emotions physically."

Erin's eyes had widened as she listened to him. In the back of her mind she had presumed that Derek wouldn't even see her article until the next day at the earliest. But instead he must have gone back to his office that afternoon and, finding it on his desk, decided to read it immediately.

Hardly breathing, she waited for him to tell her that what she had written was too subjective to count as journalism and would have to be scrapped. When he did speak his words were so far from what she was expecting that she could hardly credit them.

"Of course, you must already be aware that it's the best thing you've ever written. I knew you were good, but frankly, I never guessed you were capable of that kind of quality. Very few of us are." Almost as an afterthought, he added, "You'll get the cover, naturally, and we'll run the story with a full complement of photos. I suppose we'd better talk about your salary while we're at it, since we both know you can write your own ticket now. I'm not about to lose you to another publication just because I'm kicking myself for letting Demertov move in on what should have been strictly my own territory."

Torn between relief that he liked the article and anger at his presumption that she was some sort of prize in a male tug-of-war, Erin bristled. "Let's get something straight right now. Professionally, I'm pleased that you like my work, and I'll be happy to discuss terms for my staying with *Focus*. But personally, I couldn't care less what you think of me, and I don't appreciate your insinuations about my private life, much less this idea you seem to have that I'm up for grabs, by you or any other man. I suggest you get rid of that notion right away, or you can forget any chance of my continuing to work for you."

Derek stared at her for a long moment. His face reddened further, and an ugly gleam appeared in his eyes. Slowly he said, "I believe I've already mentioned your temper. Demertov doesn't seem to have managed to cool it down any. Maybe you need to be taken in hand by someone better equipped to manage you."

She was on the verge of an outraged exclamation when he reached behind him, pushed open the French door and, still holding onto her wrist, propelled her into the garden. A blast of icy air struck her. She shivered and tried to free herself from his grip, but unsuccessfully.

Her resistance seemed to fuel his anger. "Come on, Erin, don't play dumb with me. You know what the score is. Sure, I'll do a lot to keep you with *Focus* because you're a good reporter. But I'll do a hell of a lot more if you give me some personal reason to look after you."

Outrage, no matter how justified, had gotten her nowhere. She decided to try a different tack to put an end to the encounter before anything unforgivable happened.

"I'm not interested in being looked after, Derek—for any reason. I'm more than satisfied to be treated strictly as a competent professional." After pausing a moment to let that sink in, she added, "It's freezing out here. Let's go back inside before your guests start wondering where you've gone to."

Her very calmness seemed to take him back. He had expected an angry confrontation that might have escalated to the point where he would have felt justified in taking physical measures to subdue her. Instead, she presented the voice of sweet reason, subtly reminding him of both his desire to maintain their working relationship and how potentially damaging the gossip would be, should the events in the garden become known.

But beneath all that was an undercurrent of sympathy and tolerance that surprised them both. Even as she told herself that she should be furiously angry at Derek, she couldn't muster more than mild annoyance. Mikhail so absorbed all her thoughts and emotions as to leave little room for anything else.

A month earlier, or even a week ago, she would have turned on the man holding her as if she were a spitting cat. Instead, she was prepared to forget the entire matter—as long as it ended quickly. Turning slightly, she urged Derek back toward the door.

The icy wind had begun to penetrate even the alcohol-induced fog enveloping his brain. Its sobering effect was evident in his rueful smile. Quietly he said, "You're one terrific lady, you know that? What's Demertov thinking of to let you get away?"

"Is that what I'm doing?"

The low, dangerously calm voice startled them both. Mikhail stood at the open door, his big body blocking their view of the party going on behind him. As though in slow motion, Erin took in every detail of his appearance. The hands that had always touched her so gently, but which she suspected could be brutal when he felt it was necessary, were clenched into fists at his sides. Despite the cold, his face was pale. A pulse beat near the curve of his jaw.

Derek was nothing if not realistic. Recognizing both the futility of what he had attempted to do and the immediate danger staring him in the face, he dropped Erin's wrist. She took a quick step forward, putting herself between the two men.

"I'm cold, Mikhail," she said softly. "Let's go back inside."

For a moment she thought he would refuse. Derek must have thought so, too, because he flexed slightly, preparing himself for the blow that might well be coming. The vision of the all-out brawl that would undoubtedly result spurred Erin to act.

Determinedly she took Mikhail's hand while sending Derek a radiant smile that made it impossible for anyone to believe that anything untoward had happened between them. "I know you never thought twice about playing football in all sorts of weather, but some of us aren't quite that hardy. Much as I appreciate hearing how much you like my article, I could stand to be a little warmer."

While rattling on about inconsequential things she managed to steer both men back inside the apartment. A few curious glances came their way, but the guests were enjoying themselves too much to be easily distracted. Derek allowed himself to be drawn off by a florid-face banker and the silver-haired anchorman of a network news show, who wanted him to settle an argument they were having about what teams were likely to make the Super Bowl.

Erin offered no protest when Mikhail put a firm arm around her waist and guided her in the direction of the study, where a cheerful fire was blazing. Sitting down close to it, she let the warmth seep through her gratefully. For long moments neither one of them spoke, until at last he said, "I looked up suddenly and you were gone. Why did you leave?"

"Leave?" she echoed, a spurt of indignation flaring in her. "I'd hardly describe it that way. You were too busy with your fan club to notice anything else. And I didn't feel like hanging around to watch you being fawned over."

"You were jealous," he said with sudden understanding. "That's what caused all this."

The pleased smile that banished the last of his anger only increased hers. "I was not," she insisted hotly. "I just thought it was ironic, after all your big talk about keeping me to yourself, that you didn't even realize I wasn't with you anymore."

Lowering himself beside her on the couch, Mikhail said quietly. "Oh, I noticed all right. And as soon as I could politely disentangle myself, I went looking for you." His voice hardened perceptively. "Imagine my surprise when I found you on the terrace with our host. Hardly the night for a moonlight stroll, is it?"

"We weren't strolling. We were just talking."

"What about?"

"Work." The skeptical arching of his eyebrows forced her to elaborate. "Derek had a little too much to drink, but he still wanted me to know that he liked the article I did on you. That's all."

"How very thoughtful. Couldn't he have waited until you were in the office?"

"Apparently not. Look, I really would prefer not to talk about him. I'm still cold, I could do with some food, and frankly, this is not shaping up to be the greatest New Year's Eve I've ever spent, so let's just drop the whole subject. All right?"

Mikhail stared at her for a long moment before he slowly nodded. "Stay here. I'll get us both something from the buffet while you get warm."

Rising, he touched a gentle hand to the gleaming mass of her hair, letting a soft auburn curl wrap itself around his finger. She couldn't repress a quiver of desire as his gaze captured hers. "If our host returns, I trust you will make it clear to him this time that you are otherwise engaged?"

Bewildered by her own acquiescence, Erin nonetheless nodded. She watched as he strolled away, mingling easily with the other guests, several of whom stopped him long enough to exchange a few words. Although he was too far away for her to hear what was being said, she was by no means oblivious to the sense of excitement and fascination he sparked. Even among such sophisticated, dynamic people, Mikhail stood out. It seemed as though everyone wanted to be seen with him, but some weren't satisfied simply with that. Erin stiffened when a particularly lovely blonde rested her hand on his arm, smiling up at him.

He made no immediate effort to escape her touch, but moments later he did move away, continuing toward the long rows of tables covered in white linen and loaded down with all manner of holiday delicacies. A lovely brunette in an amber silk gown cut low enough to make Erin's own décolletage look modest apparently asked him something about the caviar, which sparked yet another of his devastating smiles.

Unable to watch anymore, Erin turned away. She stared into the fire, fighting against the doubts and insecurities that were beginning to plague her. The long, hard hours she had spent working on the article had left her tired and on edge. She told herself that she was letting trivialities upset her.

Of course Mikhail was especially popular with the female guests. Why shouldn't he be? She was far too familiar with the overwhelming impact of his masculinity not to understand that other women would be similarly affected. That didn't mean she had anything to worry about.

Not for a moment did she doubt that he was an intrinsically honorable and decent man. Although the words had not yet been said, she was certain that he considered himself committed to her in a way that would transcend any attraction he might feel for another woman.

That being the case, why did she continue to be so unaccountably anxious and disheartened? On the verge of trying to discover the reason for her unease, she was forestalled by his sudden return. Carrying two large plates and accompanied by a waiter loaded down with an ice bucket, champagne bottle and two crystal goblets, he grinned at her engagingly.

"I hope you meant it when you said you were hungry."

Eyeing the more than ample selection of patés, meats, vegetables and pastries that he had chosen, she couldn't help but laugh. "If I wasn't, I would be now. That looks delicious."

The waiter opened the bottle for them, filled the tulip-shaped glasses, leaving room for the wine to breathe, and took his leave. The high-backed couch effectively screened them from the rest of the study and the rooms beyond. Snuggled close together, they shared choice tidbits while making slow but steady inroads on the champagne.

Erin put all thoughts of the scene in the garden and Mikhail's angry response firmly aside. In the relaxed, companionable way that they had shared from the beginning, they laughed and teased each other while talking about nothing in particular. Not until the strains of a waltz reached them did they leave their secluded corner, and even then, they didn't stray far.

Cradled in his arms, her head resting against the smooth velvet of his evening jacket, Erin gave herself up to the beauty of the music. They moved effortlessly together. His hand on her waist was warm and solid. The other caressed the bare expanse of her back, lingering at the particularly sensitive points that he already knew so well.

A low sigh of mingled contentment and need escaped her. Meeting his eyes, she smiled. The same sensations shone clearly in his silvery gaze. More than simply their bodies were in accord. Their very hearts and spirits seemed to float in perfect harmony.

They were still dancing when the sudden excitement of the crowd alerted them to the fact that the new year was about to arrive. Mikhail drew her into a shadowy corner of the room. The lights were turned out and a breathless hush descended, only to explode into cheers as the clock chimed midnight.

In the midst of blaring horns, popping champagne corks and laughing shouts, he captured her effortlessly in his arms. Cradling her head in a big, gentle hand, he kissed her long and deeply.

Enthralled by the taste, scent and feel of him, her senses whirled out of control. She was powerless to do anything other than respond fully with all the warmth and passion of her generous nature. Her breasts welled against the rock-hard expanse of his chest, the nipples growing insistently taut and swollen. Her slender arms wrapped around him ardently, her fingers tangling in the thick gold of his hair.

As his tongue plunged insistently into the moist cavern of her mouth all the strength seemed to go out of her. Her legs trembled and might have given way if not for the steely strength of the arms that held her. She made no protest when he pressed her to him intimately, making her acutely aware that his need matched her own.

A sudden blast of music as the band swung into a new set drew them reluctantly back to earth. Oblivious to the amused looks of the guests closest to them and the resentful stares of a few who couldn't hide their envy at the sight of such transcending passion, they gazed at each other dazedly.

Mikhail had to take a deep breath before he could speak, and even then his voice was shaky. "Let's get out of here."

Erin nodded mutely. Every part of her was crying out in need. She couldn't bear to remain there, surrounded by other people, when all she wanted was to be alone with him. Moments later she stood wrapped in her coat just inside the lobby as the doorman flagged down a cab. When it pulled up to the curb, Mikhail helped her in before sliding in next to her and giving the driver their address.

They rode in silence without looking at each other. Once Erin glanced up to see the driver watching them with concern. She smiled faintly, guessing that he thought the couple in the back seat had argued and felt sorry for anyone starting the new year that way. If only he knew, she thought impishly. The sheer, over-whelming force of their desire compelled them to re-frain from touching each other, even with their eyes, until they were safely hidden away from all the rest of the world.

Once they were inside the apartment, she deliber-ately delayed the moment of their coming together. After carefully hanging up her coat, she moved around the living room, pulling down shades, tidying a pile of magazines, even fluffing the pillows on the couch. She was just reaching for a file that needed to be returned to her briefcase when a bronzed hand closed gently but firmly around her wrist.

Mikhail had come up behind her so silently that she gasped. The sound was abruptly cut off as, without giving her a chance to protest, he led her purposefully down the corridor and into his bedroom. The room was dark, and there was a definite chill in the air. But that wasn't what caused Erin to tremble. It was the look in his eyes, the half-menacing, half-tender gaze of the fully aroused male that made the breath catch in her throat.

Unfastening his bow tie, he strode toward her. When only inches separated them, he muttered, "Take off that dress."

Startled, she stared up at him doubtfully. Was this apparently fierce determination, so far removed from the gentle, tender lover that she knew, some sort of joke?

Seeing her disbelief, Mikhail moved quickly to convince her that he was utterly serious. After tossing his jacket on the chair beside the bed, he began to unbutton his shirt as he said, "I am not teasing you, Erin. There's simply no way I can love you slowly and patiently tonight. I can't wait that long. So unless you want that very beautiful dress removed precipitously, I suggest you get out of it now."

Gulping, she realized that he meant what he said. It was on the tip of her tongue to object, to tell him that she wasn't about to be treated to any show of roughness, when she stopped herself. Mikhail wouldn't hurt her, she was certain of that. So why pretend that they didn't both want the same thing with equal urgency?

The zipper gave way smoothly beneath her quick tug. A shrug of her shoulders was all that was needed to send the dress slipping to the floor. The instant it fell, she realized that she had forgotten all about the silk stockings she was wearing and the lacy scrap of a garter belt that held them in place. Combined with her half-cup bra and tiny bikini panties, they gave her an alluringly sensual air that wasn't lost on Mikhail.

His eyes ran over her so hungrily that she felt almost scorched by them. The heavy gold cuff links he had just removed were dropped swiftly on the bedside table as he reached for her. Through the shirt that hung open to the waist she could see the bronze skin of his massive chest, thickly covered with golden hair. The muscles of his powerful arms rippled sinuously against her softness.

"So beautiful..." he groaned, letting his callused palms run over her demandingly.

Erin trembled beneath his touch. Caught up in the waves of desire pounding through her, she was barely aware that he had insistently unclipped her bra and pulled it from her. The tiny clasps of the garter belt didn't yield as easily, and frustrated, he drew back slightly. Against her mouth he demanded, "It's sexy as hell, but take it off."

She did as she said, her eyes never leaving him as he swiftly unfastened his slacks and slipped out of them. His briefs followed immediately, leaving him a bronzed giant standing naked in the faint light filtering in from the hallway.

Erin forced herself to stand perfectly still as he approached her again. His big hands slid down the vulnerable line of her back and beneath the rim of her last garment to squeeze and knead her buttocks compellingly. Vividly aware of his strength and of the urgency of his desire, she cried out softly as he lifted her, and wrapped both her legs around his waist as he carried her to the bed.

Even as they fell onto it, he was stripping the fragile lace from her. He had said that he couldn't wait, and she believed him, so it came as a great shock when she realized that despite the strength of his need he was determined to ensure her own arousal.

His mouth was warm and gentle as it followed the slender line of her throat, his tongue darting out to taste the sweet hollow at the base of her collarbone before continuing on downward the cleft separating her breasts, where his locket still rested. His fingers traced all the way around the delicately carved gold before stroking the fullness of her nipples.

"Mikhail...please..."

His only response was a low growl. She could feel the tremors wracking his powerful body as he strove to control his own passion while fueling hers. Not that any such effort was needed. She was already on fire for him, almost mindless from the currents of pleasure darting through her. When his mouth claimed the taut peak of her breast she moaned softly. Each swollen peak was tenderly suckled before at last his mouth drifted further down her body, lingering on the soft incline of her waist, the indentation of her navel and the flat plane of her abdomen.

Twisting beneath him, unable to endure much more, Erin cried out softly. Mikhail glanced up for a moment, his eyes locking with hers as he deliberately confirmed her surrender. When he moved again an instant later it was to bring them together with a shattering power that reached to the very depths of her soul.

Far away in the back of her mind she was conscious of an added element in their lovemaking that made it different from any that had gone before. It was as though Mikhail were deliberately sealing his possession of her, branding her as his own in a way that she would never be able to erase.

The power of his movements combined with the fiery tenderness of his restraint as he deliberately held himself back until her own pleasure crested, banishing any chance she might have had of resenting his actions. She could only yield totally, finding in absolute surrender a fulfillment beyond anything she could ever have imagined.

In the instant when the world dissolved around her in a blazing explosion of light and sound, Mikhail was with her fully. He cried her name deep into her mouth as his passion spent itself.

Clinging to each other, they slid almost instantly into sleep. Their bodies didn't fully separate, even through the long hours of the night, as they lay entangled in each other's arms, their breaths mingling as naturally as their dreams.

Chapter Thirteen

It was still well before dawn when Erin awoke. She stirred reluctantly, unwilling to lose the delicious sense of well-being and security that filled her. Only gradually did her sleep-dazed mind clear sufficiently for her to acknowledge certain less serene feelings.

She was lying naked under the sheets, her body still half covered by Mikhail's long, hard length. One sinewy thigh was thrown over hers, and a bronzed hand rested near her breast. The soft sound of his breathing reverberated through her. Moving slightly, she gazed down at him.

A lock of golden hair fell across his forehead above eyes shielded by closed lids and inordinately thick lashes. His lips were slightly parted, the hard lines of his face relaxed. He looked utterly at peace and almost shockingly vulnerable.

All the vast love she felt for him welled up in her, and her hand moved lightly to trace the ridge of scar tissue on his back. A quiver of pain ran through her as she deliberately forced herself to think of all that he had suffered. His very survival was a miracle. That he had also emerged from what was truly hell on earth with his mind intact and his will unbroken was a rare testimony to the power of the human spirit.

In the days since they had become lovers she had carefully kept from thinking about how his experiences might have marked him. With his ready adaptation to his new life, his colloquial English and his obvious ability to successfully compete in the sophisticated world of the wealthy and powerful, it was very easy to think of him as someone who had always been on the winning side. But that was wrong. More than anyone else she had ever known, Mikhail was all too familiar with defeat, and even death.

How did he reconcile the extreme changes in circumstance that he had experienced over such a short period of time? Or did he even try? Wasn't it more reasonable to believe that he was simply existing from moment to moment until the shock of being lifted from one world to another eased somewhat.

And when that happened, when the inevitable day arrived and he was able to take a close look at his personal life beyond the needs of his country, how would she fit into his thoughts? Would he feel compelled to remain with her because of the intimacy they had shared? Would the love that she felt for him become simply the walls of a new prison that in the end would be as bitterly hated as any he had known before?

Tears misted her emerald eyes as she forced herself to confront the doubts and insecurities that had finally begun to surface the night before at the party. She had no difficulty in recapturing the image of Mikhail surrounded by a crowd of beautiful, adoring women. Nor could she deny the fact that any number of them would be only too willing to take her place in his bed and his life. The stubborn pride that had carried her so far in her profession tempted her to do everything possible to keep him for herself. But did she have that right? Didn't simple human decency demand that he be allowed a choice?

After slipping out of bed she scooped up the clothes that lay discarded on the floor and padded down the hall to her own room. Moments later she was in the shower, scrubbing herself vigorously and trying hard not to think about the demands of her conscience.

Wrapped in a robe, her face free of makeup and her freshly washed hair hanging loosely around her shoulders, she was standing at the kitchen counter making coffee when Mikhail appeared. Despite the early morning chill he was wearing only pajama bottoms that rode low on his lean hips. He ran a hand absently through his rumpled hair as he smiled at her.

"How come you got up so early?"

Erin forced herself to look away, unwilling to be drawn yet again by the potent force of his attractiveness just when she most needed to keep a firm hold on herself.

"It isn't really. It just seems that way because we got to bed so late."

"Hmm...." He laughed softly, and his arms slipped round her waist to draw her back against him. "And it was much later than that when we finally fell asleep." His lips nuzzled the warm curve of her shoulder. "I can't remember the last time I slept so well."

"Me neither," Erin admitted, "but..."

"But what?" he murmured distractedly, his attention focused on the ultrasensitive nape of her neck, where he dropped feather-light kisses.

Twisting, she tried to elude his grasp, but he took her movements for playfulness and didn't release her. "M-Mikhail, please....I have a lot to do."

The serious, almost desperate, note in her voice reached him. His devastatingly gentle caresses stopped as he looked up, puzzled. "Erin, what is the matter?"

"Nothing.... I told you, I just have a lot to do."

It was more difficult than she could have imagined to meet his gaze as he studied her intently, but she managed to do so for long enough to convince him that she meant what she said. For a perilous moment she thought that he intended to press her for an explanation of her sudden withdrawal. When he didn't, she breathed a sign of relief, even as she realized that the reprieve was only temporary. Mikhail was far too perceptive not to sense the tension building within her, but apparently he was willing to wait at least a little while in the hope that she would reveal the cause voluntarily.

He let her go and poured two mugs of coffee as he asked, "So, what's all this urgent business you have to take care of?"

"Well, to start with, we...uh...have to take down the tree."

It sounded absurd even to her, but Erin held on to the excuse for dear life. She simply wasn't ready to talk to him yet, not before she had a chance to get her scattered thoughts in order.

"All right," he said at last, "but first perhaps we had both better get some clothes on."

Erin nodded, well aware of how difficult it was to stand so close to him without giving in to the temptation to ignore the dictates of her conscience and sink again into the radiant glow of pleasure that they had basked in the night before. At least when there were more layers of clothing between them, she might have a fighting chance of sticking to her resolve.

She took her coffee back to the bedroom and pulled a clean pair of jeans from the closet, along with a bulky sweater that fit her so loosely that she usually didn't bother to wear a bra with it. But, unwilling to dare fate any more than she could help, she deliberately put one on. After pulling her hair back in a ponytail she added a faint touch of lip gloss before returning to the living room.

Mikhail joined her a short time later, after showering and shaving. The utter relaxation she had noted in him earlier was gone, replaced by a wary watchfulness that tore at her heart. The last thing she wanted to do was to cause him pain for any reason, but she suspected that however carefully she phrased what was on her mind, he wasn't going to take it well.

In silence they stripped the ornaments from the tree and stored them carefully away in their boxes before removing the strands of lights. Mindful of the needles that were falling onto the rug, they tied the branches with cord before removing the tree from its stand. Erin held the door as Mikhail carried the tree out to the service elevator.

While he disposed of it downstairs she vacuumed up the needles and replaced the furniture in their accustomed places. There was always a certain sadness in throwing out the remains of a Christmas tree, but she had too much else on her mind to dwell on it. All it really meant to her was that the holiday was over and that everyday life was once again taking over.

By the time he returned, she was back in the kitchen, fixing breakfast. Mikhail joined her there, but didn't speak until they were seated at the table. In between bites of ham omelets and cranberry muffins they talked about the party, recent news events, anything other than what was uppermost in both their minds.

He had cleared away the dishes and started another pot of coffee before at last he said, "Erin, I think you will admit that I am generally a patient man." A faint gleam shone in his eyes as they both remembered that he had been anything but the night before. Ruefully he admitted, "But you strain my endurance to the limit. Please tell me what has happened to the warm, loving woman I held in my arms only a few hours ago."

Now that the moment was upon her, she was hard pressed not to retreat. Only the undeniable knowledge of how much he meant to her, and of how much more important his happiness was to her than her own, gave her the courage to face him.

"Nothing's happened to me," she said softly, "except that I've been doing some thinking, and I've finally reached some conclusions we have to talk about."

Mikhail nodded curtly, but said nothing, as they took their coffee into the living room and settled down in front of the cold fireplace. Erin curled up on the couch as far away from him as she could get, aware of what her body language was telling him but unable to prevent the silent communication that made him frown.

Realizing that the situation was only going to get worse the more she delayed, she took a deep breath. "Mikhail, last night at the party...when I saw you with all those other people...I realized that ever since you got here you've had almost no opportunity to get out and make new acquaintances without interference from anyone else."

He opened his mouth to interrupt, but she went on hastily. "Interference, even when it's perfectly well meant, can do you a lot of harm. I can't really imagine how I would feel in your place, but I'm sure that I'd be very vulnerable to being...taken over by someone who might not even realize what was happening, but who could still prevent me from building other relationships that might really be better for me."

"What on earth are you talking about...?"

"Please, let me finish. What I'm trying to say is that even though you've come to...mean a great deal to me, and even though I want more than anything to believe that we can have a future together, I'm afraid that unless you have a chance to consider alternatives you'll mistake gratitude for love and end up feeling trapped and resentful. I just couldn't...bear that...."

Her voice broke. She had to duck her head to keep him from seeing the sudden tears that threatened to spill from her eyes. For a woman who had always prided herself on being able to control her emotions under even the most trying circumstances, she was having remarkably little success maintaining even the slightest degree of detachment.

The utterly feminine part of her that had come to the fore in recent days was putting up a fierce struggle against the facade of calmness she was struggling desperately to maintain. Instincts she had paid very little attention to until Mikhail brought them vividly to life were demanding that she stop such nonsense at once and enjoy whatever he was willing to give no matter what the reason.

But she couldn't do that: not because she wasn't tempted—the urge to do so was all but irresistible—but because she would have to live with herself afterward, and with the knowledge that she had violated her own fundamental principles out of purely selfish motives.

Yet even the knowledge of how guilty she would feel might not have been enough to stop her had it not been for the single, overriding fact of her love for him. For the first time in her life she truly understood what love between a man and a woman really meant. Because of it she could put Mikhail's well-being ahead of her own, knowing even as she did so that, however painful the outcome, she would never regret having done so.

Forcing herself to look at him, she said as calmly as possible, "What I'm trying to say is that, before our relationship goes any further, I think you should give yourself the opportunity to meet other women and get to know them. It's not impossible that you may find you don't really feel for me the way you think you do. You might even discover that you . . . care for someone else more. . . ."

She stopped, unable to go any further. Her fingers were clenched around her coffee mug so tightly that they ached, but she didn't notice. The hurt welling up in her heart blocked out everything else.

Mikhail was staring at her in genuine confusion. He shook his head bewilderedly. "I don't think I understand what you're saying. . . . You want me to go out with other women?"

"Y-yes. . . ."

"To date them?"

"Yes."

"Perhaps take them to bed?"

Erin bit her lip so hard that she tasted blood. Her voice was little more than a whisper as she said, "You seem to have gotten the idea. Surely it isn't necessary to go over all the details?"

"Indulge me. After all, I'm a novice at this sort of thing and frankly, I feel as though you just yanked my feet right out from under me."

His sarcasm drilled through her with razor sharpness. Wincing, she murmured, "You know perfectly well I've never been involved in anything like this...overwhelming either. It's cruel to suggest otherwise.''

"But it isn't cruel of you to suggest you want to break off our relationship?''

"That's not what I said! I just want you to have a choice...."

Mikhail's eyes flashed dangerously. He stood up, then strode over to the fireplace to stare into it silently. The rigid line of his back warned her that he was growing angrier by the moment. When he turned to her again his hands were jammed into the pockets of his jeans, and he was scowling heavily.

"I would never have imagined you were capable of this, Erin. You seemed far too honest to play such callous games.''

Baffled, she shook her head. "I'm not...I don't understand what you're saying.''

"I'm saying this whole charade wasn't necessary! If you wanted to break off with me, you had only to say so. I'm not claiming I would have liked it, but at least I would not have lost respect for you, as I have now.''

Unable to believe what she was hearing, Erin rose shakily. "You must have misunderstood me. All I'm saying is that I'm concerned about you and our feelings. I'm not playing any sort of game!''

"Aren't you?'' he sneered. "I really missed the whole point of that episode on the terrace, didn't I? I actually believed there was nothing to it.''

"There wasn't! Mikhail, please, you aren't making any sense."

"On the contrary, this is the most sensible I've been since I first set eyes on you. When I think how easily you affected me..."

He broke off, turning away again as though he couldn't bear the sight of her. Grimly he demanded, "Last night, when we got home, did you decide you were in the mood for a farewell performance, Erin? A little something to tide you over until Kent could step in?"

"That's disgusting! What on earth is happening to you? You're twisting everything I've said and done."

Angrier than she had ever been before in her life, Erin grabbed hold of his shoulder, trying to force him to face her. "I'm not going to listen to that kind of talk from anyone, no matter how much I lo—no matter what."

The icy look in his eyes when he finally deigned to look at her made her throat clench. Whatever was going through his mind, it was very ugly and very dangerous. She had only to meet his gaze to realize that.

In the back of her mind she remembered the image that she'd had of him that first evening at the airport. He had appeared to her then as an immensely proud, fierce man who, no matter how weakened and hurt, would still be capable of exacting a full measure of revenge from those he considered his enemies.

Since then that initial impression had been overlaid by far gentler, more tender memories. She had temporarily lost sight of the remorseless strength of his character until his anger was suddenly turned against her.

Too late, she realized the battle he was waging to hold on to some remnant of his self-control. His powerful hands lashed out to seize her arms, not holding her painfully, but so firmly that she had no hope of escape.

"Don't worry, Erin," he growled when he saw the spark of fear in her eyes. "You won't have to listen to me much longer. There is very little more I wish to say to you, except that I hope you do not discover that the payment for your story was too steep. Undoubtedly Kent will reward you far more generously. But then, you will at least be going to him with enough experience to be able to please a man."

His hands tightened for just a moment, almost but not quite enough to leave bruises. "Don't say it," he warned as she opened her mouth to attempt a last, desperate denial of his accusations. "I cannot be sure how I will react if I have to listen to more of your lies. Why I thought you were different is beyond me. I should have realized it wasn't possible for you to have come to care for me as deeply as you seemed to in such a short time."

He laughed bitterly, the sound echoing the pain stamped on his hard features. "I thought I had learned some difficult lessons in the past, but this is by far the worst. However, at least you have been kind enough to point out exactly how I might console myself.''

Letting her go so abruptly that she had to catch hold of the mantel to keep from falling, he stalked away toward the guest room. Over his shoulder he said, ''Be assured I intend to take your advice. I have no doubt several of the lovely ladies I met yesterday evening will be able to appreciate my company, despite how quickly you have tired of it.''

Behind him Erin slumped against the couch, her eyes wide and dazed. Instinctively she wrapped her arms around herself in a futile effort to stop the trembling that threatened to shake her body apart. The full enormity of his suspicion and anger overwhelmed her. She couldn't make the slightest sound in her own defense, nor was she willing to try.

In her grief-stricken state she saw only one explanation for Mikhail's behavior. He could never have felt for her as she did for him, or he would never have been able to turn on her so totally and with such vile accusations.

Unable to move, she was barely aware of the sounds from the bedroom or of his sudden return. Not until he was standing in front of her, fully dressed and with his duffel bag once more slung over his shoulder, did she manage to look up.

''The rest of my things will be out of here by tomorrow.''

She continued to stare dazedly at him, hoping against hope that the angry apparition in front of her would vanish and in its place would be the gentle, caring man she had come to know.

But the lover she had cherished was gone without a trace. There was nothing left but a cruel, hurting stranger whose very words tore at her heart. And then he was gone too, vanishing out the front door without a single backward look.

A slow, trembling breath escaped her. She was distantly aware that she was behaving like the victim of a traumatic accident. Shock was settling in, leaving her mercifully numb. She barely made it to the couch before all the strength went out of her. For uncounted hours she remained there, oblivious to the hot trickling of tears down her ashen cheeks.

Only when the dim winter light had faded and the room was bathed in darkness did sensation begin to return, and with it came pain beyond anything she had ever known.

Chapter Fourteen

"Mr. Kent wants to see you," Jenny said softly, her eyes dark with concern as she surveyed the pale, quiet young woman sitting at the desk. The first week of the new year was supposed to be filled with renewed energy and purpose, but Erin clearly lacked both. Jenny had never seen her so downhearted. She looked almost . . . breakable.

"Right away, I suppose," Erin murmured, glancing up from the article she had been diligently trying to read for the last hour. The neat lines of type kept dissolving in front of her eyes to be replaced by the image of Mikhail's face, stiff with anger and bitter accusation.

"No, actually, he just said you should stop by whenever you had a moment." Though she tried, Jenny couldn't keep the surprise from her voice. She had never seen the managing editor in such a quiet, almost subdued mood. Even Sheila was unable to explain the sudden change from his usual brash, demanding self.

That startling statement reached Erin even through the anguished haze that had enveloped her from the moment when Mikhail had walked out of her apartment and her life. Absently she said, "Is Derek all right?"

"Uh...I'm not sure.... Sheila thinks he may be coming down with the flu or something. He's been so quiet."

A slight frown appeared above Erin's darkly shadowed emerald eyes. "That doesn't sound like him. Maybe Sheila's right."

"Well, anyway, whether he's sick or not, he'd like to see you."

Erin shrugged. She closed the folder, then stood up and pulled on her suit jacket, though it didn't quite disguise the new fragility of her form. Her face was pale, the almost-translucent skin drawn tautly over her delicate bones. Deep shadows were visible beneath her eyes, despite her efforts to hide them with makeup.

Sheila smiled tentatively when Erin entered the managing editor's outer office, and one look was enough to worry her. "Is everything okay?" she asked softly.

Erin forced herself to smile reassuringly. She could barely confront the shambles of her relationship with Mikhail in her own mind. Talking about it would make it real in a way she could not yet endure. "Of course, or it will be, once I find out what our great leader wants."

Sheila took the hint and went off to announce Erin's arrival. Erin sat down on one of the Ultrasuede couches positioned around the room and tried to concentrate on a magazine. Since there was no set time for her appointment, she expected to wait. But the secretary came back at once to show her in before carefully closing the door and returning to her desk.

Derek was in his usual spot behind the marble-top table, his jacket off and his shirt sleeves rolled up. He looked tired, and beneath his perpetual tan his face was almost wan. A spark of concern ran through Erin even as she told herself that she had no reason to be solicitous of him after the stunt he had pulled at the party. But try as she might, she couldn't blame him for precipitating the confrontation with Mikhail. If their relationship had been all that it should have, nothing he had said or done would have had any effect.

Settled across from him in one of the visitor's chairs, she waited for Derek to explain the summons to his office. The delay struck her as unlike him. She was used to a barrage of instructions, questions and complaints with—on very rare occasions—a grudging compliment tossed in.

When he finally spoke, after scrutinizing her thoroughly, his voice was low and hesitant. "Are you feeling all right, Hennessey? You look like hell."

For the first time in days some remnant of spirit stirred within her. "Thanks a lot. That's just what I needed to hear this morning."

Derek managed a faint grin, not up to standard, but still somehow reassuring. "Now, don't get your Irish up. I just don't want one of my star reporters coming down with something when I'm about to give her a new assignment."

Perking up slightly, Erin tried to show at least a flicker of interest, but without much success.

"Don't overwhelm me with enthusiasm," Derek muttered. "I couldn't take it this morning."

Despite her resolve not to be concerned about him, she caught herself murmuring, "Speaking of coming down with something, you don't look all that great yourself."

"So what if I don't? You should be delighted to see me laid low."

Erin's eyes widened slightly. Implicit in his tone was the suggestion that her pleasure would be justified. Was he actually admitting that he had behaved badly?

"Look," she said slowly, "if you're talking about what happened at the party, just put it out of your mind. I'm certainly not going to mention it to anyone."

Derek grimaced. With an effort he met her eyes. "I never thought you would. But I still want you to know I'm sorry. You didn't deserve to be put on the spot like that."

The last thing Erin had expected from her brash, self-assured editor was an apology. It took her a moment to come to grips with it. "Consider it forgotten, okay?"

He nodded gratefully. "Thanks, but just one more thing. If I caused trouble for you with Demertov, I'll do whatever I can to patch it up. Maybe I should talk to him, or..."

"No! That isn't necessary. You didn't cause anything."

Derek looked at her doubtfully. "I'm relieved to hear it. Then you two are getting alone fine?"

"Uh...well..."

"That's what I thought." He shook his head ruefully. "I would never have pegged you for the kind who could be brought down by a man, Hennessey. Where's that old Irish spirit?"

"I think it went back to the emerald isle," Erin muttered noncommittally. Though she was genuinely over whatever anger she had felt toward Derek, she still wasn't prepared to discuss her personal problems with him.

He sensed her reluctance, and with a surprising degree of tact he changed the subject. "We were talking about your new assignment."

Desperate for something to distract her from her anguished thoughts, she would have welcomed any absorbing task. But the one Derek offered astounded her.

"Do you remember a few months ago when you drew up an outline for a series of stories about the various international organizations affiliated with the U.N., what they're supposed to be doing and what, if anything, they actually accomplish?"

Erin nodded silently. She had no trouble recalling the outline, or the fact that Derek had found the idea interesting, while doubting her ability to carry it through. He had seemed inclined to give the assignment to one of the senior political reporters, and she had reconciled herself with poor grace to that inevitability.

"I want you to get started on it right away so that we can begin running it in the first February issue."

"What made you change your mind?"

The blunt question was answered in kind. "Your coverage of Demertov. That convinced me that you're capable of the type of sustained effort and perceptive analysis this assignment will require. Plus the fact that, while you were always a good writer, you seem to have crossed over the barrier that separates the good from the outstanding."

Erin swallowed hard, more moved by his praise than she cared to admit. "Thanks, Derek," she said softly. "At least something worthwhile came out of it all."

He shrugged off her appreciation. "I figure I owe you one. Now that we're even again, I can be as tough on you as ever."

She couldn't help but laugh. "That's good. If you'd kept on being so mild and reasonable, none of us would have known what to make of you."

"Had you stumped, huh?"

"I'm afraid so. Crusty, hard-nosed editors aren't supposed to suddenly turn into softies."

"Don't worry, I'm sure I'll be back to normal in no time."

"That's good . . . I think," Erin teased. She got up to go, feeling far more kindly disposed toward him than she had when she came in. His apology had made her realize that people were rarely as easy to predict as they might seem. Granted, Derek would probably always have a broad streak of self-centeredness in his nature, but at least he was occasionally able to temper it with consideration for others.

She had no illusions that he would have given her the assignment simply to make peace between them, but neither did she doubt that he had put some effort into thinking of a concrete way to express his regret, rather than merely passing it off with words. While nothing could erase her abiding sorrow over Mikhail, Derek's thoughtfulness had at least let a little ray of light into her life.

Some of the customary energy and excitement she felt when tackling any new project were making themselves felt as she went back to her office to immerse herself in the assignment.

By midafternoon she had set up several appointments and was busy bringing together essential background information from the magazine's archives. Caught up as she was in the familiar hum of activity, she didn't notice Sheila's arrival in her small office until the secretary coughed politely.

"Things seem to be getting back to normal around here," the other woman said. "You're pounding away at the typewriter, and our glorious leader is once more snapping and growling at everyone."

Erin grinned, pleased to hear that Derek's brief bout of conscience wasn't being unduly extended. "If you've come down here to hide out, be prepared to help. I've got a ton of information to plow through."

"Far be it for me to get between a reporter and her backgrounding. I just came to add these to the pile." She dropped a handful of folders on top of a precariously balanced stack. "Derek thought these might be helpful."

"Translation: He wants to make sure I won't overlook the points covered in them."

"Right in one. Now, on to more serious matters. Am I correct in thinking that you have a particular fondness for pre-Colombian art?"

"It's my single most expensive weakness," Erin admitted dryly.

"Good, because Sidney and I have tickets to a preview of the new show that's opening at the Fiske Gallery. Want to go?"

"Do I ever! It's being billed as the finest collection of pre-Colombian art ever assembled outside Latin America. Dare I ask how Sidney got added to the guest list?"

"Who knows? With the triple life my dear husband leads as a would-be actor, part-time model and possibly the most popular substitute teacher in the city's high schools, he's liable to have come up with the tickets anywhere. He wants to go because there's some big deal producer who's planning to attend. I'm going to protect him from the fairer sex, since they have a distressing habit of drooling all over him. Somebody really ought to come with us who's actually interested in art."

Sheila's offhand explanation didn't fool Erin. Beneath both their stunningly attractive exteriors, she and the improbably named Sidney were warm, thoughtful people. He had probably accepted the tickets just so they could get her out for a few hours and cheer her up.

It would have been almost as tactless to reveal that she had seen through their ploy as to refuse the invitation. Gratefully Erin accepted. She dreaded the thought of another evening alone at home, when not even her new assignment would be able to keep her heartache at bay.

Leaving the office shortly after five o'clock, she opted to walk uptown to her apartment. The weather was cold, but she was warmly dressed in a cashmere wraparound coat and lined boots. Enveloped by the stream of people emerging from the buildings, she let herself be carried along. For once the anonymity of the city was welcome. The crowd absorbed her without a flicker of interest. Automatically matching its fast pace, she kept her mind resolutely blank as exercise soothed away some measure of her tension.

By the time she got home, she was actually feeling relaxed and looking forward to the show. After changing quickly into a simple ankle-length black sheath she coiled the heavy weight of her hair into a neat chignon at the nape of her neck, freshened her makeup and, as a finishing touch, sprayed on her favorite perfume.

The results weren't bad. Considering how poorly she had slept in the last few days and how little she had eaten, she looked better than she had any right to. Vast quantities of tears had left her eyes with a luminescent glow. Her face was pale, but that only emphasized the purity of her complexion. Even the air of fragility that she couldn't hide made her seem softer and more delicate.

Telling herself that she could take a certain pride in being able to so effectively mask the emotional turmoil seething inside her, she went downstairs to wait for Sheila and Sidney.

They arrived moments later, pulling up in the bright yellow Edsel that was Sidney's pride and joy. He had found the car in a junkyard some ten years before and spent a good part of the decade restoring it to its former glory. Now that the model had become something of a status symbol, he'd turned down numerous offers to buy it for impressive amounts of money. Sidney was nothing if not stalwart in his affections. Only Sheila counted for more with him than his Edsel.

"Hop in," he invited as the traffic behind him began to blare in protest.

Sliding in beside Sheila, Erin was quickly caught up in the couple's cheerful chatter about the day's events. Sidney had been on a shoot for a dog-food commercial. He regaled them with descriptions of the petulant collies who had refused to eat even in the face of dire threats to their lives.

"I keep telling my agent I'm the soulful, indoor type, but he keeps getting me jobs where I have to look rugged and put up with animals. Last time it was a pinto pony I swear was out for blood. I couldn't sit down for a week."

"Serves you right for looking like you do," Sheila informed him unsympathetically. "If you would only gain thirty pounds and lose some hair, people would take you seriously."

"I doubt it," Sidney griped. "Whenever I open my mouth to say something even half-way intelligent, I get the feeling I'm really shocking everyone. Just the other day I got lavishly complimented for being so articulate."

"What's wrong with that?" Erin asked.

"I was ordering lunch at the time." Stentorially he intoned, "Gimme a pastrami on rye, hold the mustard, and a cola to go."

Laughing, they pulled into a garage, where Sidney negotiated briefly to make sure the Edsel would be treated with proper respect. That task completed, he offered an arm to each lady. "Shall we?"

The gallery was already crowded, but a quick glance around was enough to tell Erin that she was one of the few people there who was actually interested in the exhibit. The rest had come to see and be seen. Many of the same faces she had noticed at Derek's party were once again in evidence. Or at least it seemed that way. After a while all the beautiful people began to look somewhat alike.

Leaving Sheila and Sidney chatting with the producer he had wanted to meet, Erin wandered off to enjoy the artwork. The evocative textures and colors of the pottery absorbed her so completely that she lost all awareness of her surroundings. The sights and sounds of the party faded away, becoming no more than a blurred backdrop.

Part of her pleasure in the exhibit came from the awareness that she was actually enjoying herself. That was a victory of sorts. Though she wasn't so foolish as to believe she would ever be able to get over Mikhail, at least she was still capable of appreciating the beauty of the world beyond the darkened limits of her own life.

Content to remain on her own in the midst of the preening, posturing crowd, she wandered along the fringes of the large room. The attentive looks of several men who would have liked to make her acquaintance passed her by completely. Her very lack of interest spurred their curiosity, but she remained oblivious to her own impact. She thought of nothing but the exhibit, until a prickling at the back of her neck distracted her and she turned to find Mikhail standing near the gallery entrance, staring at her.

He was dressed once again in evening clothes that emphasized the rugged masculinity of his build and the golden virility of his chiseled features. To Erin it was impossible to believe that any man had ever looked more desirable. But she still couldn't help but note that his burnished skin was pulled even more tautly than usual over his high-boned cheeks and that his face looked slightly drawn, as though he hadn't been sleeping or eating well.

With him was a lovely young blond woman who she vaguely remembered from the New Year's party. Muffy somebody or other. Tall and slim, she had the elegantly cool beauty of an aristocrat. The deceptively simple white dress she wore looked almost demure; until she moved. Then it parted at the sides to reveal slender, tanned legs clear to the thigh.

As she gazed up at Mikhail Erin's throat tightened. For just a moment she allowed herself to meet the hard glitter of his silvery eyes. The mingled pain and pleasure she saw there startled her. He seemed glad to see her, but reluctant to admit as much, even to himself.

In the next instant any softness she thought she had glimpsed in him vanished. His expression became shuttered, revealing nothing. Puzzled as to what could have caused the sudden change, it took her a moment to realize that Sidney had come up behind her.

Even to somebody who knew him as well as she did, he was breathtakingly handsome. His movie-star good looks, combined with obvious intelligence and self-deprecating humor, set him apart in any crowd. As he smiled at her she was aware of several women standing nearby who were torn between the urge to drink in the sight of so much sheer male splendor and the need to shoot daggers at the innocent object of his attention.

"Sheila and I are about to tackle the buffet," he said. "How about joining us?"

Standing across the room, Mikhail couldn't make out his words, but he was clearly conscious of the friendly warmth underlying the exchange. Erin glanced back at him in time to see the stiffening of his broad shoulders and the anger that flitted briefly across his face before his expression became coldly contemptuous.

Fully aware of how he had misinterpreted the situation, Erin was torn between rage at the unfairness of his judgment and an obstinate determination that he not see how much he had hurt her.

Beaming a smile at Sidney that could have melted an iceberg, she took his arm, turned her back on Mikhail and walked away.

Chapter Fifteen

"I'm in the mood for Japanese food today," Derek said. "Is that okay with you?"

Erin nodded absently. It didn't make any difference to her what sort of restaurant they went to for the usual once-a-month lunch the managing editor felt compelled to have with each member of his staff. She doubted that she would be eating much anyway.

In the week since her unexpected encounter with Mikhail at the gallery, any hope she had cherished that time would ease her anguish had evaporated. Far from lessening the sorrow she felt, each day seemed to bring only further reminders of how much she loved him and how empty her life was without him.

The restaurant was just around the corner from *Focus*'s offices. Erin had been there several times before and had always enjoyed the subdued ambiance and excellent food, but that afternoon she was barely aware of either.

Settled at a table near the window with a platter of Derek's favorite sushi in front of them, she made a valiant effort to throw off her dejection. The weather had turned unexpectedly warm, giving New Yorkers a brief respite from winter. Her work on the U.N. articles was going very well, so much so that she was tentatively planning a quick trip back to Wyoming to visit her folks. Her latest paycheck had reflected her new, considerably increased salary. She had promptly gone out and spent it on clothes in a futile effort to cheer herself up.

The violet wool suit and warm-pink silk blouse were part of the booty from that shopping expedition. Vibrant colors and the judicious use of makeup went a long way toward camouflaging the paleness of her complexion and the shadows under her emerald eyes, but they didn't entirely manage to fool Derek.

"Is it the new series that's keeping you up late these days, Hennessey, or have you just decided you can do without sleep?"

Erin sighed, well aware that there was no good answer to that. If she claimed to be working late every night she would be giving the impression that the assignment was too much for her to handle. If she admitted the truth, that she deliberately avoided going to bed until she was ready to drop, she would be opening the door to personal questions that she wanted desperately to avoid.

Reluctantly she said, "A bit of both, I suppose. The series is going very well, but it's also very absorbing. I lose track of the time."

Derek looked unconvinced, but apparently decided not to pursue the subject. Gesturing with his chopsticks at a particularly succulent slice of raw tuna set on a bed of vinegared rice, he said, "Why don't you try that, and while you're at it, have a beer. It wouldn't hurt you to start gaining back those pounds you've been losing."

Accepting the tidbit, which was delicious, she shrugged. "Isn't there a saying that a woman can never be too rich or too thin?"

Derek snorted derisively. "You can bet no man ever believed the second part." There was an unaccustomedly gentle light in his eye as he added, "I could point out that you're a damn good-looking woman who didn't need to lose an ounce, but since we've agreed our relationship is strictly professional, I won't."

Erin's eyes widened slightly. "You were in your high school or college debating club, weren't you?"

About to take a swallow of his beer, Derek froze. He glanced around quickly to make sure no one was listening. "Now how in hell did you figure that out?"

"Because there's a name for what you just did, mentioning something by saying you're not going to. I forget what it is, but it's an old debating technique everyone learns—*if* he belongs to a debating club." Smiling slightly, she asked, "So how come everyone thinks you did nothing but play football until you took that sportscasting job that led eventually to *Focus*?"

"Because that's what I want them to think. It's a lot easier for me to deal with the pseudo-intellectual types I encounter in this job if they think I'm strictly a dumb jock."

Delighted by her discovery, Erin couldn't resist the urge to pry a bit further. "You didn't by any chance work for your school newspaper, did you?"

"What if I did?" Derek growled, obviously chagrined at having been found out.

Taking pity on him, she relented slightly. "Don't worry, your secret is safe with me."

"It's a good thing I already know you can keep your mouth shut or you could find yourself *Focus*'s stringer in Bora Bora."

"Didn't any of those management books you're so fond of tell you not to threaten sensitive, creative types like me?"

"Actually, they never mentioned anyone like you," he shot back. "I'm convinced you're an original. Now, eat your sushi."

Grinning, she did as she said. Her appetite remained nonexistent, but the beautifully prepared Japanese food was such a treat that she couldn't resist it. They had started on their second platter of seafood when Derek asked, "Any problems with the series so far?"

"Some, but nothing I can't handle. A few of the agency heads aren't too happy about being interviewed, but they're astute enough to realize what it will look like if we run a story without their comments. One or two have tried to turn it into a public relations coup for them. That didn't continue past the point where they realized that I had done my homework and had a pretty fair idea of what they were trying to conceal. Since then, everything's been moving along fairly smoothly."

"Good. So we can still plan to take the first story to press in a couple of weeks?"

"I don't see why not."

Satisfied, Derek nodded. He waved over the kimono-clad waitress so he could order a plate of tempura and more beers. When she was gone, he leaned back in his chair and surveyed Erin quietly.

"There's something else we need to talk about."

The sudden somberness of his tone warned her that she wasn't going to like what he had to say. She was right.

"It's about Demertov."

Quickly Erin said, "I don't want to discuss him."

"Maybe not, but I still want you to hear what I have to say."

She started to shake her head, but was stopped by Derek's stern look. "This is strictly business," he insisted. "I'm not asking what went wrong between the two of you personally. I just want you to be aware that a twist has cropped up that may affect how he's viewed by both the media and the public."

Against her will she was driven to ask, "What twist?"

With maddening slowness Derek took time out to taste the tempura after it was placed before him. He grinned approvingly at the waitress before continuing. "On second thought the whole thing is just a rumor, so maybe I shouldn't say anything."

"You can't do that," Erin protested. "Out with it!"

"If you insist.... It seems that a French newspaper, one that's admittedly very leftist, has turned up a report to the effect that when Mikhail was in prison he collaborated with the authorities against his fellow inmates and members of the opposition underground. Supposedly that's the real reason why he's come here and why he seems none the worse off, despite all the horrors he supposedly endured. Furthermore, they're also going to charge that he was in fact a double agent, working for the C.I.A. at the same time as he was cooperating with his own former government. Covering his bets, so to speak.''

Shock darkened Erin's eyes to sea-green pools. Her stomach clenched tightly as all the color fled from her face, only to return an instant later in full fury. ''That's absurd! No one could believe such a lie! I know how much he suffered. I've seen the scars....''

She broke off, embarrassed. It made no difference that Derek was certainly aware of her intimate relationship with Mikhail. She still wasn't comfortable talking about it.

Tactfully ignoring her comment, he said, ''It really makes no difference whether the charge is true or not. Unless it's countered, it could do him a great deal of harm.''

Erin took a deep breath, fighting to get control of herself. All the mental and emotional barriers she had carefully erected to keep from thinking about Mikhail crumbled in an instant. The thought that he might be unjustly charged, held up to false accusations, threatened with public condemnation, was unbearable.

''It isn't fair,'' she murmured, afraid to speak above a whisper lest her outrage break free. ''He lived through years of absolute hell, and before that he was constantly on the run, never knowing what would happen from one day to the next. He had no chance for a family life, children, any of the things we all take for granted. Yet he persevered. He never gave up on himself or his beliefs. It's contemptible for anyone to suggest otherwise.''

Derek listened to her patiently. Not until she had run out of breath and was once again silent did he say quietly, ''You really think a lot of the guy, don't you?''

Unable to deny it, she nodded. Her eyes were bright with unshed tears. ''There has to be some way to prevent that story from being taken seriously.''

He shrugged doubtfully. ''I suppose there might be....''

Erin wasn't fooled by his hesitation. She knew him too well not to realize that he would never have mentioned the problem unless he had at least some idea of how to solve it. Schooling herself to patience, she waited for him to reveal it.

''To start with, Demertov has to be told, so he can prepare to rebut the charges, but there's nothing I can do,'' Derek explained slowly, ''simply because I doubt that he would believe anything I said. On the other hand, he might be inclined to listen to you....''

''Me? I'm the last person he'd believe.''

''Oh? Why's that?''

''Because he thinks...that is...'' Erin broke off. She wasn't about to burden Derek with the full story of what had happened after the party. ''Never mind. I just don't think he'd pay attention to anything I said.''

"That's too bad," Derek said regretfully. "Then I guess there's nothing we an do."

"You could get in touch with his publisher," she suggested. "Tell him what's going on and leave it up to him to tell Mikhail."

"No way! If you think I'm about to leak a story that far, you're crazy. I'm not even sure telling you was ethical. I only did it because I think Demertov deserves a break."

Stymied, Erin fell silent. She tried to come up with another alternative, but every plan she thought of had some intrinsic flaw. Finally she had to admit defeat. "All right, maybe I am the only person to tell him. But I still can't."

"Why not?"

"Because I don't even know where he's living."

Her boss grinned unsympathetically. "So what? You're a reporter, aren't you? Put that well-honed investigative ability to work. I bet you'll have his address by this afternoon."

Erin wasn't anywhere near as confident, but she wasn't about to admit that. Back in her office half an hour later, she shut the door and began making phone calls. Her first try was Mikhail's editor. The woman listened politely to her explanation of who she was and what she wanted, but absolutely refused to comply.

"I'm sorry, Ms. Hennessey, but I cannot release Mr. Demertov's address to anyone. I wouldn't do so with any author, but in his case security is a particular concern. I'm sure you understand.''

Erin did, reluctantly. She hung up and called Mikhail's agent. There the response was even firmer. ''Not a chance. If you want to leave a message for him with me, I'd be glad to relay it. But that's the best I can do.''

It wasn't good enough. The message could get lost or Mikhail might simply choose to ignore it. Precious hours, even days, could be lost while she waited to hear from him. Combing through her files on him, she tried futilely to come up with another lead. Nothing. He simply hadn't had enough of a chance to put down roots yet. A check with her contact at the credit bureau confirmed that all his charge cards carried the address of his publisher. The stores she knew he had shopped at had already delivered all his purchases and been paid in full. They had no reason to know his current whereabouts. Calls to the top hotels in town turned up the fact that he had spent several nights at one of them after leaving her apartment, but he had checked out the week before and left no forwarding address.

In exasperation she finally called Derek. After explaining the problem she said, ''There was a blonde at your New Year's party. Tall, slender...''

He chuckled. ''There were at least a dozen of them.''

"No, this one was different. I'm pretty sure she's not a model or an actress. She's beautiful enough for either, but she seems a little too aloof for that. My guess is she comes from money, probably serves on charity committees, that sort of thing. I think I heard someone call her Muffy."

"Melinda Trina Bradshaw," he said instantly. "She hates to be called Muffy. Hasn't answered to it since she was twelve. Very old money and very good legs. What about her?"

"I saw her the other night with Mikhail at a gallery. So maybe if I could get in touch with her, she would know where he is."

Derek didn't seem any happier than she was about the beautiful blond socialite dating Mikhail, but he was able to provide the young lady's address and phone number.

Erin took a break before trying to reach her. Sipping a tepid cup of coffee, she made a deliberate effort to get control of her wayward thoughts and emotions. Pride demanded that she give no hint of how deeply she loved Mikhail and how hurt she was by his involvement with another woman.

When she was certain that she could manage at least a semblance of professional detachment, she picked up the phone again. Ms. Bradshaw, her housekeeper announced, did happen to be at home. If Erin would wait a moment, she would tell her who was calling.

The warm, cheerful voice that promptly came on the line was a surprise. Whatever else she was, Melinda Trina Bradshaw was at least not overly taken with herself. She listened to Erin courteously before she said, "Yes, I do know where Mikhail is living. Ordinarily I wouldn't dream of giving anyone's address out, but in this case..." She hesitated a moment before asking, "Are you by any chance the person Mikhail was living with when he first arrived here?"

Erin's stomach fluttered. Despite her careful preparations she couldn't keep a tremor from her voice. "Y-yes... I am...."

"I thought you might be. Hold on a sec and I'll get his address."

It made no sense that, having learned of her true role in Mikhail's life, Melinda was willing to give her information that she would otherwise have withheld. But that was exactly what she intended to do.

After the socialite read off a street number in a nearby neighborhood on the Upper East Side, Erin tried to thank her, but the woman brushed that aside. "It must be my New England upbringing. I can't stand to see something good go to waste. Whatever the problem is, I hope you two work it out."

So did Erin, more than she could admit, even to herself. Her spirited defense of him had forced her to remember all that he had endured. After what he had been through he was bound to expect disappointment and betrayal at every turn. It was up to her to convince him otherwise, if only belatedly.

But that was easier said than done. Tired out after the hectic day, and not feeling at all at her best, she wasn't ready yet to confront him. First she went home, stripped off her clothes and stood under the shower long enough to feel somewhat revived.

After blow-drying her hair she dressed in pleated tan wool slacks that were gathered at the waist and a creamy silk blouse. The outfit was casual but elegant. She looked very good, but it wasn't obvious that she had taken great pains with her appearance.

Leaving her hair brushed loosely around her shoulders, she redid her makeup to hide the dark shadows under her eyes and put a hint of color in her cheeks. A spray of her favorite perfume was the final touch to boost her confidence. With a quick glance at herself in the mirror, she tossed on her camel's hair coat and left the apartment quickly, before she could have any second thoughts.

The taxi ride to Mikhail's place seemed endless, but finally she arrived in front of an elegant East Side town house. After paying the driver she got out and stood on the sidewalk, trying to get up the courage to ring the bell. It occurred to her that he might be out or, worse yet, not alone. She really should have called first. But it was too late to think of that. Winter darkness was rapidly closing in. A chill wind blew off the river, piercing through even her warm clothes. Shivering, she made up her mind.

Her heart was beating uncomfortably fast and her stomach tightened painfully as she pressed the door bell.

Chapter Sixteen

The chimes sounded deep within the town house, reverberating hollowly. Erin waited through long, seemingly endless moments, straining to hear any hint of approaching footsteps. Nothing. Stubbornly she rang the bell again. After another indeterminate delay she reluctantly acknowledged that Mikhail was not at home.

At a loss as to what to do next, she surveyed the rapidly emptying street. The unusually warm weather of the afternoon was gone, replaced by a bitter cold that cut to the bone. She was tired, hungry and growing steadily more anxious. Common sense told her to leave and try to reach him the next day, but such reasonable behavior was impossible in light of her feelings for him.

He had to come back sooner or later. Deciding that it wouldn't hurt to wait a bit longer, she pulled her coat more snugly around her and turned up the collar against the wind. The entrance to the town house was slightly recessed behind a stone overhang. It provided a small amount of shelter, but not much.

Half an hour passed, and it got colder and damper. Her feet, shod only in high-heeled pumps since the day had seemed too warm to require boots, were beginning to turn numb. She found a scarf in her purse and put it on, all the while mentally rehearsing what she should say to him.

A policeman strolled by on his beat. He glanced at her carefully, and she tried to look as though she were waiting for a bus. Something about her must have reassured him, because he didn't bother her.

Erin glanced at her watch. Seven o'clock. Sensible people were at home having dinner. Her own stomach growled, but she ignored it. Pacing back and forth, she tried to get some feeling back into her feet. Her fingers were becoming stiff, but a search through the pockets of her coat revealed that she had forgotten her gloves.

Seven thirty. Maybe he had gone out somewhere... with someone. Maybe he wouldn't be back for hours, or perhaps not even until the next day. She was an idiot to be standing there on a dark, deserted street, inviting all sorts of trouble. If she weren't completely crazy she would go home.

She stayed. The policeman came back. He was a young man, very pleasant, but very firm.

"Are you waiting for someone, miss?"

"Yes," she answered quietly, not taking offense at what was, after all, simply his job. "I'm hoping the man who lives in this house will be coming back soon. It's very important that I talk with him."

"You picked a bad night for it."

She grimaced. "It was so warm earlier that I didn't expect this." Without even realizing that she was doing so, she began automatically to draw him out, just as she would on an interview. "But I suppose you're used to cold. Have you been walking a beat long?"

He shook his head wryly. "Only a couple of months, though it seems longer." They fell to talking about the city, the changes they had seen in the last few years, the good points and the bad. It occurred to Erin that she wasn't the only one asking questions. With a few well-placed inquiries the young policeman managed to determine that she was unlikely to have any nefarious object behind her vigil.

"I'd better be going," he said regretfully. They had shared a simple human exchange that for a short time, at least, had broken through the barriers of their solitude. Turning to leave, he added, "I hope you're not planning to stay here much longer. It looks as though we're in for some rain.''

Erin glanced up at the sky in dismay. He was right. Leaden clouds obscured the topmost floors of nearby office towers. Even as she watched, scattered drops began to fall, splattering against her forehead and running down the bridge of her nose.

"Oh, great!" Muttering, she brushed it aside and retreated back under the stone overhang. Maybe it would be content to just drizzle.

It wasn't. Within minutes the first few drops had become a downpour. It rained so hard that the water bounced back off the pavement, soaking her shoes and the cuffs of her slacks. It was just as well that she could no longer feel her feet, Erin thought glumly, since they were sopping wet. Too bad the rest of her hadn't turned numb. She was only too aware of the sodden weight of her scarf and coat clinging to her body, the wet tendrils of hair plastered to her forehead, the icy fingers of water sliding beneath her collar to trickle down her back.

No matter how she tried, it was impossible to keep the rain off. The wind blew it at her almost horizontally, making the stone overhang useless. She tried to keep her spirits up by telling herself that it could be worse, it could be snow. But that didn't work very well. She was wet, cold, miserable and feeling more like a full-fledged idiot with each passing second.

But she still couldn't bring herself to leave. Some hitherto unsuspected streak of do-or-die stubbornness forced her to stay. Not simply because of what she had to tell Mikhail, but because she couldn't bear the thought of walking away, perhaps only moments before he returned. She badly needed to see him, to be close to him, even if his terrible anger hadn't eased at all.

Shaking her head ruefully at such singlemindedness, she peered through the rain-swept gloom, trying to see if anyone was coming. Of course not. Nobody, absolutely nobody but she, was outside. In the entire city of almost eight million people everybody else was snug and dry, well-fed and content. Everyone, including Mikhail, who was undoubtedly comfortably ensconced in some restaurant or—she flinched at the thought—some lovely lady's apartment.

Or was he? A familiar figure had turned the corner near the town house, walking, head bent, into the rain. Even obscured as he was by the darkness and the sheets of water, there was no mistaking the big body clad only in slacks, a turtle-necked sweater and a tweed jacket. His shoulders were hunched and his hands were jammed deep into his pockets. In the glare of a streetlight she could make out the burnished gold of his hair clinging wetly to his head.

Her throat tightened convulsively. In another moment he would see her, and she still had no idea what she intended to say to him.

Not that it mattered. The moment their eyes met, all ability for rational thought fled. She couldn't move or speak, could only wait as the disbelief she saw in his gaze gave way slowly to something that looked very much like the first faint stirrings of hope.

"Erin...? What are you doing here? Standing out in the rain like this... why...?"

"I need to talk to you," she said, surprised that she managed to sound calm when everything inside her was exploding with an almost painful combination of pleasure and fear. It was so good, so right, to be with him again that she forced herself to put aside her doubts about what he really thought of her sudden appearance on his doorstep. "Could we go inside?"

He hesitated for just a moment, still struggling to come to terms with her presence. When her tentative question finally registered he nodded quickly. "Yes, of course. You must be soaked."

"So are you," she pointed out rather unnecessarily as he unlocked the door and stood aside to let her in. They were both dripping water onto the wood parquet floor, but Mikhail didn't seem to mind. He was too busy staring at her.

"You're really here.... I thought perhaps I was just imaginings things."

Startled, she looked up at him. It was perfectly believable that she might call up his presence out of her heated thoughts, but for him to do so...

Seeing the surprise in her eyes, he laughed dryly. "It wouldn't be the first time. I seem to have encountered you everywhere in the last few weeks."

"I-I don't understand...."

He shrugged, looking away. "Let's get dried off first. Then we'll talk."

Erin had to agree. The puddle forming at their feet added nothing to the decor. Not that there was much to it to begin with. The entry hall was bare of furniture, as were the spacious living room and the dining room, which smelled of fresh paint. A few cartons were scattered around, with several more piled near the marble staircase that led to the second floor.

The house had the vaguely forsaken air of a place that has been empty for a long time, but that couldn't detract from its old-world elegance or the gracefulness of interiors well suited to another, more genteel age. She could easily understand why Mikhail would choose such a home for himself.

Touching her arm lightly, he said, "There are towels upstairs, and I should be able to find a robe for you."

About to tell him that wasn't necessary, Erin thought better of it. Her clothes were sticking soggily to her, and she felt chilled clear through. Besides, it was ridiculous to hesitate about facing him in only a robe when he was accustomed to seeing her in far less.

They parted at the top of the stairs, he to what she guessed was the master suite overlooking the back of the house and she to the guest room he indicated. Some of its furniture had already arrived and been put in place. A large brass bed covered by a vibrant star-pattern quilt was framed on either side by low pine tables topped in marble. A golden oak wardrobe took up most of one wall, near the door leading to the bathroom.

Erin had taken off her coat and shoes and put both in the shower to drip when Mikhail knocked. He handed her a pile of fluffy white towels and a navy-blue cashmere robe. For just an instant she thought she saw his quicksilver eyes flicker with concern as she surveyed her bedraggled form. But his tone was no warmer than any conscientious host's as he said, "You should get out of those things before you catch a chill."

She thanked him quietly, but waited until the door was closed behind him and she heard him walk away before attempting to undo the buttons of her blouse. Her stiff fingers were awkward, and she was trembling so badly that it was an effort just to stand upright. She hadn't counted on the shattering effect his presence would have on her. Being alone with him in the silent house forced her to confront the full intensity of her love. She desperately wanted to go to him at once, convince him that he had no reason to mistrust her, and find both forgetfulness and rebirth in his arms.

Only her pride stopped her. She had no confidence that he wouldn't rebuff her. It would be the height of foolishness for her to misinterpret what was only a simple act of courtesy from an innately gracious man. Just because he had allowed her into his home, it didn't follow that he was willing to reassess their personal relationship and admit that his accusations had been unjust.

When she was finally able to unfasten her blouse, she hung it up in the bathroom, along with her slacks. Even her lingerie was wet. After a moment's hesitation she took it off as well, toweled herself dry and put on the robe.

A glance in the mirror made her grimace. The dark-blue cashmere hung on her slender body. All her makeup was washed off, and her hair hung in tendrils to her shoulders. The paleness of her skin made her emerald eyes look enormous. She had the fragile, uncertain air of a waif.

And there didn't seem to be much she could do about it. The hair dryer she found in a cabinet under the sink helped a little. But nothing could disguise the vulnerable quality of her mouth or the anxious pulse beating in the alabaster column of her throat.

Reluctantly admitting that she had done everything possible to restore her appearance, she padded across the bedroom and gingerly opened the door to the hall. There was no sign of Mikhail, but from downstairs she caught a whiff of a wood fire and the distant sounds of someone moving around in a kitchen.

The steps of the marble staircase were cold beneath her bare feet. She moved down them hastily, not slowing until she reached the bottom. A sudden burst of wind rattling against the windows made her tense. The rain seemed to be getting worse. She peered out at it worriedly, wondering if she would be able to get a cab when it was time to leave.

A soft sigh escaped her. If only things were different. If only the closeness that had existed between them so briefly hadn't been destroyed by bitterness and anger. How wonderful it would be to spend that night and every night with him upstairs in his bed. No storm that raged outside would be able to equal the tempest of their passion.

Erin bit her lip hard as she felt her cheeks grow hot and flushed. Why was she tormenting herself with such thoughts? They could achieve nothing and would only make it even harder for her to face him. Determinedly forcing her mind back to the reason for her presence, she headed for the kitchen.

At some point in its long life the house must have undergone extensive remodeling that had transformed the entire rear of the first floor into a combination cooking, dining and living area. Dark-gold terrazzo tiles lined the floor beneath white stucco walls and a pressed copper ceiling. A huge brick fireplace stood in one corner, the source of the wood smoke

Erin had sniffed. In front of it were a comfortable overstuffed couch and several tables. Nearby a large trestle table and chairs sat under a brass and pewter chandelier. The silver bowl of dried fall flowers on the table picked up the red, yellow and blue shades of the hand-painted tiles decorating the kitchen.

Ordinarily she would have been too distracted by such a delightful room to notice much of anything else. But as it was, the interior details barely registered. All her attention was focused on the man standing at the kitchen counter, preparing a pot of coffee.

Mikhail was wearing only the terry-cloth robe she had seen so often from across the breakfast table. His golden hair was tousled, as though it had been roughly toweled dry. The broad sweep of his shoulders and chest tapering down to his slender waist, narrow hips and long, powerful legs made her breath catch. She remembered all too vividly the feel of his lean, hard body against her own and the havoc he so easily wreaked within her.

Feeling absurdly exposed despite the robe that covered her from below her fingertips almost to her ankles, she had to fight the urge to flee back upstairs. How had she ever imagined that she could face him calmly, without revealing the torrent of love and sorrow he had caused? The mere sight of him was almost enough to make her forget why she had gone there in the first place.

Almost, but not quite. Remembering the accusations that were about to be unleashed against him, she forced down her fears. It was imperative that they talk, no matter what the consequences for herself. An instant later he became aware of her presence and looked up, and she was able to meet his gaze calmly.

"Do you need any help with that?" Erin asked.

He shook his head, his eyes wandering over her slender, vulnerable form. "No, thank you. Why don't you sit down by the fire? It should be warm over there by now."

Erin did as he suggested. Curled up on the couch with her feet tucked under her, she waited for him to bring over the coffee. Her eyebrows rose slightly when she saw the bottle of brandy and two snifters on the tray next to their cups, but she didn't argue when he poured a generous measure for them both. The fiery liquid slid down her throat easily, warming her from within and bolstering her courage to some degree.

She took another, smaller sip before setting the brandy snifter down. "Mikhail . . . I know my turning up like this must seem strange . . . but I really do have a good reason for needing to see you."

Something flashed in his eyes. Concern . . . excitement . . . she wasn't sure which. "I'm sure you do, Erin," he said quietly. "You don't have to convince me of that. Just take your time and tell me what is worrying you."

After the scene in her apartment on New Year's Day, the last thing she had expected from him was consideration or patience. But he seemed disposed to offer both.

Taking a deep breath, she said slowly, "I found out something today that I'm sure will be a...shock to you.... It sounds so unbelievable...but I'm afraid it's true, and I thought you should know...because you're the only one who could—"

His sudden interruption made her break off. "You don't have to say that, Erin. I know I'm the only one."

"Oh...well, good...I mean it's not as though there aren't other people who will want to help and all that...but basically it's going to be up to you to decide what to do."

He frowned slightly. "Up to both of us, don't you mean?" Before she could answer, he went on quickly. "And there really isn't any question of what to do. At least, not as far as I'm concerned. It's my responsibility. After all, I'm the one who was supposed to be making sure that..." He stopped, his gaze dark with some emotion that she couldn't fathom. "I'm just very...grateful that, after my despicable behavior, you were still willing to come here and tell me."

Puzzled, Erin tried to pin down what it was about his words that confused her. Mikhail seemed already to know what she had come to tell him. Perhaps that meant he had already formulated a plan to defuse the accusations. But what did he mean about it being his responsibility? What had he been supposed to make sure of?

Even as those questions flitted through her mind, they faded before the realization of how he had characterized his actions. Tentatively she murmured, "Does that mean you believe now that there was never anything between Derek and me?"

He nodded gravely. "I think I always knew it, but I was so frightened of my feelings for you that I let my own fears run away with me." Carefully, as though unsure of her response, he reached over and took one of her hands in his. A lean, calloused finger rubbed her palm gently as he said, "Erin, words are inadequate to express how sorry I am for the things I said to you. Believe me, I have berated myself a hundred times since then for being such an insensitive idiot. It isn't possible for you to think worse of me than I do of myself."

"But I don't! That is, I was hurt and angry, of course. But I never stopped...I mean..." The unmistakable contrition and yearning she saw in his gaze dissolved her last defenses. She could no longer deny her feelings, nor was she willing to try. "I never stopped loving you, Mikhail. I think I've loved you from the moment we met, even though it took me a while to admit it to myself." A soft, wistful smile curved her mouth. "However you feel about me, nothing will ever change that."

"However I...? But I love you. I always have. I took one look at you that afternoon at the airport and thought I had flown straight to heaven." The emotions that she hadn't been able to read in his eyes before were suddenly evident. She saw relief, passion, elation, all intermingling with the glow of deep, abiding love, mirroring her own gaze.

Erin's lips parted on a soundless sigh of pure joy. Hardly daring to believe, she reached out to him shakily. "Mikhail...are you sure? That night of the party, I was so worried that you hadn't had a chance to...consider alternatives. And then, when I saw you at the gallery with Melinda, I told myself I'd been right...that you really did want to go out with other women."

"Foolish angel," he murmured huskily, drawing her into the enchanted circle of his arms. "Melinda is a very kind young lady who took pity on me. She realized immediately that I was in love with someone else and tried her best to convince me that everything would work out. She even helped me find this place. I'm renting it, by the way, with an option to buy. So if you really like it, we can stay here for good." He shook his head ruefully. "I'm afraid I was terrible company for Melinda, especially when I saw you at the art exhibit with that man."

"Sidney? But he's Sheila's husband. They invited me to go to the gallery with them because I was so down in the dumps about you."

"Ah, that was it. And to think I could cheerfully have strangled him. As it was, I took Melinda home, came back here and did away with the better part of a bottle of vodka." A wry grimace touched his mouth. "I'll never know why that stuff is so popular. It gave me the worst headache I've ever had in my life."

Erin couldn't quite suppress a little chuckle of delight. Happiness beyond anything she had ever imagined glowed within her. "I think we both owe Melinda a vote of thanks. She told me where you were."

"Thank God for that! When I came back here tonight after finding your apartment empty, I didn't know where to look next."

"My apartment? Was that where you were?"

He nodded sheepishly. "You will never know how relieved I was to see you standing outside." His expression grew stern as he added, "But you really should not have waited in the rain. You don't take good enough care of yourself under normal circumstances, but now..." A dull flash suffused his cheeks. "Erin, are you very upset about my failure to protect you as well as I thought I was doing?"

Baffled, she shook her head. "Protect? I don't understand. What are you s—?" She broke off suddenly, the meaning of their strangely askewed conversation at last reaching her. *"Oh! You thought..."* Swallowing hard, she forced herself to face him. "Mikhail, I didn't come here to tell you I'm pregnant. I'm not...at least I don't *think* I am...."

"Then why?" he asked in bewilderment. "What was all that about my being the only one?"

Briefly she explained to him what Derek had told her about the charges being prepared against him. When she was done, Mikhail's eyes were wide with astonishment. He leaned back on the couch, staring at her. "Kent told you this?"

She nodded.

"When?"

"This afternoon, over lunch." Why was he wasting time asking her such questions when he should be concentrating on how best to meet the accusations?

"And that's why you came here?"

"Yes, I just told you. Oh, Mikhail, it's unthinkable that anyone would believe such charges. But I'm afraid that if they're printed there will be some people who'll take them as an excuse to turn against you. Your credibility will be undermined, and you may be subject to all sorts of verbal, even physical, attacks. There has to be something you can do to prevent that."

"Hmmm . . . I see what you mean. Yes, I suppose I really should respond in some way."

"Of course you should!" As he stood up and headed for the phone, she asked anxiously, "What are you going to do?"

"You'll see." He consulted the phone book, punched out a number and waited a moment before saying, "Ah, good, you're home. It's Demertov. I just called to thank you.... Yes, she's here. We've been talking.... That's some tale you told her.''

He grinned over at Erin, whose eyes were darkening with rapidly growing suspicion. ''I owe you quite a favor, but I've no doubt you'll come up with some way to collect.... What's that? Melinda? Delightful girl. Listened to me talk about Erin for hours. You know, I couldn't help but notice that the few times I shut up long enough for her to get a word in, you seemed to be on her mind.... No, I'm quite sure.... That might be a good idea. She'd undoubtedly love to help you celebrate. After all, how often does someone get named editor of the year? Just one thing, though. You should know that she's as intelligent as she is lovely. You won't be able to get away with much.''

A low, masculine chuckle reached Erin's burning ears. ''Yes, I guess it will make a rather nice change for you. You'll have to bring her to the wedding. Well, I won't keep you. I just wanted you to know how much we both appreciate your...creativity.''

''That's not what I want to tell him!'' Erin began, only to be cut short by Mikhail, who politely made his farewells and hung up. When he turned back to her he was smiling broadly.

''I've completely changed my opinion of Kent. He's not so bad after all.''

''He's a con man! He sat there in that restaurant and spun that whole tale of woe about you and that newspaper and...! Oooohhh! How could I have been so stupid? The whole thing was a lie, wasn't it?''

"Not entirely," Mikhail said calmly. "There was an attempt to launch an attack against me using the charges you mention. It happened earlier this week, when I gather you were embroiled with a new assignment and didn't hear about it. The attack fell apart almost before it got started when other men I had been in prison with ridiculed the very idea of me as a collaborator. They knew I had caused the prison officials and myself considerable trouble because I wouldn't cooperate. Also, the so-called journalist making the charge was found to have accepted payments from my country's former regime. That revelation destroyed *his* credibility. My guess is that whatever is left of the old regime won't try anything like it again for fear of drawing even more attention to me and to what I have to say."

"Then . . . you're safe . . . ?"

"Completely. Not that it seemed to matter before you showed up here. Now, however, it means the world." Sitting down beside her, he gently took hold of her clenched hands and drew her close against him. His gaze was infinitely tender as he said, "Erin, I love you with all my heart and soul, and I want you to be my wife."

She swallowed hard, desperate to contain the overpowering surge of joy that spread through every cell of her being. She couldn't let it break free yet, not until she knew.... "Even though there may not be any baby?"

Her voice was so low that he had to lean forward to hear her. When he did, he tilted her head back and smiled down at her, his silvery eyes glowing with a fire brighter than any she had ever seen before. "Would you like to have children?"

"Yes... your children... I love you so...."

"Then you will have to marry me. I am very traditional in that respect. The woman I adore must be my wife before she becomes the mother of our children."

It got very quiet in the room. The only sounds were the splatter of rain against the windows, the crackle of the fire and soft sighs of lovers.

When Mikhail stood up with her in his arms Erin offered no protest. She snuggled contentedly against his broad chest, listening to the steady beat of his heart as he carried her up the stairs and into his room. A single light burned beside the massive, four-poster bed. By its golden glow they rediscovered each other. The robes fell forgotten to the bed as their hands and lips touched and caressed and savored until the fires of passion raged beyond all control.

Erin cried out softly as he brought them together in unbridled joy. Her body opened to accept his without restraint. They moved as one, climbing higher and higher toward a glimmering peak of pleasure made all the more acute by the knowledge of their mutual love.

When the undulating coils of rapture at last exploded within her, the cry of his name was echoed in her soul. His own being responded an instant later as he joined her in shattering release.

Throughout the long, rain-washed night they came together again and again, setting the seal on a future bright with the promise of abiding love. Not until it was almost morning did they at last drift into a peaceful sleep, nestled in each other's arms, secure in the knowledge that in that embrace they had found the greatest freedom the world could offer.

*   *   *   *   *

WELCOME TO

The quintessential small town,
where everyone knows everybody else!

Each book set in Tyler is a self-contained love story; together,
the twelve novels stitch the fabric of the community.

"Scintillating romance!"
"Immensely appealing characters...wonderful intensity and humor."
Romantic Times

Join your friends in Tyler for the eleventh book,
COURTHOUSE STEPS by Ginger Chambers, available in January.

Was Margaret's husband responsible for her murder?
What memories come flooding back to Alyssa?

GREAT READING...GREAT SAVINGS...AND A FABULOUS FREE GIFT!

With Tyler you can receive a fabulous gift, ABSOLUTELY FREE,
by collecting proofs-of-purchase found in each Tyler book.
And use our special Tyler coupons to save on your next
TYLER book purchase.

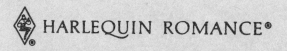

HARLEQUIN ROMANCE®

Norah Bloomfield's father is recovering from his heart attack, and her sisters are getting married. So Norah's feeling a bit unneeded these days, a bit left out....

Orchard Valley

And then a cantankerous "cowboy" called Rowdy Cassidy crashes into her life!

"The Orchard Valley trilogy features three delightful, spirited sisters and a trio of equally fascinating men. The stories are rich with the romance, warmth of heart and humor readers expect, and invariably receive, from Debbie Macomber."

—Linda Lael Miller

Don't miss the Orchard Valley trilogy by Debbie Macomber:

VALERIE   Harlequin Romance #3232 (November 1992)
STEPHANIE   Harlequin Romance #3239 (December 1992)
NORAH   Harlequin Romance #3244 (January 1993)

Look for the special cover flash on each book!

Available wherever Harlequin books are sold.   ORC-3

In February 1993, Maura Seger, like her characters, will break all convention when she launches a four-book series based on the lives and loves of the people in the fictional town of Belle Haven, Connecticut.

Look for THE TAMING OF AMELIA (HH#159) in February 1993, THE SEDUCTION OF DEANNA (HH#183) in August 1993, and one other historical in early 1994. The fourth book in the saga will be a contemporary for the Silhouette Intimate Moments line.

And if you enjoyed Maura's Christmas novel, don't miss her short story in the Harlequin *Historical Christmas Stories 1992* collection. The collection, which also includes works by Bronwyn Williams and Erin Yorke, is available now wherever Harlequin books are sold.